# PILOT

First Edition

Written by
Jamie P. Barker

# Fuera de la Oficina de Jeff

*Fuck fuck fuck fuck fuck*, I thought. *Fuck fuck fuck fuck.* I'd just knocked on the door and absolutely nothing had happened. Getting into the office was supposed to be the easy part. *Fuck.* I stopped thinking *fuck* and instead actually thought about the problem. I shook my arm slightly and clenched and unclenched my hand a few times, then looked over to the Box for assistance, but it wasn't any. It had gone back to sleep. "Hey!" I said, making that word as short and polite as I could. I moved my head up and down, hoping my movement might trigger its peripheral sensor. It didn't sense me. I guess I was out of range. *What now? Keep knocking like an idiot? Just walk in like an idiot?* I had another look around and then I did a little double tap on the door, took a deep breath, and this time, not waiting for a response, I opened it.

The door was harder to open than I'd expected because the carpet was so thick that the bottom of the door rubbed across it. I had to really shove it as I stepped inside and looked around. It was empty. *Fuck. What now?* I asked myself. *Back out and sit down? Wait another half an hour?*

I still had my left hand on the door handle when I heard a toilet flush. I was now sure I should back out but before I could, a different door inside his office burst open and Jeff burst out. That sounds a bit dramatic, right? But he burst through the door with such force it banged off the wall. That door didn't rub on the carpet.

"Mikey!" said Jeff, clicking his fingers and pointing at me, not the least bit surprised that I was there. He said 'Mikey' like we were friends and my name was Mikey. Neither of those things are true. I'd never once spoken to Jeff and my name's Michael. Then he was walking at me as I stood in the doorhole. He flicked the fingers of both hands out behind him as he approached, like he was trying to dry them. Kind of looked like a determined swan, the way he was leaning forward.

The speed he was walking I wouldn't have been surprised if he'd just gone right past me. Out into the reception, down the hall and out. He didn't show signs of slowing down at all until he stopped and thrust a hand towards me. I shook it. Well, he shook mine. Really pumped it. His hand was cold and still wet.

"Nice to meet you too," I said, even though he hadn't said it was nice to meet me. I followed that with a small cough while I thought *fuck*.

"Get in here!" he said, standing to the side. I let go of the door handle and stepped fully inside his office. I heard the door brush the carpet as he pushed it closed, then he placed a hand gently on my back and steered me over to a small couch, which I sat on while he sat on the corner of his desk. There were chairs in the office. Heavy, solid-looking chairs. Office chairs. I don't know why we didn't use them.

"I'm Jeff," said Jeff, pointing at himself as he loomed over me.

"It's nice to meet you," I said for the second time and again followed it up with a small cough. I seemed to have too much throat stuff in my throat. Phlegm. Jeff's name *is* Jeff.

"Hey, I always have time for my guys," said Jeff, smiling, and then his face turned calmer and more receptive. "You have a concern that you'd like to raise with me?"

"Yeah," I replied with a little nod and a little cough. "I told the… the Box. It's not a big deal-"

"Hit me. If I can help I will."

"Okay, well… you know, I want to keep my unit."

"You want to keep your unit? Is that it?" he asked with his head cocked. He asked it like *he* was posing a question. Like I hadn't just said exactly that.

"Yeah," I said and then, because he didn't reply for a bit and was still smiling at me and I felt uncomfortable, I added more. I'd been prepared for an argument and so had more to say. "We work well together. I know he's not state of the art or anything but, hey, neither am I!" I chuckled. I'd hoped that I might get a laugh with that. I didn't. I coughed. "I know how he works and I think he's-"

"He?" asked Jeff, the start of a smile appearing at the corners of his mouth.

I smiled and shook my head at my own idiocy. "It. I call it… you know? I know som-"

Jeff held up a finger and said, "Hold that thought." I didn't really know which thought he meant. He got off his desk and marched over to the door he'd burst from. I watched him go. I thought he was going to get something pertinent to our meeting, you know? Because he marched with such purpose. Instead, he opened that door, less violently this time, stepped inside and after a bit of muttering I heard the toilet flush again. I tapped my left forefinger on my left thigh as I looked at the dent in the wooden panelling, caused by repeated hits from the door handle. Jeff stepped out and I looked away. I looked at the walls instead. They were flat. Nice. Good quality walls. When I did look at him, he was on his desk and looking perplexed.

I raised my eyebrows. "Everything okay?" I asked. My throat was dry.

"Yeah, it's..." He cocked his thumb and pointed it over his shoulder at the toilet door and squinted. "Ah, don't worry about it," he said, flapping his hand at me, the smile returning to his face. I tried to get comfortable on the couch. Not easy because it was so low. Jeff's legs began to swing. "What were we..."

"Keeping my unit."

"That's right. You want to keep your unit," he said.

"Yeah, so..." I said, nodding. I didn't have anything else to add. I wanted to keep my unit. That was basically it. No big deal. No drama. I relaxed slightly.

"You want to keep your unit," said Jeff.

"Yeah."

"Even though I've ordered replacements which will completely revolutionise the industry?"

"Well…"

"Is that it? I'm not missing anything? I just want to get that straight in my head." The way Jeff pulled a goofy face, held his hands near the side of his head and shook them when he said the word 'head' made me tense up again.

"Well, like I said, we work well toge-"

"You've said that," said Jeff.

"Well, you know, and… what's the saying? If it-"

"I don't know what the saying is." He was smiling again, but it was a different smile.

"It's… it's, you know? If it's not broken then don't fix it."

"That's a saying?"

"Yeah, you haven't…"

"No, I haven't ever heard that."

"Well, we work well together, so-"

"You keep saying you work well together."

"Yeah," I agreed and slowly rubbed my lips.

Jeff's odd. I mean *really* odd. Physically too. Sometimes he looked really young, but then, when he pulled a different facial expression, he looked nearly my age.

He sighed. "Look," he smoothly swivelled his bum on his polished desktop and picked up a piece of paper from behind him. I took this opportunity to attempt to sit up straighter. I was being swallowed by the couch. It was just the fact my stomach was so tense that was stopping me from disappearing down between the cushions. He ran his finger down the document then turned it to me. "That one," he said, leaning forward and pointing to a number on a list of similar sized numbers. I leant forward, which wasn't that easy to do on the soft couch and pretended to inspect the rows of numbers. He wasn't really pointing to a specific number. His finger was wider than the numbers and it was a page full of numbers.

"Oh yeah, I see," I said when I felt I'd pretended to look at the numbers for long enough. "That's… what? Serial numbers?"

"You're damn right they're serial numbers, and yours is on the *list*." He tapped the page a few more times then flicked the back of the paper which made a loud crack and caused me to blink. He smiled at my reaction. I tried to smile back. He then tried to throw the paper over his shoulder, but because he hadn't screwed it up it didn't go over his shoulder and instead fluttered gently to the floor. He looked down at it like it was an injured dove. "It's on the list," he repeated, softly. I picked up the sheet for him and he thanked me, then he talked me through the entire process. It was worse than I'd imagined and I'd imagined it would be shit.

Outside his office I weakly thanked the Box. I don't think it was on. I rubbed the fingertips of my right hand against my thumb as I walked slowly along the carpeted corridor to the lift. In the lift I pushed my hips forward because my back hurt, and then I pressed my forehead against the cold wall. That felt nice. When the doors of the lift were closed, I shouted "Fuck!" into the wall. The lift descended to the second floor where the floors are bare and metal, and the walls are metal, and where it's noisier but easier to walk. I walked slowly to the canteen where the tables are metal. There is a lot of clanging down here. I watched Simon for a bit through the canteen window. He was at the table where I always sat.

"So?" asked Simon before I could even put my tray down. "How did it go?"

"Guess."

"Really, really, really, really, *really* well?"

"Yeah, no, the other one."

"Dang."

"Yeah."

"How bad, because you tend to ex-"

I looked at him. "It couldn't have gone worse," I said.

"One to ten?"

"Not even a number. Shit. Just bad, *so* bad." I looked at the lumpy orange saucy offering that was dinner. Curry. "The guy's an idiot. He kept checking his toilet while we were... I think he blocked it. And he wanted me to know."

"Power move," said Simon, deadpan.

"Yeah definitely, and I had to sit on this, like, mini sofa."

"Mini?"

"Yeah, so he could look down on me."

"Did you say what we practised? You made the points?"

"Yeah… well, no, it was okay. The guy's a cretin." I found a lump in the sauce and tried to stab it but ended up just pushing it around.

"Well, you tried."

"Ah, don't worry about it."

"I'm not worried," said Simon and he didn't look worried. That annoyed me.

"You should be worried."

"Why?"

I thought about telling him about the process Jeff had in store for him. Decided against it. "Ah, it'll be alright." I ate a lump. "I didn't know you had precious metal in you. You kept that quiet."

"Think there's some gold," said Simon, looking down as best he could at his torso. "It's what makes me so *fab-u-lous!*" He sang the last word and I stared at him. "Just a few grams."

"Seriously, it'll be fine, don't worry about it."

"The more you say don't worry, the more worried I'm getting."

"Don't be, remember," I looked around but nobody was interested in us. Most of them were still out. "There's still plan B," I whispered.

"What was plan A?"

"What was..." I stared at him again. Was he messing with me? He was doing good acting if he was. "That was, just then, me… with Jeff. In his office." I stared at Simon.

Eventually he nodded. "Of course."

"Shut up. Play pool after this, yeah?" I looked around again for no real reason. "Can't do anything about it tonight."

"Yeah, play pool after this."

I'd put my fork down, I wasn't hungry and my heart was thumping, and after about seven whole seconds a TCU approached. "I am still eating! Eating!" I told it as I picked up my fork and stabbed theatrically at my plate. It backed away, beeping apologetically. "They wanna replace those things," I told Simon. "They're useless."

"They do the job."

"Exactly!" I said, excited. "Just like we do, *that's* what I tried to tell him."

"He wasn't having it?"

"Wasn't having it."

"How's the curry?"

"Better than it looks, actually. Maybe a bit sweet." I ate some more. "Flavours aren't fully developed but, yeah, it's okay. Crucially, it's not *too* spicy."

"*Mmmmm*," said Simon, narrowing his eyes.

---

"Just take it down two levels!" I shouted, leaning in close because of the terrible singing from the stage. It was karaoke night and too loud. I wiped my spit off him. "Just two levels," I repeated. "No, three. No, two. Two!"

"That's against protocol, Michael," replied Simon, looking at the balls as he moved around the pool table with the grace of a semi-famous dancer. He enjoyed saying that and I smiled at his sassmouth.

"I know, I know but I'm not feeling it today. I kinda want to win! I need a win," I shouted.

"No."

"What do you mean, no?"

"I'm sorry."

"What do you mean, you're sorry?"

"You told me not to. Even if you asked. I'm to ignore you. You said this. Even if you beg like a dog."

"No I didn't." I was a bit annoyed so I made a disgusted face. I was disgusted with his lies. I hate liars.

"You didn't?" said Simon, coming back towards me.

"No." I was indignant. Simon came and stood all up in my personal space. "What?"

Simon tilted his head. "Mate, don't lower your accuracy, even if I ask. You're better than that. Makes playing you *boring* and *stupid*, just... just, like, don't! Ignore me, yeah. It's like, mate, you

17

*unintelligible* with the... You're better than that, you can record this I don't even care," said Simon in a slurred voice. Well, it came out of Simon, but it was my voice. I'd said it and by the sounds of it I'd been pretty drunk. I hate playbacks of my drunk talking, although I'm a pretty cool drunk, generally. Funny. Not angry. I don't like my voice.

"Simon, lower your accuracy parameters to a three. *Confirm*." If I say confirm he has to comply. The idiot. That's just the way he's programmed.

"Accuracy level three," he repeated, sadly, while shaking his head slightly.

"And don't record me, confirm." Simon nodded and I held my cue like a staff for support and watched Simon move around the table. "Hey, I didn't mention a dog."

He bumped into a chair. "I must have added that bit," he said and I drank more beer. I was careful not to drink so much that I got sloppy, but I felt I had to drink enough to keep up appearances of normality.

Even with his lowered accuracy he potted the black – it was right over the pocket, should have lowered it sooner – and he held the cue above his head and spun around in celebration, bumping the hanging light with it. "Uno mas?" he asked.

I didn't want to play any more but Simon did. I hate playing pool. I like the *idea* of playing pool, but I don't like playing pool. Luckily Carlos' face appeared over the pool table, illuminated by the swaying light above it. Carlos only started here a few months back. Or maybe a year. Maybe longer. He was a fairly recent recruit and a nice guy. The only one I've got any time for. He doesn't make me tense as he can hardly speak English.

"I play Simon?" he said, his smiling face swimming in and

out of the shadow. He pronounces *Simon* so it rhymes with *firemen*. I nodded and sat in the booth and watched them play. I was irked when Carlos rubbed Simon's head in celebration. He knew I'd lowered Simon's parameters so it was a hollow victory, not even something to celebrate, but I liked Carlos' smile. And his moustache. He's very smiley. Afterwards we drank and talked more about the east.

---

*Fuck. Fuck. Fuck. Fuck,* I thought. A fuck for each step I took across the hangar. It had been fine up until then, my walking. Yeah, I'd been a bit unsteady when I first got up, but I'd been fine in the corridor. Fine in the hall. Fine in the other corridor. Fine on the ramp. But in the hangar the simple act of walking became problematic. The more innocently I tried to walk, the more I was kind of stomping. I felt I was, anyway. My knees were stiff. And I didn't know what to do with my face. My pack was heavy, which didn't help my efforts in walking like I wasn't about to steal a truck. And, of course, a unit.

My gran had a toy. It was this sort of small figure on a round pedestal. Light brown. Wood or plastic, I'm not sure. The string running through the small person would pull its limbs taut, but if you pressed the base of the pedestal the string would loosen and the tiny person would collapse in a heap. Just collapse. Straight down. And now I knew how it felt. My muscles were the strings, too taut for me to walk naturally, ready to buckle if anybody asked me where I was going. If Pete jumped out of the shadows and asked me why I was out so early then I'd just collapse into a heap like somebody pressed my pedestal. What was in my bag? In a heap.

*Pete won't ask, why would he?* I often go out early, before we're loaded. Not often, but it has happened. No big deal! This wasn't *that* unusual. I often had a bag. The only difference today was that I was guilty and I knew that it showed. I wasn't really guilty, not yet, we hadn't gone! It was fine. I'd done nothing wrong. I was just going out for a bit. *Don't collapse. Don't collapse. Don't collapse.*

I saw the Lady out in the yard and tried harder to relax as I walked towards it. I wanted to accelerate. I wanted to run but knew I couldn't. Instead I slowed.

One foot in front of the other.

I glanced over at Pete's office. His shed. There was no sign of him. I had an excuse ready to tell him, if he appeared, but as excuses went it wasn't great. I wasn't confident I could deliver it naturally. I hoped he wouldn't appear. I couldn't hear his legs. I took one more glance at the Lady then I just stared at the floor a few steps ahead of me and walked. I had my thumbs hooked into the straps of my pack. Without my thumbs there it felt like the sides of my face were being pulled down into a guilty grimace. It wasn't too bad with my thumbs taking some of the load. I was leaning slightly forward and my walking totally went to pieces when I crossed from the shadow-covered floor of the hangar out into the natural light of the yard.

I shambled halfway across the yard before I looked up and saw Simon staring at me from his side window. He looked concerned and I shook my head and looked at the enticingly open door. It wasn't far. I could make it. I had made it, practically. I could run the rest of the way if Pete appeared. I looked back down to the floor. I was sweating but I'd made it. It was right there. Twenty steps, I guessed. Twenty at the most. I started to count my steps. At fourteen the tannoy crackled. I closed my eyes and my left foot stuttered ever so slightly.

"Hey!" It was Pete's voice through the speakers which were positioned in the four corners of the yard. There were about nine steps to the truck's doorhole. If that. I looked at the distance then stopped and turned towards his hut, which was just inside of the shadow divide. Just inside the hangar doors. I nodded over to it. The general direction. I couldn't see him, of course.

"Me?" I mouthed. I pointed at myself. Thumbs hooked under the straps of my pack left my fingers in the perfect position to point at myself.

"Have you shit yourself?" boomed the speakers. That wasn't the question I was expecting and it took a couple of seconds to process.

"Hahaha," I said. I exaggerated the fake happiness on my face so that it would be visible from further away, but I knew, close up, my expression was that of an insane ventriloquist's stupid-looking dummy. I pulled out my right hand and put my thumb up with what I knew was a ghastly grin on my face.

"Pri-" I heard before the tannoy crackled its way back to silence. I still had my thumb up, I noticed, and so I lowered it but kept the grin on my face. I had no control over my face. I turned my grinning face towards the Lady, pointed my face at Simon, who looked very concerned, took the last few steps and climbed aboard. I threw my bag behind the seats. Then I did collapse. I crumpled into my chair and buckled myself in.

My right leg bounced up and down. I looked at Simon because we weren't moving. He was looking at me. "You okay?"

he asked.

I clicked the fingers of my left hand while holding it towards his face. Three times I clicked. "Let's go!" My leg bounced as we waited wordlessly for a gap in the traffic above. I leant forward and looked over at the black rectangle which was the opening to the hangar. My leg bounced faster.

"Hold on," said Simon and we lurched up into the HiWay.

"That was easy," I said, checking the wing mirror when we were clear.

"I make it look easy."

"I mean..." I'd meant our escape. I rested my head against the side window as we climbed up into the channel. "We've done it." I looked down at the yard then rested my head again.

"It's approaching nine," said Simon.

I was staring at a greedy bird. "I know. I've got a watch." Without looking at him I jangled the wrist that had the watch on it in front of his face. I always wear a watch but I usually just ask Simon the time, it's easier than lifting my wrist. "Approaching! Listen to Mr Vocabulary!"

"Approaching? What's wrong with that? What should I say?"

"Say nearly."

"It's nearly nine."

"Better. Anyway, in a hurry to get somewhere, are you?"

"Are we?"

I licked the ice-cream and nodded my head towards the only

other person on the stretch of bank. A bit further along from us I'd noticed a grey-haired guy with a horrible body. He'd been stripping and was now completely naked. His clothes folded neatly. We watched him walk to the water. He wasn't completely naked, he had a large blue knee bandage. It wasn't holding him back. "Soles of his feet must be bulletproof," I said because the bank was made of garbage. I was sitting on the back of a screen.

"So what's the plan?" asked Simon and I blinked slowly to stay calm. It didn't work too well.

"Urgh, why are you so negative all the time?"

"What?"

"You, you're always so negative."

"I just asked, what are we going to do next?"

"I can't eat an ice-cream in peace."

"*What?*" asked Simon.

"Let me eat this and we'll be on our way. Jesus Christ, just give me a few minutes, you know?"

"I literally didn't say anything except to ask what's the plan."

I exhaled through my nose. There was warm air being pumped from somewhere and my ice-cream was melting quickly. I licked around the cone but a blob still dripped onto my overall trousers. I dabbed it off with a finger. The guy was already swimming. Head up out of the water. That stroke. The one old people do. Guy probably wasn't much older than me but despite all his swimming I was in much better shape. "Would you like to swim?"

"I can't float."

"If, I'm asking *if.* You know, rhetorical question? *If* you could, would you like to swim?"

"I don't know. Can you swim?"

"I don't know," I replied. I assumed I could. It doesn't look difficult. "I wonder how many condoms he's swallowed out there."

"Twenty-two," said Simon, confidently.

"Hmm, that's a lot. Twenty-two?"

"Yeah, twenty-two."

"Too many. Twelve, I reckon. Thirteen at the most."

"Maybe."

"After the first ten you'd develop a strategy, you know, to avoid swallowing them. Then two more when you let your guard down."

"Possible," conceded Simon. "What's a condom?" The swimmer was quite far out.

I ate all of the cone, just to spite the gull which was on Simon's head. I didn't like the way it sneakily got closer, its head turned sideways, all the while ready to take flight. Devious. If it had just come up and stood in front of me, well, I still wouldn't have given it the cone. It was still watching me. It must have thought I had another cone in my pocket or something. Like I carried them around with me. "Stupid bird." I pointed up and Simon raised an arm. The bird lazily took to the air, banked and glided along the water looking for something else to scavenge.

"You okay?" asked Simon.

"Fine!" I snapped back. I hate that question, but I instantly felt bad for being shitty. I glanced at him. He was looking at me and we both turned our gaze out to the heaving pond of polluted water. We were basically sitting next to a large gutter. "Yeah, I'm fine, you?"

"Just following orders," he replied. One of his jokes.

"Well, I've got no choice either, so, you know." Having no choice, like following orders, took away a lot of stress. We *had* to go.

We couldn't go back. There was no choice.

"We can always go back," said Simon. I nodded to this while doing another long blink. "I bet we do." He was still looking out at the water. I couldn't see the swimmer. *He dead*, I thought.

"How much?"

"Ten pounds," he said. I reached across with my right hand and shook his.

"We can't go back. And you don't have money."

"Got gold."

"Oh yeah. I forgot." I'd forgotten about the gold. The swimmer was still there but further out. His head popping up through a layer of debris. The detritus. I stood and yawned and turned and saw the monstrosity that is the City towering over us. From the trench you can see a lot of the distinct layers. Where they've just built on top of old layers. Parts pancaked, crumpled and collapsed. Like seams in old rocks, or a cross-section of a crushed, sunken ocean liner.

We got back in the truck. The LD-950. If you're lucky enough to work with them you call them Ladys. Because the LD sounds a bit like the word Lady. The vehicle probably holds the record for the most ninety-degree angles ever used in the construction of a single machine. It's basically a cube. They weren't built for speed, they were built for transporting goods and for stacking with other LD-950s, in a hangar. Most of the space inside is empty, even when we have it full. There is a lot of headroom in a Lady. A lot of excess headroom. It's *so* the opposite of aerodynamic that it can only be driven by another machine. Its four small engines can move along any of the Lady's twelve edges. Simon controls it like it's his hand. Glenn reckons he got 200mph out of his. Not sure where he'd get his pilot to do that in the City without getting shot down, so take that with a pinch of salt.

Simon sits in the middle. Because he's the pilot. I sit to his right. I've got the screen and glove box. My chair moves sideways on rails so I can look out of the side window, if I want to. It doesn't swivel. Our Ladys are yellow with the corporation's logo on the side.

"Sit still," I told Simon when he was back at the controls. I took the folded piece of paper from my thigh pocket. I sat on his lap so I had access to the three buttons on his chest and unfolded the paper. "Actually, turn it on first."

"Turn it on?"

"Yeah, they won't be looking for us yet. But... just check. See what's going on. Turn on communications, confirm."

"Turning on communications," said Simon. A burst of static came from him and then, after about ten seconds, the word 'dickhead' was spoken in Pete's voice. He was saying it gently. Like he was trying to coax a cat named Dickhead out from somewhere in his room. "Dickhead, are you there?" That was blunter. I looked at Simon's face, confused. He pointed at me. I shook my head. Simon nodded and I shook my head again. Pete could be trying to contact anybody. "Dickhead, I know you can hear this. You better get back here." I again stared at Simon who was smiling and nodding at me.

"Who are you looking for? Over," I asked, deepening my voice.

"I'm looking for a dickhead called Michael. Over," said Pete and there was somebody talking to him in the background. And then Jeff was screaming something. He must have had his mouth too close to the microphone. I could just make out crazy shouting and muffled bumping.

"Do you hear me?!" screamed Jeff.

"Yeah?" I said. "I didn't catch the first bit of what you said though."

"Listen, Mikey, you get back here. Get back in the next hour and I'll... otherwise..." and then there was just heavy breathing. Perhaps Pete was laughing in the background.

"Okay," I said. The heavy breathing continued. I looked at the paper and then pressed the buttons in the order described. The breathing continued. I tried again and there was a click. I looked at Simon. "Ha! Did that work?"

"Yeah."

"Tracking and communications?"

"Both disabled."

"Shit, didn't think that would work. Maybe our luck is changing." I stood up.

"What? Did you *hear* Jeff?" asked Simon.

"Yeah. That was unlucky. But since *then*, maybe it's changed." I sat in my chair, looked at the dark screen and turned it on. "Brown," I said to myself while waiting for the narrow band of light across the middle of it to expand with a pop and fill the whole square. It hummed and then popped and the screen was showing our location. The Oasis, ha! A lovely name for what was no more than a weeping boil on the face of the City. It did have an ice-cream machine going for it. I was looking for brown. I pressed the bottom button and zoomed out from where we were. I kept my finger on the button as the district names appeared. I was going bigger in scale than that, much bigger, and as I continued to zoom, those district names were overlaid by territory names. I moved the screen with the dial to reveal the biggest brownest area to the east and then I zoomed in with the top button, moving the dial away from any major-looking towns that appeared. Towns I'd never been to or even heard of. Then I avoided the small towns. After a few seconds of leaning in close I saw an expanse with no names. I put the marker in the middle of it and read out the coordinates. "How far?" I asked.

"Guess," said Simon. He likes it when I guess things. Especially distances. Normally they're short distances, within the City, but this one was *big time*. I looked at the map. Turned the dial to zoom out and zoomed in again.

"Miles or kilometres?"

"Miles."

"Okay, six thousand, one hundred and-"

"Ooh! And what?" asked Simon, interrupting me mid guess. He was nodding, encouragingly, and that got me all excited.

I licked my lips. The number twenty-seven was talking to me. But so was thirty-two. "And thirty-two miles! Six thousand, one hundred and thirty-two miles!" I looked at Simon who made a klaxon sound and turned his mouth down. We didn't know why he could make a klaxon sound, it never ever came in handy outside of our quizzes. Don't know why I can turn his accuracy down either, but I can. Seems dangerous. I can mute him too. I'm not supposed to be able to turn off tracking and communications, but then I wasn't supposed to have got hold of that code. "Twenty-seven miles! Six one two seven!"

KLAXON SOUND. Simon looked down at the screen. "Eleven miles."

"Damn, nearly said eleven."

"Three thousand, eight hundred and eleven miles."

I too looked at the screen. "Wait. What? Three thou... What? So it was all wrong?"

"Yeah, you were *way* off. You always are," said Simon doing that annoying smirk.

"So... why did you go 'ooh' when I said part of it?"

"What?"

"When I started to guess you went *'oooooh'*, like an idiot."

"I just like it when you guess."

I looked at him. Sometimes he perplexed me. I was now perplexed. "That was a complete waste of time," I said. Simon was smiling. "Anyway, I nearly said eleven, honestly. I'm not joking."

"Yeah sure."

I moved the map around randomly. "Not so smart now, are you?" I was back in charge. "You're all ones and zeros," I said.

"Three, seven. Forty-two," he replied. Looking at me with his eyebrows raised and his chin down. "Eighty."

"That's not what I meant. Advanced AI? *De*vanced, more like. Hey, add those numbers together if you're so smart."

"Devanced isn't a word," he said and started the tiny engines.

I stood and stretched then sat down again and did my harness up, then pulled it hard to tighten it. I took the dictionary from the glove box – I had to stretch my arms out because of the harness – and checked a word. Then I put it back. I wasn't checking if devanced was a word. I was looking up something else.

"Jeff didn't sound happy."

"He didn't, did he?" I agreed. "I'm surprised." I was surprised. Yesterday I'd sat in his office while he told me that Simon was so useless, he wanted him melted and entombed. You'd think I was doing Jeff a favour by taking him. It was weird. And scary. It was also okay. If I'd given it much prior thought, I would have dreaded hearing Jeff ranting. But it happened and it was okay. A bit of a shock but it also galvanised us. We definitely couldn't go back, not now.

From the Oasis we flew over the sprawl, heading as far away from the Hub as we could get. Over the different shades and textures of grey. Some gloss, some matte, some light and some silver. After an hour or so we could see down to a sight we rarely saw. Fragments of the bottom level. The actual bottom. The surface of planet Earth. It was always pretty cool to actually see land, to see the ground, and for a bit of fun we went down through the old residential areas on the outskirts. Red bricks, broken windows, fire escapes and massive shadows. Shafts of light here and there shining on green trees clawing up at them, but mostly shadows making geometric black voids. Simon put our headlights on. They don't come on automatically. The streets were crazy narrow and some still had the words and symbols visible. STOP and arrows pointing this way and that. Simon's fans had come on as we picked our way through, heading roughly east. I didn't help him navigate. I know when to keep quiet.

I like it when Simon's fans come on. So he gets stressed like a person. Don't we all? I'm not an engineer and neither is Jeff. I've known Simon for years, I know his quirks. I think I'd know if he was going to explode, you know? The King Street incident, which, yeah, had been bad and left Pete, then a rep himself, with no arms or legs, had happened *ages* ago. Not long after Simon and the others were operational. Even in that disaster nobody had been killed. And look at Pete now! Happy as can be, running the hangar with his mechanical limbs. A news cam came to film him so he got a bit of fame out of it too. You can see us in the footage.

We're pretending to load the Lady in the background about two minutes in. I've got the tape somewhere. Ha! And because he swears so much they had to chop the audio, so it sounds a bit like he's got a stutter. He has a very foul mouth now, Pete has. Always ready with a friendly insult. That's just since the accident. It must have damaged the part of his brain which stops him insulting people. I don't really remember him before, though we definitely worked together. Nobody died, is the main thing. The buildings were built over, and after the incident they'd issued a firmware update and not one had exploded since. Nah, Simon isn't exploding anytime soon. I'd know. Pete blamed UPS for the accident, more than he blamed his Pilot. Apparently a UPS truck had taken his slot and that's why his Pilot overheated. Pete couldn't find the kill switch so it was partly bad training too. A combination of things. It all seemed like one big accident to me.

Teething troubles. There are always going to be teething troubles. Exploding, accidentally eating sweets and getting gummed up, that kind of thing. Kinks which need ironing out. The new ones, no matter how great they are, aren't going to be any different. Some people just want shiny new things.

Eventually the holes and crevasses that revealed only glimpses of the ground or sky grew bigger and more common, until they began to merge and formed open spaces. These open spaces grew bigger and more common with each mile we travelled. Occasionally there'd be a cluster of life. A flow of traffic heading to some large destination in the suburbs, but we were forging our own path, heading to the future, and soon the City was a dot behind us. I almost started to relax. That relaxation was ruined by Simon asking if we were really doing this. He thought I'd been playing a prank on him. It was okay, though. I muted him and pointed ahead.

Below us there were a few trees. Sand-covered derelict buildings. We zipped over things that were once silos or farms. Rusted carcasses of all sizes, from small tractors to giant harvesters. A lot of this land would have been green. Verdant. Like the Boulevard near Central. There were sections of fences that once would have prevented cows from getting splattered by lorries or school buses. I once stroked a cow. Or it might have been a horse.

The problem was, I was telling him everything was going to be okay. And he believed me. But I'm not sure I believed it. He didn't understand the gravity of the situation. The situation had a lot of gravity. All the gravity. You're decommissioned, smelted and entombed under concrete and, well, things don't get much worse than that.

"It's going okay so far," I said. Simon looked at me then turned back to the front. I didn't unmute him. I liked the quiet. The whine of the engines. The wind against the windscreen. "I'll look after you." Simon nodded and looked over to the left side window, so now his face was away from me. I could still see his reflection. He was rolling his eyes. "We should be enjoying this," I said, squinting to the horizon, our destination. "Let's enjoy it."

I guess the reason it pissed me off when Simon asked me what the plan was, was because *he* knew it as well as I did! Any parts I hadn't *explicitly* told him, he should have just known. He'd experienced what I had over the last few years. We were a team. We hadn't been apart. I know some people think it's weird I bring him to the canteen or bar. I think it's weird to treat him like he is a truck. A tool.

Anyway, it was simple. It wasn't a complex scheme. We'd take the truck. Engage on a sort of road trip. See a bit of the world, sample some cuisine and then find somewhere in the east where we could live out a nice peaceful life. First part was already done and I was getting hungry. Unfortunately out here it was barren. It was good that it was, in the respect that we were off the grid, but yeah, I needed something to eat. As we flew I told Simon what was going to happen.

"You'll make bread," I said and smiled at the thought. Simon was just staring ahead. I stared ahead at the spoiled earth beneath us. The horizon was still no closer. The sky was blue but there was weather ahead. I sort of zoned out of the view, zoned into our future.

"'What's this one?' I'll ask you and I'll click the mag I'm reading, the one about carpentry or something, back into its dock and take the plate from you. There'll be, like, tiny wisps of steam, blown around by the breeze coming in from the open window, dancing up from the slice of bread." I wiggled my fingers like they were steam. "The bread's on the small plate you gave me. It's the crust, right? The best bit. And the window overlooks a meadow." I could see the meadow. "We've got to have a meadow. 'Guess', you'll say, about the bread, and I'll lift the warm slice of bread. It's heavy, you know? I like my bread like I like my robots — dense as fuck." I turned to Simon. "That's a joke. I joke now, because life is good. I don't like dense robots. Anyway, you're not dense." Then I was back there, with the bread. "I'll smell the slice and then take a bite." I imagined my lower teeth cracking through the crisp, perfectly baked crust, my upper teeth sinking gently into the buttery pillowy bit of the bread which isn't the crust. "Mmm." God, that imaginary bread tasted good. "'What is it?' You'll ask, because you want me to guess the flavours. You've got the ingredients yourself." Sat there in the Lady I imagined chewing the imaginary bread, trying to work out what Simon had put into the bread which wasn't really there, to make it taste so good. "'Yeah, what? What?!' You'll ask, all excited, and I'll tell you to take it easy. 'I know it. It's honey and pump…' and you'll get ready with the klaxon, but I was fucking with you! Because it's sunflower seed!" I looked at Simon. He did a tiny shake of his head. "'Yeah, it is! Sunflower!' you'll say and then you'll go, 'Michael, you're *amazing* at eating bread' and I'll say, 'Thanks Simon, you're amazing at *baking* bread.' You'll be all sheepish and say something like 'Ah, I don't know, I think I left it in too long.'" I shook my head. "You're too self-critical, you know?" I said and looked at Simon. He was smiling slightly. I turned back to my window and saw the church and said "Ooh!"

The sky was cloudy but it didn't look like rain. I'm by no means a top cloud expert, just an amateur, but these were the wrong kind of clouds for rain. These were high and flat, and so I got out without my coat. Simon followed. "Check this out!" I told him while doing a spin in the car park. Nepton, as it was marked on the map, when you zoomed in far enough, was really quite pretty, in a faded-photo kind of way. "It's pretty, isn't it?"

We were only half a day outside the City and already we were having a tremendous adventure. The road trip had begun. It was a different world out here. There was nowhere like this in the City, not any more, but I suppose the way the City spread and consumed, it probably wouldn't be too long until it reached out here. The clearing where we parked was in front of a real-life church, made of real-life dead wood which was painted white. The parking area was massive and old. The church and the town had once been popular.

We'd parked on the far side. Away from the building and other vehicles as I wanted to keep our contact with humans to a minimum, until we'd gone a bit further. Just to be safe. "Simon! It's pretty?" I asked before I remembered. "Ha, unmute, confirm."

"I'm not making you bread."

"You are," I corrected, "but this is pretty. A bit different."

"Is it?" He looked around.

"Yeah! Well, it was, once. And the church is pretty," I said, pointing to it. He looked at it.

"It's white."

"You should write poetry, mate," I told him with a playful arm slap. Don't know what it was. Hunger. Thinking about the meadow. Don't know, but I was upbeat and that's why Simon was suspicious. "You really paint a picture with your words," I told him.

"The town is abandoned."

"Yeah, a bit," I agreed. "Apart from the church." It had looked better from the air and four miles away. That's why I'd made him turn around. "It's a bit rough now but I can picture what this would have been like."

"That's nice for me."

Simon hates being muted. That's why he was pretending not to be interested. I could picture it. I could see cars with wheels and people going about their lives. Going to work. Getting paint.

Sleeves rolled up. I looked at him. He wasn't getting it. I looked over at what was just about still the town square.

"It once bustled."

"Bustled?"

"This place would have *bustled*, once."

"Bustled?"

"Oh yeah, people would have been bustling around here. Up that street," I said, pointing at the street. "Bustling around here," I said, pointing around the car park with a circular point. "Bustling about."

"Oh, cool. Like everywhere in the City."

"Nah, that's not bustling, they do something else in the City. Bustling is…" I couldn't really describe it. "It isn't aggressive, and it's, like, independent. You know?"

"No, not really."

"You know my insect theory?"

"Yes," he sighed. He knew my insect theory. How we're now behaving like insects working for the Queen when in fact, as mammals, we should just be chilling out like monkeys or dogs. I go on about it a lot.

"Well, when this place was thriving, people weren't quite so insecty, or, like, the Queen wasn't quite so queeny."

"Just looks like a ruin."

"Now, but this is where I grew up," I said, heading over to the square. He followed me.

"No you didn't."

"Well, not here, but a town like this." A main street ran from the square down the side of the church and on it were four, three, and a couple of six-storey buildings. Most had large windows on the ground floor. Some with the glass still intact. I didn't know what the main street in Nepton was called, or if it even had a name, there was no sign, but it may as well have been called *Remembory Street* and let me tell you, I wasn't just walking down it, oh no, I was *sashaying* down it like a regular Miss Ikarus. Gah! Miss Ikarus. She'd visited the Hub last year. God, that had been awkward. Poor girl. They shouldn't still do that.

"These were once shops, right?" I said as we strolled. It was only in my mind that I was sashaying. I was strolling and being an excellent tour guide. I stopped at a window, cupped my hands around my face and leant onto the dirty glass. Apart from papers and posters on the floor and an overturned table, it was completely empty. Light was coming through from an open door at the back. We could probably go in. I stood back and saw our reflections. Simon was looking around, disinterested. "This one might have been a clothes shop. You could go in, try on a few pairs of trousers."

"Amazing!" he replied, not even trying to hide his lack of wonder.

"You're right, it *is* amazing, *actually*," I said. "You could just go in and buy things, and they had all different things. No waiting for the thing you want to come up on rotation, you know?" Simon was looking at the shop fronts as we passed. Probably checking out his reflection in any bits of glass. I was doing that too. "You didn't have to go down the Bizaare to get things. You could buy things. In shops. On the surface!"

"There's nowhere here to eat," he said.

"Nah, town's gone," I agreed. I stopped at another window and saw darkness. The flooring had gone and there was bare concrete. Who bothers taking flooring? Where the fuck does flooring go? "This one might have been a cafe." We walked to the next one. "Maybe a florist or a Chinese," I said, pointing to it. "A florist is where you buy flowers."

"Why would you buy flowers?"

"Why?" I asked, making sure that was what he'd asked.

"To eat?"

"No. Nah, you can't eat flowers. Actually, some you can, I think. You'd... you'd buy them as a present." He stopped and his face went blank. He moved his head smoothly and slowly from side to side. "What?"

Eventually his facial features moved and he nodded. "I can hear singing."

"Really?"

"Yeah."

We started walking again. Slowly. I was looking down, mainly, at the fissured tarmac a couple of metres ahead. I was hungry. All I'd eaten was the ice-cream. "There was a Chinese where I grew up. That's noodles and chicken and things. The chips were weird. They must've used a different oil. Different cooking oil so the chips were weird."

"Different oils taste different?"

"Yeah."

"Interesting."

"Thanks."

"You're welcome."

"The owner gave me and this other kid a job, to clean the grease from his kitchen windows."

"I definitely detect singing," said Simon.

I ignored him. "This was a big job, you know?"

"I don't know. How could I know? You haven't told me dimensions or anything."

"The kid I was with, I think it was Tom. He lasted, like, three hours. Covered in grease, clothes ruined. It was grim so he quit. Yeah? Just went home."

"I don't care. Your stories are boring. They never have a point."

"This one does, listen. Or I'll mute you. He quit, I didn't think he'd get anything but the guy gave him twenty-five pounds, and this was back when twenty-five pounds wasn't much, not even to a young guy. Twenty-five pounds for three hours! You couldn't buy anything with twenty-five pounds. Two tapes, maybe."

"Well, what did he expect? He hadn't finished the job. That's why he was compensated so poorly. Is that that point?"

"Not exactly. Listen, so he quit. Couldn't handle it. But do you know who *didn't* quit?"

"You? You're the only other person I know in this story."

"There's the Chinese man who gave us the job."

"Did he quit?"

"Why would he quit? It was his restaurant."

"Because his windows were greasy?"

"What? No! I hate telling you stories. People don't… Who would give up a business because of greasy windows?"

"Greasy windows are bad, apparently. I don't know."

"Yeah, but not *that* bad."

"You then. You didn't quit."

"Duh-huh! Yeah, I didn't quit. Didn't even think about it. Two full days it took. I actually went back the next day in clean clothes. Ruined more clothes. *Two* sets of clothes. Grease doesn't come out. But when I was finished, the windows were *spotless*. Well, no, not spotless. There were bits you couldn't get to. But, you know… Simon… Simon!"

"It's coming from the church."

"Are you listening to me?"

"Yeah, clothes ruined. Windows still greasy."

"*Two* sets. But as I went for my pay I felt that... you won't know because it's a feeling, but that sense of satisfaction you feel when you've done something difficult. When you didn't just give up. And I'd done it for myself, not to make somebody else richer. It was for *me*."

"Cool."

"I'm talking about *not* taking the easy option. So I went to Mr Chinese Man an-"

"He was called Mister Chi-"

"Shut up. Guess what he gave me?"

Simon's fans whirred. "One hundred pounds."

"You'd think, wouldn't you? You would think. Nope, he gave me twenty-five fucking pounds."

"Ooof," said Simon.

"I just took it. I probably thanked him," I said, sniffing. "Fuck."

"Is that it?"

"Yeah, there's got to be a moral in there."

"It's beneficial to quit? The Chinese are exploitative?"

"People are shit, is probably it. And greedy. I'm still glad I saw it through."

"You like noodles."

"Yeah, I really fucking do! Anyway, his place will be like this now." I looked at the ground as we sauntered. We were sauntering now. "That's what fucked everything up."

"Hard work?"

"Greed."

"Oh."

"Yeah, it was… there was a thing where people wanted big houses. That's what everybody wanted. Big houses and loads of stuff. There was a point where it seemed really important to have loads of stuff."

"Stuff."

"Just… yeah, people wanted stuff. Not stuff you need, like trousers, but other stuff. Stuff they didn't need."

"Why?"

"Just so they'd have more stuff than other people. Can you believe that? And so they'd work hard so they could buy stuff. Work like insects just so they could have more stuff. Then of course you're buying the stuff from these corporations that just grew and, well, yeah, this."

"There's nowhere to eat here," said Simon.

"It's a ghost town," I agreed. I looked up and down the street. "Starbucks."

"What?"

"One of these would have been a Starbucks." Simon didn't ask what that was. We'd gone far enough. "Wonder what's happening in the church."

"What happens in a church?"

"Oh, mad shit. You wanna go and see?"

"They're singing."

"Yeah, they do that. Is it Eggfest?"

"Eggfest?"

"Yeah, that's around this time of year. It's *mental*. You want to have a look?"

"Do you?"

"Do *you?* You decide, I've been in one."

"I don't know, are you allowed to just go in?"

"Of course, it's a church." We were walking back on the other side of the street. "Easter, not Eggfest. The proper name is Easter."

"Do you want to go in?" he asked.

"Just *once* it would be nice if *you* made a decision," I said. We went down the side of the church. Looking up I could see its pointed steeple had been patched with all manner of material. The white paint was peeling.

"I didn't really want to leave the Hub," he said.

"It would just be *nice* if you made a decision that *I* agreed with. It'd take the pressure off me a bit."

"I want to look in the church."

"Cool. Quick look. They're boring, really. Then we need to find food," I said. My arms were getting cold.

Quick look! Yeah, nice one, Simon. Why couldn't he have said no? I warned him it was boring. We sat through the last ninety minutes of somebody called Ned's funeral, so it wasn't just boring. It was depressing as well as tedious. The problem was, once we'd opened the doors and people in pews had turned around, we'd *had* to go in or we would have looked foolish. Ninety minutes! And we'd missed the first bit so fuck knows how long the whole thing was in total. After a bit I was glad Ned was dead, for putting us through it, he deserved whatever had happened to him. Simon liked the singing but I just mouthed along. The relief when they opened the doors! Had to push past a couple of very slow-moving people to get out first. I think we were supposed to wait for the coffin to be carried out but you can only take so much, you know? Outside I respectfully looked sad and nodded at mourners with my hands clasped in front of me. There was a lot of sad nodding at each other. Then I elbowed Simon and we started over to the Lady. I walked sadly the whole way. Walking sadly means walking slowly.

We were about to step into the Lady when I heard a call. Somebody was heading over from the church. "Fuck!" I said. It was a woman and she was waving at us. I waved back, unsure, and looked at Simon who shook his head. "Fuck," I said again. It was a big car park so it took her a while to get to us. She had a limp and walked with a stick. It didn't slow her down much, though. "Hello!" I said when she was close enough. A part of me thought she was going to invite us to a buffet then offer us a job. That was instantly dispelled.

"What do you think you're doing?" she asked.

"What do I think I'm doing?"

"Why did you bring that into the church?" she asked, pointing her stick at Simon.

"Why did I bring this into a church?" I asked, pointing at Simon.

"You can't bring that into a church."

"I can't bring this into a church?" I'd totally got stuck just parroting back her questions.

"It's an affront to God, especially after what happened to Ned."

"Poor Ned," I said. "We missed the first bit, so I'm not sure what ev-"

"Did you even know Ned?"

"Did I know Ned?" I said, blowing out my cheeks. "I mean, I *feel* I do. After all that. Did. Did know him. Or do know him."

"Is this a... a sick joke?"

"Is this?"

"Those things arc... arc…"

"Are?" I said. She was annoying me.

"Fucking dangerous!" she said, looking at me but pointing at Simon.

"Well he's not. He's friendly. He's got a... like a directive. He can't harm a human."

"I don't have one of those," said Simon. I looked at Simon.

"You don't?"

"No."

"I thought you had a, you know, harm no human thing. Like a failsafe."

"Nope. I could fuck you up."

"You sure?"

"Yeah I'm sure, I'm just nice," he said and I stared at him to see if he was joking. Apparently not. I raised my eyebrows. You learn something new every day.

"Why are you talking to it?" said the woman. "Do you need psychiatric help?"

"Nope, we're just fine, thanks. We just... we're on holiday. Just wanted to look in the church, that's all. Didn't think it would be a big deal."

"Well, please leave. And never take one of those into a house of worship again."

"Well, we *were* leaving, until you stopped us. And he's got the right to go into a church as much as anybody."

"Oh no it hasn't."

"Yeah, he has. At least he's nice. That's more than could be said for you! You're being *really* horrible. It's unnecessary."

"Go. GO!" She'd flipped. She really shouted that second 'go' and also hit Simon with her walking stick.

"Oh my Go… oodness, what is your problem? We're going. You need to go and, like, repent or something." I don't like talking to people, but I don't mind arguing with crazy people and I felt I was doing well. Telling her to repent. That was pretty good.

She hit Simon twice more with her stick then stabbed the end of it just under my left nipple. I batted it away then rubbed my chest while backing up. "You're the mentalcase!"

"Go! Go! GO!" she shrieked. She seemed on the verge of tears. We climbed into the Lady backwards. I had my palms out.

"Fuck!" I said as I buckled in and heard her stick bash the side. "If she's dented it… nutter. Quick, up!" I said and a couple of seconds later we were up. I looked down in time to see the woman spin around in the car park. She spun differently to how I had when we arrived.

"Shall I run her over?" asked Simon.

"Yeah, go on," I said and locked my chair as he climbed and looped, then lined up with the woman and descended. The woman was limping away but somehow twisted and craned her neck and saw us. She sped up more and reached the maximum speed her damaged body could maintain. Perhaps she was just above that speed because she looked on the verge of falling. She was moving like she was out of control. "Up!" I said and Simon climbed up and away from the out-of-control woman.

On our way over Nepton I saw it for what it was. Most buildings were missing at least part of their backs. It wasn't obvious if they'd been knocked down or fallen, but the town was a ruin. It was a wreck, much like its resident car-park termagant, and I felt badly let down. I released the catch which was between my legs and using my left leg I pushed my chair over to the side window. I looked out, my forehead resting on the side window as the landscape flicked past. I thought about how nothing was permanent. How everything was precariously balanced and how incredibly easy it would be for everything to just spiral out of control and for us to become a pair of Bill Higginses.

Floaty Bill. Poor Floaty Bill. Hadn't thought about nor heard mention of Floaty Bill for years. I looked at the barren landscape flying past below us. I must have been about ten or so. Still in primary school, but I remember watching the disaster very slowly unfold on each nightly news broadcast. Captain William Higgins had become untethered and floated away from one of the very first commercial space flights. He'd gone outside to fix the aerial and had become detached and floated away. There was joy and surprise, twenty-four hours later, when he floated past again. The joy didn't last as nobody was prepared and past he went, waving his arms which did nothing to alter his trajectory. His course was set. On the fourth day, when he passed for the fourth time, he did so slightly shaking his head and with his padded arms folded in his space suit. You could just see it, the barely perceptible shake of his head inside the motionless helmet. He didn't attempt to grab the pole which the crew and passengers had fashioned out of baguettes, because it was clearly way too short. Arms crossed. Stoic. Resigned. Bill Higgins had floated past and the ship had returned to Earth. He was lauded as a hero. They promoted him posthumously. He was also used as a cautionary tale. He's now a tourist attraction, like a hot spring.

Rain began to speckle the windscreen and off to the side there was a rainbow. Simon pointed to it, excited.

---

We saw it from miles away. Glittering like a jewel in the overcast afternoon. Lights in the City just give me a migraine, but this looked nice against the blank brown background. I suppose if somebody was covered in diamonds and gold and crowns and stuff, you wouldn't notice if they were wearing a really nice bracelet. If they were naked you'd notice the bracelet. Less is more, that's what I'm getting at. The diner looked nice, okay? That! That's what I'm saying. I was also literally starving, so that added to its appeal. It probably wasn't shimmering quite as brightly as it seemed. Part of that could have been my low blood sugar levels.

And it was busy. There was a steady stream of crafts swirling around it. The influx and outflux of vehicles confirmed the diner was open. It's one of my biggest fears, trying to get in somewhere that's closed. Trying the door, shaking it. People inside giving me the sad face, pitying me and apologising through the glass while I pretend everything is cool and I didn't want to go in anyway.

It was open.

Of course that meant it could be full. Then you run the risk of getting turned away once you're already inside. And more people see it happen. Close up. I was prepared to risk it.

The smell hit us before we'd opened the door of the Lady and stepped aground. The smell of grease being pumped powerfully from the vents was immense and seeped into the Lady. There were background notes of wet sand. It was properly raining now and, though only mid-afternoon, it was dark enough for headlights.

"That smells good," I said, putting on my big coat, my tummy rumbling like a bastard.

"Does it?" he asked.

Simon's sense of smell is over forty-eight times less powerful than that of a dog. That was a bullet point in the manual. The one in the glove box which I'd sometimes skim through if I was incredibly bored, during his early days especially. It stuck in my mind because it was an odd way of saying his sense of smell was four times better than a human's. You'd say it that way – focus on the positives. The rest of the book had been pretty technical and dry. I'd just used the quick-start guide as that seemed to have the important stuff. Resetting him. Muting him etc.

Being able to smell was wasted on Simon. He could smell but he didn't know *what* he was smelling, and further to that, he didn't even know if the smell was pleasant or rank. Pretty pointless. "I'm going to die if I don't eat something soon," I said, unfolding his rain cover.

"They might have sausages," offered Simon, jinxing it before we'd even got in there.

"Yeah, let's not get our hopes up."

"I think they do."

"Can you smell sausages?"

"Now?"

I did a long blink. "No, just in general. Can you *ever* smell sausages?" I asked. I was holding the clear rain cover like a matador holds that red thing. I shook it.

"I don't know."

"Then why ask, Simon? Why ask? *Why?*" I stared at Simon for a while but he ignored me. I get grumpy when I'm hungry. "Yeah, I could really go for a sausage, come on." Simon held his arms out and I clipped on the cover. He knows I love sausages. I've spoken about them many times, back in the canteen, where they have them, like once every two years.

In normal circumstances I'd send Simon to the window first, so he could check that we could definitely get a seat, but it was too rainy for that, so after we shut everything down we ran splashing and giggling across to the diner. The place was big, with loads of empty tables, so that was absolutely perfect.

I wasn't worried that they were looking for us. I should have been but I wasn't. The resources it would take! If they actually *did* start looking then it'd take a hundred years just to check the City. They probably weren't even looking. Not yet. Probably still just monitoring the transmissions. See, Ladys would often be found abandoned all over the City. Well, not often, but it happened sometimes. Sometimes you'd hear that so-and-so had abandoned his Lady, or sometimes just the Pilot would return. It never seemed like *that* big a deal. Not that we didn't have to be careful. No point taking unnecessary risks, but eating was now life or death. I wiped my feet as best I could on the mat's rotators but we still tracked mud across the white, speckled floor. I felt a bit bad about that.

Simon was across from me. He still had his rain cover on and looked a bit stupid. I had red tea and was waiting for my soup. Soup? Yeah, I know! They'd run out of sausages and I'd panicked while pretending I wasn't too upset about sausages anyway, and I'd somehow ordered soup. Fucking soup! At least it came with bread. I had the bread. I ripped a piece in half and began to eat. The soup hadn't arrived yet.

"If you hadn't said they probably have sausages then they'd

have had sausages. Probably." I'd been trying not to say that. I was just thinking it. I knew it was irrational.

"What?"

"Nothing."

"They ran out of sausages because I said they might have sausages?"

"..."

"Michael!"

"No, I'm not saying that. I'm saying that if you'd said that they definitely *weren't* going to have sausages, then we'd all be in a better mood."

"You still wouldn't have sausages!"

"And I could live with that. Honestly, expect to be disappointed and you'll never be *that* disappointed. Expect the worst, all the time, and then if anything good happens then it's a, you know, a bonus. You got my hopes up and they were crushed."

"Sorry," said Simon.

"Ah, it's not your fault. I just don't understand how an establishment whose sole purpose is to sell food can run out of food. That's all. It just... it boggles my mind." There were sausages on the menu, that was the worst thing! And I was happy for a moment, but when I tried to order, the rug was pulled from beneath me and I came crashing down to a place lower than I'd been to begin with. That's when I'd gone back to the menu and picked the next thing I saw. Soup.

The table we sat at was turquoise, rounded and thick, with a rippled chrome trim. "Are you going to review the bread?" asked Simon.

I looked at the bread in my hand and shook my head. "Maybe when the soup gets here. *If* it gets here." I looked around the diner. Everybody here could be on the run, for all I knew. We didn't stand out. "We're just tools, anyway."

"No!" protested Simon. "We're cool!"

"Ha! No, I mean we're just *tools*, you know? Like implements. To the Corporation. We're like... shovels. It won't be a big emergency that we're AWOL. It's not a big panic when somebody loses a hammer, is it? We're not important. We think we're important, but we're not."

"AWOL?"

"Away Without... something." I thought I knew what the L stood for but it took me a couple of seconds to remember. "Let."

"Away Without Let?"

"Like, they haven't *let* us go, we just went, away."

"That's AWL."

"It's from when they had soldiers."

"Oh right, well that explains it."

"Yeah," I agreed. "The bread is very dry. And hard. I need something to dip it in." I dropped the bread and I drank some tea. The tea was good. I looked around, over the rim of my cup. "We'll need to get rid of the logos." I figured we could peel them off the side of the Lady. "How long does it take to put soup in a bowl?"

"How far is the soup from the bowl? What are they using to transf-"

"Shut up."

"Hey, you know what *I* think is going to happen?" asked Simon, smiling.

"What? What do you think is going to happen?"

"I think it's already happening. I think that Jeff *is* looking for us. I think he's very annoyed. Furious. I think that he sees what you've done as an insult."

"Yeah? He probably does, fuck him."

"I don't think he'll stop at *anything* until he finds us." Simon was nearly giggling.

"Okay."

"I think he *does* have the resources. First I think he'll get Carlos into his office. He'll know you and Carlos were talking last night before you did Karaoke. He'll find out you were talking about the east. He'll make Carlos talk." Simon raised his eyebrows at me. It was strange. Simon was being strange. "Maybe we'll get a bit further. Maybe we'll think we've got away. Might be a year from now but Jeff *will* show up," said Simon. I put my tea down and sat back and watched Simon talk. I was waiting for the punchline. "When he finds us he'll want to hurt you. He might kill you. He might just torture you, but he *will* make you pay."

"Where are you going with this?"

"I think he'll strap you to a chair, and you'll be naked. Blood around your eyes, from the beating."

"The beating?"

"The beating. And your arms will be strapped to the armrests. Your palms will be facing up and Jeff will take a knife, a very sharp blade, and cut a straight line from your shoulder to your wrist. Down the inside of your arm. And you'll be screaming and he'll enjoy the sound as he peels apart the cut in your skin and puts his fingers in, digging them in and grabbing the tendons and veins and muscles, and pulling th-"

"What the fuck is wrong with you?"

"What?"

"Why... why are you saying this?"

"That's what I think will happen," said Simon, nodding

slightly and smiling. Smiling! That was the unsettling part.

"Are you okay, Simon? Have you blown a capacitor?"

"And he'll burn your feet to stumps!" he blurted, like *that* was the punchline. I stared at him.

"I…" was all I could manage and he saw some of the fear in my eyes.

"I was trying to think of the worst thing that could happen! So it... so it won't."

"Fucking *hell*, I was talking about sausages and things. That was just... depressing. And strangely specific."

"Oh, I thought-"

"I'll do the thinking. You just be... Simon, yeah? Fucking hell, that was *dark*. What do you watch when I'm asleep?" A server was trundling in our direction, but I'd given up on ever getting soup so I expected it to go to a table behind us but... it didn't! And I was happy. And as an added bonus the soup looked *great*. Much better than I'd expected. It was more like a stew.

At first I'd been coy about eating in front of Simon. For the first few weeks of us being together I'd felt guilty about it, so I'd never express an opinion about what I was eating, even if it was delicious. It turned out he *loved it* when I ate something nice. He liked it even more when I reviewed food. The soup looked tasty and I pulled a very satisfied face at him. I mouthed *ooooh* as I reached for the spoon. "First impressions are generally positi-"

"Is that Ikarus truck yours?" asked the person attached to the hand that was suddenly on my shoulder.

I stopped reaching for the spoon and ran my tongue across my front top teeth with my mouth tightly shut. My hand involuntarily became a fist. *This could be bad. Very bad. How to play this?*

"Hello!" said Simon, brightly, and my hand relaxed.

"Is it yours? The yellow one?" asked the man. He'd released my shoulder. I didn't answer him immediately. I thought about his question while I stared at Simon. "The yellow truck? It's not yours? Habla usted inglés? El camión amarillo?"

"I'm sorry, what?" I asked.

"Is that your Ikarus truck outside?" said the man, slowly and clearly.

"Ha! No, I think I'd know if I had a big yellow truck," I said and then snorted a laugh as I stared at Simon. Simon's face was fixed. I picked up the spoon and stirred my stew. The man was still there. Ignoring him wasn't making him go away. I put some stew in my mouth even though it was too hot. I'd felt it was too hot even before it got in my mouth. My nose sensed it. "Well, thanks," I said and smiled before returning to stirring my stew, but the man was still standing next to me. I could hear water drip from him. "Big yellow truck," I said, shaking my head and taking a sharp intake of breath so the air entering my mouth ran over and cooled my tongue. Then I dared look up at the man's face. It was quite red and under quite a large cap. I could see he was looking at the emblem on my overalls. Deliberately looking. The same emblem which was emblazoned massively on the side of our big yellow truck. "Why? Why? You know? Why? Why, why do you ask?"

"Somebody's stealing the engines," he said and I nodded. I nodded for quite a long time. If this was a trick then it was a good one. His face didn't give much away. I put the spoon down and dabbed my face with the serviette, even though I hadn't got any soup on my face. I screwed up the serviette and threw it in a disgusted manner onto the table. "Damn. Bloody criminals, well, we'd better go and check *our* truck is okay, our... our blue one," I said. "Thanks for the heads up." The man moved on to the next table and asked the people sitting there the same question he'd asked us. But he looked back at me as I was putting my coat on.

"You're not going to eat your soup?" said Simon.

"It's boiling. They must have heated it up in a... foundry or something." I made for the door with Simon following.

There were two small figures trying to steal our engines. They were hunched over, trying to wrestle the back left one off. I shook my head which just rubbed my head against the inside of my hood. I had my big coat on so I had to twist my whole upper body to look around for Simon. He was standing beside me beneath his clear plastic shield. His face obscured by thousands of darting droplets. I pointed at the thieves, unsure how to proceed. The rain on the outside of my hood was like a thousand tiny fingers flicking it. I walked down the side of the Lady, making sure Simon was right behind me. Sensing my approach one of the thieves looked up. It was a woman, which surprised me. I kinda thought they were feral children. She looked at me and nodded. Brazen. I nodded back. "Can I help you?" I asked.

"Have you got a twelve millimetre socket?" she asked, pushing her hood up with the back of her wrist. Her hood wasn't waterproof. It was stuck to her head and her hair was stuck to her face. I turned towards Simon by twisting at the waist. This was all very unexpected. I turned back.

"This is our truck," I said, almost apologetically. "Do you wanna maybe stop doing that?" They ignored me. "We need those for, you know, propulsion."

"Do you want a fucking hole in your head?" asked the other figure, standing straight and revealing her face. She was a lot younger than the other one. She was also holding much more of a pistol than the other one was. She swiped the top of it and it charged. I held my hands up and took a step back. I grabbed for Simon's rainshield and then stood behind him so that I could make sure nobody snuck up behind us. I tried to drag him backwards but he didn't get the message. He stood there. I wasn't cowering, I simply crouched down so I could see under his rainshield. I'd tell you if I'd been cowering. Not at all. That's why I was crouched behind Simon when it happened. Yeah, at that moment I'd had my eyes closed so I didn't see it happen. But even though I was crouched with my eyes closed behind Simon, I was still ready for action.

They were impressed with Simon. They spoke about how much they could get for him. Wasn't much, actually, they could have got more, I'm sure. I heard one of them undo the poppers on his cover and then there was a bang. And the sound of humans going *doof*! I saw the flash through my eyelids. And yeah, I might have screamed. When I peeked out from behind Simon I saw the thieves in a heap, up past the Lady. A smouldering, writhing heap of thieves. "Fuck!" I said.

"I'm sorry," said Simon. He hadn't killed them. One of them was already sitting up. I screamed again and slipped to my knees, then got to my feet and ran and scrambled to the doorhole on the Lady. Simon hadn't followed me. I saw one of the thieves already standing. She was leaning over with her hands on her knees, but she was standing.

"Simon!" I shouted.

"I thought this wasn't yours," said the man from the diner who'd chosen only now to come outside and actually do something about the whole fucking thief thing.

56

"This blue truck is ours," I said, looking at Simon. He was still just standing there. "And I like your orange shirt," I said, thinking fast. His shirt was actually green. "Simon!" I shouted and he snapped out of whatever he was in. He looked around then came over and I moved aside to let him in.

"I'm sorry," he said again.

"Don't be, they were dicks. Get us up." I closed the door on the diner guy.

"I'm sorry! I'm sorry!" Simon was saying in a voice I'd never heard before. He sounded on the verge of tears as I buckled in.

"Let's just get out of here. Hope they didn't get the engine off."

There was a small bump as Simon spun the Lady but it still flew.

"What did you do?!"

"I'm sorry!"

"That did *not* go well," I said. I looked in Simon's wing mirror. Simon wasn't hanging around and the light from the diner was already shrinking to a pin prick, but nothing was following us, it seemed. I stood and took my coat off. "Mate, you could have killed them. Thought you didn't hurt people?"

"It was an accident!" said Simon.

"Nah, don't worry. It was them or us. Shit though! First time I've had a gun pointed at me!"

"But I didn't..."

"You have to pick your battles. You don't know your own strength."

I stripped down to my underpants and vest and got a towel from my pack. I rubbed the towel over my head. My head wasn't even that wet because of my big coat, but it felt nice to rub it. I kept laughing as I did it. Relief laughing. Relaughing. My coat had done an excellent job of keeping the top half of me dry but it had simply channelled the rain directly onto the bottom of my overalls. They were sodden and would need to be in front of the heaters for a while. I draped them over my right forearm and got lost for a moment, staring out over nothing but dark wet mud. I checked the mirrors again. Nothing.

"I didn't even..." Simon said again. I could hear his fans over the wipers. They were really going, his fans.

"Okay, don't worry about it. They deserved it. I thought they'd shot you... What did you do? Punch them into next week?"

"One of them... there was just a bright flash, then... I didn't... the flash was in me!"

He seemed to be in shock. The way he was repeating that he didn't. I stood behind him. I looked out of the windscreen from his side. Not something I usually do while we're flying. I saw what he saw, through the rapidly beating wipers. The sky was lighter ahead. There was a narrow band of gold between the burgundy ground and the bruised purple sky. "You know what it was?"

"What?"

"The *Rage*. That was just pure undiluted rage. That's what that bright flash was. That's what happens. I get it sometimes when it's just... gah! You know? And you were worried about me too."

"Where did you go?"

"I was right there with you, buddy. It's probably a good thing you got them before I did." I undid the poppers on his rain hood and lifted it off and shook it in the space behind the chairs, then threw it into the corner. "This rain cover is fucked," I said. It doesn't really rain in the City. The air above it is too hot. Simon's shoulders were soaking. I went to wipe off some water and as I touched him the world shook then disappeared.

It was dark and I was being jostled and there were screams echoing all around. I'd probably have fallen over if I wasn't just jostled into somebody else. There wasn't enough room to fall over. I was pushed from behind into the back of the person in front and when I turned to express my displeasure I was knocked sideways. People were screaming. Wailing. Shouting out names. If you fell over here you were done for. You'd have your ticket punched for sure. I tried to hold an arm out, trying to make some space, and somebody's knee hit the back of mine and my leg folded unexpectedly. I went down while clinging on to the back of somebody's jacket. I lost my grip. I tried to get up but there were already people stepping over me. Knees. Bums. Feet. Somebody stumbled over, actually sat on my shoulder. It didn't hurt. I stayed down for... dunno, but my face was stamped on a few times. *I can't breathe*, I thought. Now annoyed, I ignored the weight pressing down on me and, tensing myself, I slowly stood, knocking people sideways. Then I grabbed on to a person on each side of me to stop myself falling again. The crowd I was part of was moving slowly in a direction. Most people were facing the same way.

I didn't realise I was in a tunnel until I saw the end of it. For the last part I was crushed so tightly against other people that my feet weren't on the ground. The screaming was mainly coming from behind me. People around me were just grunting. "Keep it moving!" shouted somebody from ahead. From the exit.

Something had happened. Was I on a transit? Had I been? And the transit had, what? Derailed? Was it the Snake? We weren't in the City. The last thing I remembered was... where was Simon? I tried to shout his name but could only gasp out a croak.

Everybody fell over when they got to the end of the tunnel. Not just me. Everybody did as we spilled out. Some running for a bit, trying to stay upright before faceplanting. Most going straight down. "Keep it moving! C'mon, c'mon!" somebody was shouting in a loud and clear voice. "Move to the side! To the side!"

Out of the tunnel there was slightly more room. Slightly. When you got up you could walk in. The tunnel led to a white room so big you couldn't see the sides or the top. You wouldn't know you were inside, but I knew I wasn't outside. I suppose when I noticed everybody was now wearing white gowns, me included, that I realised what had happened. I knew where I was. "Fuck," I muttered. I was in a massive mental asylum. Was I shocked? No, not really. Disappointed certainly.

We shuffled forwards and I wondered where exactly I'd finally lost my mind. I didn't know. I wasn't sure I'd ever had it. I could have been in here for years. The crowd spread more the further we shuffled. There was a person ahead I'd chosen to shamble after. Figured they might know where we should be going, because I didn't have a clue.

"Horse riding is full, I repeat, horse riding is full!" came the same loud voice as before. The person I was following stopped upon hearing this and their shoulders slumped before they changed direction. I stood there for a while and then continued the way I'd been going.

I got to a woman with long hair. Her white gown had gold on it. "Horse riding is full," she said before I could ask her anything. I wasn't sure what I was going to ask her so it was good she said something.

"I don't want to go horse riding," I said.

"Well you can't, it's full."

"What... what should I do?"

"I don't know, what do you like doing?" she asked. She smiled but I didn't buy it. Looked a bit forced.

"What do I like doing?"

"What do you want to do while you're here? What about surfing? Do you like surfing?"

"I don't... I've never done it."

"Surfing is full too. Look, have a think about it. Think what you'd like to do for eternity."

"Eternity?"

"But you can't do horse riding. It's full. Or surfing. So is trampolining. Actually most things that you need equipment for are oversubscribed. Well, all of them, honestly, but you could do dancing."

"Dancing?"

"How about modern interpretive dance? You look like a modern interpretive dance kind of guy."

"I don't know what that is."

"It's good. You dance your feelings. You want to do that?"

"For eternity?"

"For eternity."

"I mean... no, probably not that. Do I get drugs? Is there somewhere I should be getting drugs?"

"There are no drugs up here, mate."

"I think I should maybe take some medication. I think you're supposed to give me medication." I needed something to make all of this go away. "Are you a doctor?"

"No."

"Where's the doctor? I don't think I can breathe." I didn't seem to be breathing. "Do you know where Simon is?"

"There are nearly forty billion souls up here, of course I know where Simon is!"

"Where is h-"

"Is that him?" she asked, pointing at a man who seemed to be waiting behind me, for his turn to speak to this woman.

"No."

"Well, you'll find him, just keep the faith. Dance is over there," she said, pointing over there somewhere. "Enjoy it, yeah?"

"Okay, thanks," I said. I began walking then stopped and turned. "I like karaoke," I said but she shook her head sadly. *This place is fucked*, I thought. "Simon," I said. "Simon!" I shouted.


"Michael?"

"What?" I was at an unusual angle.

"You're alive!"

I tried to get up but couldn't. I just managed to roll over onto my side a bit. I lay back down. I was lying behind the seats on the checker-plate floor with Simon looking down on me. "Did we do karaoke?"

"I electrocuted you!" he exclaimed. Not something you should really exclaim. I could smell burnt... something. I touched my head and, sure enough, there were hard bits on the ends of my hair. My fingertips were tingling.

"Oh great."

"I saw your bones! I saw them in the reflection! In the windscreen!"

"You didn't see my bones."

"They lit up! All your bones!"

"They didn't. That doesn't happen." I was still lying there.

"You were dead."

"I'm not dead, you didn't see my bones. Do I look dead?" I got up on my elbows. "I'm not dead. If I was dead I wouldn't be talking…"

"I electrocuted you back again! By accident!" he said, sounding delighted.

"By accident?"

"Yeah, you were dead and I was going to move you and there was a spark and you flopped around for a bit and then you were alive again!"

"Well…" That was a lot to take in.

"Yeah."

"Where were you moving me to?"

"I am glad you're alive."

"Well, thanks." I got up using my legs and also my arms, hooking them around my chair and using it as a climbing frame. I had to rest when I was halfway up my chair. Simon came over, looking like he was going to help me up. The hair on my head and arms stood up as he approached. "No!" I said, holding out my left hand. Holding on to the chair tightly with my right.

"Oh yeah," he said, sheepishly, and then sort of tried to help me up without touching me. It didn't help. He was just moving his arms up and down. Offering moral support instead of physical. Willing me up.

Eventually I was upright. Propping myself up on the top of the chair. I looked out of the windscreen. We were facing a rock face and the sky above was a deep pink. You couldn't tell it had rained. Down below, a long way down, through my side window, I could see part of a plain that seemed to go on forever. We were up high, on a plateau. "Where are we?"

"Near the Mines."

"The Mines? Wh... why? How? What time is it?" We'd been hours away from the Mines when... whatever happened happened.

"To hide, flew, and eight o'six."

"Eight o'six? What, are you a pirate now?"

"Si... seven minutes past eight."

"Fuck, I was out for ages," I said rubbing my face.

"You were dead."

"I mean, I wasn't but… whatever. I had a weird dream," I said but already it was fading. "Where are my clothes?"

"I was actually very concerned."

"You didn't go back, though. That's good," I said, shaking a shaky finger at him.

"I considered it."

"Didn't go to a hospital either. That's not so good."

"Sorry."

"Nobody followed us?"

"I went full speed. One of the engines is damaged but it flew."

"And we made it to the Mines!" I said. We were at the Mines. We were east. I went to slap his back, then remembered and didn't. "I need some fresh air."

Outside was nice. A nice breeze and the sun was only starting to set. Down on the plain, about seven or fifteen or forty miles away, were what looked like South American soccer stadiums. Two of them. One red, one blue.

"The hell are they?" I asked, squinting.

"They're incredible," said Simon, getting a bit closer to me. A bit too close. I stared at him until he realised.

"What are they?"

"Burrowers, the biggest machines ever made."

I looked at him as he smiled at the Burrowers. "Where did the water go in?"

"My neck," he said, then shivered. He tried to shiver, but he can't, so he shuddered.

"You need to dry out, Simon," I said. "If only we had four tonnes of rice."

"I could spin around."

"Ha! Any excuse," I said. I felt good. Better than I had in a while. Jovial. Rested. "Do that, spin a bit."

Simon moved backwards then, slowly at first, began to rotate from his waist. He held his arms out. He rumbled a bit but that was to be expected. His bearings were old. He's old. "They're machines?" I asked, looking out.

"*YeEeEsEs,*" he replied.

And then I saw it. "And the fuck is that?" I asked.

"That?" he replied, slowing his rotations and pointing down at the freshly dug grave-shaped grave, briefly, on each passing revolution.

"Yeah, that. What is that?"

"That's nothing, Michael. *Protocol.*"

"Fuck. You dug that?"

"Yeah."

"You can dig?"

"Apparently."

"Well, looks like it would have been nice. It's a nice spot." I shook my head. "Don't ever bury me in a grave until a doctor has confirmed that I'm dead, confirm."

"That's not a recognised directive."

"Just do it, for me."

"Deal. I'm glad you're not dead."

"Thanks. And I'm glad you didn't short circuit your memory banks, or whatever. God, I'm hungry. I always wake up starving if I've had a nap."

"You could eat these flowers!"

"Aw, look! You got some flowers!"

"You want to eat them?"

"I'm not sure I can. I told you, you can only eat certain kinds. It's probably not worth the risk."

Simon sped up then spun for forty minutes until it was nearly dark, pausing only to allow me to hang my jumpsuit and socks on his arm. He hung them, I threw them at him. I couldn't watch him for long without getting nauseous, so after I checked the map I sat looking out over the plain. The sunset was beautiful and the Mines, the man-made hills on the horizon, lent the vista a magical touch. A beer and a sandwich and I'd have gladly sat there all night. We should have packed some food. I was snapped out of this calm moment by a giant flappy eagle attacking the back of my head. I jumped up screaming, nearly slipping from the ledge I was sitting on.

"Your clothes," said Simon, staring at me.

"Yeah, I know," I lied. "There's a buckle on the belt, idiot, it hurt." Simon watched me for a bit. "You dry?"

"I think so."

I missed, the first few times I dared to try poking him with a stick. Didn't quite reach him with my darty pokes. Then I touched him. For a split second. Then for a bit longer. And then I dropped the stick and placed my hand on him. He was warm. "Michael?"

"Yes Simon?"

"*DeZeeeZuh!*" he said, jerking, and I pulled my hand back.

"Prick. Why would you do that? That's not funny."

"Sorry."

"How did you think that was funny?"

"You'd do it."

"Nah. No, that wasn't funny."

"Sorry. Goodbye."

"You what?"

"You know, goodbye. In case you fall off a cliff or something, and I don't get the chance to say it. I thought I'd missed my chance."

"Oh yeah, well, goodbye to you too," I said, stepping a bit further away from the edge. "It's been good to know you." I patted him carefully. "Let's not die, eh?"

Dinner that night was three out-of-date Marathon bars that I'd found jammed in a grate in the back of the Lady.

I'm sure people think I'm dour, but I'm not, and here's a great example of how my seemingly pessimistic ethos can result in good times. I'd been dreading trying to get the decals off the truck. Absolutely dreading it, so I put it off for a bit by picking the woven badge off my overalls. That wasn't easy either. See, nothing's easy. The truck stickers, though… oh boy, they were going to be nearly impossible to remove.

I started and thought about just getting paint instead. Paint over them. That would be easier. Then, after I'd spent ages getting a tiny corner of the first sticker up I *knew* I was going to pull it and it would rip. Only a small bit would come off. A tiny, mocking sliver. And I'd have to scrape at it with my ID card again, and there'd be no corner then. I'd get another small bit up, pull, rip and I'd be doing that for eternity. And I couldn't give up after I'd started, otherwise we'd be going around with ripped stickers and that would look more suspicious than no stickers at all. Dreading it. And Simon couldn't help because of what his hands are. Everything was down to me, *again*, as usual.

I was really huffing as I worked at the corner of the first sticker but it turned out the stickers were made of, I don't know, kevlar or something. I think they were made of the same material as the straps in the back, because after I got a corner up, Simon could help. He could peel the whole letter off in one go. The stickers were unbreakable and it was actually a nice thing to do. Satisfying. A pleasant activity, out in the morning sun, just Simon and me, working together. I'd get the corner up and then hand over to him to peel the whole thing off. He could do that in his smooth, mechanical way. We soon developed a rhythm.

"We could do this for a living," I said just an hour later when we were on to the front, which just had our registration. I was almost sad to have nearly finished.

"Peel stickers off?" said Simon, but he was distracted and looking out at the Burrowers.

"The size of them!" I mused as I stood aside after peeling the corner from the last number. The Burrowers were insane. Too huge. I couldn't believe they were machines. "Do they have Pilots? Or are *they*, like, the pilots?"

"They probably have Pilots," said Simon, smoothly removing

the last stickers and then looking back over at them.

"Hope they drive better than you. You've hit something there," I said, pointing to the green scratches of paint in the corner under his window. Simon looked, then shrugged and we stepped back to survey our work. I'd thought that the Lady would look cooler without the stickers, but to be honest, it didn't. There was now too much yellow. Just a big yellow cube. And worse still, on the side that was receiving the sun you could clearly see where the stickers had been. It was matte yellow, and slightly darker than the rest of the truck. Wouldn't matter soon, when we got our business up and running, but, yeah, I wasn't over the moon with the result.

On the plus side, Simon had made a perfectly spherical ball with all the stickers we'd removed. I mean *perfect* perfect. Incredible. In the bar I'd sometimes wondered how they make pool balls, but I've never got any further than just wondering. How do they make perfectly round balls? They must have to put them down. What's the process there? I can't even begin to imagine and yet the ball Simon made was better than a giant pool ball.

I'd never seen him make a ball of stickers before, because he'd never done it before. That's what happens when you're outside your comfort zone, you realise you're capable of so much more than you thought. After we packed up, and just for a bit of fun, we took the ball to the cliff edge, just to see how far he could throw it. See what else he was capable of.

He stood there, holding the ball in both hands, then his elbows clicked back. It sounded like a massive stapler. I counted down from five and, well, it turned out he could throw it a very long way. Miles. How many I don't know, we lost sight of it almost immediately, and it was still going up. I clapped my hands together, "Well, a nice end to a good morning!" and then, because I was in a good mood, I added, "To the Spannertorium!" I held up a finger when I said that.

"What are you doing?" asked Simon.

"I'm being fun, Simon. I'm being fun." We needed a twelve millimetre spanner to tighten the engine back up. The thieves had only loosened it.

The point is, if I'd have expected the truck stickers to come off easily, they wouldn't have. I guarantee it.

"Spanner, food, toilet roll. Anything else?" I asked as we fizzed around the outer rim of the plain, against the cliffs. Keeping near the edge felt safer. We were less exposed. His fans came on, just for a moment, before he shook his head. The Lady wasn't flying right, but even then it wasn't as bad as the time I'd forgotten to restore his accuracy after playing pool the night before. Por dios! Trying to join the stream that day I'd just had time to regret a lot of decisions I'd made in my life! He'd taken off somebody's wing mirror.

Even struggling to fly he kept glancing sideways, over to the massive machines, whose positions didn't seem to change in relation to the horizon behind them, really showing their massive scale. Each leg was at *least* as big as a pile of hospitals. "Might find somewhere where we can get you some new seals."

"That would be good," he replied. The tone of his voice suggested he didn't think that it would happen. I didn't think it would happen either. And if by some miracle we did find them, I didn't know how to fit them. It was a problem for another day. We had to get supplies first. And a spanner. We had a focus, a goal, and it was sunny. Hardly a cloud in the sky.

"Hey, those thieves got a bit of a shock," I said and giggled at my own great joke. "I wonder if they can speak French now?"

"Speak French?" Simon looked at me briefly and he was smiling.

"Yeah, because sometimes if you get knocked out, you wake up with a new skill. It's a phenomenon. Like... or you can suddenly play the piano."

"Nah."

"Seriously! I've heard of it."

"Really?" he looked over again. "Nah."

"Why would I make that up?"

"So can _you_ speak French now?"

I hadn't considered it. "I dunno," I said. I sat there and considered it for a weirdly long time before saying, "Nah." I should have said, 'Non'.

"Maybe you can play the piano."

"Maybe," I agreed, I didn't think I could. I tapped my fingers on my knee and looked out. Below us there was the odd small hut, sometimes a cluster of huts, the odd vehicle, a dust plume, but mainly it was earth and rocks.

We were heading to Graymall. I'd guessed it would take us one hundred and seventy-seven minutes to get there. We'd been going for twelve. I opened the glove box, just for something to do, and saw the pill-shaped case tucked at the back. I'd bought the sunglasses three or four years before. In the Bizaare. Back then I'd intended to wear them a lot. They were going to be my new look. They were cool. Pretty big. Gold rims and blue mirrored lenses, but so far I'd hardly worn them. I'd worn them once, in fact, and that first and only time I'd put them on, Simon had looked at me and I'd thought he was going to say that they were cool, but instead he'd made a sort of static noise. A little burst of static.

I took the case out quietly, opened it and looked at my reflection in the lenses. I looked old. *If I couldn't wear them now, then when? Sunny day. Second day of our new life.* I took the sunglasses out and snapped the case shut. I put them on, with no fanfare, while looking out of my side window, then I leant forward to put the case away. I sensed Simon look at me. *So what?* I saw his reflection just as he was turning away from me. I tensed as I heard his fans come on for a moment, and then they were still.

"Have you got something to say?" I asked.

"No. Why? What?"

"Fuck it." I took the sunglasses off, folded the arms and reached for the case.

"Leave them on!" said Simon. I ignored him, despite his increasingly passionate protests that they looked good. I put them in my rucksack and took out the dictionary from the open glove box and we went through words. I found one I liked. **Termagant**: a violent, turbulent or brawling woman. It made me think of the woman from the church. I liked the word. Using unusual words lets people know you're not a dumbass.


I also liked Graymall. Its name on the map had suggested it might be a bit depressing and gloomy. Because, you know, the 'gray' bit. But even from a distance you could see it was actually picturesque, perched up on a hill. Sure, it was being eaten away in patches, covered over with steel and plastic, but there was still enough of the old citadel visible to give you good vibes.

The centre of the town stood behind a ring of huge stone walls. Ramparts? Walls with a walkway on the top. Big sections of the wall were still visible. Walls that had been built to keep invaders out, but weren't designed to stop development spilling over from within.

"Imagine building them. How long it took them. With no machines."

"Twelve years," said Simon, who was following the beacon to the parking and was not really interested.

"Twelve years. Imagine that. Every day for twelve years, you, and hundreds of others, all breaking rocks, lifting them, day after day. How did they even lift them?"

"And then they go and invent flying cars."

"Yeah, and then they invent flying cars and it's like, well, that was a waste of time that was."

"How long are we going to be?"

"Why?"

"There's two-hour parking down there, but it's expensive."

"I don't mind walking a bit," I said. I actually *wanted* to walk a bit, so we parked near the station. I really like seeing stations in strange places. I like wondering where the tracks go. There was no Snake in Graymall so after parking we walked for a bit, then got the shuttle the rest of the way to Retail. Graymall, like my face, was worse close up, but still alright.

People weren't exactly bustling about but they definitely moved more casually than you see back... nearly said home. The City was never home. There was a queue for the Vems, it was about lunchtime. I waited and got a burger and juice. I didn't have high hopes for it but it wasn't too bad, probably less than a day old which I guess you'd expect. It would have come from a small, nearby depot. It couldn't be far because Graymall wasn't massive.

I ate it near a statue of a man sitting on a rearing horse while two dots annoyed pigeons. The pigeons didn't seem *that* annoyed, more resigned, as they pecked at nothing on the ground, waiting until the last minute of the dot's mindless, bouncing approach. I was more annoyed, because when the birds took off they did so in my direction.

'Approach,' better not tell Simon I used that word.

"Can we get one?"

"A pigeon? Sure, go for it. They're free. Get a fat one."

"A dot."

"Yeah, su-"

"Oh, cool!"

"Let me finish, you didn't let me finish. If you had, you would have detected that I'm being sar-cas-tic."

"So, can w-"

"Haven't I got enough to worry about? Looking after you?" I said. I wiped my mouth with the back of my hand, not expecting the smear of sauce to appear. Must've been on my cheek. And now it was on the back of my hand. I wiped it off as best I could with the cellophane the burger came wrapped in, then rubbed the back of my hand against the low wall I'd been leaning on. "The bun was perhaps a bit too sweet." With warm food in me I felt I could better handle shopping.

"You don't have to look after me," said Simon. I smiled, but just like *that* it hit my mood. That was all it took. It annoyed me. I took a deep breath. *What did I do if I didn't look after him, you know?* It wasn't a big deal and a better person would have ignored it. I tried. With the smile. But I knew it was going to develop into an argument at some point soon. I knew it, because I knew that I'd start it. But then it's not like they were planning on entombing me in concrete. You know?

The store was tiny compared to the Ikarus one in Central, but the layout was similar. And the queues were similar, there were just fewer of them. I went to the far side hoping nobody else had thought of that, but they had. At least the lines were moving well enough and soon there were people behind us.

"Tell me, Michael, how much would you expect to pay for a dot?" asked Simon as we took another step forward.

"It's weird when you say my name."

"How much?"

"I don't know."

"Guess."

"I'm not in the mood."

"Twenty pounds?"

"Yeah, about that."

"You think? *You'd* pay twenty?"

"Ha! Yeah, nice try." We shuffled forwards.

"Would you pay ten?"

"Nope. I wouldn't pay anything. We're not getting one."

"Well they're *seven* pounds. Can you believe that?"

"How do you even know?" No way were they only seven pounds.

"Look!" he said, gesturing up to the big screens at the front as we again shuffled forward. On the screens sex dolls were replaced with a flask that, for some reason, turned whatever you put in it into a jelly, and then night-vision magnifying glasses. "Wait," said Simon. An electric knife appeared. "It's after this." It wasn't. Dungarees were next. I should get new clothes. Then the dots appeared. And they actually were only seven pounds. "So shall we get one? We'll get one, yeah? Yeah, let's get one."

"We? You mean me? It's *we* when it's... something easy. When it's tough decision time, it's me."

"But they're cheap. We'd be making thirteen pounds."

I looked at Simon, he was looking at me with raised eyebrows. Raised everything. His face was raised. "Look, it's not part of the plan. Let's... you know, let's get settled first. When we've got somewhere to live..."

"Let's get it now and we won't turn it on."

"Yeah, sure." I could imagine that. *Having a dot in a box in the back of the truck and Simon not pleading with me to turn it on every three seconds. Yeah sure.* "What would you call it?" I asked as we took another step forward. "Come up with a good and original name, and you can get one. Promise."

"That's not fair."

"Think of an original name."

Simon's fans came on. "Dot..." they whirred louder. Then louder again. "Dot."

"Nice."

"So can we get one?"

"*When* we're settled."

"We're not going to get settled," he said in his normal voice, instead of his quiet voice and that was it. That was the interaction I'd been waiting for to start a petty and pointless argument, because sometimes I just can't stop myself. I can never stop myself.

"Shut up." I looked at the heels of the people in front of us. "And what do you mean, we're not going to get settled? Why are you saying that now?" I asked, looking down and to the side.

"I said it all along."

"No, you totally didn't."

"I wanted to st-"

"Because you don't know what they're going to do to you! And... even if you did you're too... too simple to understand the... the... fucking ramifications." I shook my head and stepped forwards.

"You don't ha-"

"Mute, confirm." The people behind us were getting all in my personal space and I turned my head again. My heel had been kicked at least three times. I didn't actually look at the people kicking me, I looked off at the wall, but I knew just turning my head would show them that I was a human being with human being feelings, and they should back the fuck up, because standing so close to me wasn't going to get them a sex doll any quicker. I looked at Simon who was looking up at the screens, or pretending to, more like. I looked down at the heels of the people in front of me and shuffled forward again. The person in front of me was wearing a pair of very dirty slippers.

We shuffled forwards.

*I don't have to look after him?* I thought, sarcastically. *And he'd doubled down on it!* I shook my head slightly. Just enough so Simon would know I was thinking about what a jerk he was. *Stupid ungrateful robot.* I decided the next time he mentioned going back, we'd go back. Immediately. Fuck it. I'd mute him and we'd go back. No skin off my nose. See how close we got to the Hub before he started panicking. *Jerk.* I was at the counter facing the smiling server.

"What would you like?"

"An easy life," I replied and the server threw back its head and laughed. Then its head flipped forward again. "What would you like?"

I thought about saying 'an easy life' again, to see if it would indulge me again, but instead I said, "toilet roll."

"How many users?"

"Just one. Bread and white spread."

"One user?"

"Yep, oh, and water."

"One user?"

"One user. And a twelve millimetre spanner."

"Anything else?"

"Was there anything else Simon?" I asked him, and he pointed to his mouth and threw his hand up like a petulant massive metal baby Frenchman.

"How much are the dots?"

"Seven pounds."

I shook my head to this but I said, "Okay," as I shook it. The server didn't respond so I said, "Yeah, a dot please." I'd get Simon a dot and I'd make sure to moan about it for eternity. I figured that would teach him a lesson.

"Which colour would you like?"

"Gah!" I said to show that already having a dot was a pain. "Blue?"

"SYNTAX ERROR!" the server screamed so loudly that I instinctively ducked. "Which colour would you like?" It asked. I saw its eyes flick up and look past us at people who were doing giggles behind.

"Green?"

"Anything else?"

"That's it," I said while doing little nods and blinking rapidly. Those little nods turned into little shakes as the server disappeared sideways and down, only to be replaced immediately by a server rising up from the other side. This one was carrying our box. I took my wallet from my back pocket and fed twenty-seven pounds into the slot. "You can carry it," I told Simon, pushing the box over to him.

I thanked the server, even though the original one was underground now. A lot of people don't bother thanking machines, but I always do. A lot of people don't thank humans either. The humans behind were pressuring me to move as I was still putting my wallet away. So I moved aside and did it there. With my wallet in the pocket on the side of my thigh I walked to the door. Normally I'd head through a crowd slowly, because Simon is so big and it's more difficult for him. *But hey, if he's so good at looking after himself... If he doesn't need me then he should be fine.* I picked my way through the crowd to the front doors as quickly as I could, without it looking like I was rushing. I didn't care about bumping into a few people as I danced my way out.

Outside I walked a bit further, so that when Simon eventually caught up he'd feel bad about being so slow and making me wait, and he'd see that I was waiting because I'm a good guy with his best interests at heart and I was doing everything for him and that he was a dick. I was pretty disappointed to find that, when I did stop, he was right there with me.

As we walked wordlessly back towards the shuttle I knew that *I* was the dick. I knew it all along, really. I knew I should unmute him and apologise. I couldn't. That would be to admit I was the dick. Nobody likes to admit they're a dick so it went as it always went. In this case I pointed to an unusual building while we were on the shuttle. He looked at it and nodded, and then we were communicating again. "You're taking it for walks," I said. I didn't unmute him there and then, because at that point I was still fragile and he might have said something that would have caused me to remute him immediately. But we were communicating. Sometimes it took twenty four hours to get to this stage. We didn't really have time for that.

I did unmute him on the shuttle. I made it seem like I'd forgotten he was muted. He didn't make a big deal out of it. That's how it happens and then we just relax back into it. "We'll have to think of a name, for the dot," I said. This was my apology, you know? He knew. He nodded.

"I'm not good at th-"

"No, I know. *We'll* think of something."

I watched Graymall fly past the windows. There were a lot of old-looking pro-independence signs up. This whole area was between two competing territories. It had all gone quiet, for now, but who knew what was going on in boardrooms. And Graymall was a bit big for us. I pictured us living somewhere smaller, if we wanted to live under the... hold that thought. Hold that thought! "Hey, Radar's a good name."

"Radar?"

"Yeah, for the dot. Radar. Come here, Radar!" I said, slapping a thigh. "Good boy, Radar! That's a good name. It's kind of mechanical. I like it. You like it?"

"Radar," said Simon, turning to me slowly, giving me a thumbs up and a satisfied nod.

The skin on my side bristled when I saw the little meaty man checking out the Lady. I gave Simon a doubtful glance and we slowed our pace. "What do you reckon?"

"He's just looking," said Simon. "It's okay." The guy was

wearing a white vest and golden shorts. It was a strong look. Confident. People in authority don't wear tight white vests and golden shorts but I was still wary. We continued across to the Lady at our slower pace.

I haven't got the physique to go out in public wearing a vest like that, and neither did this guy really. He was very meaty. His vest was tight over his massive belly, but it was hard fat under there. Not jiggly fat. He was one of those men who are fat as a bell, but the fat's unyielding like muscle. Don't know the science behind that but he had the kind of belly you just wanted to poke. To feel how hard it was. His vest pulled across it, taut like a drum. He was bald and toasted by the sun, and when he looked up – he was really checking out the Lady – delicious looking folds of smooth fat appeared at the base of his skull. The folds swallowed his thick gold-coloured chain. I wanted to pinch that fat between my thumb and forefinger and feel how it felt. I could well imagine what it would feel like. It would surely feel like gripping two warm rubber belts. He was a very touchable man. A little, fat, meaty and touchable man. Maybe part of that is they don't have fat people in the City. I guess for the same reason you don't see fat ants. In the City everybody just gets what they need from the corporation, nothing more.

"Okay?" I asked the little, fat, meaty man.

"Hello!" said Simon, brightly.

The man turned and looked at us. He had a beard that went down to a point. It was like a fuzzy ice-cream cone. A very strokable beard. "Dis yours?" he asked.

"This?" I asked, looking at the Lady then back at the man. I was trying to read him. "Is it ours?" I asked as I heard the doorhole open. I did a long blink then turned to the doorhole and watched Simon get out, minus the box he'd dropped inside. "Yup," I said. "Yup," I repeated.

"I look for one adeez."

"Are you a bounty hunter?" I asked. I was forlorn.

"One hit my car," he said. "One adeez."

"Oh yeah?" I asked. "Where dat happen?" I asked, adopting the man's accent because of… I don't know, stress?

"A diner out by-"

"Never heard of it."

"Chu see dis?" I didn't need to see dis, I knew what he meant, he was going to point at the scrape on the corner. We walked over to it. He had a cool walk. As his hip dropped, his shoulder went up on the same side and did the opposite on the other. So his walking looked like a form of rolling.

"Fuck," I said to Simon who'd said the guy was only looking. Simon can't read situations that well. Yeah he can carry heavy things and drive, but beyond that? He's fucking *useless*.

"That's been there for ages, hasn't it Simon?" I immediately regretted how guilty that question made us seem. *Hasn't it, Simon? Why did I ask that?* The man looked at Simon. Simon looked at me and then back at the man.

I feared Simon might blow it but, after smiling, Simon simply said, "Hello!" I exhaled.

"Is my colour, man," the man said, and shook his head and stroked his beard. He bounced down into a squat while fingering the green paint. *No shit, buddy, it's literally your paint! We hit you! You know that, right?* "Is *exactly* my paint." He stood easily – strong thighs – and pointed a meaty arm over to the green car we hit while escaping from the diner. It was a cool car.

"Cool car," I said and he thanked me. "So a truck similar to this hit you?" I shook my head with disgust. "That is so shit."

"Yeah, jus like dis one."

"But not this one, right?" I said, slapping the Lady. "You don't think it was this one?"

"No. No dis one. It had beeg signs on."

"Signs?" I asked, even though I knew exactly what he meant. I thought that was good. I didn't just brush it off. I asked for more details. I wouldn't have done that if it was *us* who had hit his car and then spent the morning peeling the signs off our truck, no way! I'd be steering the conversation *away* from signs, and certainly not asking *about* signs. I wasn't guilty at all. Thank god we were in the shade. The man just nodded and I looked at the open doorhole on the Lady and felt its pull. "Like I said, it wasn't us, and you agreed to that."

The man nodded. "The one dat hit me had a fookin' military robot. Fookin' lasers, man."

"Well!" I said with a finger extended. 'Well' is short for 'Well, time for us to get on with our separate lives!' The extended finger was for poking the man's belly. I unextended my finger. The man just nodded, so I nodded and gestured for Simon to get on board and start it up. I nearly clapped the man on the back but I didn't. I didn't touch him at all. We'd only spent about two minutes together. We weren't friends and that made our separating a bit awkward. Didn't really want him just standing there and watching me climb aboard, but he was showing no sign of not doing exactly that. "Okay," I said, clapping my hands together, nodding my head forwards and actually heading to the Lady. I was in the doorhole when he shouted.

"Hey, hey! I just tink..." he shouted and I held my eyes

tightly shut for a moment before turning to him, but I held my hand over the door closer.

---

"Un. Fucking. Believable," I said, because it was. I think I was in shock. We'd been flying for a few minutes in silence while I struggled to articulate my thoughts. "It's just... un. Fucking. Believable."

"Why?" asked Simon, banking, causing the box to slide across the floor behind our seats. The Lady was flying fine now.

"Why?" I scoffed. "I'll tell you why. *This* doesn't happen."

"But it did happen."

"I know, I know and it's... it's... un. Fucking. Believable."

"Just go with it."

"I mean I am, but..." I shook my head. "You know?"

"Yeah, I know."

"It's like..."

"Yeah," he agreed.

"You just..." We didn't talk for a while. Occasionally I'd look over at Simon who was framed by the setting sun.

"I'll be honest with you," I said when the sun was over the horizon and there was only a little light left in the sky. "I didn't really think this was going to work." He didn't reply. "I thought it was going to be a big disaster. A big terrible disaster. This whole thing."

"There's still time."

"Ha! Yeah, true that. But... *unbelievable*." And it was

unbelievable. I wouldn't believe it. When Hub Cap had shouted at me in the car park I was certain he'd worked out that it was us who'd hit his car, but I hadn't closed the door, and he hadn't killed us. Instead he'd offered us our first job. Nah.

The fact that we'd hit his car... and we met him hundreds of miles away... and he was the world's most gullible person, nah, that doesn't happen. But it *did* happen and the back of the Lady contained two little pianos. "Hub Cap's a nice guy, huh?"

"Isn't he nice," agreed Simon.

"Isn't he?"

"Nice guy, Hub Cap is," said Simon.

"A bit gullible, that's okay, though."

"He seemed a bit..."

"He did seem quite stupid, didn't he?" I felt bad thinking of him as stupid. After what he'd done for us. "But he's just trusting. It's a better way to be. Isn't it? It's different out here. People aren't so cynical."

"It's nice."

"Instead of just thinking everything is against you. We said we didn't hit his car, and he believed us. He was happy with that. We were happy."

"But we *did* hit his car."

"Yeah, struggling with that bit. But then, I guess, we are delivering his pianos for free, you know? He'll get his car fixed with the money saved and... you know?"

"Win-win, isn't it."

"Yeah. Win-win," I agreed. "It's just... this is how I imagined it would happen. My dream. We'd get a job and it would lead to another one and... dreams don't usually come true."

"Tell me the story," said Simon. "But I'm not making bread."

"You are. Or I'll replace you. And you're going to start gardening." It was dark out and I imagined our future. "We're in our house. You've just made some bread..."

...and I was there again, in the place I rarely dared go to, sitting back and finishing the delicious slice of bread, while Simon went back to the kitchen to clean up the plate. I caught the crumbs with my left hand. A nice bird landed on the windowsill overlooking the meadow. You know, a nice bird, not a pigeon. Or a gull. It was a nice little brown one. Lovely little dicky bird. "Here you go, little fella!" I said, scattering the crumbs I'd caught in front of it, and then I sat smiling as it gratefully pecked them all up. The serenity of that moment was broken when Radar came bounding into the room and jumped into my lap, nearly making the chair tip back. "Woah there little guy!" I laughed, putting him down on the floor where he went in circles. "Somebody's ready for a walk," I said, beaming and nodding my head slowly. I stood and stretched. I don't get dizzy anymore if I stand up too fast, that must have been a stress thing. Running a successful delivery company is a different kind of stress, a good one, and my blood pressure is now 'really nice and low', according to the local apothecary.

"Are these fresh vegetables which we're growing ready yet?" I asked Simon as we walked down our garden path, Radar zipping ahead. Simon has taken over the garden. At first it was a shared thing but he can remember stuff better than me and now we know he can dig.

"Yes," replied Simon.

"That's dinner sorted, then."

We walked along the river with Radar ahead of us, chasing butterflies and geckos. Simon hardly took his eyes off the little dot because the other day it had nearly chased a butterfly into the river! That would have really fucked it. The dot seemed to have learned that water was bad for it. Being submerged is bad for it. It's okay in light rain showers, that's according to the quick-start manual. We hadn't tested it because it was early summer and only seemed to rain during the night. That was nice, lying in bed, in the dark, and hearing the rain tap at the windows, which were in wooden frames and which we'd painted a really nice colour. Hub Cap's Car Green, actually.

It hadn't rained last night and I occasionally stopped on the path and turned my face up to the sun. Though early, it already had energy and it warmed my eyelids. We got to the clump of trees, which is as far as we go, unless it's a Sunday. It wasn't a Sunday. Two of the trees have grown through each other. It's kind of cool. I don't know what kind of trees they are but you have to marvel at the amount of time that it would have taken for that to happen. I kicked a pine cone and Radar chased it. So cute! Simon and I laughed.

"Hey, Michael," said Simon just as I skipped a stone over the river and it did, like, twenty bounces. I made sure Radar wasn't looking before I threw it!

"Yeah? Did you see that? Twenty odd."

"I just want to thank you."

"What are you on about, you big idiot?" I said, leaning away and looking at him like his stupidity was a contagious disease.

"I just think about all the times I doubted you..." he said, gazing across the water.

"You did doubt me a lot," I agreed. "But it's... it's fine."

I opened my eyes and looked at Simon's reflection as he flew the Lady. He was shaking his head but smiling. I closed my eyes...

"I'm glad we didn't go back," said Simon.

"Me too. Come on, let's get a wiggle on, we've got deliveries to make."

Walking back to the house Simon asked me to guess the world record for stone skimming. Turns out it was the one I just did!

We arrived at Mrs Bathingthorpe's house just before ten, as agreed. House is an understatement. It was a really big house. She was a pleasant old duffer. She seemed to take delight in most things. Everything was marvellous to her, particularly Simon, and she'd take every opportunity to stroke his arms.

"So you want this vintage armoire delivered to your other house?" I asked her, pointing to the vintage armoire.

"That would be *marvellous!*" she shrieked, and then Simon carried it out while I followed him.

"And how much do I owe you?" she asked as she followed me.

"Eighty pounds?"

"Oh, you are so reasonable, and that's why I've told all my friends about you and they all use you for their deliveries!"

"I know, you told me that weeks ago," I said, disappointed with Mrs Bathingthorpe's clumsy exposition. It's no good charging too much and not having any business. That's obvious.

"Oh sorry, I must have dementia!" she laughed. We stopped at the door and watched Simon load the truck. The truck that we'd got restored at that place which also sorted out Simon's seal and other potential issues with him. He's got another fifty years in him, apparently. Simon had painted the new logo and name on the side of the truck. I thought he was going to do it brilliantly, because he's mechanical, but it was like a slow child had done it, some of the letters were back to front. We kept it, though. Made us seem more approachable. "Well, if you won't take extra money then please take these," she said, producing a package wrapped in white shiny paper from her pocket. I took the package. It was cold.

"Mrs Bathingthorpe!" I said, with mock chiding, slightly turning my head to her. "What is this?" She giggled and clasped her hands under her chin and for a moment I saw how she would have looked fifty years ago – still a bit rough, to be honest, but less wrinkly. "Are these what I think they are?"

"Do you think they're delicious sausages?" she asked.

"I do now!" I said.

"Well they are!" she screamed and started clapping her hands under her chin.

"Where did you get real meat from?" I asked with a playful squint. She tapped the side of her nose while stifling a giggle. Simon was done, "Well, it's been a pleasure," I said.

"You two really are marvellous," she said.

"Ah, we're just doing our job," I replied and looked around her gravel driveway. It had a fountain in the middle.

"Well, you're very good."

"Thanks," I said, looking at her.

"..." she said.

"Eighty pounds!" I said, clicking my fingers near her face.

"Oh yes, I totally... sorry," she said, grabbing for her purse in a panicky way. She dropped it. I picked it up for her and finally she found the eighty pounds. I folded it and put it in my cape pocket. "By the way, I found twelve tapes of Oriental pornography, they were Clive's, my dead husband. Would you like them?"

I looked at my watch and winced. "Ooh, no time now, tell you what, I'll get them next time. Can't keep my clients waiting!" I said, skipping down the steps then crunching over to the truck. She was still in the doorhole of her house waving when we took off and headed to her other house.

Then we had two more jobs, similar sort of thing, moving stuff for rich eccentrics and we were finished by three, which gave Simon loads of time to pick the vegetables we were having with our sausages. That was one of the best things about this life, we could choose our own hours.

Over dinner I taught Simon what mustard was because he was asking if there was anything which could make the meal better. I told him mustard was yellow and tasted like batteries. He found that absolutely fascinating.

After dinner we sat on the porch. I had my pipe and a glass of wine. Simon was content just to be there. To be alive. Radar was exhausted and was plugged in, in the living room. Usually he would be out here on the porch with us. I gazed out over the plain. Between the pear tree and the shed I could see the Burrowers in the far, far distance...

"I don't know a thing about vegetables."

"How hard could it be?"

"That's it, over there," said Simon, nodding his head out into the pitch black darkness. Took me a while to see it. Where that diner had shone like a single gem in the desert, the town of Morlay glittered like God had dropped a jewellery box. Its streets looked like a spilled golden necklace. Simon banked.

My guess as to how far Morlay was from Graymall was miles better than Hub Cap's. Literally. Sixty-six miles better. Not listed, he'd only given us an approximate position for Morlay, out past the Burrowers, up on top of the rim and he'd claimed we could get there before nightfall. Even that exaggeration or mistake or whatever turned out to be a positive, because despite Simon's powerful eyes, the town would have been difficult to spot in daylight. It was easy for him to see it in the dark. He hasn't got night vision or anything, just really really good eyes.

We landed in a small paddock and I stretched pretty violently. My arms going directly up. I reckon I could actually snap something while stretching. Snap a vital tendon if I tried hard enough, that's old age, that is. We shut everything down and after a moment of enjoying the total silence offered by a turned-off Lady, he climbed out. After grabbing my jacket I followed.

Morlay smelled nice. It smelled of burning wood and I inhaled deeply and it struck me that I hadn't smelled burning wood in a long time. Years. Burning smells in the City are not good burning smells. They're more your melting smells, or friction smells. Grinding. Something overheating. Burning smells in the City seem accidental, like something's gone wrong, but the smell of burning wood out here was deliciously deliberate. It wasn't just the scent of burning logs hanging in the nighttime air, there was also a strong flavour of tobacco and charred food. Just needed fresh bread and fresh coffee and this place would be the best-smelling town to ever stink up the planet. And coconuts. Throw some of those in too. I fucking love the smell of coconuts.

"Smells nice," I told Simon.

"Does it?"

"Yes," I said. Two smoking men were leaning casually on the log fence which made the paddock a paddock. Without the fence it'd just be, you know, the ground. We'd seen the men when coming in and they hadn't moved at all, from what I could tell. These guys were languid. They weren't bothered by us. We started over to them. I walked slightly slower than Simon.

I wasn't *overly* keen on just how casually the men were leaning on the fence and smoking. I don't know, but if *I* had been leaning on a fence when a guy and a massive robot were walking towards me, I might just have started leaning a little less casually. To be polite. "Hey, this is Morlay, right?" I asked.

"Wotcha," said one man with a bread and braces over his white shirt, holding up his trousers. Ha! Bread. I meant beard. I was hungry.

"Wotcha," said the other, who also had a beard and braces over his white shirt holding his trousers up. I took that to be their greeting.

"Oh, wotcha. This is Morlay, right?" I knew it was but I couldn't see any harm in getting confirmation. And it was an icebreaker. The other conversation starter I had but didn't use was about what a lovely evening it was.

"This is Morlay," said one of the casually leaning men.

"Cool. We've got some small pianos. For…" I clicked my fingers at Simon but remembered before he helped me out. "LP's Music?"

"*Small* pianos, is it?" said one of the men, the thus far more talkative one, before removing his cigarette for a second so he could gob on the floor. Kinda gross.

I suppose it was exactly then I realised the men were themselves quite small. Well, very small. I'm not sure what's the acceptable term for people who are... well they're not big. It didn't even matter so let's forget it. The fact is the whole gorgeous looking town seemed small. And not small as in not many houses, though there weren't that many houses, the ones that I could see from the paddock looked small. It was hard to tell for certain, because we weren't right next to them, but I was sure the houses were not quite full-sized houses. I looked back to the men.

"Well, pianos," I said.

"Can't deliver anything now. It's closed, isn't it?" said the talkative man. The other nodded. "It's dark."

"Yeah, no, of course," I said because I'm not stupid and wasn't really expecting to deliver them at night. "It's a... it's a lovely evening," I added and pressed my hands deeper into my jacket's pockets. I got no response. "Well, is there somewhere to get something to eat around here?" I asked.

"Is it snowing up there?" asked the other man, the quieter one, with a laugh, and his laughter turned into a coughing fit which he caught in his hand.

"Ignore him. You want something to eat?"

"If there's somewhere open."

"Bettsy's, a couple of streets over. Then go up the road a bit," he said, still leaning and just casually cocking his head back. Directing us with his scalp.

"Okay, yeah, thanks, that sounds... that sounds great," I said, nodding at the men and then to Simon. Simon's face didn't suggest it sounded great. And I suppose I didn't have enough information to know if it would be great. It might have been shit.

All I really had was the cafe's name and directions which I'd already forgotten. I hate talking to people. "And it's..." I pointed.

The man sighed out a cloud. Didn't even bother taking his cigarette out of his mouth this time. Just rolled it to one side with his tongue. "Over there, halfway down, Bettsy's," he said, and then he did take his cigarette out and he sniffed quite violently.

"Cool," I said to sound cool. "And that's okay there, is it?" I asked, actually going to the effort of cocking my thumb back over my shoulder at the Lady, rather than just lazily tilting my head.

"Why wouldn't it be?" he asked.

"Well… I don't know," I said and the man took a long draw on his cigarette while staring at me. "Cool, well, thanks!" I lied. I found his response to my reasonable question a little bit shitty, still, I gave him a double thumbs up. I've got to stop doing that. Thumbs ups, they look ridiculous. They just pop out.

I tutted when we were on cobbles. "I hate that, sighing," I said as we began our search for the cafe. I did a big sigh, for Simon, for effect. "Oh, it's so difficult for me to be a… a fucking courteous fucking person!" I said, quietly, in a stupid-person voice, doing an impression of somebody who might sigh.

"Easy, Michael," said Simon.

"Yeah, you're right. And we're strangers. They're a bit wary of us. It's fair enough. Can't believe I said small pianos." Baby pianos. They were called baby grand pianos, I now remembered. Hub Cap had told us as we'd loaded them. And as I suspected, despite being electrocuted I still couldn't play them. I'd had a quick go. I could slide my finger up and down the keys, and that made a pleasing sound, but no more than that.

The town was actually completely lovely. The little town. It was a little town and all the people were too, all that we saw, but that's okay. I was a good forty centimetres taller than anybody I saw. And Simon's quite a bit taller than me.

We walked down the first street smiling at the inhabitants. These were night people and they all wore basically the same outfit, every one of them, men, women and children. Braces, white shirts and trousers. Sometimes a waistcoat. They looked smart. I think it was Simon who fascinated them most, though I too was getting stared at. They didn't get many robots around Morlay, was my guess.

"Down here?" There was a left, a side street, you might say, and we went down it. Or maybe we went up it? It was narrow, unlit and uneven. Simon didn't like the cobbles and he clattered. The houses weren't *tiny*, tiny. They weren't like toy houses or anything, they were made of boulders and wood. They were solid but everything was no more than seventy-five percent of the size you might expect things to be. Maybe only sixty percent. It might have been a large small village, rather than a small small town.

At the end of the side street was the next street over. Had to be. It was literally that. I stopped at the small junction which was lit by an orange burning lamp which smelled of exhaust. "What did he say now?" I asked, looking both ways.

"You know he gave you two different directions?"

"What?"

"He gave you two different directions."

"Did he?"

"Yeah."

"Well I didn't hear either one. I panic when people are giving me directions."

"It's fortuitous that part of your job isn't navigating."

I barked a laugh at Simon's attempted joke and use of a big fancy word all in one sentence. "Ah, I don't mind the screen telling me. And it's a fortuitousness that I've got you. So which way, smart guy?"

"I don't know."

They weren't dead straight, these streets. They meandered and you couldn't see far either way. There was no grid system here. "He said halfway up, definitely."

"Which way is up?" asked Simon.

"Fuck knows, let's just walk around." And we did. We walked around. None of the buildings looked like a cafe, though the smell of food wafted from many. We walked up, or maybe down a few streets until we got to the men smoking on the fence. "Yeah, this isn't right," I said to Simon, hoping to push him back behind the corner before they saw us. Too late. Hearing Simon, the two men looked at us and I gave one of the biggest thumbs ups I've ever goddamn given. In fact... yeah, it was definitely the biggest. Arm straight out towards them. The men nodded but I knew the nods would turn to shakes as soon as we turned our backs. That was disappointing. I saluted for some goddamn unknown reason. A little salute. I don't know how to salute! I just put a finger over my right eye and brought it forward and hated myself. I don't even know if they were looking at me when I saluted. Simon was. "Shut up," I said. It's because I don't enjoy meeting new people that I often react with exuberant hand gestures, to compensate for... something. I don't know. Sometimes I get the urge to touch people. Poke them. Weird. "I have no idea where we are," I sighed.

We walked back up, or down, the street we'd walked down or up. "Will the truck even fit down any of these?"

"No."

"You're carrying pianos tomorrow then!"

"No problemo. I am strong."

"I'll help." I slapped the back of his arm. "Couldn't help you now. I'm getting weak. We don't find the cafe soon and we'll go and eat the bread in the truck. "

"Ask somebody."

"I will if we don't find it soon."


Twentyish minutes later, after one more pass of the paddock, we reached a little junction. It seemed like the same one as the first, but it couldn't have been as this time I saw the cafe. It had a red awning and its large window was framed on the inside with red and white chequered curtains.

The lane was quiet. Not much foot traffic, and I wouldn't normally consider entering an eatery on such a quiet street but these weren't normal times. "Let's walk past first," I told him and we walked past the window first, nice and casually. I glanced inside and saw a lot of beards. A hell of a lot of beards staring out at us. I also saw at least one free table but maybe only one. Risky. "What do you reckon?" I asked him when we stopped a bit further up the street from the cafe, at a point where the buildings on each side joined in the middle and formed an arch over the lane that Simon would struggle to fit through, never mind the Lady. "Shall we go in?" I asked him. I looked at my watch. It wasn't five to two. My watch wasn't working. I shook it. "Time is it?"

"Eight twenty."

"Eight twenty? Okay. That's okay. They're not going to close at eight thirty so, yeah, we'll go in?"

"Yes?" he replied, and that was good enough for me. I agreed with him. Tacitly, I agreed, which means without actually saying it. Sure, they *might* have stopped serving. The empty table *might* be reserved, but it was a joint decision. Mainly Simon's.

We went back and I entered the cafe. I was chatting to Simon as I opened the door, to give off the air of nonchalance. He had to really compress, to get through the door, and even then it was tight.

"Just yourself?" asked the woman with the apron who I'm going to say was Bettsy herself.

"Well, yeah," I replied because although robots don't eat, I wasn't going to leave him outside. She winced a bit and tilted her head back and forth before pointing us towards the back.

Getting there meant people moving, scraping their tables and jockeying their chairs sideways, so we could pass. There was some sighing and a bit of harrumphing and a lot of me apologising, but we made it and I took my coat off and hung it on the back of my chair. My knees wouldn't go under the table so I sat sidesaddle and looked at the menu.

"Sausages," I said, casually. I showed the menu to Simon. Which meant holding it up as high as I could. I was showing him the bit where it said sausages.

"Don't get your hopes up. And pick a backup."

I nodded, he was learning, and I picked a backup. Mushroom quesadillas. I put the menu down and looked around at what other people were eating. Just being nosy. They weren't eating sausages, as far as I could see. "This is alright, eh?" I said to Simon, and then, more for the benefit of those on nearby tables I added, "it's a lovely town." I was complimenting their town. It was a nice town. I picked the menu up again and then put it down. I looked up at Simon. "Do I go up?" I asked, even though he couldn't possibly know. I turned around. There was now a man with the woman behind the counter. The counter was up a few steps. Part of a kitchen was visible through a hatch behind that. "Do I go up to the counter?" I asked him again. "Or is it, you know, table service?"

"I don't know. Ask."

"We'll wait," I said and picked up the menu. I put it down. "Okay, I'll go up," I agreed, grasping the proverbial nettle and also the actual menu. "Shall I?"

"Can't do any harm," said Simon.

"Yeah, I'm going to go up," I said and after some more chair scraping I was bending slightly in front of the counter. The woman was busy and so I stood there while she did things. "Do I order here?" I asked, politely, when she was close.

"You can if you want!" she said, which I guess, reading into that, suggested that ordering here wasn't actually the accepted method of ordering food. I really should have asked her what the exact process for ordering food was, but instead I banged my head on a beam. Simon wouldn't have been able to order food up here. He simply wouldn't fit.

"Oh no! Oh dear! Are you okay?" asked Bettsy as I smiled and stopped rubbing my head. I resisted the urge to look at my fingers for blood.

"Yeah, fine, it didn't hurt," I said. It did hurt, but the little shock was worse. That shock when you bang your head and your body jerks away.

"Oh dear, oh dear. Your poor head! Oh, I'm sorry, are you *sure* you're okay?"

"Really I'm fine!" I assured her.

"Oh, that bloody beam!" she placed her fists on her waist.

"Honestly, it didn't hurt at all."

"Brian!" shouted the woman, and the man who had been next to her moments earlier came out from the kitchen. He looked tired. "This poor man just smashed his brains out on the beam, I *told* you that would happen."

"I didn't," I laughed. "It's fine," I squealed, not meaning to go that high, as the man looked at me with an expression I didn't want to place. It wasn't warmth, nor was it respect, I can tell you that.

"He said he's fine," Brian told Bettsy. I think they were man and wife.

"I am, I'm absolutely fine!" I agreed, though I didn't really want to take sides.

"That beam holds the building up," the man said. He was addressing me. "How can I take it down?"

"Ha! No, really, it's... I'm..." I rubbed my head to show it didn't hurt. It really hurt and my left eye might have closed involuntarily for a split second when my hand ran over the bump, but I mostly hid it.

"We'll have to get rid of it," said the woman, balling up and then unballing a tea towel.

"We can't," growled Brian.

"Don't, it's fine, seriously."

"He's just lazy," said the woman as she watched Brian trudge back through the swinging kitchen doors.

"It's…"

"You must hit your head a lot," said Bettsy, regaining focus.

"Oh, all the time, seriously it's-"

"What do you want then, you big wanker?"

"Oh, erm, the sausages?"

"What do you want *with* them?"

Jesus Christ, they had sausages! I swallowed hard. "Erm, maybe, like, *more* sausages!" I said, probingly, exploring what were surely the outer reaches of their finite sausage supply.

"A double portion," she replied like it wasn't even anything. Jesus Christ. "Rice? Bread?"

"Bread."

"Bread."

"Actually, and rice. Why not?"

"Somebody is certainly a hungry big greedy pig," she said smiling.

"Yeah, I'm..." I said, taking out my wallet.

"Pay afterwards."

I put my wallet away. "Can I get a beer?"

"Can you grow a beard?"

"Ha! Er, no, a beer, can I..."

"Why *wouldn't* you be able to grow a beard? You're a man, aren't you?"

"I..."

She rubbed her chin and laughed hysterically. Then, when a normal person would have stopped pretending to laugh, she doubled over laughing, the notepad she was holding touching the floor as her arms dangled straight down. People on nearby tables started laughing. I guess it was contagious. I laughed a little too and looked over at Simon. He saw me laughing and smiled. His eyes weren't smiling. Everybody laughed for a while. Just as I was growing concerned for the woman's health she stopped. Then she started again, a few times, but she eventually managed to talk. "So you'd like a beer?" she finally asked, dabbing her eyes on her apron, then she ripped off what she'd written, balled it up and threw it through the hatch into the kitchen. I heard a curse from the kitchen then headed back to Simon.

"Sorry about this," I said to the people whose dinner I was ruining by making them move as I tried to return to my table. They weren't laughing now. I sat down and raised my eyebrows at Simon. He raised his at me. I looked over at the counter. Shit, she had my beer and was holding it up at me. I was supposed to have brought it to the table myself. "*Fuck*," I sighed and with scraping and now mumbling mixed with some cursing I got it and returned, apologising sincerely.

I sipped the bitter ale then touched the cold glass to the side of my head where I'd just cracked it on the beam. I put it down and touched my hair where it was burnt at the ends. "It's nice here," I said, taking another sip. "This is definitely more like it," I said. I was finally relaxed and not even the sound of guitar playing from the front of the cafe changed that, and I hate guitar-playing people. I smiled and nodded along and sipped more beer. "I think she called me a wanker."

"Shhh," said Simon because he could see her coming.

"Here you go, love," said Bettsy while putting the plate down. She was an enigma. I liked it when she called me love, but she also seemed to hate me a little bit. I was probably overthinking things, I do that, and anyway, whether she liked me or not, the fact was she delivered six sausages.

I saw Simon's face as he counted them. He's very good at counting *things*. Items he can see. It's his secondary function, after flying. It's just things that he can't physically see that he can't count.

To think, although I hadn't voiced it, I'd been worried that the plate would only have two sausages. That a single portion of sausages was as few as a single sausage, but no, that was *way* off. No, the amount of sausages wasn't an issue. There was an issue, but I hid it from Bettsy like I'd hidden my injured head.

"Mmmmmm," I lied, looking up from the sausages to Bettsy whose face was level with mine.

"Do you want any sauce?"

"Sauce?" I asked. Sauce could be a solution. I hoped saying sauce in a questioning way would be enough for Bettsy to tell me what sauces were available.

It wasn't."Do. You. Want. Any. Sauce?" she asked, like I had just damaged my brain.

"No. These are… they look… they look… *Mmmmmm*." Bettsy smiled and then waltzed back through the tables.

I moved a sausage with my fork.

"They *do* look good!" said Simon, surveying my plate.

I smiled and looked around before looking up at him.

"No, Simon, they don't."

"But you-"

I moved another sausage around. "In what way do they look good?" I hissed, my face incredulous. I looked up at him to show I was actually expecting an answer. His fans came on.

"They're... they're... they're sausage shaped!"

"I told you, it's not all about the shape. Or the amount."

"Sorry."

"That's okay."

"You're going to eat them?"

"Yeah, I'm going to eat them. I'm so hungry I'd eat a... a fucking... deep-sea diver's poo." That's what they looked like. I pointed at them with my cutlery. "They look like they're made of... wetsuit." I picked up my knife and started cutting. "*Annnd*, they're as tough as they look." Luckily the knife was sharp and soon a greyish mush oozed out from the hole I'd made. "The consistency of the interior is... yeah, it is disappointing. Perhaps better eaten with a spoon."

"It might taste better than it looks," said Simon, hopefully. "You've said that before."

"These won't." I lifted what I could get onto my fork up towards my face. I sniffed and my head jerked in a similar way it had when I'd hit it on the beam. "It smells..."

"Good?"

"Ha. Nope, no." I braved another sniff. "It smells... organic? It smells pretty organic."

"Oh yeah?"

"But it also smells of more... like, more abstract things. It smells like the... the scene of a crime." Most of it had dripped off before I put the fork into my tensed mouth. I suspected people on other tables were sneaking peeks at me by the way the volume dropped as my fork went in. I couldn't do anything about that.

"Well?"

I nodded. Or shook as my right foot tapped on the tiled floor. "Misery. I can taste misery. And... despair."

"You should have got some sauce," said Simon as I slowly chewed. I thought about my life choices as I slowly chewed. I thought about a lot of things as I slowly chewed.

"I know what I've done." I said and nodded and chewed and winced and tried to swallow.

"What?" he asked.

I didn't answer, I couldn't, not just yet, and I held a finger up to him. The skin was really chewy but better yet, there was something hard in it! A small bonus texture. I managed to swallow most of what was in my mouth. Everything but the hard bit. I turned my head and subtly spat the hard thing out into the palm of my hand while pretending to stroke my upper lip.

"What is it?" asked Simon. I looked at the hard thing, then held it up to him. "Yeah."

"What?" asked Simon, very curious.

"Yeah, see I thought it was mo*le*, you know, like that stuff Carlos had in the jar that time. But, yeah, it's moley. You know? Like… like chickeny."

"*What?*" asked Simon.

"There's a little... it's an animal and it... anyway, yeah. I mean, it said moley sausages so I can't... but I thought-"

"The animal?"

"Yeah, look," I said, rolling what was clearly a mole's nose around in the palm of my hand.

"Tastes bad?"

"Oh yeah." I put the nose on the side of my plate then took another forkful and I chewed rapidly and with a lop-sided face then, with eyes tightly shut, I swallowed. "It's… it's… it's abhorrent."

"Aw," said Simon, "you were looking forward to them."

"Just when things were going well."

"Damn.

When I'd finished, I put my fork down and shuddered for a minute or so. Bettsy returned and took my plate which was empty, save for some recognisable parts of a mole which I pressed onto the side of the plate. A few more noses. A claw. Some eyelashes.

"Everything okay?" she asked and I nodded because I had a mouthful of beer which I was using to rinse. I gave her a thumbs up.

Before leaving I used the cafe's small toilet and spent time staring at my tired face in the mirror. I tried to flatten my hair down with water from the tap. I was only semi-successful. A few tufts just wouldn't stay flat, no matter what.

Outside the cafe we stood on the foreign, dark, twisting and lumpy lane and as I did my coat up I heard an eruption of laughter from inside the cafe. The guitar player then started playing a much more uptempo song.

People smoked outside at night in Morlay and we strolled through fragrant plumes back to the truck. People stared at us. I smiled back. The smoking men on the fence had gone but the Lady hadn't. From the paddock, away from the town I could see red and blue flashing lights out in the black, apart from that there was nothing. We could have been floating in space.

In the Lady I made a bed out of clothes on the floor behind the seats. Simon slept at the controls. I saw he'd put the box containing the dot next to him.

"This is going okay," I said as I gazed up at the roof with my hands clasped under my head. *Was it though? Yes it was, shush.* Tomorrow we'd do something else. Deliver pianos. And then... *Shush.* "It's going okay!" I said again. Simon didn't reply and I dreamt that I had a house. It wasn't the house near the meadow. This house was a wreck. This house had steps which got steeper and more rickety as you climbed them. It must have had three or four floors. There were gaps in the steps and a small hatch to climb through. I wasn't sure I'd be able to get back to the stairs if I went through it. It was muy precario. That turned into a dream where I had sex with a tiny woman. Attempted sex. Not with a small woman, but with a really tiny woman. Microscopic. You couldn't even see her.

Looking up at the roof of the truck it took me just a few seconds too long to remember where we were and what was outside, and panic began to roll in. If I'd have had fans they would have come on. Then I remembered. I sighed. It was light. "Time is it?" I asked. I huffed and looked at my watch. Five to two. That wasn't right. "Fuck," I sighed. "Simon!" There was no answer. He was there, though. I raised my head. I could see him. "Simon!" He didn't move. "Simon!" Nothing. "Fuck," I muttered, grasping around on the floor. I threw the first thing my hand found which turned out to be my shoe. It missed and hit the windscreen then the dashboard. "Fuck!" I propped myself up on my elbows and looked around for something else to lob. There wasn't really anything. A sock wouldn't make it that far. "Simon!" I stood up, using my chair as a crutch, and looked out at the paddock. It looked cold. I looked at Simon's face. "Simon!" I shouted into it. "Fuck!" I shouted. Simon was sleeping. His sleep light was on, blinking yellow. "Piece of *crap*," I said, looking around for an implement.

On the side of Simon's neck, just below his right ear, there's a tiny hole with a tiny button in it. You have to put something in there and press the tiny button. Why they decided to put a tiny button in there I don't know. I checked my pockets. Nothing. I kicked my makeshift bed around. Nothing. "Fuck!" I shouted, and then, "Simon!" though I knew that it wouldn't work. I needed a pin or a toothpick. Or a thin nail, which I guess is another name for a pin or a... a... What I did not need was this shit.

It happened *fairly* regularly, but that was always in the bunker where I had a small bowl with pins and toothpicks and coins.

I checked the shelves at the back, throwing things around. Nada. I went over to the tray on top of my glove box and moved around my shit. I opened the glove box and just pushed things aside. I wasn't really looking any more. I was just moving things while trying to think of where there would be something suitable in this fucking shitty transport. "Wake up, dickhead!" I said as I picked up my coat and checked the pockets. The floor at the back. Between the seat cushions. My pockets again. The shelves again, though not all of them. The glove box again. I kicked the dot's box, just gently. Pushed it with my foot. "Don't have time for this!" I said. I stood and clapped my hands and looked around. "Really, *really* don't have time for this," I announced. I put my socks on and then a shoe while shaking my head. I then kicked over my bed and looked around for the other one. My other shoe, sometime in the night, had *fucking* dissolved. "Well that's ju-" I said, then remembered. It was a tight squeeze reaching down to get it from Simon's footwell.

I opened the door and stepped outside. Lovely morning. Not as cold as it looked. A thin mist hung close to the ground, but off to my left, not too far away there was an edge to the haze, where the ground just dropped away beneath it. The flashing lights I'd seen in the darkness were warning lights on the Burrowers whose tops were visible over the lip. I did all that taking-in-of-the-sights in just two or three seconds.

I looked around the ground. Found a piece of straw which was soft, damp and flaccid. I held it for too long before I threw it down and kicked my feet around. A twig would do but of course when you need a twig there's no fucking twig! I went over to where the men had been smoking when we arrived. There was a hell of a pile of butts there. A bit scummy, I thought, and the first black mark against the town. Actually the second. Because of the sausages. I bent down and ran my hand through the cigarette ends, looking for something long, thin and hard. I brushed the butts aside. "Fuck!" I said.

"Here," said a voice. I looked up. Approaching me was a man with a beard and waistcoat. He was holding out a cigarette while smoking one himself.

"Oh no, I'm not... I need a needle or something."

"That shit will kill you."

"What? No, it's for... Robot needs resetting. Rebooting. I need a pin... or something," I said, making a jabbing motion while still looking down. *He needs booting*, I thought but didn't say.

"Something like *this*?" asked the man, fiddling in his pockets. I was excited until he produced a key. He seemed pleased with himself. Like he'd saved the day.

"No, it needs to be like, you know... a sewing needle. Or a tooth pick. Because you have to..." I did the jabbing motion again while looking at the floor. Nothing. I ran my hand along the log fence, looking for a splinter. "You know, like a pin or something?" I said.

"Wait there," said the man who took off jogging. For a few feet he jogged, before he started coughing, and then he was just walking away. I could hear him coughing. I wasn't going anywhere. I continued my forlorn search, which involved me kicking the ground and swearing, until the man returned with a small cushion, from which jutted at least thirty sewing needles. *At least*. Some had tiny balls on the end. "Oh, you lifesaver!" I said.

"They're my wife's, so be careful."

"Just need one," I explained, perusing the cushion he held out and selecting a medium-sized pin. I got into the Lady and the man followed, even though I hadn't said he could. Fair enough I suppose, I had his pin, and at least, after one last long drag, he'd had the decency to flick away his cigarette. The man stood in the doorhole and watched me.

On the third attempt I pushed the pin into the hole on the side of Simon's neck and held it there. The man tried talking to me so I moved my slow count to twenty from inside my mind to outside it. "Twelve, thirteen," I said with a small nod between each number, "fourteen, fifteen, sixteen, seventeen, eighteen, nineteen, tw-" Simon bleeped and his fans started up. "Oh mate, really, you saved my life," I said, holding out the pin and not knowing if I should stick it in the cushion myself, or hand it to him, so he could stick it in. It was a bit awkward as I held out the pin and he held out the cushion. I didn't know if the pins had their own specific places. In the end he took it and put it in the cushion himself. It takes Simon ages to start up after a reboot, and he bleeps a lot, but I could relax knowing that he was turning on. I would have been able to relax even more if the man took his pins and fucked off but that didn't happen.

"It's a lovely town," I said because the man was hanging around. He wanted to make sure Simon came on, I suppose, what with him being an integral part of the process, thanks to his wife's pin cushion.

"We like it," he replied. I nodded. "You eventually found the cafe then?"

"Ha! Yeah!" I said, relieved the man had identified himself as one of the two from the previous night. I hadn't been one hundred percent sure. Bearded men all look pretty similar to me.

"We thought you'd be wandering around all night!"

"Well, your directions were pretty vague," I said and laughed.

"Up there, next street over. Then halfway down."

"Anyway, lovely cafe. Had the-"

"Moleys, yeah, I heard."

"You heard?" I asked. Weird.

He didn't elaborate on how or why he'd heard. "What did you think of them?"

"They were... yeah. I liked them! Honestly, I thought they were... yeah. No, they were good." There was a reason I doubled down on that ridiculous lie. You don't insult local delicacies. If I'd said 'Your sausages are fucking ghastly' then I'd bascially be saying, *what the hell is wrong with you people?* People don't want to hear that and he would have got all defensive. I value honesty but sometimes you just gotta lie. "Nice town." That wasn't a lie. "It's not on the map." Nor was that.

"No sir, haven't been incorporated."

"Oh, well that's good." I liked everything about his sentence. I liked being called sir. I liked that he sounded proud that they hadn't been incorporated, even though I didn't *really* know what that meant. What practical difference it made. He made it sound like a good thing.

"You're from Ikarus?" he asked. Simon was still bleeping, but now only occasionally. He'd be on any second, thank fuck.

"I'm sorry?" I asked, even though I'd heard him perfectly. I needed a bit of thinking time.

"You're from Ikarus?"

"I'm sorry, the bleeps. I'm what?"

"You're from Ikarus?" he asked.

"What-"

"You... This is an Ikarus transport. That's an Ikarus robot. There's a..." said the man, pointing at my chest where the ghost of the logo I'd picked off still remained.

"No," I said. I'd kind of wasted my thinking time. The guy didn't look like he bought my explanation. "We did. I mean we were but don't... This is just a... they were... they were selling it off. We deliver. It's our own business. We're deliverers."

"They sold you all this?" he asked, pointing around the cab, his pointing finger lingering on Simon. Was I being questioned? Or was he just curious? I couldn't tell but I didn't like it.

"Yeah, they're replacing it all. Getting a new... you know, a new crew. I could probably get you one... I think they have..." I was struggling. Wilting. "Hey, that reminds me," I clicked my fingers at him and went to the dashboard. People can't talk if you click your fingers at them, I hoped. I was only going over to the clip next to my screen. I pulled out the note from Hub Cap. "So, LP's Music, where's... where is that? Got a delivery. That's why we're here." I noisily blew air through my lips to show it was a bit of a chore, delivering stuff, but, hell, we were delivery men and it's what we did. "Campers Lane? Where is that?"

"You probably passed it last night about four times!" said the man and I was relieved. I'd successfully deflected attention. Two more probing questions and I'd probably have told the man my entire life story.

"Ha!" I said. I went to clap the man on the arm.

"Hello Mike!" said Simon.

I winced and lowered my arm. "Fuck," I said to the man who'd given me a pin.

"Your name not Mike?" he asked while I considered pushing him out of the doorhole. I decided against it.

"Erm... well, yeah, it kind of is. It's not, it's Michael really," I said, doing a wide upside-down smile, "but *that's... that's... that's...* not Simon." No, that was Jeff's voice coming out of Simon. The reboot had obviously reactivated communications. "It's Jeff," I whispered and bit the end of my thumb.

"Who's Simon?"

"He is." I only mouthed that, and pointed.

"Where are you, Mike?" asked Jeff, through Simon.

"I'm, err," I said, removing my thumb from my mouth and pressing it to my forehead. And then – and this was pure luck or instinct – I shot out my hand and covered the man's hair-surrounded mouth before he could helpfully chime in with our whereabouts. '*Sorry,*' I mouthed to him. "We're not far. We're on our way back," I said then coughed. "Be there in an hour or so, yeah? It's, erm… yeah, so I'll see you there and explain everything. It's a funny… Anyway. Cool?"

"So I'll see you soon?" asked Jeff. He was much calmer than last time. He sounded happy.

"Yeah, good! An hour. We're... we're... still in the City, so..." I was staring into the bearded man's eyes, I realised. I was concentrating so hard on the voice I hadn't noticed. And my hand was still on his mouth. I dropped my hand and my gaze. I was relieved Jeff had accepted my fake promise to return so easily.

"I want my machine back," said Jeff, through Simon.

Simon was looking at me through concerned eyes as I carefully and as quietly as I could mouthed, "Turn. The. Fucking. Communications. Off. Con. Firm." I made a chopping gesture at my neck with curled fingers. He nodded.

"Yep, of course, well, be an hourorsobye!" I said, the last few words running together.

"I'm coming to get y-" There was a click.

We all waited to see if anything else came out of Simon. After a few seconds nothing had and I exhaled. "Oh man!" I said.

"Who was that?" asked the man.

"That? Oh, just Jeff. It's not what it... What's your name by the way?" I should have asked him his name earlier but I hadn't. It was now or never. There's only a certain period you can spend in somebody's company before it's too late to ask them their name and I was approaching that point with this guy.

"Carl."

It turned out he was named Carl. I generally don't ask people their name because, well, I generally don't care.

"Carl. Thanks again for the pin. I'm Michael," I said, holding out my hand. He was still holding the pins so he shook my right hand with his left hand. Not ideal but I'd already touched his face and felt the wiry tickles from his facial hair prickle my palm, so it's not like it was our most awkward interaction of the last ninety seconds. "And this is Simon, and Jeff... Jeff is from... from?" *Where could I say he was from?* "He's from head office," I said. I probably shouldn't have.

"I thought that was talking for a minute," said Carl, nodding at Simon.

"*Was* from head office. A head office. He's still from head office, but, like, not ours." I did a series of big blinks. The conversation was getting away from me. "Because we're not... you know? Anymore. We don't have a head office."

"So what did he want?" asked Carl.

"I've literally no idea, and that's the truth," I said. "I mean it all is. It's all the truth, but that bit, you know... especially. Well no, all of it is."

"Where's an hour away?"

"Where's an hour away?"

"You're going to be back in an hour."

"Yeah, just... just... just... you know?"

"No."

"I know what it is. Just, probably the paperwork hasn't gone through, for the... To re-register the... well, you know how it is." I sucked my lips into my mouth and nodded.

"Are you on the run? Because we can't have trouble here."

"Of course, of course," I agreed. "What?" I asked, all consternated, should have said that first. "There won't be. It's just... just... just..." Oh my good god, I was stuck in a loop of saying the word just! I *had* to get out of it. "It's just... it's just, you know, paperwork!" I blurted. "I need to sign something for the... the... you know. The registration. It's fine. I honestly don't know what his problem is. He hasn't got one, actually. A problem. He's a nice guy." I was aware I was starting to babble. "Don't even worry about it," I said, wrinkling my nose. "He couldn't possibly find us here. *I* didn't even know we were coming here, it was just... just... just... He wouldn't come here, it's fine, you know?" I said, placing a hand on Carl's shoulder which meant YOU GO NOW CARL! Thanks for the pin and all, but GO!

"How did *Jeff?*" asked Carl, who paused to make sure he had the name right. I nodded, "Jeff know that you'd just turned it on?"

"I don't know," I said. I thought about it. "Maybe a light comes on somewhere?"

"And he was just waiting there? Monitoring a light."

"Must have been."

In the distance a siren sounded.

"They're awake," said Carl. I peered out of the windscreen, leaning on the back of my chair, and looked towards the Burrowers. The mist had cleared from the paddock and the Burrowers were clearer. They were moving. Possibly. Slowly. Massively. I stared at a single point on one of the machines and matched it to a point on the mountains behind. They were moving. Or the mountains were. Either seemed unlikely. It was certainly not something you see every day.

"They're incredible, huh?" I mused, mainly to Simon, happy to not be talking about Jeff.

"They're shit," said Carl.

I nodded my head at an angle, because everybody's entitled to their opinion, and I continued to stare at them. Mainly to ignore the man who couldn't read a room. Another siren sounded and there was a flash of blue light, a pillar of it, as the earth was punched by the formidable fist of science and commerce. You could see the shock wave coming across the ground, like a hand sliding under an expensive bed sheet. I lost sight of the wave as it barreled towards the crater's edge beneath us. The dust hit the cliff and broke like a wave. A cloud of dust burst up then fell back on itself and there was a moment of peace before the Lady shook, just ever so slightly, and a shower of small stones pinged, binged and tinged off the windscreen and bodywork. Then we heard the roar. To be fair to Carl, I could see how showers of pebbles might one day lose its lustre.

"They shouldn't be that close," said Carl, shaking his head.

"Why did you build the town so close to the edge?" I asked.

"We didn't," he said. I was still looking out at them. Every time I blinked I saw the pillar. "LP's is a couple of streets over, and then down."

"Thanks Carl," I said. I turned to him and watched as he put a cigarette in his mouth and lit it with the same hand, before stepping outside. His other hand had a pin cushion in it. He should have done that the other way around – stepped out, *then* lit his cigarette – but at least he was gone. I gave his back a thumbs up.

I turned to Simon. "The fuck happened?"

"I got stuck in sleep mode!" he replied, petulantly, like I already knew the answer, which, to be fair, I did.

"Well... don't."

"Oh yeah, I did it on purpose! My cache doesn't empty, *does it*?"

"I know, we'll get that fixed."

"Sure we will."

"We will, buddy, I promise. They've probably got an engineer around here." It was on the list of things to do. Getting Simon's cache fixed. I hadn't written it down. The list was in my mind and his cache was pretty far down it, but it was there. I looked out of the doorhole but couldn't see Carl.

"He's still looking for us then."

"Yeah, but it's only been a couple of days. It's what I expected. He'll... you know?"

"What now then?"

"We've got pianos to deliver. Let's do that first. Then… yeah, if we have to move on, we will."

"Sounds like a plan."

"We should go and find this music shop. Walk there first. Should we?"

"Should we what?"

"Find the shop. Walk there. Then come back and get the pianos? So we know where we're going. Or should we fly nearer?"

Simon's fans hummed. "Let's walk."


"You're just not talking to me?" asked Simon, *now* suddenly perceptive. I continued to ignore him. We could have done with some of that perception when he said walking was a good plan. Then, maybe, we wouldn't have been kidnapped. Despite my protests and bargaining, we'd been marched down here by Carl and his cohorts while we looked for the music shop. That wouldn't have happened if we were flying.

Let's walk! Nice one. We should have left *immediately*, just chucked the pianos out, but no, Simon thought it would *make sense* to walk. Nice one, Simon! Yeah, sure. *Whatever*.

Down here, where we were being held captive, was the entrance to a mine which was accessed from the square in the centre of the town. The centre of town was up through where the two buildings joined over the lane. Near the cafe. The mine entrance looked like a not-quite-full-scale entrance to a subway, but inside the passage soon turned to bare rock, which led to a large wooden door. We were now behind that large wooden door, in a cavern, and we were to remain here while Carl, treacherous, devious dickhead Carl, contacted Jeff. So no, Simon, I'm not talking to you. *Let's walk*. Idiot.

And talking of idiots. Bloody Carl! He'd given me a sandwich and thought I'd be thankful. He seemed to think that made this whole thing more acceptable. I'd told him I thought Moleys were disgusting. I didn't care about his feelings anymore. He'd apologised and asked if I wanted an egg sandwich instead and I'd said, 'What, a rat egg sandwich?'

Before he'd closed the door Carl had said that it was nothing personal, but I didn't buy that. I found that very hard to believe. It seemed *quite* personal. When he had *personally* forced *this* person into a mine, well, it was hard to not take that slightly personally.

Moleys were somehow much worse when they were cold.

He hadn't wanted Simon to come with me, but they couldn't stop him. Only I can do that and I told them I couldn't. I told them it's in his programming to follow me. *I should have left you out there*, I thought as I ignored him.

"Michael!" said Simon, but I was biting my fingernails. One particular nail. "I'm sorry," he said and I took my finger out of my mouth.

"*Why? Why* are you sorry?" I asked with my teeth holding a bit of nail I'd torn off. I looked at him, then had to look away when he turned to me, but not before he'd blinded me with his eye lights and cast my shadow large on the rock face behind.

"Because you think it's my fault?"

"Think? It's not my fault, is it?" I said, trying to blink away my second deep-pink retina burn of the day.

"Sorry."

"Stop saying things you don't mean. You think I think it's your fault? What does that mean? It's not my fault, is it? It has to be somebody's fault."

"Well, okay it's my fault.

"I'm trying to do my best." The ground shook slightly, and dust and tiny pebbles fell, sounding like a shower. I wiped the dust from my hair with a sharp horizontal chopping motion. Those bits were still sticking up.

"Sorry."

"I'm doing this for *you*. You think I enjoy this?" I asked. Once again I was being a dick, but I couldn't stop. I don't know why, but it happens sometimes. I know it's happening and it's out of my mouth before I can stop it. Bullshit comes out. "I could be… be back at the Hub. I could get a new unit," I said. I did know why I was being a dick. Things had gone wrong and it was *my* fault. But then Simon could have stopped me. He should have stopped me.

We sat in silence. The cavern was statically lit with a few flickering lanterns. There were roughly hewn, pitch dark tunnels leading off from the cavern. Carl hadn't even bothered to tell us to not go down them, because it was so obvious that we shouldn't. I didn't think Simon could with the state of the floor. Frigid air billowed from them.

The cavern's details were mostly illuminated by Simon's eyes. I could see him looking around. He turned to me again and I managed to shield my eyes in time.

"Just take me back, then."

"Is that what you want? Really?" I asked.

"Yes."

"Okay, fine, we'll do that. When we get out."

"*If* we get out."

"Don't be dramatic, they're not going to kill us."

"I can't-"

"Me then, they're not going to kill *me*. It's all bluff."

Simon's lights, his eyes, they stopped moving around and instead just lit up the floor in front of us. We sat like that for a while.

"It's fucking people. People are shit," I said, flicking a piece of grit off my thigh. "They're just liars and... greedy. Selfish. And stupid. People are very stupid."

"You're not that greedy," said Simon and I exhaled a laugh through my nose.

"Thanks pal."

"You're welcome."

"It's like... nobody is happy with what they have, you know? They want *more* and they'll fuck you over. You can't trust anybody. Because for you to have more, somebody else has to have less. It's..." The doors opened behind us and a silhouette was there. Simon turned and illuminated Carl's face. "Oh here's the little dickhead!" I said, only giving him the briefest of glances. I didn't stand up. He didn't deserve it. I didn't mean to say little, either. "Massive dickhead."

"Wotcha. Look, we need to move your wagon," he said, coming over and actually putting a hand on my shoulder! Nerve of the guy. I shrugged it off.

"We'll move it by getting in it and flying away from this shitty town, how about that?"

"Yeah," said Carl who then immediately added, "No. We just need to hide it, just for a while."

"What's going on, Carl? Why are you doing this? What do

you hope to achieve?"

Carl did a big sigh and came and sat on a rock to the side of us. I moved away from him because he was disgusting. I looked over at the door that he'd left open and then to Simon and considered making a dash for it, but not seriously. I looked over at Carl who was rubbing a hand over his beard and neck. He lit a cigarette. "Okay," he said, his throat sounding thick with phlegm, and then he explained the situation. The situation was that Morlay was being threatened by the company. Morlay had been a mining community for a long time and then the Burrowers arrived, and they'd coexisted for a period but now the town was blah blah blah. Something about incorporation. I tuned out at this point but I got the gist. It was apparent Carl wanted to selfishly use us as something to bargain with. A pair of chips, and the fucking idiot had only gone and contacted Jeff!

"And what did Jeff say to this?" I asked.

"He didn't seem *that* interested in reaching a solution," said Carl.

"No?" I said, raising my eyebrows. "Well, if you'd have asked me I could have told you. You can't negotiate with him. Guy like that isn't bothered about people like us. Hope it works out for you," I said. I nodded at Simon and cocked my head towards the door. "We're going to shoot, yeah?"

"No, sorry," replied Carl. "He wants you. Well, that thing." He looked at Simon briefly which annoyed me. "Yeah, he was pretty adamant about that. He got quite animated." He took a long drag then exhaled. Simon lit the smoke and its shadow danced on the rock face behind. "Yeah, I don't know what you've done but..." said Carl, shaking his head. He did a thick-sounding swallow. Carl lit another cigarette. He had two. I waved my hand at the smoke and leant back. Carl didn't care.

"Well, look Carl. You tried. The guy is weird so we'll go and you prob-"

"He's coming."

"What? He's coming out here?" I sat up straight at this news.

"He said."

"Nah."

"So I need you to move the wagon," said Carl, looking down and shaking his head and taking a long draw.

"Why?"

"We'll hide you until he *does* care. About the town. Until he *has* to make a deal."

"That's all very well, Carl, but we have places to be. We can't just... just... And I told you, you can't negotiate with him. Really. How long until he-"

"Just move the wagon. We have to hide you properly. Just until we get this sorted and then..."

"And then what?"

"..."

"I thought so. Nah, fuck it, move it yourself."

"We trie-"

"Tried?" I asked and Simon's head spun, instantly throwing Carl's shadow on the wall behind him. "You haven't crashed it, have you?"

"No!" said Carl. "Well, *I* haven't."

"I really don't appreciate being led places," I told Carl and the others as they led us places. You're never led anywhere good, I've found. "Just point me to where we should go." Twenty or so men had been waiting behind the wooden door to escort us. When we were out in the bright town square I held my hand up to shield my eyes from the sun and then waved it to clear the smoke the gang were producing. I didn't know which bothered my eyes more. "And you know, Simon here, I haven't mentioned this yet but he's actually a *weapon*." I announced. "I didn't tell you that before but one word from me and…" I blew out some air which caused the cloud of smoke to twirl and whirl. I looked around with my eyebrows raised. "I wouldn't want to be in your shoes. Oh boy, you'd be fu… finished." I didn't swear during my threat because there were children within our whatever it was, procession? Jamboree?

"Is that true?" asked a child walking next to Simon. She was gazing up at him as he clattered along the cobbled lane.

"It *is* true," I said, staring down at the child until she looked away. "He's just not allowed to admit it, protocol. He's a, erm…" I couldn't think of the word. I clicked my fingers at the child.

"Robot?" she offered.

"No. Well yeah, but there's a word." I was trying to think of that word. You know that word. The one which means a sort of, like, test model. You know? Like a test model. Not final. I couldn't think of it. We walked down the street, through where the houses formed an arch and past the cafe. Bettsy was staring out, arms folded, an impassive expression on her face. I smiled, she didn't.

"A weapon, is it?" asked Carl. "Yeah, we believe that, after all, we're all very simple folk who don't know much about the world."

"I said that about three minutes ago, *Carl*." *Keep up*, I thought.

"We were just about to run away screaming. A weapon!" said Carl.

"Prototype!" I pointed at Carl triumphantly because I'd remembered the word. "Simon's a prototype weapon." Even if Simon wasn't a weapon, what Carl hadn't appreciated was that as soon as he got behind the controls to the Lady we were *gone*. "Hey, we've got that guy's pianos!" I said, pointing to the shop behind Carl. I wondered if one of the people with us was LP. "It's hot, isn't it?" I said. It was hot and I could feel the warmth of the sun on my neck every time we left a shadow. We went around a bend and I saw it at the end of the lane. The Lady, formerly a cube and therefore square in profile, was now a diamond and leaning against a building. "Oh for fuck's sake," I said, not bothered about offending children.

"Yeah, so if you move it and we'll..." Carl didn't finish that and I didn't press him. We walked the rest of the way with me just shaking my head. I stopped in front of the teetering Lady and put my hands on my hips and continued to shake my head. I wanted to make the men feel stupid for crashing it. Bad and stupid. I said already that Ladys are impossible for a human to drive. I'd tried once, in the yard. The thing had lurched sideways and I'd only gone about five metres and that had been enough for me.

One of these guys had somehow got it from the paddock and into this house where one of the corners was through a first-floor window hole. That's how it was balanced. A corner on the floor and one through the window hole. *Whoever did that must have absolutely shit themselves*, I thought as I looked around it, looked under it, bending at the waist, my hands still on my hips. Damage to the truck seemed slight, luckily, but I knew it couldn't be doing it any good, propped up like that. Most of its weight on one corner. I looked over to the paddock. The section of fence where Carl had been standing last night was gone and there were seven large divots leading to us. I shook my head. I mean, in a way it was impressive, to get it so far. But it also wasn't. "This is terrific, Carl. Good job," I gave him a thumbs up.

"Get it down, we can..." said Carl, again trailing off.

"We can what?" I asked but Carl's interest was taken by somebody running towards us from the paddock. "What?" I repeated, a bit insulted that he wasn't giving me his undivided attention.

"Twelve clicks!" shouted a running boy. He didn't have a beard and could run. That's how I knew it was a kid from a distance. His white shirt, too big for him, billowed. "Twelve clicks!" the running boy shouted again and the crowd murmured. Carl walked towards him.

"Erm! Excuse me!" I shouted. "We've got a bit of a situation here to deal with!" Carl looked at me but only for a second. He was talking to the boy then looking out over the plain. "*Hello!*" I shouted but he didn't turn back.

I walked over and pointed my face where theirs were now pointed. Towards the Burrowers. They'd sort of stopped guarding us so something was afoot. I went over to Simon. "Seen that?" I asked, nodding back at our Lady. He glanced over for a moment and nodded. He was more interested in looking where the men were looking. "What are we looking at?" I asked, hoping his good eyes could see something. Simon simply stared. "Is it Jeff?" I asked. I didn't think it was because they weren't trying to hide us from whoever was twelve clicks away.

"They're coming this way," said Carl and it was his turn to shake his head.

"Who are?"

"Who are?" laughed Carl like I was a moron. It was somebody in the crowd who had basic courtesy and said it was the Burrowers. *So what?* I thought. They looked no closer than they had been, to me. They were still miles and miles away.

"They're not coming," I said.

"They're not coming?" asked Carl.

"No, I don't think so." I looked again. Squinted. "Nah."

Carl clapped his hands. "It's okay, everyone! Everyone! Shush! This man here, who saw a Burrower for the first time in his *life* today-"

"Two days ago, *actually*," I said, putting the record straight.

"Oh I am sorry," said Carl but he wasn't. He very obviously wasn't. "Well, it turns out he's now an expert. Perhaps the leading authority in the territory on the subject, *actually*, and he says that, despite all the readings and measurements, which we've been keeping for, what? Coming up to thirty-seven years? Well, they are, in fact, no closer. George! Where's George?" asked Carl.

"Here!" shouted a man that I had to assume was George.

"You're fired, George, your readings aren't accurate. This guy here says so."

"They don't look closer, is all I said," I said.

"So it's all fine and let's all go have a big party." Carl started clapping and smiling at me.

"Is it true, is he an expert?" asked the child next to Simon.

"You know, Carl, there's no need to be like this. You've been a dick to us since we got here. They don't *look* any closer, *to me*. And even if they were coming this way it would take them days. What are they going to do, jump up here?" Nobody laughed at that. "So… so let's worry about the here and now, yeah? Let's get the..." I tilted my head back towards where the Lady was embedded.

"Oh!" said Carl, very animated and I knew he was going to launch into another sarcastic rant, and I wasn't disappointed, although actually I was disappointed, because he did. I closed my eyes in readiness. "It's okay everyone. It's going to take them *days* to get here, the expert said so, and you know what that means! Let's go and have a party!"

"Yeah, let's," I agreed, opening my eyes and nodding, "a party would be nice. It's Jeff we should be worried about."

"Jeff can come to the party, because it's not like it's the blast *radius* that will destroy the town. It's not like they only have to move one thousand metres closer for the blast *radius* to destroy the town and everybody in it. Because you think it's their legs we have to worry about? Well, it's not, but it won't matter because we'll all be having a great big party!"

"God, what a jerk," I whispered to Simon while leaning close to him. "Are they... are they closer?" I asked him. Simon nodded. "Actually they are closer," I announced to the crowd.

"Oh!" said Carl. "The big expert sa-"

"Carl. We get it," I said. "Anyway, if anybody shouldn't be in the mood for a party then it's us. *We're* the wronged… wronged, you know, party here." I guess I used the word party because we were talking about parties. Wouldn't normally call us a party. Carl was winding me right up. Word was spreading and more of the townspeople were coming to see what was going on. Must have been sixty or seventy people now. I smiled at a few before Carl grabbed me by the chest of my T-shirt. He also had some of my skin but I just grimaced and ground my molars together instead of screaming.

"*You're* the wronged party?" he shouted. Spit flying. Gross. I thought about how best to answer. I mean, we'd been held in a cave for a while. Though I had been given a sandwich. And somebody had crashed our truck. And yeah. The cave was the big thing. When we got kidnapped. We were definitely the victims of whatever this was.

"We've been nothing but nice. And we're treated like... I know what it is, it's because we're bigger. There's a word for that, Carl. Treating people badly because they're different."

"What's the word?" asked Carl, still holding my chest skin.

"Uncool."

People were telling Carl to calm down but that wasn't helping. I agreed with that sentiment, tacitly. Carl finally let go of me with a push and I fell back against Simon who caught me.

"You deserved that," whispered Simon.

"Thanks for the back up," I said, holding my hand against my chest to reattach the skin he'd loosened.

Carl was talking to men. Holding court. He was in charge, for sure and for whatever reason the Burrowers were his main concern. I was still more concerned about *our* vehicle. That's what we were here to move, right? And it was stuck in a house! That was my priority. Is that selfish? Maybe, but I tapped Simon and we left the throng and walked over to the jammed Lady.

"That's great, isn't it?" I said, peering in the ground floor window of the house. From what I could see the ground floor looked unscathed. The small cosy lounge looked okay. "How the hell are we going to get that down?" I asked as I stood back and we both stared up at the hanging open side door of the Lady. No way could Simon get up to it. I maybe could if I climbed on Simon. Then what? I pushed the Lady as hard as I could. It didn't move.

"That didn't work," said Simon.

"Well why don't you use your big computer head and come up with a solution, huh?" Simon accepted the challenge and he stared at the front of the building. His fans came on and he stared. I was worried he'd frozen. Now would *not* be a good time for him to freeze. I didn't have a pin and there was no way I was going to ask Carl for one. "Simon!" I said and he moved toward the side of the Lady. He'd completed some complex computations. I thought he'd worked out the exact spot where he'd be able to exert force on the Lady to free it. I watched as he extended himself to his full height. With his arms up he could just reach the bottom of the Lady's door hole. He gripped the angled sill and with a burdened whirring of his servos he managed to shorten his arms until he was off the floor. At first he scuffed the floor but then with a bit more whirring, which turned into clicking, he was swinging freely. I was watching. Soon he was five centimetres off the floor and swinging, and I could smell something acrid.

And then nothing else happened.

I watched him swing there for a while before I realised nothing else *was going* to happen. "Is that it? That was your plan?"

"I thought I might have been able to climb in."

"Fu... Get down." Simon lowered himself much quicker than he'd risen. "Good job, mate!"

Carl, followed by some of the others, marched over to us. I groaned and moved a bit closer to Simon. Slightly behind him. "You have to call Jeff," said Carl.

"Yeah, I *really* don't want to do that," I said, honestly. "Help us get this down and we'll do the hiding thing."

"It's too late for that," said Carl. "Call him," he said to Simon. "Communication on," he said, dictating clearly but ineffectually. Simon only listens to me.

"And say what, exactly?" I asked.

"You're going to tell him that what you're doing, whatever that is, is nothing to do with us and you're sorry and you're giving yourself up."

"It *is* nothing to do with you. He knows. And look, Carl," I said, using his name so he'd know I meant business, "we'd be gone by now if you hadn't kidnapped us. *You're* the one who called him. Help us get this down, yeah? We'll go and you... do what you do." I slapped Simon on his front with the back of my hand and went to walk away. Don't know where I planned to walk to. I planned to just walk a bit away and let Carl come up with another plan. One that didn't involve us.

"Just tell him!"

"Calm down," I turned back. I'd only taken two steps. I guess I did feel partly responsible. "And then what?"

"Then, hopefully, he'll leave us alone."

"There's no guarantee. And he's kind of stubborn. I know I keep saying this but he doesn't really listen to me, you know? If I thought it would work I'd call him, I *would*," I lied. I probably wouldn't. I definitely wouldn't. "Best thing would be for us to be gone. He'll forget about you."

"He's going to destroy the town," said Carl and I saw in his eyes that he was serious. Somebody in the crowd gasped.

"You... you can't just destroy towns. He'd... he'd have to give you... notice or something, surely," and then Carl handed me a printed piece of paper. And there it was. "Well..." I said, handing it back to him. "Get a lawyer."

"I am a lawyer!" said Carl.

"Oh... I thought... I thought you were a miner." I looked around. I thought they were all miners, but that was presumptuous of me, I now realised. Uncool.

"Communications on," Carl said to Simon. It still didn't work.

"Sorry Carl, he only responds to my voice."

"Tell him!"

"Let's just all relax a second. It's getting a bit... It's getting a bit... Let's think this through first. What's the date on that?"

"Today's date."

"Okay," I said and pretended to think.

"Turn on communications!" said Carl.

"Stop it, you're pressuring me and I... I really don't work well under pressure." I just needed time to think. If I had time to think then I'd think of something. But he wasn't giving me time. I couldn't think.

"Turn them on," said Carl, tensing all over, balling his hand into a fist and putting that fist near my face. "Do it!"

"No!"

"Do it!"

"Nah."

"Fine!" said Carl, lowering his arm and relaxing. "Don't do it."

"I wasn't going to."

"You weren't going to what?"

"*What?*" I asked. *Was he doing reverse psychology? Did he think I was a child?*

"What's the *thing* you weren't going to do?" he asked. He really wanted an answer.

"Fucking... have you had a stroke? Turn on communications,

that's wh-"

"Hello Mike," said Jeff, through Simon.

"What? Fuck! *Simon!*" I said, betrayed.

"It's me, Jeff." He sounded muffled and out of breath. I thought maybe he was lying down in the corridor outside his office. His face pressed into the sumptuous carpet. That would be okay. Weird, but okay.

"Oh, hi Jeff!" I said and then I began to pace around, one hand on Simon. Simon shadowed me and the men milled around us like a smoky soup, getting out of the way as I paced in small circles, then filling the space behind us.

"I'm coming to get your machine," said Jeff. "I'm on my way. I'm getting ready, huh-huh-huh!"

I looked at Simon. The noises Jeff was making were more disturbing than his words. "Yeah, about that. Look, what is it you want us to do? *Specifically?* I feel this is getting... getting… like, getting out of hand? Somewhat? So… What's the next step? How do we... how do we get out of this?" I asked. "It's just a robot, you know?" I wrinkled my nose at Simon as I paced and shook my head to show him I didn't mean that.

"Ask him about the town," said Carl and I nodded but paced. I'd work that in.

"You don't have to do *anything*, Mike! Hgggnh huh huh."

"Okay, but, you know, to end this? What should we do?"

"Nothing. Don't do anything," said Jeff, and then he made a really weird sound. Sounded like he was straining on a toilet. "Run, don't run, it doesn't matter, because I'm coming. I'll be there before it's dark."

"You definitely know where we are? We might be somewhere else by now. Have you thought about that?"

"You're in Morlay. Carl is keeping hold of you for me. You still think you can get away?"

I shook my head at blabbermouth Carl. "Okay, look, Jeff, I've got a load of worried miners here. And, well, this is nothing to do with them. There's at least one lawyer too," I said, nodding at Carl. "So, you know, whatever's going on with us, you know?" I gestured to myself and Simon even though Jeff couldn't see. "We can sort that out but... you know?"

"I don't know."

"Well, what I just said," I said. "So, we'll come back?" I said. "Or... or meet you somewhere? You have my word."

"I'm coming for you."

"Right, okay, but we're going to leave now, I'll just get these guys to help us... we've a little problem with the truck, but once we get it down... okay?" I glanced at the Lady.

"Hgggggnh!" said Jeff while Carl grabbed my sleeve. I shook him off.

"And you'll leave the town alone because we'll be on our way back?"

"Nope," said Jeff.

I stopped pacing. And Simon stopped. I looked at Carl and held my hand out. "Jeff, it's Carl," he said, then he took up the pacing with Simon following.

"Hey Carl."

"Hello, erm, I was thinking, what about if we, erm, killed... killed Mike for you."

"Michael," I mouthed at him while I glared at him. Hard to tell if he was serious as he wouldn't look at me.

"That's tempting, Carl. That really is but it's the robot I'm really after. Mikey's just *there*, he doesn't realise it but he's nothing."

"Well, shall we do it anyway?" pressed Carl.

"Hey!" I said.

"You know what's funny, Carl?" asked Jeff.

"No."

"Mikey thinks he's important."

"I get that impression," said Carl, fully turning his back to me.

"He's only there because we have a quota of humans! He lives in a bunker! Like a... a..." Jeff couldn't think of anything else that lived in a bunker.

"We could smash up the robot?" said Carl, and Simon furrowed his eyebrows as best he could. Mine were still furrowed. More furrowed than ever.

"Thanks Carl, I really do appreciate the offer, but I've got this. You're a good guy."

"We'll do it."

"I know you would."

"So... we're okay?" asked Carl, hopefully.

"*Hgggggggggggnh!*" said Jeff.

"Are you okay?" asked Carl.

"I'm fine, just practising some kung fu moves."

"Oh. So we're okay?" asked Carl.

"We're groovy."

"Okay, okay, well, that's a relief," said Carl, nodding and looking around, trying to pass on his nodding to the others.

"You should be packing up, though. You haven't got long," said Jeff and Carl stopped nodding.

"I'm sorry?" said Carl, leaning closer to Simon's speaker.

"Don't be."

"I…" said Carl. That's all he had.

*Nice one, Carl*, I thought. "Jeff? It's Michael again," I said without having planned what I was going to say next.

"Yes?"

"Why are you being such a..." I said, in my mind going through all the insults I know. "A knobhead?" I settled on. Carl's shoulders slumped and he sarcastically applauded me, I turned away from him. It's not like being nice was working. "You're an absolute knobhead."

"Listen to this," said Jeff and in the distance, not through Simon, but in our world, an enormous siren sounded.

"Jeff, Carl again," he said, panicked. There was no reply, just panting and straining. "Jeff! Sir, if I may." Just breathing.

"Jeff, how do you know when we turn on communications?" I asked.

"A light comes on, in my helmet," said Jeff and despite Carl's pleading he didn't reply again. But he was there, breathing and grunting until I turned off the communications.

"How long have we got?" I asked Carl.

"Three hours, according to the notice," he said. He now seemed depressed. He'd been powered by anger earlier, but his vigour had escaped from him like the inside of a hot Moley through its sliced skin.

"Well look, three hours? That's ages. We could just move everybody then... then sort it out and... It's a bluff, right? I mean there are laws against this kind of thing, right?"

"Yeah, but it takes-"

"What vehicles do you have?"

"A few bicycles but nothing with an engine," he said.

"Damn!" I said. *It's all very well living a backward lifestyle if you don't have to flee real quick*, I thought.

"Where could we go?"

"I don't know," said Carl.

"The Outpost?" said the girl who had been looking up at Simon a lot.

"Outpost? How far is that?" I asked but she went shy and shook her head. She was holding Simon's arm.

"About twenty-five clicks," said Carl.

"Okay, twenty-five clicks," I said, thinking, trying to do the maths. "What's a click?"

"What's a click?"

"Yeah, how far is a click?"

"It's a kilometre."

"Okay, okay," I said, trying to do the maths. "And how many people?"

"Around three hundred."

"Three hundred times twenty-five is... then there's minutes... Sixty minutes in one hour. So... yeah?" I didn't really count anything but nobody corrected me. "Carl, get everybody here." I'd worked out if we crammed as many people in the back of the Lady as we could then we could move them all. Probably.

With the help of logs, fifty men and Simon, it took less than ten minutes to get the Lady down. It came down with a crash but didn't squash anybody. More surprisingly it didn't pull the front of the house off. The houses, like the people who lived in them, were solid. Even Carl had pulled himself together.

Simon tested the controls while me and some others launched the now damaged pianos out of the back. So much for *that* job.

"We did basically deliver them," I told the helpers.

"It was my house," said one man.

"Sorry about your window," I said as I threw out splintered bits of wood. "It wasn't our fault."

"It was broken anyway."

"Oh, well, that's kind of lucky?"

"Yeah, I was in bed yesterday morning and this bloomin' red cannonball came smashing in. Just missed me. And today a truck!"

"A what?" I asked. "Red cannonball?" I stood straight for a second. That seemed familiar. I couldn't think from what though, and then I kicked out the rest of the splintered wood from the floor. "Come on," I said and we all jumped out of the back.

Carl was reinvigorated and shouting orders, and the crowd around him was kicking up dust.

Underneath the town there was a network of tunnels with rails and powercarts, but obviously it was underground where the Burrowers did their damage. Word had been sent to try and retrieve the guys who were already down there. *That* was going to be the big problem, but we could only go as fast as we could go.

It only took another ten minutes to comfortably fill the back of the Lady. And that was with a fair bit of faffing about. We didn't have a system for this operation yet. So we weren't at full efficiency. And that's what it was. An operation. In a war it would have a cool name, like 'Operation Armoured Eagle Talon' or 'Operation Mega Mole Man Move'. No, the eagle one is better. Anyway, yeah, we were conducting an operation and we were being pretty fucking heroic about it. There were fifty-three people in the back. Could have been more if we'd really jammed them. Even more if they were on each other's shoulders.

"Go!" said Carl, ready to close the door.

"You'll have to show us where it is!" Fucking Carl and his vague directions.

"Just go that way," he said, pointing but not holding his finger up long enough for me to get an exact bearing. "Twenty-five clicks."

"Which way, exactly?" I asked.

"Brendan will show you," said Carl pushing a bearded man into the cab.

"Okay, we'll be, like..." I turned to Simon, "half an hour?" I asked. He tilted his head. "Twenty minutes?" He started the Lady. "Twenty minutes, be ready!" I shouted out of the doorhole.

We'd try and do it faster but maybe even twenty was a bit optimistic, there and back plus unloading. We'd get faster, I was sure. And the time didn't start until we took off and it didn't include the two minutes or so it took us to tell everybody to hold tight, close the doors, and for Brendan to politely introduce himself. He was sent by Carl to show us the way but also, I felt, to make sure we returned. After introducing himself he held up a hammer. It was unnecessary, he didn't need to threaten us, I was well into this. It was my idea. I kinda felt bad sitting down while Brendan was standing but there was no chair for him.

Because of the crowd Simon had to turn real careful, which meant my window passed Carl pretty close by and I saluted him, but this time it felt *right*. Simon gently accelerated, so as not to smush the people against the back door and Brendan, who was standing behind us, in the middle, swayed backwards gently as he held on to our chairs. Soon we were smoothly travelling at one hundred and seventy miles per hour, the Lady's maximum speed, it turned out. Not too shabby for a brick full of humans. It probably would do two hundred empty.

"Are you a miner, Brandon?" I asked as he pointed the way to Simon.

"Brendan."

"Brendan, are you a miner?"

"No."

"Oh," I said. *Got the chatty one here,* I thought, and I failed to think of a follow-up question. "Have to get everybody out quick, okay?" We skirted along, close to the ground, filling the rear-view mirror with dust. I played with the map screen. Just zoomed in and out a bit so it looked to Brendan like I was doing something important. I wasn't. "Hey, Carl's a bit... isn't he?" I asked, looking up but not quite all the way around to Brendan's face.

"A bit what?" he asked.

"Oh, you know, he's a bit, well, you know?"

"..."

"He's a bit of a dick?"

"No."

"Well, you know him better than us," I said, "though, you know we've been nothing but nice. I'm a nice guy. Look at me helping you. You'd think Carl would be-"

"We wouldn't have had to do this if you hadn't turned up," said Brendan.

"Well... I mean, that's not strictly... Carl did call Jeff, so, you know?"

"He wouldn't have, if you hadn't turned up."

"I mean, we can point fingers... the point is I'm a nice guy." Brendan didn't reply to that. "This is our second delivery job," I said. "Hey, you're probably going to reward us with a load of gold!" I laughed then looked up, again not quite looking at Brendan, then looked over at Simon who was intently staring ahead. It was a joke, of course. I wasn't entirely serious. "You've probably got loads of it. But you don't need it, what with your simple lifestyle," but this time, when I vocalised it, it didn't seem quite so fanciful. These guys were bound to dig up valuable nuggets and one massive ruby would set Simon and me up for life. And what? They *weren't* going to give us a massive ruby? After moving a whole town? Why wouldn't they? Brendan didn't confirm that we'd be rewarded, but neither did he deny it. That was okay, get the job done first, then quibble about rewards. I shifted in my chair to get more comfortable.

Brendan pointed again and Simon began to decelerate, gently, so as not to smush the people in the back against the front wall of the Lady's storage section. "Already?" I said. It had only been about five minutes. The operation was going to be much quicker than I'd thought.

The five shacks which made up the Outpost, coated in dust, were almost perfectly camouflaged. I'd never have spotted them from further away. Don't even think Simon would've. We looped around the back of the Outpost and landed facing towards Morlay. "Have you been here before, Bran... Bren..." I just gave up on his name. I don't understand how people can be precious about other people getting their names right.

"Brendan, and yes."

I waited a moment for him to add to that. He didn't. "Cool." I replied with a nod. "May as well keep it running," I said to Simon, which meant he wouldn't have to get out. I opened the door and Brendan and I jumped off.

There were only five shacks. That was it. No fences or

anything. Possibly a small entrance to a pit. I couldn't quite see from where I was, but there was a frame that looked like the entrance to a shaft. I was looking around when Brandon grabbed my arms. "Oh yeah," I said, remembering our tight schedule. He couldn't reach the rear latch.

I opened the back door and unsteady people, mainly women, a few kids, and at least one very old man, stepped off. "Hope that wasn't too uncomfortable," I said as I held my arm up and people used it as a bannister. Nobody really thanked me. They looked around, kind of horrified, as they headed over to Brendan. The adults looked horrified. The kids seemed hyped. "Quick, quick!" I said, as gently as I could. My smile was doing nothing to reassure the displaced and soon I didn't want to look at their eyes. I just scanned over their faces. Of course they were scared. Maybe horrified. "Hey, you'll be going back later," I said to one particularly worried-looking woman who stepped off with her hand covering her mouth. "Better safe than-"

In the distance a huge siren sounded. The horrified woman looked at me and I did look into her eyes for a moment, while remaining absolutely motionless. I stood like that as the sound from the siren echoed all around us. I hurried the remaining few off then closed the back doors and went to the cab. Nobody was moving. Even the kids, who had gathered next to Simon's window, stood quietly in the thin swirls of dust which had followed us. Then Brendan moved. He walked out ahead of the Lady.

I followed him. "Are you staying here?" I asked. He was walking with his right arm up, hooked over the top of his head. And he was holding on to the black hair on the back of his head. "Brendan!" He didn't respond and so I went back and climbed in. "Quick!" I said and this time Simon didn't bother accelerating gently.

We were halfway to Morlay when the Burrower fired. It was very different to how it had fired that morning. It wasn't a blast. It was like... if you've seen footage of old bombs, then you'll know they're sort of organic looking. The flash then the mushroom. All billowy and somehow slow. This was like that but modern. The blue pillar of light gone before you were certain you'd seen it. No cloud but the sky seemed to silently ripple. Simon was climbing steeply but it still hit us. Knocked Simon's hands off the controls. Never seen that happen before. Never seen him panic as he's tried to find the controls again. My chair hit the bottom of its spring with a shocking, hard jolt. Again, a new experience. Then I guess we bounced off the wave of whatever it was. If Simon hadn't been climbing we would have met it head on and that would have been that.

So, yeah, that happened.

*I'm not equipped to deal with this*, I thought. A selfish thought considering what had happened, but, yeah, that's where I was. Morlay was... well it wasn't. It just wasn't. There was a cloud of brown dust. We flew around it. The freshly exposed cliff face beyond where Morlay once perched was already visible through the cloud. Soon the rest of the cloud would blow away and be gone and... yeah, it was just gone and it was the time for somebody to step in. Step up. I didn't know who, exactly, but somebody who wasn't me, because, I was thinking, *I'm not equipped to deal with this.*

Simon was silent. No fans. He was just flying. I was rubbing my right knee and right lower thigh with my right hand as we flew around the crater. I was feeling the bones in my knee and the muscle around it. Digging my fingertips in. I looked over at the Burrowers as I worked my fingers around. I turned to Simon. After a moment he noticed and turned. I nodded while looking back at my hand on my knee and he climbed.

They'd already moved back some clicks. Red's tracks were clearly defined and if there was somebody to look into it then that would be great evidence. It was only from above that you could see the blasters' true shape. They were massive, which we knew, but from above you could see they were more oval than circular. I'd thought they were round. The nearest one, Red, would have been brightly coloured when it was new. I knew that because there were still a few patches of that original colour clinging on. Mostly it sat caked in rust and dust, with bare shiny metal showing in the places where it had been sandblasted. Storms, maybe, or maybe it was blasts from Blue that had taken Red's paint off. Blue, off in the distance, was no doubt in a similar condition. They were slightly rounded on the edge of their top, their underbellies hanging downwards into more of a point. A droop. No right angles on these things. Six huge mechanical legs and a circular void which went down through the machine's centre. There was something produced in that hole which made the blast. Some kind of focused beam. It formed in there.

Flying closer I could see the oversized rivets which held its sheet metal skin in place. The rivets, probably made of a different metal, one which didn't hold paint as well as the machine's skin, gave the otherwise smooth surface a covering of small shiny lumps and that made it look even more like a disgustingly diseased creature.

There was something else on its back and without me saying anything Simon headed to it. I guess he could make out what it was, but we were practically over it before it revealed itself to me. A cage. Not much bigger than an upright coffin. It was the only thing on the Burrower's back. Inside the cage was what looked like a sitting figure. "Is that a per-"

"Pilot," said Simon. I tried to keep my eyes on it as we passed but my harness held me down. There was no movement from the cage and Simon looped back while I looked out through my side window, slower this time, completing a figure of eight as we passed the back of it. And then we stopped. Twenty metres away from the cage, and twenty metres is just my guess. If I say a distance and Simon hasn't confirmed it then they're always only estimates and could be wildly out. It was *about* twenty or thirty metres away from the cage where we gently landed. There was still a huge clung as we touched down. Simon feathered the controls and moved us slightly, scraping on the Burrower's back until he found a part of the surface which seemed like it could bear our weight. There was another metallic straining sound from beneath us and Simon was ready at the controls to lift if needed, but then the groans settled as the Lady did. Simon shut it down.

I picked up Brendan's hammer and tossed it in the air like I was a cowboy and it was my revolver, dropped it, picked it up and tucked it into my belt.

Something was going to happen but the sky wasn't all moody. It wasn't all heavy and oppressive. Storm clouds weren't gathering. It was pleasant. It wasn't dramatic. It was just a nice afternoon, if a bit windier than I expected when I stepped out. It was easy to imagine how away from the plain everything was ticking along like normal. Over in Graymall people would be queing in the retail. People would be eating in diners. That's where I wanted to be – somewhere where things were ticking away like normal.

The surface flexed alarmingly if I stepped off a seam and out into the middle of a sheet, something I did only once. Simon didn't do it once, luckily, because he would have gone straight through, never to be seen again. He weighs a tonne, at least. So keeping to the lines of rivets, Simon and I, with many a ninety-degree turn, made our way over to the cage with the Burrower's skeletal frame supporting us. The wind made it even more of a tightrope walk.

It was insulting, if I'm honest. After what it had done I couldn't help but feel insulted at how unimpressive this thing actually was when we were standing on it. I had, and I know Simon had, felt genuine awe seeing it from a distance, due to its scale. It looked so fucking *big* and *solid*. Now, up close, creaking... I'm not joking but I reckon I could've dismantled it with just the hammer in my pants and enough time. The thing was more like a blimp. A metal-skinned balloon. You don't want to be killed, but you *definitely* don't want to be killed by a balloon, even if that balloon could crack the Earth's crust. It's like slipping on a banana skin. It's a bad way to go.

The cage, in keeping with the rest of the machine, didn't look like it would take much effort to demolish as the figure inside sat motionless. The robot was as decrepit and rusted and muddied as the rest of the machine, moreso, and it must've predated Simon by at least a decade. At least. I couldn't believe it still worked. I thought it was a relic. Preserved in dirty, dried grease and attached to the surface of the Burrower like a grotesque hood ornament. I banged my hammer on the bar of the cage but there was no movement.

"Is it alive?" I asked Simon, thinking he might be able to tell, you know, because he's also a robot and there might be… I don't know, a kind of wireless electronic connection of some kind. His shrug suggested there was no such connection between machines. "Hey!" I shouted, hitting the side of the cage. Between the thin metal bars was a wire mesh. Maybe to keep birds out. I hit it again. It made a chink but the robot didn't stir. "Hey!" Nothing. I looked at Simon. *Was that it?* I'd expected more from being on top of a Burrower. Now that nothing was happening I wanted something to happen.

Simon sounded his klaxon and that made me jump. He apologised. Simon, who could have ripped the cage apart in a second if I'd asked, was as polite as ever. The robot inside slowly and jutteringly lifted its head to us and its eyes flickered into life. Took about seven seconds for them both to come on. It was a bit creepy. And that was before it made a sound.

"Wuuuaaaa..." it garbled deeply and I took a step back. Simon stopped me stepping too far. Yeah, it was a pretty scary sound to hear coming from what seemed to be a mummified machine. The noise rose in pitch and turned into "...uuuaaaaaaaceell, hello there, fellas! What y'all doing up here? I don't get many visitors up here. Y'all have clearance?" It asked in a crackly voice. Its mouth movements didn't match the words it was saying, it just opened and closed as it spoke, and when it finished its mouth just hung open.

"Do... do you know what you've done?" I shouted as the wind tried to whip my words away. "Do you *actually* know what you've done, you…" I was saying angry words but I wasn't angry with it, I felt I *should* be angry. I looked across to where the plume of dust was now a faint smudge. I felt the metal underfoot give a little, and looked down and moved sideways so I was back on top of a joint. "Do you know?" I asked again, hitting the cage with the hammer then pointing the hammer at the robot.

"Yes, every single thing," replied the robot, its mouth opening and closing maybe twice.

"You've killed people," I said, pointing towards where Morlay stood. Once stood.

"Oh jeepers!" said the robot, looking out to where I pointed, then down at the aged console in front of it, and then back to us with its ratchety clockwork movements.

"Jeepers?"

"I have a first aid kit. Y'all need first aid or an eye wash?" It looked around in its cage. Not all of its cage, as its head didn't turn much more than one hundred and eighty degrees. It got that far then started clicking. "Oh jeepers, I had a first aid kit or an eye wash. Now I no longer have a first aid kit or an eye wash. I suggest y'all seek medical attention." It's mouth again hung open.

"What controls you?" I shouted. The robot had an aerial on the side of its head, it was bent but I reckoned *it* did. The robot didn't answer.

"Do y'all have clearance?" it asked.

"Here's my clearance," I said, waving the hammer.

"Rejected!" it squawked, once again surveying the controls in front of it and then looking back to us.

"I'm going to knock y'alls head off if you don't give me some... some fucking answers, you rusted... shit." I made another couple of menacing chinks on the cage with it.

"Michael!" said Simon.

"No Simon, you can't stop me, I'm going to do it!"

"Michael!"

"Simon! I'm trying to scare him, for fuck's sake," I said, dropping my arm that was holding the hammer. The hammer was heavy and my arm was tired

The robot inside stared at me and its eyes flickered. I brought the hammer back up, and just as I thought it was going to say something else it instead pushed a button on its console and four shutters exploded up from the bottom of the exterior of the cage, catching my hammer and sending it flying straight upwards. I stumbled backwards, leaving the robot encased behind some kind of protective shield. The floor bowed. "Fuck!" I said as I regained my balance like a surfer and looked around for my hammer. I knocked on the shield with the knuckles of my fingers on the hand I'd been very close to losing when the shield closed. The shield was solid. So *something* on this thing was. I turned to Simon who was listening to something. His head slowly moved from side to side. I thought maybe he was listening out for the sound of my hammer landing but then I heard it too. A screech, I suppose best describes it. A faint scream. It was getting louder and I looked around and then saw something moving at incredible speed. Too fast. A black dot, but it was growing. Heading towards us. Then it disappeared. It was beneath us. "The fuck was..." but in my peripheral vision I saw something else. A figure encased in a black leather suit and wearing a black full-face helmet was walking towards us. Behind him a scooter was now parked. He too seemed to be following the rivets but he was doing it without looking down. "Fuck!" I said again. Now that something was happening I no longer wanted something to happen.

"This is it," said Simon.

"Yeah, I think so," I agreed. "Fucking lost my hammer." I squinted into the wind at the approaching Jeff. I really could have done with a weapon. It's not like I would have used it, but it had been reassuring to have something to hold. I held on to Simon and we watched Jeff extend his arm and catch my hammer without breaking stride. I braced myself against a gust of wind.

Jeff stopped on the other side of a large sheet. On the rivets. About fifteen metres away. He tapped the hammer gently on the side of his helmet, which made his visor disappear to reveal what we knew to be under there. His fucking face. I moved along my row of rivets to the end. Simon didn't move. Nor did Jeff.

"Hello boys!" he said, smiling. "Surprised?"

"Not even a little bit," I replied. "What the fuck is wrong with you?" I shouted.

"Did you get everybody out?" he asked. He was asking me but staring at Simon. I didn't reply. I didn't need to, he knew. He nodded. "That's a shame. I know how much you wanted to be the hero," he said, now looking at me. "That guilt... that's going to stay with you for as long as you live. But there's a- "

"Okay!" I shouted.

"I haven't finished," shouted Jeff. "Let me *finish*," his calm demeanour slipping momentarily before he regained it and his smile returned. "I was saying, the guilt, it'll stay with you, but there's a plus side."

"Okay!"

Jeff looked sideways for a moment and then back to me. "Ask me what the plus side is," he said.

"No, we're cool."

"ASK ME!" he boomed. This time it was a real struggle for him to get his smile back, but he did.

"You're going to say, on the plus side you've only got a few minutes to live, something like that, and it's going to be boring and predictable, and... you know, it's... it's... I'm embarrassed for you for even thinking it up."

"Well," he said, not quite hiding his disappointment that he didn't get to say it, "that's right, you *do* only-"

"You shouldn't have said 'ask me why,' that just made it obvious."

Jeff walked parallel to us on the other side of the sheet, along his line of rivets, over to my side. He pointed my hammer at me, shook it, and then smiled and walked back towards Simon's side. I wondered if we could do this forever. Stay opposite each other. Run around in square circles. Like a child's game. Probably not.

"How do you want to do this?" he shouted.

"I wouldn't mind smashing your head in with that hammer, could we try that? Or you could smash your own head in."

"That doesn't work for me," said Jeff.

"Well, how do you want to do it?" I shouted. "We gave you a chance! None of this needed to happen, you know?"

"He was on the list, Michael, you saw it."

"So fucking what if he's on a list?" I shouted and Jeff did the face I recognised from doing it so often myself. It was the condescending 'I can't even be bothered to explain it to you' face. He went across then forward as he headed towards Simon, all the while along a line of rivets. I moved to the opposite corner and

Simon should have followed me. Instead he turned to face Jeff. I could just see Simon's back.

"Smash him, Simon!" I shouted, but he just stood there, motionless, as Jeff rounded the corner on to Simon's line. I could see the top of Jeff's helmet over Simon's shoulder. They were face to face. I looked around. At the cage. The shutters had retracted at some point. Then at the Lady. I was looking for something, anything, but there was nothing.

I heard the tinkle of glass breaking and couldn't imagine what had smashed. Jeff and Simon weren't doing much. They might have been standing there just talking and so I dared to get closer. Jeff sensed me and his face appeared out to the side of Simon. Simon turned and I saw his smashed eye. Simon's left eye was gone and it was, like, what do you do? It just gets to a point where…

Simon was facing me while I stood and watched as Jeff climbed on his back. He had one arm, the one holding the hammer, around Simon's neck, his free hand was delving around and into Simon's eyehole.

"Stop," I said, holding my hand up, and Jeff looked at me but his face was pure concentration as his fingers worked themselves into Simon's head. I stepped forward and reached up and tried to pull away his arm that was around Simon, but it was like it was attached. I wasn't moving it.

It would have been pretty cool if I'd been thinking of a plan while this was happening. While Simon was dying in front of me. I wasn't. I *might* have thought about getting water and tipping it on Simon and electrocuting Jeff, but more likely I thought of that later. I didn't have water. I didn't have anything. This was going on around me. The best I could do was say stop.

"Jeff, stop!" I said, clawing at his arm. "Please." I tried to prise the hammer out of his hand. I couldn't. Did I even try? I didn't use all of my strength. You know when you're beaten, you know? "Simon, come on, do something." I punched Jeff's arm. He probably didn't even feel it. "Come on, Simon." Simon looked down at me out of his working eye.

"Nearly done," said Jeff, "now for the other one." Jeff repositioned himself on Simon's shoulders which meant moving the arm around his neck, which meant I could grab the hammer from him. I don't know if it was me or Jeff who was more surprised when that happened. The hammer was just in front of my face and I took it. And now I had a hammer. "Hey!" said Jeff, like I'd just played a trick on him.

*What the fuck was I going to do with a hammer?*

Jeff reached down and clicked his fingers. "Yeah, right," I said, I'd begun to back up.

"I don't even need it," he shouted.

"Good, because you haven't got it. It's mine."

"Yeah, actually I do want it," said Jeff.

"Come and get it," I said, backing up further, quickly daring to look down and behind to check where the rivets went as Jeff was jumping down in front of Simon. Then Jeff was walking towards me. His arm extended.

"Give me it."

"Nah."

Jeff stopped and took his helmet off. He placed it off to the side of the rivets and shook his head the way somebody would if they had long hair. He didn't have long hair. He bent his left knee with his right leg stretched out straight behind him, the toes on that rear foot bent ninety degrees and resting on the metal skin.

He drew shapes in the air on the back of the Burrower with his hands held rigid and sideways. He looked a bit like a mad Minotaur. Then he was upright and I didn't know if he was doing modern interpretive dance or kung fu. He was doing *something* and moving towards me. I backed up. I knew I must have been nearing the end of the sheet but I was kind of mesmerised by whatever Jeff was doing. I could hear his leather suit creaking and the whoosh as his hands cut through the air.

I felt the floor give a little and instinctively looked down, and that's when Jeff kicked me in the head and I dropped the hammer. The kung fu practise, which had sounded stupid when I'd heard him grunting on the communicator, had paid off for him, big time. He was good. I was now sitting well off the rivets. I was sitting in a dent, looking up at Jeff's silhouette. The sun was somewhere behind him. I saw him bend and pick up the hammer. "Okay, you've won. You can go now."

"Thanks, but this doesn't really involve you, you know that? I don't know why you're *buzzing* around." He drew shapes in the air when he said buzzing.

"Fuck off," I said, but he didn't. It would have been good if *that* had worked. Instead he laughed. "People are going to be looking for us. They're going to find out what happened."

"Who exactly is going to look for you?" his silhouette shouted, incredulous.

*It was a fair question. Who was going to look for us? Let's see. Jeff was, but he'd found us and was standing over me with a hammer. Somebody else must have noticed we'd gone. Pete definitely must have noticed. He'd been on the communicator. And Carlos maybe missed us.*

"Nobody even cares that you've gone! Shame that, because..." Jeff waved the hammer at me, "pretty soon you're going to be all on your own. Just need to get in behind its other eye, so if you'll excuse me."

"Your kung fu is really good," I said.

"Well... thanks." He sounded genuinely touched. It was good kung fu, but I only told him that to distract him for another second because Simon's silhouette was slowly creeping up behind him. Jeff turned and launched a massive kung fu chop that looked like it could have smashed through a brick. Simon caught his arm but Jeff, practised, spun and launched a kung fu kick that looked like it could have knocked the hat off a priest. Simon caught his leg. Simon now held Jeff's left wrist and his left ankle. He twisted and struggled to get free. Simon began to spin, slowly at first but soon the centrifugal force was enough that Jeff couldn't struggle, and not long after that he was limp. Jeff's protests sounded like a siren as he came around again and again and again and again. Faster and faster.

I lay back and rolled over to a seam of rivets then stood up. I danced over to the cage and knocked.

It took me two attempts to open the wire-mesh door even though there was no lock on it. There wasn't much room for me inside. The old robot smelled of grease and was bolted to the floor. I could see now that its legs, torso and left arm were all just one solid lump of metal, moulded to look like independent body parts. I could see a jumble of dirty wires through a hole in its side. A hole that once probably had a cover, now long lost. Only its head and right arm moved. It tried to close the door with its right arm but it wasn't articulated that way. I closed it. The old robot's arm could only move the distance across the console.

"How long have you been up here?" I asked.

"Forever," it said. "Do y'all have clearance?"

155

"No."

I looked at the console. If there were symbols on the controls they were covered in grime. I didn't need symbols, I could work it out. It wasn't complex. There weren't many options. There was a stick for moving the whole thing, a dial for power and a big red button, a couple more little buttons in a row on one side. One must have been the siren, one was the shield. I watched the robot adjust the power. I wanted to turn it up, so I reached out my hand, but the robot awkwardly waved it away. I looked over at the tornado that was Simon and Jeff. Somehow Jeff's arm and leg were still attached.

I slapped the big red button and the Burrower instantly shook and rattled and groaned. Under that was the beginning of a roar which sounded animal. To begin with it did, but then it rose and rose until I could only feel it. I felt the wind change direction and the mesh cage jingled as the wind was sucked through it towards the hole. Its strength was increasing until it was tearing through the cage, jangling it instead of just jingling it.

Soon the roar of the air ripping through the cage was impossible and my T-shirt was pulled up around my shoulders as I tried to cover my ears. I was pressed against the cage, only capable of breathing if I angled my head down. I crouched and looked over just as Simon let go of Jeff who went pinwheeling towards the hole. The slope into the hole starts off gently and it didn't look like Simon had thrown him far enough, but the suction was stronger than his scrambling. Jeff was clawing at the floor and then I couldn't see him. I saw Simon crouch as much as he could, as Jeff's scooter tumbled across the back of the dirt-red Burrower. Then it was black.

I slid down onto the floor. Onto the sandy grease. I felt the blue light. Didn't see it but I knew it had happened. I felt like I was very, very hot, without actually being hot, and the muscles at the back of my skull and neck tensed.

I stayed crumpled on the floor until the cage wasn't completely black inside. There was an orange glow when the robot looked down at me. It didn't say anything. And then the shields opened and it was daylight.

The wind had completely gone, from both directions. There was a curtain of billowing orange dust fully surrounding the Burrower, blocking out the world and leaving us floating on a red disc. Something big, maybe Jeff's scooter, maybe just a part of it, the engine? *Something* had taken out a whole sheet, revealing just how dark and huge and empty this thing was on the inside.

I led Simon, who wasn't quite where I'd last seen him, to the truck which wasn't quite where we'd parked it. It took a long while to get there. We took it really slowly, but we got there.

Flying away I saw the robot. He was in the cage, head down and still.

# Acto Dos

I woke in the light to see Simon touching his face. I quietly turned away and then pretended to noisily wake up. "You okay, buddy?" I asked, looking over. He'd dropped his hand.

"Yup," he lied and that was fair enough.

I used to have a fat neighbour, when I was a kid. Fatso had a vintage white sports car. One with wheels, you know? Anyway, what made it a sports car and not a regular car wasn't that you did sports in it. Oh no, this guy didn't do sports. What made it a sports car was its pop-up headlights which were cool as fuck. They didn't just look cool, they had a purpose, and that purpose was to increase aerodynamic efficiency in daylight. The lights on this type of car would retract down into the front when not in use. I guess it didn't need to be quite so aerodynamic at night.

People didn't drive so fast in the dark.

One day, one of those headlights ceased functioning. It just stopped retracting. After a few weeks of seeing it outside his house with one eye open it was clear he wasn't getting it fixed anytime soon. And the car didn't just look half as cool as it had because of this small headlight retraction defect, it looked bad. Real bad. The rumour was the fat guy was in prison for driving slowly past women at night. Can't comment on that, though a lot of rumours you heard as a kid turned out to be true. At the time I didn't see how that could get you sent to prison, but his car just sat there. Moss began to grow on the rubber seals. Around the windows. As a kid I thought I'd somehow get money and buy the car and fix it, but I didn't, in part because of a miserly Chinese man. The car looked ill. Like it had had a stroke or something. The car looked thick. One day it was gone and it was a relief that we didn't have to look at it anymore.

I'm not saying that thoughts of that broken car came to me when Simon turned to me and tried to smile, but...

"Did you sleep?" I asked and then tried to act nonchalant. I stood, yawned and went and sat in my chair. My chair felt different. Maybe a bit lower than it usually was. I couldn't tell for sure but when you sit in the same chair for years you notice when it's very slightly different. "Did you sleep?" I asked him again and he turned to me, and this time I didn't wince, I made sure of that. I stared all around his face.

"No."

"You know, it's not too bad. It's not as bad as you think. Just get a replacement. Do they... screw in?"

"Bayonet."

"Yeah, no problem, we'll get one."

"Yeah," he agreed.

"Actually..." I said, and then I went and rifled through the shelves on the back wall of the truck.

"There are no eyes in there," said Simon.

"Ha!" I said and continued to rifle through the garbagerie we'd accumulated over the years. I knew what I was looking for. I'd seen it, or felt it while searching through the shelves for a pin. Or maybe it was when I stuffed everything back in there after it fell out when the Lady crashed. Whenever it was, I was sure that I'd seen it and I was going to find it.

It was on the bottom shelf, at the back. I reached in for it, the side of my head pressed against the upper shelves as I grasped for its unmistakable shape. "Remember these, Simon?" I asked, showing him the tin of sweets. I shook it but it didn't rattle, even though there was definitely something in it. It was heavier than an empty tin would be.

"Don't!" he said and his smile looked more genuine.

"Blast from the past," I said.

"Better get them away from me!" he joked, his smile not lasting long. It was like when you have a sore throat, you know? You can act happy and talk fine for a moment, but as soon as you have to swallow, the pain returns. Simon was behaving like that. Like he had a sore throat. He was being braver than I would have been. Luckily he had me as a distraction.

"God, remember?"

"Yes," he nodded.

I turned the round tin over in my hand. "I thought that was it. Ruined. Ruined a brand new unit because it couldn't eat a sweet."

"But you've got a mouth! What's your mouth for?" said Simon, mocking me.

"Ha, yeah. Funny," I agreed, but actually, even now, even with what I now knew, I didn't think it was totally idiotic. To think that Simon could eat. What's his mouth for then? "That's how I knew you were a good guy. You didn't snitch."

"I would've! I couldn't. You told me not to."

"Yeah, another flaw in the software, that. Bet the new units can snitch."

"You were nearly crying!"

"Yeah, I really wasn't. I was a bit worried. Thought they were going to make me pay for you, is all."

"Oh really?" Simon said. His fans came on and his face went blank.

"Don't bother," I said. It was obvious he was searching his remembory bank for a recording. He's so unsubtle. It was taking a while. He was really looking. "Alright, Simon, yesterday was traumatic for all of us. No need to be a prick." He was still searching. "Look, you didn't snitch. That's the important thing."

"They knew it was you. Julian knew."

"Yeah, of course," I said. "Good times, huh?"

"Not for me."

"I suppose not, not for me either. It's a remembory though." I couldn't open the tin because time had sealed it. I was not nearly strong enough, so I tossed it to him. He juggled it then dropped it and it took too long for him to find it again, which made me wince again. I didn't help him. He opened it easily once he'd found it. Inside, the remaining sweets had congealed into one solid mass. Stuck to the bottom. That was a shame. The bottom would have been much better as a patch. Shiny. Almost like a monocle, but with the sweets stuck to it, it was a no go. And it was a bit rusty. The lid would do fine. Maybe it was better than the base because it was yellow with a thin red stripe of writing across the centre. The writing looked like a solid line from a distance. Like a closed eye, and without measuring with lasers it looked exactly the right size. It was pretty much the same size as his good eye.

"You'll look like you've been in a fight," I told him as I held the lid up to his face. "Well, you were." I wondered how I was going to attach it. "You should see the other guy," I said, just thinking out loud. There was nothing of the other guy left to see. I found the tape.

The tin lid fit over his socket pretty much perfectly. I could jiggle it maybe a millimetre or two, so if it had been smaller it wouldn't have worked. It fit and it didn't look absolutely fucking insane. Well it wouldn't, when I got the angle right.

First I tried it so the writing was horizontal, but it made his eye look like it was yellow with a red slit across it and that was a bit gross. It was his left eye, by the way. Did I say that? It was no better with the red line of writing going vertically down, in fact that was probably even more macabre. This wasn't so straightforward, I was discovering. I was left with a choice of it slanting down towards the middle of his face, or slanting up. Slanting down towards the middle made him look angry, but slanting up made him look dopey.

I twisted it so the writing was at an angle. Very slightly sloping downwards, towards the middle of his face. He had every right to be a bit angry. I carefully wrapped the tape around the edge of the tin and his eye socket as he held it in place. It was more difficult than it sounds, taping around the edge, as I had to miss his eyebrow and hand. He cut the end of the tape and I stood back. It had twisted slightly somewhere in the taping process. He was looking a bit angrier than I wanted. I thought about taking the tape off and trying again. "Ah, fuck it, that looks fine." It looked better than a shattered, gaping hole, but then most things do. "Good as new."

Simon leant over until he could see himself in his side mirror. "Fuck," he said.

"Language!"

He looked at me and shook his head. But it was just a weary shake. Not a suicidal one. "I think we should g-"

"Yeah," I agreed. There was no real choice. "It sounds weird when you swear."

Simon held his hand out to me. I nearly high-fived him but high-fiving wasn't something we did. "What?"

"Ten pounds," he said. I think he'd have clicked his fingers at me, if he could.

"You're dreaming."

---

"What the *fuck* have you pair of three-point-five-inch floppy dicks done to that?" asked Pete, chlunking hydraulically over to us from within the shadows of the depot, pointing at the Lady. Then he saw Simon and did a double take that would have been comical in other circumstances. "And what in Christ's hairy hole's name have you done to this big fibre-optic whopper cock?" he asked, pointing at Simon, staring into his face. Simon didn't know how to respond to being called one of those. "What's that?" he asked, flicking the sweet-tin lid and making a *p-tang* sound. He's got good control over his hands for a half-man, half-machine monster, I'll give him that. He could have flicked Simon's head clean off. His reaction was much better than I expected. Better than we'd hoped. I'd thought there would be a big furore when we turned up. People running around, waving their arms, screaming.

"We had a crash," I said. We were standing in a rectangle of light in the enclosed yard in front of the depot, with our shadows stretching off at an angle. "Truck hit us so hard the stickers came off."

"No!" said Pete.

"For real, hey, guess who it was? Guess. Guess who hit us?" I asked, then did a little cough.

"Nah!" said Pete, he knew what was coming.

"UPS."

"UPS?"

"Fucking UPS," I said, shaking my head. Pete *hates* UPS.

"Fucking U, P fucking S," he agreed, running his giant hand over the front of the Lady. It all made sense to him now, as long as he concentrated on his dislike for UPS, rather than the ridiculousness of our excuse. He ran his piston-driven fingers over the dents where it had hit the house. The holes from the blast. "I hope you got him good."

"You should see the other guy," I said and looked at Simon. Pete extended his legs and checked the roof before lowering back down with a *p-tish* sound and a satisfying little bounce.

He pointed to Simon. "And how did this happen?" he asked, pointing at Simon's face. I'd practised this on the journey back from the mines. The key was to not offer up too much information.

"It just fell out."

"What, his eye fell out?"

"Yeah. In the crash."

"Like an egg out of a chicken's arse when you squeeze its tits?"

"Well... I mean... it just fell out. Then he trod on it."

"Oh for fuck's sake. What a pair of fucking twats!"

"So I stuck that tin over it," I said, pointing to the sweet-tin lid I'd taped over Simon's eyehole.

Pete stared at Simon. Simon looked back at Pete. Pete's arms slowly extended from the shoulder joint and I could hear him breathing through his nose. Took me too long to realise what was happening. "You got a problem with m-"

"No! Pete, it's just the angle I stuck it on." I covered up Simon's angry eye with my hand. "See?"

Pete grunted and his shoulders relaxed. "What a fucking mess!" He shook his head.

"You should have seen this UPS truck," I said, hoping to distract him.

"Yeah? Bad was it? Smashed to bits?"

"Yeah, fucked. I swear to god, it was flying all over the place. Pilot must've had something fucking wrong with it, a malfunction. We couldn't miss it, right Simon? It was all over the place. It hit us. The stupid shit." Even though I was trying to speak his language by incorporating lots of cursing, Pete wasn't listening, he was back to looking over the Lady. I raised my eyebrows at Simon and nodded.

"You better hope Jeff doesn't turn up," said Pete and I instantly went dizzy. Like I sometimes do when I stand up too quickly.

"What?" I said with ringing ears, which meant I didn't have full control over the volume I spoke. He repeated it. He had finished looking over the Lady, now he was looking over me. "Why? What?" I asked, then coughed and tried to laugh. Then I took a deep breath. "Why?"

"He'd rip your dick off for this."

"What?"

"He'd rip your dick right off and then get two hammers and smash your dead dick between them. Smash it to a pulp, your dick, and then he'd get one of the hammers and shove it into the hole where your dick was."

"Okay," I said, but I was trying to unpack what he'd said about Jeff.

"And then he'd get the other hammer and shove the handle of that one up your arschole, so you'd have two hammers dangling between your legs and they'd hit together when you walked."

"Yeah," I said.

"And the hammers would hit your nuts. Because they'd still be on. Every step."

"I think the hammers would be too long," I said. "My nuts wouldn't be that low."

"They will, when Jeff's finished with you. And he'd get your dick – flattened it is now – off the floor and tie it around your head, around your eyes. Like a... blindfold... and he'd... he'd..."

"Okay, okay. Anyway, what? Jeff's... what? Not here? Where is..."

Pete considered my question then leaned back a bit and went to fold his arms, but couldn't because they were massive and hydraulic. He tried both ways. Left over right and then right over left before putting them down by his side, looking slightly disappointed. "Cunt's gone."

"Cunt's gone? Where?" I felt Simon look at me disapprovingly.

"Nobody knows, just fucked off. Some kind of nutty mental breakdown. The soft wanker." I noticed Pete glance around after he'd said that.

"He's just gone?"

"Yeah, lucky for you. Tell you, if he saw this... this fucking mess, he'd get a screwdriver and-"

"Okay Pete. I better go check in."

"He'd get a... a screwdriver and he'd... get a pallet board and he'd... he'd..." Pete was starting to hyperventilate.

"Is it okay there?" I asked.

He took a few deep breaths. "Yeah," he gasped. "I'll see what I can do about this. Hey, Michael?"

Uh-oh, he'd used my actual name. "Yeah?"

"Are you okay?" he asked. Pete asked. Pete was actually asking me if I was okay.

"Yeah," I said, suspicious.

"I know how things can get..."

"Fuck off, Pete," I said and he turned to the Lady.

"You were lucky."

*Kind of. So far*, I thought as Simon and I stepped into the shadow of the hangar. I rolled my eyes at Simon. The depot was quiet. It was mid-afternoon and the stack of Ladys was low. Looking through into the inner bay I saw a row of pine crates lined up. Each about the size of that cage on the... you know. There were twenty or twenty-five of them.

"Oh hi, Julian," I shouted, my palms flat on the counter that you weren't allowed to go past unless you were a technician. He was bent over, looking at a screen with another technician whose name I didn't know. We were deep inside the Hub now. He looked over and then his head drooped. His head hung there for a second, then he raised it, pointed at the screen, said something to his colleague and then came over.

"What now?" he asked, which was kind of weird because I hadn't been down here for years. I passed Julian now and again. Usually I said hello or nodded, but I definitely wasn't a big part of his life.

"Look at this!" I said, pointing at Simon's face.

Julian looked. "That's really great, yeah, good job guys. It's funny. Thanks for... thanks..." He turned and started walking away.

"No," I said. "No!" I laughed and then did a little cough. *Does he think I've just stuck a tin on Simon's face and come down to show him? That's what he must think.* "It's just... with tape because I broke his eye. Under it. That's just a... just a... a cover." The light down here was somehow all black and green. It really needed brightening up.

"You broke his eye?"

"Yeah, well, it got broken. Crazy... crazy crash. Pete knows all about it. It's just... you don't have a spare, do you?"

"A spare eye?" asked Julian.

"Yeah."

"Of course I have, I've got a big box of them. Just let me get them."

"Are you being sarcastic?" I asked.

"Noooo!" he said.

"Is... is that... sarcasm?"

"Yeah," replied Julian.

"So... Just so I'm... you *haven't* got a box of them?"

"Why would I have a box of eyes? They're twenty years old."

"But you can get one, right? Order it?" I looked at Simon with pursed lips, to show I was concerned and confused but still on top of things. Conversations sometimes get away from me.

"No, the only place you'll find one is at the Bizaare."

"Really? The Bizaare?" I wasn't expecting that. I really thought he'd have some. In a box. One at least. Just screw it in. Press and twist it in and done. So much for getting him sorted this afternoon. Julian went to walk away. "Well, will you get some seals, too? If you haven't got them."

"Ha! Me?" barked Julian. "I'm not going."

"You want *us* to go? To the Bizaare?"

"If you want an eye. It can't fly with *one*."

"He can actually," I said. Judging by his face, Julian seemed to take my reply as a challenge. It wasn't supposed to be. It was just a fact. I blew my cheeks out. "How much will an eye be?"

"I don't know."

"And what do I ask for? An eye for a... a..." I gestured at Simon. "An eye for a?"

"A tooth for a tooth," replied Julian.

"A... *what?*"

"Forget it. Take him with you, you always do," said Julian, half turned away, his arms fixed in a walking position, not trying to hide the fact he was not interested.

"Okay, erm, what about seals? Some... some water got in."

"Go and see."

"Oh," I said. I pinched my lower lip and pulled it down then let go. I pursed my lips and inhaled through them, making a squeak. The squeak tickled my lips but I didn't stop. I was thinking. I couldn't inhale any more air. "You haven't got seals?"

"No."

"This is a pain," I said.

"Just wait for a new one," said Julian, tapping Simon but looking at me.

"Is that… Just saw Pete, he said Jeff is missing or..."

"Apparently."

"So they're still doing the... the erm, replacement Pilots?"

"Just waiting for Jeff to okay it."

"Okay, okay... that... that could be days or..."

"Is that it?" he asked. I was beginning to sense Julian didn't like me. I had always thought he liked me. Why didn't he like me? I'd hardly spoken to the guy. This open hostility was a surprise.

"Will you fit it, if I get it?"

"I suppose."

"I'll try and get the eye."

"Yay!" said Julian, clenching his fist in a small sarcastic celebration.

"And some seals," I said, but he really was walking away this time, shaking his head slightly. I looked at Simon for a bit then ushered him out.

Two down, one to go, and the third one really had the potential to be *disastrous*. If there was going to be a problem it was going to be with Bella. Yeah, it was going okay *so far*, no dramas, not too much fuss, but Bella is HoS and that means Head of Security. Get past Pete. Get past Julian and that was meant to be it. We'd go and hide in our bunker, but of course the door wouldn't open. Of course! Why did I expect anything different? Why do I let myself think that things might turn out okay?

Robots aren't allowed on the higher floors and so I left Simon in the canteen, not really knowing if I'd see him again. Or if the last time he'd see me was when I was being dragged along the corridor outside, kicking and screaming and protesting my innocence. Would I bother protesting my innocence while they dragged me? I probably wouldn't. We did it.

"Bella?" I asked, my head poking through the gap I'd made in the doorhole by opening the door slightly.

"Hello?" she replied.

I went in, even though she hadn't invited me. I shook her hand, which seemed to surprise her, then I didn't know what to do with my hands and arms. I clasped my hands together in front of me but I felt that looked odd, so I hooked my thumbs into my pockets.

Bella's office was no bigger than the truck but, unlike the truck, it had a whole wall of monitors and no chairs. There were, at a guess, fifty screens. Each showing a different scene. I knew the scenes were live because I could see Simon waiting for me in the canteen. I watched him interact with a TCU that passed him. A lot of the monitors were showing feeds from places I'd never been. Rooms I'd never been into. The kitchen of the canteen. Offices. Stock rooms. Only a quarter or so had people moving on the screen. Most were just static and could have been photographs placed by audacious burglars. It was hard not to look at the screens but I did my best. It would be an okay job, looking at the screens all day. I could do it but I'd want a chair.

"Can I help you?" asked Bella. None of the screens seemed to show the interior of the bunkers.

"Were you… are you looking for me?" The last word there came out high pitched.

"I've no idea who you are," she said. "Why would I be looking for you?"

"Well, my door won't open. The code…"

"Seven, five, three, nine. They've been reset, because of the powercut."

"Excuse me?"

"The codes were reset because of the power cut."

"Right," I said, nodding.

"Seven, five, three, nine."

"Right, because of the power cut," I said.

"Can you remember those four numbers or do you want me to write them down?" she asked, and she wasn't being sarcastic. It would have been better if she was being sarcastic, but judging by her face she was genuinely concerned I didn't have the mental capacity to remember four numbers.

"No, no, I can remember four numbers, thanks!" I laughed.

"What are they?"

I coughed. "Four-"

"*Seven. Five. Three. Nine.*"

"Seven, five, three, nine." I nodded. "Seven, five, three, nine." Bella pointed at the door and I nodded. I recited the numbers quietly until I got back to the canteen. I really wished she'd written them down.

"Seven, five, three, nine, remember that," I said, then went and got a cup of red tea from the machine. I carried it back and sat down.

"She just gav-"

"Yeah, no big deal. Hey, I saw you flirting with the TCU, on the *security camera*." Simon understood and nodded slowly.

I stared up at the television as the spoon chinked on the side of my cup. I kept stirring. It kept chinking. I stirred my tea while a picture of Jeff Jefferson appeared. I looked down at my tea, then back up. It was a photograph of Jeff wearing a shirt with the sleeves rolled up and a tie, no jacket, standing with his arms folded outside the company headquarters in Central. Not here at the Hub. The photo was taken from low down so the whole of the building was also in the shot. A row of flag poles bearing the company's insignia between him and the tower. Jeff looked satisfied. I stirred my tea slower because I'd been stirring it faster and faster, without realising, and I looked at Simon who was looking up at the TV. There was no sound from the screen. I looked down at my tea and stirred it, the spoon chinking on the sides of the cup. Then the TV was displaying inspirational quotes again.

"We're lucky," I said, looking at his damaged face, then at the back of my hands. The back of my hands looked particularly old. I shifted in my chair because the chair was uncomfortable and my hip was painful.

---

I had a check around the bunker for cameras even though I knew that was just paranoia. Anyway, if they'd wanted to really hide them I wasn't going to find them, whatever I did. Still, I whispered to Simon. "This," I whispered, pointing to the floor, "this is what we'd have left behind if *we'd* gone down the hole."

"What?"

"I'm saying," I said and then lowered my volume, "I'm saying, if *we'd* gone down the hole, you know, on the... at the... then *this* would be our legacy. A pile of dirty clothes and my cup." The bunker was exactly as we'd left it. "Nobody cared that we'd gone." I sat on the bed and took my shoes off, held them, and watched my toes wiggle through my socks.

"Pete seemed to care," said Simon. I looked at the soles of my shoes then tucked them under my bed, then I stretched my legs out as far as I could, still wiggling my toes.

"Ah, he only cared about the damage. Not about us. That guy loves damage."

"It's good?"

"Oh yeah, of course, this is... this is good, perfect, it's just a bit surprising."

"Is somebody feeling underappreciated?" he asked. I looked at him, he was smiling with his head tilted down a bit.

"I don't know. It's just a bit shit that the only person who was *really* ever bothered about what we did was a fucking psychopath."

"Pete's o-"

"Not Pete, *Jeff*." I said his name quietly. "Why wasn't it a... like a... a baker, you know? Why wasn't it a baker who was obsessed with us?"

"What on earth are you babbling about?" asked Simon.

"You know, why wasn't it a baker chasing us around? Trying to feed us bread and pastries, why wasn't it that guy? Instead we get a nutjob."

"Are you hungry?"

"A bit." I wasn't explaining myself very well. "The one person who cared was trying to kill you."

"Do you want friends? Is that where this is going?"

"What? No! I don't want *more* friends, I'm not saying that."

"More?"

"Yeah, more, I've got loads." I looked at him. His fans came on for a moment but he decided against saying it. "There's Carlos. I'm just saying it's just a bit anticlimaxtic. Anticlimatix... anticlimax-" I'd launched into that word, confident I knew how to say it, but I'd overestimated myself.

"Anticlimactic," offered Simon.

"Anti-cli-mac-tic. Anticlimatic."

"Mactic. Anticli*mac*tic."

"Anticli*mac*tic. Anticli*mac*tic."

"You've got it."

"It's just a bit anticlimactic."

"You're hard to please."

"Ha, I know, it's just weird. Hey, turn on communications." Simon looked at me. I nodded and held my lower lip in a point.

"Communications enabled."

I ran my hand over my stubbly face. Slowly down over both cheeks, before swiping under my chin, enjoying the noise the bristles made against my fingers, enjoying the fact it was the only sound. There was no noise coming from Simon. Two or three minutes I sat there, staring at the empty floor between my feet and the table. "Nothing?" He shook his head and I nodded mine. "Turn it off, quick," I said.

"Communications disabled."

"Good, that's good," I said. "Good?" I asked.

"I don't know."

"Yup, it's good," I confirmed, standing up. "Good." I stretched by planting my hands on my hips and forcing my elbows back while I rolled my head around on my neck. My neck was kind of crunchy. "We'll go out in a minute."

"Where are we going?" he asked.

"It's a surprise," I replied, staring at the ceiling.

"Are we going to the Bizaare to get me an eye?"

"Maybe."

"Are we?"

"Yeah, but I'm getting a shower first." I finished stretching with a monkey yelp noise and took Simon by surprise by suddenly aiming a martial-arts-style kick at his chest. I was surprised to find my leg didn't go that high. I connected gently just above his pivot. "Cha!" I said and then I found my wash bag.

*It's amazing how dirty your feet can get even though you've had socks and shoes on*, I thought. *How does it get in there?* I stood in the shower, leaning against the wall, propped by my forehead, and watched the red dirt as it formed swirlies and eddies in the water around my feet, before performing a different dance as it was sucked down the plughole through pipes which were connected, via some crazy route of pipes, to every other plughole in the City.

Simon was looking in the mirror over the sink when I came back in. The tape holding the tin was now neater. It looked better. I threw my wash bag on the bed and my dirty clothes on the floor. "Checking yourself out?" I asked. He didn't reply. "It looks fine, you ready?"

"Do I have to go?" he asked. I'm not sure he'd ever said

that before.

"Of course you have to go," I said, standing next to him while I rubbed my head with a towel. I got dressed. "Simon, ask me if you have to go again."

"What?"

"Say 'Do I have to go?'"

"Do I have to go?"

"Yes, you do, because… there's no I in that side of your head."

"What?"

"There's no I in team, the motto, on the screens?"

"Yeah?"

"I changed it. Because of… you know?"

"No."

"Forget it. It was a joke."

I found my Snake pass. It was in my top drawer, next to my bed. The drawer was full of crap, mainly. The tape demonstrating the new units was still in its plastic wrapper. Even if I hadn't lost the cable for the player I still wouldn't have watched it. Simon was again looking at himself in the mirror. "You ready?" I asked but he didn't reply. "Come on. Don't worry about your eye! Jesus, after what we've been through? If there's anything good to have come out of this, and I don't think there is, but if there is then it's, you know? It puts things in perspective."

"You were just crying that you didn't have any friends!"

"What? No I wasn't," I said, my face screwed up. "I don't know why you keep saying you've seen me crying because I don't cry." I thought I'd explained to him what I meant about the anticlimax. Obviously not. I wasn't going to waste any more time on it. "Fuck it, don't sweat the small stuff, you know? You look fine."

Simon's fans spun hard. "There's no *I* in friends you don't have," he finally delivered.

"No, I mean, I applaud the effort but that's… forget about that. And I've got you, haven't I?"

"I don't care how my face looks."

"Nor should you," I said, putting a hand on his shoulder. "After what we went through we can look however the fuck we want."

"You wear your sunglasses."

"Wear my sunglasses?"

"You wear them. If you don't care how you look."

"I don't care and I was going to wear them anyway, so I don't even know what you're on about, but I think they're in the Lady."

"They're in your bag. Put them on."

"I'll wear them, no problem," I explained. "It's different, though, isn't it? It's dark in the Bizaare, so they're impractical. And they might get stolen, so... Nobody's going to steal your..."

"My?"

"Your face. Nobody's going to steal that."

"So you're not wearing them? You *are* worried about what people think. Hypocrite."

"No, I *am* going to wear them." I pretended to be surprised when I found them by squeezing my rucksack. I took out the pill-shaped container and then I took the sunglasses out from within. "You want to stop looking at me?" I said. Sometimes it really bothers me when Simon just stands there and stares at me. Like a dummy. He turned ninety degrees away.

"Are you going to wear them?" he asked.

"Yeah. Why not?"

"*Really?*"

"They're just sunglasses. Everybody wears them."

"You don't."

"I'm going to, today, they look cool as fuck," I said, and put them on and went over to the mirror above the sink. They did look cool as fuck. What does a robot know about cool? Who cares what people think? I liked the sunglasses and I was going to wear the cool sunglasses.

I got my wallet, put the pass in it and looked around. The bunker was okay. It wasn't a terrible place to live. We headed out, down through the depot, past Pete's hut and out into the yard, undetected. I was glad we'd made it to the yard without bumping into Pete, but then I saw Pete in the yard and I was no longer glad. He stood and looked at us for a few seconds. It would have been nice if he'd have given us a progress update on the Lady. That would have been a cool and adult and civilised thing to do, but I didn't really expect that. I was expecting him to shout some moronic insult. I was ready for it. Ready to nod, smile and wave and just take it, but instead, upon seeing us, he took off running. I didn't expect that. He bounded towards his office. It's impressive to see him run. Sounds impressive too, it's really noisy.

"It's a lov-" I managed. I was going to say to Simon that it was a lovely afternoon, when the tannoy crackled and I did an involuntary nod and exhaled through my nose as we walked.

"You look like a penis in those!" he said through the speakers in the four corners of the yard. I did that nod again but deliberately this time. It was supposed to be a proper nod but it was jerky. We continued walking out towards the gate, which led to the gangway, which led to the bridge, which led to the platform. I looked around the yard. A few of the storemen looked away when I looked towards them. Just before we got to the gate, the tannoys around the yard crackled into life again. Clearly Pete had spent a few seconds thinking. "*Attention! Attention! There's a big famous movie star in the yard. You may have seen him in such films as 'I Fuck Robo'.*" That just dissolved into crackly laughter, which turned into coughing before there was a loud click and no more tannoy. I held a hand up in acknowledgement. I showed him the back of my raised hand.

"They look fine," said Simon as we crossed the gangway.

"I know they do, do you think I care what he thinks?" I said, then looked down. I was looking through the holes in the grating. Down at the criss-cross of gangways and tunnels and tracks until you couldn't see any deeper. A blast of warm air going up my trouser leg as below us a Snake shot past. "Anyway, he can talk! He can't even reach his mouth when he smokes. Has to put cigarettes on his... on his forearm."

"He did blow up."

"Has to use a telescopic knife and fork to reach his mouth!" I said, looking back. "Yeah, I know. It's fine, really. I don't care. Everybody has their problems."

There was a queue on the platform, but that was okay as it meant a Snake was due, so I didn't bother checking the board. I hoped it was a long one and we walked down the platform and joined one of the shorter queues. Simon had trouble navigating through the crowds and I took his hand until they thinned. It amazes me that some people will wait for the most packed carriage before they'll walk a couple of hundred metres.

We stopped behind a woman. I looked at Simon, he wasn't looking at me. He was looking down at a child that was peeking from behind its mother's waist. I smiled at the young girl and looked at Simon. Simon smiled at her, and the child's already ugly face slowly screwed itself up until it was that of a frightened gargoyle. The mother looked down, picked the child up, turned to me and gave me a suspicious look, then turned the other way and recoiled as she saw Simon. She shook her head as she pressed the child's head into her shoulders. The Snake glided to a halt and we all took a step forward.

"He's friendly!" I said but the woman didn't turn, the child continued to sob, and the doors whooshed open and we all took a step forward. I looked at Simon and shook my head. "He's not a monster, are you Simon?"

"Hello!"

"See! You're friendly. He's friendly! Just hurt his face, by accident, that's all."

"Where are your sunglasses?" asked Simon, sounding panicked.

"In my pocket," I told him and we stepped into the Snake. Our short walk down the platform was rewarded with plenty of standing room. I held on to the pole. Simon didn't need to. His gyroscopes kept him upright. The Snake glided from the station with a soft hiss and I tensed my arm muscles as I gripped the pole so that I didn't sway too much. When it was up to speed I relaxed. "It hisses like a snake!" I said, swaying towards Simon, excited and surprised that it was only now I realised. "That's a coincidence."

"What's a coincidence?"

"That the Snake hisses. When it moves."

"It's the magnets."

"But it hisses, like a snake. A snake hisses. The animal. This thing doesn't... quack like a duck. It could quack and still be called the Snake. But it actually hisses."

"It's called the Multilevel Rapid City Transit."

"I know, but everybody calls it the Snake."

"Because it looks and *sounds* like a snake."

"I suppose. They'd still call it the Snake if it made different sounds," I said as I looked around the carriage. The child was still being comforted by its mother. They were about as far away from us as they could get. It was looking at Simon with the corner of a blanky or hanky in its mouth. I thought about the kids at the Outpost but only for a second. "I think it's called the Snake because of its shape. The noise is a coincidence."

"Are you trying to start an argument?"

"No." I looked out of the window. A blur of metal walls just centimetres away from us disappeared, revealing a slowly panning view across the City. Central rising up out of the middle of the sprawl like a fairytale castle, before it was blocked again by a racing metal wall. The walls exploding into view like the shutters on the cage, but sideways.

"We have to be careful talking, back at the Hub."

"I know," said Simon. "I'm not basic."

"I know, I was just saying." I held the pole tightly as we were coming to the Palace, and that's where the Snake would drop and loop through a tunnel, and begin its weaving way through the lower levels before surfacing again near Uptown. It was here, this bit, where five hundred and twenty-two people died when the stabilisers or hydraulics on the carriage at the front jammed. A year or so ago. Maybe longer. Probably more like five years ago. The carriage had spun with the tracks. So when the Snake went under the tracks, the carriage was upside down. A carriage packed with people and robots. Spinning. Mashing together for fifteen or twenty minutes, before the Snake got to the Port

Authority and the doors opened and the poor people literally spilled out onto the platform. It was a mop job. So I held on to the pole until I was certain this one was staying level, then I loosened my grip a little. "You'd think they'd have seatbelts," I said, looking at Simon. I love the way his head remains motionless while the rest of him sways slightly. It's hypnotic. You could balance a ball on it.

At the time of the disaster, the Ikarus Transport guy had said something like, '*Although it is a tragedy we have to remember that before the Snake, over 200 people a year would die by throwing themselves on the tracks in front of trains, and as the Snake doesn't actually touch the track that's 200 people every year now saved.*'

You can't argue with numbers.

People jumped off gangways these days, but it was difficult not to just land on a lower gangway. You could do that a few times, I suppose, death by a few little jumps. Give yourself a chance to change your mind as you bounced down and then hauled yourself up over the next railing to bounce down onto the next one. Not for me. If I wanted to end it I'd save up for the Hammer.

The vehicles flew low in the narrow streets around the Port Authority and I'd instinctively duck when I heard the whir of an approaching truck or car. It was definitely better driving up there than walking down here.

The streets were awkward to walk down, and not only because of the people and machines who didn't know how to bustle, the streets were lumpy. Sheets overlapping sheets. Street corners had holes with ladders going down. Simon would have struggled with twenty eyes, nevermind one. And it was too loud.

With so many people around it was loud.

Simon had been advised to 'watch it' by two different people before he got into a stand-off with a Sweep. Simon and the Sweep had tried to pass each other about seven times, the first three times apologising, the next four increasingly aggressive, before I took his hand and guided him so he was walking behind me. It was uncomfortable to walk with my arm extended that far back, but it did make getting through the streets a bit easier. It didn't stop somebody just screaming in my face though. Some young guy with hair like long springs. I carried on walking, towing Simon who was far from the most fucked-up-looking thing on these streets.

Oh boy, some of the clothes people were wearing! You've never seen anything like it. I guessed there were some people just dressed like people from lower levels, to be cool. But there were people actually from the lower levels who dressed like people from lower levels, because they were from lower levels. There were a lot of people wearing stupid clothes, is what I'm saying, and I couldn't tell whether it was by design.

I had my work clothes on because I don't really have any others. I like my uniform. I like all the pockets. And Simon, my robot companion, had a sweet, sweet-tin eye. We were as cool as anybody on these shitty streets and as I led Simon through the crowds I dexterously took my sunglasses from my chest pocket with my right hand. I tried to flick the arms out but couldn't, so I had to open the other arm with my mouth. A bit further along somebody said, "Nice glasses, buddy," as they passed, so I put the sunglasses up on my forehead. We were in the shade. At the next corner we stopped. I let go of Simon and took off my sunglasses. After folding them I put them in the pocket on the side of my right thigh and ducked as a car whizzed low overhead.

Things got better when we reached the Boulevard. We could walk side by side. If I'd have had fans they would have slowed. The Boulevard's the biggest open space in the city. It's about three miles long and a few hundred metres wide, free of buildings. A field of grass runs down the middle of it. Real grass too, not astroturf. They water it. Most of the company's offices line the Boulevard but there are also apartments. Apartments for people not quite special enough to live in Central but they still have views of Central, which stands tall at the west end. On each side of the grass are metal parades, and dotted along these shining roads are shafts down to the lower levels, not unlike the hole we'd left in the Burrower's skin.

The sun was low and we walked down the Boulevard in a pleasant pink and golden light. We could have gone down pretty much any shaft, and made our way through the whole Bizaare from end to end, but I wanted to spend as little time as possible down there. Well, I didn't want to go down there *at all*, but we needed an old robot eye. Needs must.

"Why didn't you put your hand up?" I asked. That had been building up inside me for a while. With every jostle. Every person who wasn't giving us enough room. It created frustration in me and I released it by asking a shitty question. I felt put out, having to do this. Traipsing around the Bizaare is not my idea of a good time. It wasn't Simon's fault, I knew I was being a bit of a jerk, but what can you do? Sometimes I'm a bit of a jerk. "Like, you could have stopped him smashing your eye."

"Didn't know it would happen," said Simon.

"Next time somebody goes to smash your face up, with a hammer, put your hands up. Just an idea."

"Okay," said Simon. He could tell I was looking to relieve some stress so he didn't argue.

I knew the shaft we were looking for was about halfway down the Boulevard. From memory it had huge blue and red illuminated arrows pointing to it. I'd been down there looking for a cable for the tape player. I didn't get one because I'd foolishly failed to check what kind of a connection I needed. That was a long time ago now. It was near a fountain, the one that had the moving lion on it. I still checked all the signs we passed and peered down a lot of the shafts, looking down at the tops of people's heads and the flashing signs which went as deep as I could see. Some entrances are quite fancy. It all depends on what part of the Bizaare the shaft feeds. There wasn't a single fancy area where the good shafts went, it was all completely random.

I stopped and looked down the shaft to Shoe Town. Four levels of shoes, the sign boasted. I was okay for shoes. We wanted Electric Town and Electric Town went right down to the ground, though I was certain we wouldn't have to go very deep. The first level or two aren't bad. Some bits are nice. You don't want to go more than three levels down. Maybe that's being harsh on those that are down there. Maybe it's mostly an urban myth but why risk it? God knows what kind of shoes are on the bottom floor of Shoe Town. Flippers for hooves or something and that's only four floors.

"It'll be dark soon," I said. It didn't matter to us because it was always dark in the Bizaare, but it was something to say. I knew I wasn't chatting. I was too much inside my own head. We could see the arrows and the fountain, which was a landmark and had a name. A stupid name. Somebody's Dream, it was called. Steve's Dream? Something like that. Somebody's Dream. People were drawn to it. They sat around on its wall like it was a completely normal place to come and sit, not even paying attention to the enormous mechanical Lion which was cavorting in the water behind them. I thought the fountain looked stupid.

The queue for the baskets to Electric Town was long. Unlike Shoe Town, and I guess because it goes so deep, Electric Town had an elevator. An endless chain of egg-shaped booths. Booths on a giant chain. They went down one side of the shaft, came up the other, and then swung over and swapped sides. Whatever drove the chains was far below us and, I'm betting, massive, noisy and very very smelly. And reliable. The lift never stopped. Apart from the twenty seconds or so it waited at every level before groaning to the next one.

Men from Electric Town with no real authority stood in front of the booths, opening the doors and ushering people on and off, to keep the whole operation running smoothly.

"Thanks for doing this," said Simon as we waited our turn. He could have said lots of things, but he chose that. There's nothing he could have said that would have annoyed me more, I don't think.

"*What?*" I replied. We shuffled forwards. I'd heard him, I was giving him another chance. He didn't take it.

"Thanks."

"What do you mean *thanks?* Why are you talking like an idiot?"

"Thank you, I appreciate it," he said.

"Simon, this is for us, right? Not just you. It's us, right?"

"But you don't have to do it."

"How *don't...*" *Oh, fucking hell,* I thought. *"*How don't I have to do it? How exactly *don't* I have to do this?"

"Have I said something wrong?"

"Forget it." We shuffled forwards.

"I don't understand."

"It's... you thank me then it's like..." It was hard to explain. I just knew I was annoyed and not just because of the crowds and the shuffling and the shitty fucking City. "It's an insult. We had four eyes. You know?" I explained, pointing at him, then me and then him again. "And now we've, *we've* got three. So it's an insult. Like I'm your helper or something, you know?"

"It wasn't supposed to be," he said and I knew he meant it. I knew what he was saying. He was just saying thanks, but, I don't know, by thanking me he was saying he was on his own. You thank Julian if he fits the eye. A TCU if it clears the table. You don't thank me because it's *us*.

"Just don't thank me. They might not even have one."

I was a bit worried they wouldn't even let Simon on when I saw the weigh square we had to cross. Without him down there it could turn into the tape player cable fiasco, but nobody seemed alarmed and we were ushered into an egg with twenty or so other people. The door clanged closed and after a moment it dropped. You could feel the grinding vibrations of the chain on the cogs. Most people got off with us on the first level down. Five or six people stayed on and I tried not to touch them as we disembarked. You had to wonder where they were going and for what reason. They were all men. My bet was they were looking for something electronically sexual. Urgh, grim.

As soon as we could, after the WELCOME TO ELECTRIC

TOWN banner, we fought our way to the side and I had a little panic when my wallet wasn't in my back right pocket. It was in my back left and I moved it to a front pocket. Having so many pockets often led to little panics like that. Even off at the side we were blocking people.

"Oh, it's mayhem," I said. "We'll just find an eye, yeah? If we get split up, meet back here." I looked around. We were next to a closed Wonder stand and in front of a mess of pipes leading down. When it rained on the surface those pipes took the water somewhere. The Wonder stand was closed but I could still smell burnt fat and sugar. It smelled good. "Yeah?"

"Okay, let's try to stay together," he said. He was definitely less confident with one eye.

"Of course." I waited for a gap and led Simon by the hand out into the stream of people.

You can get *anything* in the Bizaare, which is good, but they have everything in the Bizaare which makes finding what you want impossible. There's no map. It's not laid out rationally, with robot parts in one area, tape players in another. Most stalls and shops had a mixture of junk. So we looked over each one. Went in each one.

"Why don't you ask?" asked Simon after we'd left the millionth shop empty-handed. I'd spent a while looking at a red food mixer. I didn't need one but it was a cool shape and I felt it had merit as a piece of art.

"They'd be out if they had them," I explained. "On display." I hadn't seen any, therefore they didn't have any. "I mean, what? They hide them out the back or something? In a box? Silly Simon." I gave a stall a cursory once-over then went into the next shop. It was in the corner of the top floor of an old tower block that didn't quite reach the surface anymore. It was called Tower Robots so I had high hopes, and when I saw the shopkeeper had one brass mechanical eye, my hopes rose further.

I'd look in one cabinet, top to bottom, or bottom to top, then step sideways and do the opposite. Didn't see any eyes but the cabinet nearest the counter contained the heads of seven robots and Simon saw them before I could push him away.

"They're not real," I told him.

"Oh they're real alright!" said the helpful man with the mechanical monocle, coming around the counter to stand next to us. I was ready to leave but couldn't now. Because the man was there. *I want to leave*, I thought.

"Roger That," said the man and for a terrifying moment I thought he was reading my mind. Then I realised that was the name of the model of the robot he was pointing at. The first head, top left, had a little sign in front of it that read 'Roger That – The first Pilot'. The sign was written in old fashioned joined-up pirate writing. It was kind of hard to read.

"It's your dad, Simon!" I said, tapping the glass, and then regretted it. It wasn't the time for jokes, no matter how funny they were. The head he was pointing at was basic and its eyes protruded like old-fashioned light bulbs. Simon was leaning in close to the glass. I swallowed away my embarrassment.

"They could remember forty-seven miles. That's it," the man said, leaning in like Simon was and twisting a dial on his eye.

"Is that all? Forty-seven miles? We've come a long way," I said, feigning interest. The man's eye bothered me. The brassiness of it. It was brass and glass. Just get a real-looking replacement eye, you know? You don't have to show the world how interesting you are by fitting something like that to your face. And it smelled. The man smelt like the inside of my watch strap. Get a real-looking eye, failing that, get a hygienic plastic one. And print your signs so that they're easy to read. That's really the purpose of a sign. They're not. Supposed. To be. Fucking. Puzzles.

It's lucky the man couldn't read minds.

"Oh yes, but they were revolutionary," the man said, and the way he said the word revolutionary made me look at him briefly. He said it like he was agreeing with somebody who had just marvelled at it. I hadn't. It was only now I sensed he was actually talking to Simon. Not to me. That didn't generally happen.

"Who's that guy?" I asked, but I remembered before he answered. On the bottom row was a head with a huge grin. This one wasn't caked in dust and rust and that's why I didn't recognise it immediately.

"A Driver Mark Two," said the man. "They were just heads and an arm, bolted to vehicles, not like this big boy!" He patted Simon on the back of his arm. A bit too familiar for me. "But that was all they needed. Function over form. Five megabytes of remembory."

"Five," I said, not knowing if that amount of megabytes was big or small. I guessed small but wasn't sure so just repeated the number. I leant in close to the glass as the man stood upright. "Cool."

"You've had an accident," said the man, leaning close to Simon's face. He again turned the dial on his eye. He was no older than me but dressed older. He wore a suit. The suit, the mechanical eye. It was all fake. It was just a look. He should have known better at his age. I wasn't convinced his accent was real either. He was definitely exaggerating it.

"Yeah, an accident. That's why we're here," I said. Now we were interacting with him I could ask. That was okay.

"I can't buy him," he said.

"No, I know. I'm not selling him. We're looking for an eye."

"Aren't we all!" said the man, turning to me for a second.

*Good one*, I thought. I didn't know if he expected me to laugh or not, so I didn't. I didn't really want to let the man know that I'd even noticed his stupid, ostentatious eye. "Well... *we* certainly are. Do you have any?" I said 'certainly' because it was the kind of word this man would say.

"What year are you?" he asked.

"He's a fifty-three."

"A fifty-three Pilot," said the man, thinking. "You might be in luck, I'll have a look."

We stood, silently considering the heads until the man went through some beaded curtains. "Look!" I whispered, tapping gently on the glass in front of the Driver.

"Yeah, I saw him," said Simon, sadly.

"Bit macabre," I said.

"It's life," said Simon. The man returned with a box and we both turned.

"It's your lucky day. Which colour?"

"You've got one?" I'd given up. I'd been practising my reaction to him clittering through the curtains apologising!

"These are for a forty-five to fifty, but I believe they'll fit. The colour?"

"Pardon?"

"What colour is his eye?"

"There are different colours?"

"Indeed. Hence my question," he sighed and I felt bad again. This was poor customer service.

I stared into Simon's remaining eye. "Blue," I said. "Bluey grey."

"Sea foam," said the man, pulling small square boxes out from the bigger box and turning them over in his hand before carefully stacking them on the counter like tiny Ladys. "I've got a lot of greens," he said, continuing his box checking. "There's a dark blue one but it's for a Patrol. Infrared, shows up blood. Doesn't work in the daylight."

"That's no good."

"I know that," he chided. "I was just telling you. Educating you. They have a different fitting."

"We need a bayonet," I said, showing that I wasn't a total fucking dumb-dumb. I didn't like how the man was suggesting I didn't know anything about the robot I'd lived with for nearly twenty years. I didn't like how he spoke to me like I was negligent. We really needed an eye though, so I stayed polite. "How much are they?" I asked.

"Nine pounds."

"*Nine?*" I was expecting them to be less than a pound, for some reason.

"You're lucky I've got any. How much for *your* eye?" he asked. "How much would you give to have two eyes?"

"Yep, fair enough. Have you got a blue?"

"Not yet," sighed the man.

"We could get two greens?" I suggested to Simon but he shook his head. "It's okay, I'm sure he'll give us a good deal," I said, loud enough for the man to hear. I said it for his benefit.

"He wants to keep his original eye," said the man. I looked at Simon who didn't protest.

"Fair enough."

"Sea foam!" said the man, triumphant. He held up a little box before opening it carefully, putting it down, then looking into the box while twisting his own eye.

"You've got one?"

"One. And to think, I was going to throw this box away."

"It is our lucky day," I said as we went over to the counter. "Have you got seals too?" I asked, removing my wallet. After measuring Simon with a cloth tape measure, he cut us off a length of seal, rolled it neatly and put our purchases in a carrier bag. £10! He didn't give us a deal but he wished Simon more good luck as we made his door bell ring and left.

It was dripping outside his shop. Raining on the surface, so we looked around for a while before heading up. I looked at the mixer again before we found the hats. It was full dark back on the surface but the shower had passed and steam was rising from the metal floor. Steam lit up in different colours due to the competing signs. It's never cold in the City. It's one giant radiator.

I was excited about getting the eye. I could just as easily *not* have found one. It would have been easier not to find one. And the seals too, so yeah, I was excited. Julian wasn't at all happy about being called so late, from the Snake, to be told the good news. Not sure what I was disturbing him from. Don't know what a nerd does at night. Nothing important, I'm sure, and after he got his little tantrum out of his system, we eventually agreed on a more convenient time to call him and make arrangements so he could put Simon's new eye in. Tomorrow morning after eight.

I yawned as I held on to the pole, only covering my mouth

with my free hand halfway through. I was very tired. I sniffed.
The steamy City makes me snotty. Simon wasn't chatting and that
was fine. He looked great in his blue plastic sun visor. My
reflection, only visible when we were in a tunnel, was blurred but
I probably looked great too. I took another churro from the bag
he was holding out. They were stale and tasted a bit weird,
probably fried in a weird oil, but they were still nice. I took the tin
of Nature's Tears from his other hand, took a swig and put it
back.

We went through the front of the Hub because the yard was
locked. I glanced through the rounded oblong window into the
bar as we passed but wasn't tempted to go in. Oblong. That's a
crazy word. We passed the empty canteen and went straight to
the bunker where, after carefully putting the bag on the drawers, I
collapsed face down on my bed before turning over and kicking
my shoes off.

"Everything might be back to normal tomorrow," I said and
yawned again, not covering my mouth at all this time and with
my hand up my shirt, "we might get out in the afternoon." Slowly
rubbing my chest, I felt a sore spot on my ribs and didn't
immediately remember the woman and the cane. My hip was
okay. All the walking had loosened that up. "Truck'll be fixed,
hopefully."

"He might give us a spare."

"Urgh, I hope not." The spare Ladys are *disgusting*.

"You're coming to the lab?"

"No, you can go on your own," I said. I was joking, he knew.

"Thanks pal."

"De nada."

"Brush your teeth."

"Yeah." I rubbed my chest and closed my eyes. There was a faint ringing in my head and I tried to force a yawn to clear it. Wiggled my jaw. There was a knock on the door and the fizzing in my ears grew louder. Then another knock and I tried to sit up, but couldn't. The ringing in my head was fierce now and I could see it. Speckles around my peripheral vision, and the more I tried to move, the louder the ringing grew. The harder I struggled, the more static there was in my head and the less clear everything became. I stopped struggling.

I relaxed for a moment until I could move and I sat up and looked at Simon. I did my puzzled face. "Hello?" I shouted. No reply so I swung my feet off the bed and tried to put my shoes on. I knew I'd need shoes on if there was trouble. I can't relax when I'm out of bed and don't have my shoes on. I really struggled. I couldn't get my feet in them and the laces were all tangled and coming out of their lace holes. *Nobody knocks on a door this late.* I thought maybe the knocks had stopped but then there was another knock. "Hello!" I shouted, warily shuffling towards the door, my feet half out of my shoes, my toes curled, trying to grip the inner soles.

I reached out for the door handle. I wanted to stay out of the arc of the opening door in case it was kicked open, into my face. "Who is it?" I shouted. I looked down and saw a black helmet on the floor and knew that it shouldn't be there. I grabbed it and it was much lighter than I'd thought it would be. I threw it under my bed. There was a small pile of black hair where the helmet had been. A few piles of it. I grabbed the hair but it was hard to grip and it stuck to my hand. I wiped it with my other hand until both hands were covered in fine black hair.

Another knock.

I looked to Simon for help but he was standing with his hands covering his face. "Chickenshit." I tried to wipe my hands on my chest but I was just spreading it around. It was like I was producing it and now there were clumps of hair on the wall. I crept over to the door. My shoes had gone and my feet were pushing through a deep carpet of hair. It felt nice, actually. After placing my now bare foot about twenty-four centimetres back from the door, so it would act as a brace against a sudden shoulder charge, I slowly opened it. The corridor was full, right to the far end, with small, smouldering, tattered men. Torn clothes and skin. Beards hanging off. I tried to tell them that they had to go but no words came out.

"Fuck!" I panted. I was on my bed in the dark bunker. I propped myself up on my elbows and looked over to Simon. His sleep light was blinking. "Fuck," I said again, collapsing back hard, too hard and falling through the bed and then the sky above the Boulevard as I flailed and tried to spin in mid-air so I could see where I was falling. Then I tried to turn back. It was better not to know, and I curled into a ball and tried to wake up before hitting the top layer, which gave and shattered like an eggshell. I spun and grasped as I exploded through floors at an increasing rate, each floor I hit felt like no more than a tap, only really feeling that it was getting colder the deeper I went.

I was in my bed. On top of the covers. "Yep, I don't like this," I said to the room. I laughed at the weirdness. Simon's light blinked. I didn't move. I didn't dare move. I don't have nightmares. Double nightmares, though? *Nobody* has those. It's shit you see in movies. It's not even a thing. I didn't dare move, though, until I was sure I was in the real world. I listened to my breathing. I was breathing through my nose. I could feel it and I got under the covers and waited for something to happen.

They weren't my covers. They were rough and scratchy and the blinking light wasn't on Simon, it was on a monitor. "Oh, fuck off." The screen flickered a few times before it popped on and I turned away.

*Fuck this dream.*

I was sitting in my seat, the one from the Lady, but I was in front of this monitor I'd never seen. It was all copper and had dials, and the picture was black and white. Carl and the others were on the screen. There was no sound but they were talking. Shouting. He was gesturing and then I heard the siren. I didn't *hear* it because it was silent, but I heard it. Carl looked behind and silently shouted. I swallowed as I watched. I was supposed to watch. I leant forward. I put my right elbow on my thigh and my fist under my chin as I watched. Then I swapped so my left elbow was on my thigh and my fingernails were in my mouth. I didn't look away until I heard Simon shouting for me. Something in his voice I'd never heard before. It sounded weak. I watched as Carl and the others were swallowed.

"Michael!"

I opened my eyes and didn't see what I wanted so I closed them again. Again I heard Simon shout my name. "Fucking wake me up, Simon!" I shouted. I wasn't scared at what I was seeing. I'd known it was a crazy vivid dream when I couldn't get my shoes on. I was aware, you know? It was the bits when I thought I was awake that were unnerving.

"Go through," somebody or something said, and I relaxed. There was a large iron door and I didn't much care for the look of it. Dream or no dream there was nothing good behind those doors.

"Nah, I'm good," I said. It was snowing. The snow was going up instead of down. That wasn't a surprise and the door wasn't a door. It was the Lady. Crashed and crumpled. Inside there was something on fire.

"Michael!" cried Simon and I opened my eyes. I was in my bunker. On top of the covers.

"*Fuck*," I panted, too scared to move but wanting to move. Wanting to get up and walk this whole episode off.

Simon's sleep light blinked and I didn't know what to do. I didn't know if getting up would trigger more shit. Getting under the covers, would that set something off? It was a bit chilly. I lay on top of the covers. Not moving. Just breathing. I was glad when the alarm went off and the lights came on. I was under the covers and I lay in bed and watched Simon fuck around. He fucks around in the morning. Straightens things. He makes sure the table is straight. And nothing is too close to the edge. He doesn't clean, nor would I want him to, he just straightens. I stared at him for a long time. He was just straightening things. "Hey," I said, as a test.

"What?"

"Am I awake?"

"You what, mate?" he replied, and I shook my head.

"Hope that eye works," I yawned. "Might have sold us a dud."

"You've woken up in a positive mood. Go back to sleep."

"I've gone off sleeping." I scratched my head, got a flake of skin under a fingernail which I looked at and then flicked away. "The fuck was in those churros? They poisoned me. *Crazy* dreams."

Simon got the bag from on top of the drawers. "Careful with

that," I said and then I saw that Simon had balanced everything that was on the table in a stack, hanging half off the table. "Be careful, eh?"

"Let's see about this eye, shall we?" he said and I couldn't move. I couldn't lift my arms up as Simon came over. I was low down or he was massive.

"Shit."

"Shh," he said. A short shush. He leant over me. I didn't expect to be able to feel, as his cold, sharp fingers worked their way in all around my right eye. It didn't hurt, I just felt a pressure build as his fingers went deeper into my skull and then a noise like the TCUs make. Then cold, and I was watching this happen from the ceiling but I felt the sharp spiky prongs of the metal eye being pressed into the socket. "Does it work?"

"Yeah, I think. Blurry." I tried to blink away the blurriness but couldn't. It was like I had oil in my eye.

"You're crying."

"Yeah," I agreed. The eye felt far too big for my face. It was stretching my face.

"What can you see?"

"It's, like, double vision. I can't really..." I could see an overlapping figure wearing all black.

"Well it works," he said, leaning over me.

"Don't take it out!" I said, grabbing his arm. "The old one won't go back in, you idiot." He was so strong I made no difference to his movement. "Simon! All the... veins... snapped!" I cried, looking at him and the figure all merging together. I clawed at his arm as the room exploded into flames with a gaseous scream.

I was in bed. On the covers. It was chilly and I looked over and saw Simon's sleep light blinking. I inhaled slow shallow breaths until my heart slowed.

Simon doesn't arrange things on the table, so I'm not sure what that bit was about. It *all* probably meant something. Dreams are meant to mean something, but I don't think it was anything I wasn't already well aware of. So it was basically my brain just being a dick when I was trying to relax. Simon doesn't know if he has dreams. I bet he does, he just can't recognise them. It wasn't until I was eating breakfast that I was certain I was awake. The bag with the eye was in the middle of the table. Well away from the edge.

I gave Julian the box with the eye and put the bag with the seals down on the counter. He looked at the bag, then to me and then back to the bag. He made a big thing of looking and so I picked the bag up. Julian doesn't like you putting things on his counter, it turns out. "How much did that cost you?" he asked, turning the box over in his hands. I really wanted to tell him to be careful with it, but I didn't.

"Nine pounds. Think we got robbed. Did we?"

He didn't tell me if we got robbed or not. "It's old. Where did you get it from?"

"Some guy with one eye. Well, one in his head, he had a whole box of... of those." Julian opened the box and took the eye out, carefully holding it by its edge. "Don't drop it!" I said, joking but absolutely not joking. I did a small cough. I thought Julian was going to pretend to drop it. I thought he was going to do that thing that people do when they pretend to drop things. Bend his knees slightly and make a panicked noise. I'm sure he considered it. I was glad when he didn't do that. "Do you shut him down?"

"Yeah."

"And then… what? Just stick it in?"

"It's a little bit more involved than that, leave it to me," he said. I ignored his patronising tone because I really needed him. I was eager to get this done so I could go back to having no dealings with Julian. Get things back to normal and I wouldn't need to be dealing with anybody.

"You want him on the table?" I asked.

"Do you want to go away? I've got it from here."

"I'll stay. Can I? Simon, you want me to stay?"

"*I* want you to go," said Julian before Simon could answer.

"Simon, do you want-"

"Look, I'm not going to do it with you here, so..." said Julian.

"Okay, and you're going to do the seals too?" I lifted up the bag.

"Leave the seals," said Julian and I looked around for a suitable place to leave the bag. A place that wouldn't contaminate Julian's sterile countertop environment. I handed the bag to Simon.

"And, like, nothing can go wrong?"

"Like what?"

"I don't know, you're the… you know?"

"An hour."

"Okay, see you in an hour," I said to Simon.

"Don't come back before," said Julian, standing, waiting for me to be gone.

I nodded and looked at Simon. "Yeah. You'll see me in a hour, through two eyes!" I said, pointing at my eyes with my forefinger and next finger of my right hand before patting him. I could sense Julian rolling his eyes and so I gave Simon a small hug. He sort of hugged me back. He moved his arm. The carrier bag hit my back. "You want anything? Coffee?" I asked Julian, but he shook his head. "A cake?" He didn't even shake his head to that. "Yeah, okay, see you in an hour." I looked at my watch, which still didn't work, and then I gave Julian a strong new contender for the biggest thumbs up I've ever given.

I was halfway back to the bunker before I changed my mind. *What was I going to do in there on my own?* I wanted fresh-ish air, I decided.

There were seven trucks in the stack and three more on the floor being loaded. I didn't know if ours was one of them or if ours was still getting fixed. I didn't want to ask Pete, who was directing the pickers, so I walked out across the yard and across the gangway. I made my way to the platform where there was a clock. Seventeen minutes had passed since I left Simon, I guessed. I sat down on a bench until ten more minutes clicked by. Two Snakes came and went while I sat there, and then I headed back.

"I said an hour."

"I thought..." I said, looking at my watch and shaking my head. "Sorry, how much longer?"

"He's just starting up. So slow to boot."

I could see Simon behind him. He was standing. "Ha! Look at that!" I said when I saw Simon had two eyes again. He probably had to be standing so that Julian could do the seals. "That's brilliant. Did you do the seals too?"

"Listen Mike," said Julian, ushering me through the counter

with a tilt of his head. I followed him to where Simon stood beeping. I wasn't bothered that he'd truncated my name.

"I got the right seals?"

"Yeah, yeah, listen though. It's wrecked."

"What is."

"This! This unit."

"Ah, we're all getting older."

"I don't know what happened. I don't know what you've done but something has broken its remembory casing."

"It wasn't... I don't know. The crash..." I saw a couple of sparkles in the outside corners of my eyes.

"You weren't poking around in there? With a screwdriver?"

"No," I guffawed. Yeah, it was a guffaw. My upper teeth stuck out as I laughed and I felt sick.

"Well, something's cracked it. And they're armoured so, I don't know," explained Julian, and I shook my head to show that nothing had happened. Nothing had pierced it. Yeah, there was the crash but that was it. "There are gaps in the casing," he continued.

"So?" I asked, still shaking my head. I felt just saying 'so' was enough, but Julian didn't respond. "So, can you... you know? Fix it?" I asked. Suggested, more than asked. I mean, that was the obvious solution and it was his fucking job, after all. Do your job, Julian, and fix him, I was suggesting.

"Air is the most dangerous compound there is," lied Julian. I mean, it's just not. "Once air gets in it's too late," he said, giving me problems rather than solutions. "It starts eating away at the sectors."

"He's fine though," I explained. "It's been a few days and-"

"Eventually it'll get to the OS and…" Julian raised his eyebrows.

"Then what?"

"Well, that's it." He shook his head very slightly.

"Okay," I said, also shaking my head slightly, trying to keep calm. "What do you mean, *eventually?* How… what is, you know?" For a scientist, Julian wasn't making with the scientific factualities. Exact times and whatnots, things that you'd want a scientist to produce. Hard data.

"How long's a piece of string?" asked Julian, looking at Simon.

"He could tell you!" I said as Simon beeped and I lowered my voice. "I'll get a new… part? New remembory? The guy with one eye, he had all sorts."

"You can't replace them. There'd be no point."

"What do you mean, no point? I mean, how long… guess."

"A couple of months. I don't know."

"We'll fix him," I said.

Julian looked around then lowered his voice. "Look, shut up, there's one thing I can do, but don't go blabbing about it. Yeah?"

"Yeah, okay, of course. Anything."

"There's a unit in the storeroom. I can swap the arms over with this one. I'll have to swap the serial number over but if I can get it to start then you can have that one. For a hundred pounds."

"A hundred pounds?"

"I'll have to do it out of hours. I can do it tonight."

"Right," I agreed. It sounded like an agreement but I hadn't really understood the offer. "One hundred pounds," I said as I replayed the conversation. I nodded and made it look like I was considering the sum of money involved, rather than everything else he'd said. *So, Julian was talking about what? Taking off Simon's arms and putting them onto a unit he had in a storeroom? Then I'd have… a unit with Simon's arms? For a hundred pounds?* "That would mean I'd have a different unit?" I said, each word higher than the one it preceded.

"The same arms. It's only got about a thousand hours on it so it'll last longer than this one."

"But it won't *be* this one?"

"No. And this is if I can start it up. It hasn't been on for years."

"Right," I said. I was getting to grips with the offer now. Another tech came and checked something on a screen next to us. It didn't bother Julian. I thought we were conducting some secret business and he would change the subject with somebody else within earshot. Apparently not.

"So? A hundred pounds?"

"I really want this one," I said. I narrowed my eyes. I was explaining something which I felt didn't need explaining. I was worried I was missing something and I might be sounding stupid.

"Okay, eighty pounds."

"Yeah, no, it's… it's… it's… you know?"

"Hello!" said Simon, rather sheepishly. I don't know how much of that he heard.

"Here he is!" I said, relieved. "How's that, buddy?" Simon was moving his head around. Angling it.

"They're all *exactly* the same. You can talk to a different one and you won't know the difference," said Julian. The tech looking at the screen laughed. I put that down to there being something funny on the screen he was looking at.

"I think I'll stick with this one, thanks."

"I'll do it for fifty."

"We'll see."

"Do you want this?" he asked, pointing to the tin lid with

tape tentacles coming from it. It was on top of the empty bag on a chair.

"Erm, no," I said. "Actually maybe." I thought more. "No," I decided, noting that he was looking at me with raised eyebrows. "Actually yeah, I'll take it, and thanks for the..." I said, picking up the tin lid and bundling Simon out of the room.

"How does that... how do you feel?" I asked Simon as we walked down the corridor.

"Good," he replied, and it was then I realised Julian did have an eye, in the unit he was trying to palm off on me.

"What a wanker," I said.

"You wanna do it?" asked Simon as we stood before the stack.

"What do you think?" I asked, boomeranging his question right back into his face. He was upbeat, I guess that's what getting a brand new eye will do for a person, but I was already bored of work and we hadn't even started. Getting his eye had been a big thing. Something to focus on and now I felt a bit, you know, horribly depressed. And even though having half a day was a good thing, it meant we were left with the drops the others had dodged.

"Come on, there's nobody here!" he said. He was trying to goad me into doing it. The thing is I *can't* do it, so he could goad all he wanted, it wasn't going to change that fact. We've tried a few times and I just can't do it. I don't know which part of the brain manipulates distant objects in 3D space, but I do know that

I haven't got it. He can get the Lady down in the fewest moves possible, even if the stack is full. I couldn't do it if there were three Ladys, unless ours was at the bottom. Today ours wasn't at the bottom and there were seven other Ladys in the stack to get ours jammed against. I just can't think that many moves ahead. Also, this isn't an excuse, but it's usually busy, so I don't get the chance to practise. Maybe with practise it would click. It was around eleven and not busy, but still, I wasn't in the mood. "I bet you can do it. I'll help."

"Just get it down," I said.

"*Oooooh!*" he replied. "Have one go."

"Simon."

"C'mon."

"Just get the fucking thing down, will you?" I barked. Simon looked at me with his new eye. His old eye squinting, his new eye wide open. He was doing it on purpose. It's something he can do. He was looking at me with suspicion. Trying to work out why I was being a dick. Good luck with that! I didn't know. The slight happiness he'd displayed was gone. I'd dragged him down to my level of unhappiness. He turned back to the joystick on a plinth which was fixed to the floor. "Fine! One go," I said, going to take over the controls, but Simon didn't move. "Move."

"No. I've done it now," he lied. He hadn't started. Then he did it.

"That's exactly how I would have done it," I explained.

"Yeah, sure."

"Honestly!" The Lady was in the stack exit. Simon got in it and finessed it over to the loading bay. I waved at him as he passed but he ignored me. I walked over with my hands in my pockets. Pete had a clipboard.

"Got seven for you, dong face," he said. "Ease you back in."

"My name's Michael, Pete. Could you call me Michael, do you think? It's just… it's my name, you know? Just… just, like, give me that respect?" I tried to say that lightly but midway through it became serious. Pete stared at me.

"Whatever you want, Princess Fuckface."

"Seven?" I sighed. Pete wordlessly ripped off the top sheet from his clipboard and handed it to me before schlomping back to his cabin. Simon came around and opened the back doors. "Just this seven," I said just to say something, because he was still ignoring me. As Simon loaded them, I went over to the hut which contained Pete. I took a deep breath, knocked on the door and opened the door about twenty-five centimetres. I stood to the side, away from the gap I'd made. Ajar. The door was ajar. I was holding it ajar. "Got any samples?" I shouted. My eyes darted around as I tried to focus my ears, then three bars of chocolate shot through the gap in the door, where my face could have been had I not known from experience just how hard Pete can launch them. They went skittering over the depot floor. "Thanks for fixing the truck, it looks great!" I shouted. I could only find two of the chocolate bars. Simon found the third when he moved the pallet to the pallet board stack. I put them in the chest pocket of my new overalls. The ones I'd been saving. I did like our new uniforms. I thought of them as new but, yeah, they'd changed years before. They're about the only change they managed to get right. I walked out to the yard. People aren't allowed in the Ladys while they're in the hangar. Simon pulled up and I got in and buckled up.

"They could have cleaned in here, while they were fixing it," I said. Really I was glad they hadn't.

"Hold on," said Simon and we lurched up into the late morning traffic.

"They are blue," I said. In the daylight you could really notice.

"Sea moss," he said, checking his wing mirror. For traffic. He wasn't checking himself out.

"Never noticed before. Thought they were just... you know, eye coloured."

"Am I pretty?" he asked.

"Fuck off."

We were friends again. I looked at the sheet. I always picked the route, even though Simon could definitely do it more efficiently. But we were working, and efficiency wasn't our goal. Working is very different to taking a Lady out of the stack. There's so much more to consider. It's not about getting it done as fast as possible. If it was, then yeah, he should choose the route. Working is more about going where *I* feel like going and spreading it out, so it takes all day. Simon can't do that. He can't decide which way I feel like going. And unlike taking a Lady down from the stack, when we're out and about I can't get us jammed in a corner. So that's why I looked at the sheet and announced glumly, "Fish Market, I suppose."

"How far?"

"Hmmm," I hmmmed, and just between you and me, it was a false and unnecessary hmmm. I know *exactly* how far it is to the Fish Market, because when we go, we always go straight from the depot. The answer is twelve point seven miles. But let's have some fun with Simon. Let's let him sound his klaxon, before I pull the rug out from under him, not that you could pull a rug out from under Simon. You'd need an engine of some sort for that.

"Guess!" he demanded, like an overconfident spider to a devious fly that was playing possum in his web.

"Eleven... no, twelve. Twelve and a half?" I rubbed my forehead, acting like it was helping soothe my throbbing brain. "No, no, a little bit more? Twelve point *six* miles?"

"KLAXON"

"Oh, how foolish of me, I mean twelve point... eight!"

"KLAXON"

"Gah, well then, is it twelve point seven miles, perchance, fuckface?"

"KLAXON"

"What? It is! I remember it. They weren't *guesses*. Why do you think I said the number on each side? I was *toying* with you! Twelve point seven to the Fish Market from the depot. I'm telling you."

"Twelve point seven is to the *Stadium*. Twelve point *four* to the Fish Market."

I thought about what he'd said, without letting my emotions get in the way. I scratched my skull, just above the temple on my right side. Yeah, that sounded about right, now that he'd said it. "Does the eye feel any different?" I asked. He was flying confidently. With panache.

"No different. It's nice to have two."

"Yeah, I bet. Well, yeah it is. I know."

"Only thing is I can see ghosts now." Simon slowly and smoothly turned his head to me, no expression on his face. "There's one behind yo-"

"Yeah, that's not funny. Watch where you're going." His face was still impassive and I felt cold. "Imagine if we really had a crash now."

"It was a little bit funny," he said, his face expanding into a smile as he turned it back to the windscreen. He leant over to pat me, but I pushed myself away.

"I'll explain jokes properly to you one day. That they're supposed to be funny. Remind me."

"Your face was pretty funny."

"Was it? Was it really?" I asked, nodding, trying to think up a retaliatory insult. There were none. None that wouldn't be too close to the bone. "Hurry up."

"I'm adhering to the speed limit for this altitude, Michael."

"I think I liked you better with one eye. You're all cocky now."

"This isn't so bad," he said, looking around at the towers and tunnels. "I like that we go out."

"You actually like it?"

"It's better than being in a cage. Or a display case."

"Oh yeah, it's better than that," I agreed. "Well, I'm glad you enjoy it because we've got fifty fucking years of this."

"You're going to live for another fifty years?"

"Well… twenty then." I opened the glove box and took out the dictionary.

I looked up 'couple'. Two or a few.

I looked up 'few'. Not many but more than one.

I put the dictionary back.

"Thirty-three," said Simon, looking at me then nodding.

"I'll take that. I'll be sick of being alive by then." I was worried Simon would ask me how long I thought *he* had left. So I spoke more. "Double or quits on the ten pounds I owe you for coming back. If I die in thirty-three years' time I'll give you twenty pounds, and that's a promise. Deal?"

"Deal."

I leant over and shook Simon's hand. We flew over a Snake. I watched it disappear down into a hole then checked the sheet of paper again and clipped it to the dashboard.

Twelve-point-whatever miles later we landed, ready to make the first of our drops. We land high up on the roof of the Fish Market because the entrances on the lower floors are full of important commerce and fish trucks and people covered in fish. Yeah, people totally covered in fish. Head to toe. I don't know what's wrong with them. You know? You see a librarian and they're not covered in books. They don't rub books all over themselves, but these fish people… with something that smells so bad… oh boy. Landing on the roof means there's a fair bit of walking. It's probably the walkiest drop we do, well, one of the walkiest.

Just the walking would be reason enough to do the Fish Market first. You don't want to spend the day dreading doing some walking. Get it out of the way. But there's also the stink to consider. Simon knows that fish smell. That's all he knows about the reek of fish, that it exists. He doesn't care that when the stench gets on you, forget soap, the only thing which will truly eradicate it is time. That's another reason for going there first. Give the stink time to disasipate. Disipate. Give the stink time to fade away.

Do the hard drops first. Get the hard ones out of the way and leave the easier ones until later. Then your day gets easier and easier. Even if it means flying further. It makes total sense, but only *human* sense. To Simon it's all the same, there's no difference between difficult and easy, and I knew that he was thinking we should have gone to the college first. His fans didn't hum, but I *knew*. He can be a nightmare like that sometimes. When he doesn't approve of my way of doing things. Don't get me wrong, he's important too. We've both got our strengths and weaknesses. His strengths are his massive strength and his piloting skill, and my weaknesses are, I suppose, that I'm a perfectionist and also quite weak. And I can't be trusted with tokens. I mean I *could* be trusted, but I'm not allowed to count tokens. That's why we make a great team.

If Simon chose the route then the bunker would stink and we'd get back to the depot at about two in the afternoon, only to be sent back out again. Fuck that.

I was taking my last few breaths of the Lady's unpolluted air before unbuckling and getting out, when Simon asked, "Remember the squid?" and my careful ventilating was ruined as I burst out a little laugh, spit hitting my knee. I wiped it off. I took my mask from the glove box and got out, while Simon got the first pallet from the back. I waited for him over by the railings.

The Fish Market, horseshoe shaped and old, was once a sea fort or a barracks. I'm no professional architecture historian, but it looks like it's from around the same time that they built the redundant walls around Graymall. Its shape would have sheltered boats but it was a long time since a boat had visited here. It would have faced the open ocean, but now it faces a collection of industrial buildings. Some float, bob slightly, while others are held by struts buried in the seabed. Looking out for too long at that sea of wobbling warehouses can make your legs feel weird. The only water visible is the pool, twelve stories down, where the subtrawlers regurgitate the monsters and fish and junk, and whatever else they've managed to suck up, out onto the dock.

That's where it all begins – the process of getting processed. You can watch most of it unfold, if you want, while descending the platforms and ramps that are attached to the fort's frontage.

There are only vending machines on the top six levels. The bottom six are not somewhere you'd want to go. Especially not if you're a fish. Especially not if you're anything, actually. Or anybody.

"Check it," said Simon.

I left the railing and looked at the pallet and nodded. I didn't count anything, of course. Simon can count things that he can see more accurately than I ever could, but Simon asking me to check the pallet wasn't something I could disable, or if it was, I hadn't found the code. It was hardwired into him and I couldn't simply ignore his request or he wouldn't move. I had to pretend to check it or else he'd just ask me again and again and again. A nod was the only affirmation he required. I nodded. "Vamos!" I said. I made sure my mask was tight and we went through the doors and past the security who wasn't even on.

We began our descent. Me near the railing. Most of what sploshed out of the subs went straight back down a large black pipe. Some of it had probably made that journey more than once. A shampoo bottle, for example. It looked noisy and relentless, and we'd seen it could be very dangerous. Even without the sea monsters I was glad I didn't work down there. Who were the monsters? The actual real-life monsters, or the men? That's a question. The fishy guys clearly worked hard, and they probably deserved more respect than I was willing to give them. Maybe if they weren't so covered in fish guts? They didn't seem to care about themselves, and if you don't respect yourself... you know? There's probably a saying about that. And they were rude, and it never seemed like it would take much to push them over into frenzied violence. I just ignored them.

Simon smells. Not, he *can* smell – he can, I've said that already – but he has an odour. Simon smells like the air from a laundry, but because I'm with him nearly 24 hours a day I'm used to it. Can't smell it. Can't really remember the last time I noticed it. I stink sometimes, my armpits do. I quite like it when my armpits stink.

"Remember the squid?" asked Simon and this time I didn't burst out laughing. If there's an opposite to bursting out laughing, then I did that. Compressed inwards crying? Not exactly, but it felt more like that than laughing. My hand had been sliding over the handrail as we walked, but now it bounced.

"What?" I asked as I bounced my hand on the railings.

"Pardon?"

I stopped walking and pulled my mask away from my face. The straps pulled on my ears. It was a little bit painful. "What did you just say?"

"Remember? When the squid came up? And all the men we-"

"You've asked me that already," I said. I didn't say that compassionately, or with concern. I said it angrily. Really quite angrily. He looked at me for a moment then nodded. "Two minutes ago, you asked me." I pointed up at the sky because he'd asked me on the roof.

"I know," he said, "you didn't reply."

I put the mask back over my lower face then pulled it away again. "Yeah, I remember, chaos," I said, carefully watching him as we began to walk again. I let the mask hug my face. He seemed okay and it was true, I hadn't replied.

Simon stopped at the first vending machine which everybody

knows should be the *last* vending machine. He was fucking up all over the place. Was this it? Had his remembory gone already? Was he about to explode? He parked the pallet next to the machine which was set into an alcove in the old wall.

"We're doing it this way?" I asked. Fan noise came from Simon as he looked at the machine, then to me, then back to the machine. "We're doing *this* one first?" I continued. "We're not doing the bottom one first? You know, the bottom one first, like we *always* do?"

"We don't *always* do the bottom one first," he replied, staring at me.

"We *usually* do," I said, and his fans came on, but I hadn't finished my defence so I kept talking. "Bottom one first, that's the way to do it. This way, *your* way, starting here and we finish at the bottom and then we have to walk fucking miles back with nothing to do. That's madness. Absolute mad-"

"Fifty-three percent of the time we've started at the bottom," he said.

"I *knew* you were going to do that," I said, disappointed. "So, I'm right, we usually start at the bottom. I mean, I am literally right, right?"

"You said we always do."

"I said *usually*. And you better not have recorded me." I was annoyed because he'd given me a fright by asking the same question twice, and I didn't like the noise he was making. Why had Julian even told me? If he couldn't fix it then why even mention it? I didn't think I'd normally be able to hear his fans outside, above the wind and shouting and scraping.

I'd had a fright and it turns out I become a bit of a jerk when I'm frightened and I can't help it. "You're all over the place today," I said, not because he was, not for certain, it could have just been in my imagination. I was probably seeing signs that weren't there because I was on edge. Telling him he was all over the place wasn't meant to put him down or make him feel foolish, it was so he could redouble his efforts not to be all over the place, and then I wouldn't be frightened. I was looking out for *him*.

"Let's go down then," he said, lifting the pallet.

"Nah, you've put it down now," I said. "I was just... trying to be efficient, but we'll do it your way," I said, clicking my fingers at him and pointing at the vending machine until he pressed his finger into the keyhole and the door popped open.

"Going to the bottom first means I have to pull the full pallet further," he said.

"It's not all about you, Simon."

"So-"

"It's fine, it's fine, stop thinking up excuses," I said. I felt I was now in the awkward position of trying to be enough of a jerk so that he wouldn't think anything was wrong, but I didn't want to be *so* much of a jerk that I caused him stress. I was walking a real jerkrope. I looked over the pallet for the box with the corresponding serial number on it, but Simon pointed to it before I found it. That was reassuring. He was functioning. I hunkered down and my knees popped as Simon went over to the railings.

"Don't fall," I said without looking at him.

I shuffled forwards on my knees, pulling the box that held Moonbeams and Jojos, Lucky Lucifers, Krisks, DoubleDans, Froops and Tinglers. The fishy men love Moonbeams, even though they taste like dried piss pellets from somebody on heavy medication. Maybe the taste of Moonbeams mixed with fish vapours somehow makes a nice taste? I will *never ever* find out.

Vaprellas are new and they're doing okay. It's too soon to say for certain if they'll stick around. I hope they do because the packets are a nice shape and easy to load. They fit into the hoops nicely. You never know, though. People went wild for Brownds when they first came out, but where the fuck are they now?

I'd never been passionate about restocking vending machines from a big yellow cubic truck with a robot companion, but, yeah, seeing a vending machine all full and neat and knowing I'd done it gave me a fizz of satisfaction. I got to my feet, using the machine's door for support, and surveyed my good work.

"Come on!" I clicked my fingers impatiently at Simon's back but his silhouette against the white sky didn't move. I pulled my mask away. "Simon!" I shouted and he moved, thank fuck. I shook my head slightly. He beckoned me over with a small head movement. Simon was looking down at the dock. He wasn't excited, though, so I knew he wasn't seeing an animal attack. He was looking down the way you might look down at a birthday cake somebody had dropped on the floor.

Imagine it, somebody was carrying a birthday cake, it doesn't matter who, and they didn't necessarily make it, but they're carrying it. Through a doorhole and towards a small crowd. The crowd are all singing Happy Birthday. The birthday person is sitting next to a table with a slightly awkward smile, not knowing what to do with themselves, almost wishing they could join in with the singing, as that, at least, would give them something to do. Nobody is looking at the birthday person. They're looking at the cake and at the person carrying the cake. The cake is quite tall, not crazy tall, but quite tall, and the cake carrier's trying to smile and is human. They're walking carefully, not singing themselves, although maybe they are with their eyes, or maybe they mouth the odd word. They're concentrating. Their legs never fully straighten as they walk, so as not to jar the cake. Their knees are shock absorbers. Their back slightly hunched, shielding the candles and then... Then! Even with all the cake carrier's attention and precautions, the cake starts to slip towards one side of the tray. The carrier wasn't holding the tray completely level, perhaps they were concentrating too much on not shaking the cake, but for whatever reason, it started to slip and, of course, it's now *inevitable* that they overcompensate. They do because it was inevitable and the cake goes the other way and then, with a final frantic failed last-ditch flip of the tray, the cake is fucked. It's going. The cake is going. The carrier grabs at the cake but only gets a chunk and some icing and the cake is upside down on the floor. Nobody is singing or even ready to make light of the disaster. The cake is on the floor. Yeah? Well, Simon was looking down at the dock in the Fish Market the way you might look down at that cake.

On the side of the dock, lying on its front, was a very pale corpse. I didn't see how it got to the side, it was already there when I peered over, but I supposed it had been pushed there by the men with the poles. The poles with the long bit on the bottom, like brooms without bristles, that they use to separate out the piles. "Oof!" I said.

"You see the-"

"Yup," I said. The bandage hadn't expanded the way the rest of the swimmer's leg had. I should have been surprised, really. I wasn't. Not at all. "Come on," I said, going back to the machine. "I didn't need to see that."

He came over and emptied the token drawer by clipping his hand under the box. His eyes fluttered as the tokens worked their way into his wrist safe. I pressed reset and then I pressed the door until it clicked. I stomped on the empty box and winced as I felt a sharp pain in my hip.

"Are you okay?" asked Simon.

"A little bit tense if I'm honest, Simon. A little bit tense." I said, not looking at him, my voice muffled from the mask.

"You'll get into it." He rolled onto the box and then put it on the pallet.

It's always windier on the other side of the horseshoe. The shape of the building seems to create its own wind. The machine over the other side on the top floor has never done anything. Seven tokens this week, and that's more than normal. It's a complete waste of time. There are still Johnny Pineapples with the old wrapper in there. Still, I left it looking all neat and Simon squashed the box before we went down the ramp to the level below. I stayed away from the railing.

The lower we went, the more men there were to avoid. There were probably fishy women too, it was hard to tell, but the lower we went, the busier it got on the walkway and the closer I walked to Simon. I didn't want to make eye contact with anybody, they can take that as a challenge. Even the ones who wore proper clothes, rather than the overalls and knife belts, looked rough and tough as fuck, and stunk. You didn't mess with any of these people and there were many of them.

We got to the last machine without talking to each other, or to anybody else. As Simon took the tokens from the last machine, which should have been the first machine, I looked down over the railings. The corpse had gone, and that was good because being closer would have allowed us to see some detail. Now there was a shark or some kind of big fish flopping around on the decking as a couple of the fishy people walked around it. They were shouting and gesturing. Something had gone wrong in the unloading process, I guessed, because the shouting was indecipherable but accusatory. Maybe just the fact the animal was still alive was the problem. I'd missed exactly what error had occurred but the fuck up was quickly rectified by a man putting an axe type thing through the shark's head. It wasn't instant, and with an axe as well as a fin sticking up out of it, the shark flopped lazily until, after one final big flop, it stopped flopping and three men pulled it by its tail to a big blue pipe. Before pushing it in, a man wrestled for a while, trying to get his axe back out of the fish.

The squid had put up a much better fight, but then it did have the massive advantage of having loads of really long arms. The shark didn't have any. That had been a *really* great day, the day we'd seen the squid. I don't think I'd ever laughed so much. I'd laughed until my throat hurt and I was nearly laughing just thinking about it, but my smile vanished when I saw a man approaching Simon. I left the railing and went over to save him.

"Sorry, we don't have samples," I said through my mask. I glanced at Simon to ensure he could see my serious eyes. I turned my eyes back to the man. I didn't know where the rumour of us carrying around samples had started, but we were often asked for them. I mean, there are samples. We do *have* samples, but I eat them. We're not just going to hand them out like they're... they're... We're not just going to hand them out. I was polite because anybody who is prepared to make a scene over confectionery had very little to lose.

"This machine ate my token," said the man. That's the other classic, if they're not asking for samples then it's, 'Your machine ate my token.' *Yeah, I've never heard that one before. Good one, buddy! I am a gullible fool so, yeah, just say anything to me and I'll hand over some tokens, even though I'll get docked if we're short. But it's fine, right? Us being short, because you're so selfish you'd steal from your fellow man. Just take something that isn't yours. No guilt. No empathy. How does that happen? Is it butchering fish all day, does that? Does it desensitise you to life and its beauty? To sharing? Or were you born a fucking scumbag and found your dream vocation? You wanted something where you could wallow around in guts and this came along? Okay, your job sucks, I agree, I wouldn't do it, but then it's not like I'm living it up in Central. What have I got? A broken watch and a broken robot. And a broken tape player. Well, that's not broken but it may as well be without the lead, and you want to rob me?* I thought. *Not today.* I didn't think it as coherently as that, but that was the nub of what I thought.

"Well, if you write to that address and explain," I said, pointing to the label on the machine, "they might be able to do something." I accidentally shook my head when I said that. They wouldn't do anything if he wrote to that address. He didn't notice my faux pas. He held out his hand and went to grab my arm, and I flailed and stepped back. "Listen, you fish… person. This machine *didn't* take your token. It can't. It's impossible. And you… you've seen things? Ha! *I've* seen things. Yeah you think you've seen things? I've seen *things*. Not a few dead fish."

"I just wa-," said the man.

"You threatening me now? I could… I could… I could rain fire down on you… and any…" I shook my head again. He was a bit shorter than me, so I didn't fully see his incredible tortoiseshell eyes until he looked up and the shadow cast by the brim of his trucker's cap shrank back. He had a neat moustache, but that was easy to miss because of the ways his eyes held you. They held you tight. I'm not a big male beauty expert but I'd say he was perfect.

He was a walking, talking work of art. Caked in fish shit but still beautiful.

"I'm sorry, Brother," said the man.

"Look, what are you doing? It's just shit," I said.

"It *is* shit," he agreed. He looked around then took his cap off and ran his hand over his hair, not through it, before reseating his headgear. God he was beautiful. Should have been a pianist. His face was wasted on him. On this place. This guy didn't spend his nights composing great mystical symphonies about the sea. He probably spent the nights with his hand splayed on a bar-room table, while his uncultured friends rapidly stabbed knives between his fingers, marking up the bar top, all hooting and swaying like they were on a ship.

"Look," I said again, this time giving him something to look at and getting him involved. "See this?" I pointed at the control panel, without looking at the control panel. I was looking at him because he was unpredictable. I didn't want to turn my back on the thief. "This tells you how many tokens have gone in, and how many items have come out."

"It's wrong!" he cried.

"It can't be," I said. "Computers can't be wrong. Are *you* better than a computer?"

"What?"

"Are you?" I asked, careful not to back him into too much of a corner, where his base instinct of erupting might come to the fore. "What's... eighty times... ninety-six?"

"Seven thousand, six hunned and eighty," he replied, almost instantly. I looked at Simon who was deliberately looking down the gangway. He knew I was trying to get his attention, but he was ignoring me and looking away.

"Yeah, well, that was an easy one," I said. I didn't know if it was right or wrong. I could have worked it out on a slate, probably, and Simon was ignoring me because he knew full well he would be no help. Fun fact about Simon, he can't add numbers together. He can't add two and two. Ask him to add two and two and his fans will come on and if he doesn't crash he'll ask you 'two whats?' and you're not getting out of that conversation until you introduce an object. Or a distance. He can add up distances or sausages or something. Fish. Tokens. Just not numbers. I hoped he wouldn't soon have to add up some stab wounds in me, because, somewhat ominously, the man was licking his lips. This was going to go either way and it was going pretty soon.

"You're not giving me my token?" asked the man.

I looked him dead in his great eyes. "Go away," I said. The man looked at us both. I held my head back a bit but didn't take my eyes off him. I was challenging him. He raised his arm. On the end of it wasn't a cleaver, or even a fist. It was a finger and he pointed it at me.

"Asshole," he said. I nodded. He just looked at us both and then walked off and I felt like I'd done a magic trick.

"Jesus, thought he was-" I managed, going limp, before the man stopped and turned back. I stood up straight. He did that cap off hair thing again. I stared and he walked away. Down the ramp. "...thought he was going to murder us!" I finished, my hands on my thighs.

"What was *that?* What the heck was that?" asked Simon.

"I need to sit down," I said, and I went to sit down on the pallet. I was nearly sitting down when I stood up again. "We've got to get out of here." I waved my hand at the pallet to tell

Simon we had to get out of there. "Just…"

"Rain fire?" asked Simon.

"I don't know. It just came out. Quick, in case he comes back. We've got to…" I waved my hand at the pallet again.

"Take it easy, Michael."

"I'm telling you now," I panted. My hands were on the top of my hips and I was walking in small circles. "I'm not taking shit from anybody anymore," I said. "Life's too short. Trying to steal tokens?" I waved my hand dismissively towards the ramp the man had gone down. "Fucking pathetic. We're… tempered steel."

"There are extra tokens," said Simon.

"You what?"

"There are four extra tokens."

"What?" I could hear ringing in my ears. Cutting through the Fish Market's mayhem like a bell.

"Why didn't you..." I couldn't even finish that as my face was so screwed up and quizzical, because I was so incredulous, that it made it difficult to talk.

"*He* told you."

"Him?"

"He wasn't lying."

"Oh, do ya fink so?" I said. I looked around. I looked to the left which led up and to the Lady, then right which led down and to the wronged man. "Give me a token."

"Can't, they're in my arm."

"Fucking hell."

I went over to the railing. "Hey!" I shouted, leaning over. I could see part of the level below. Just the railing, basically. "Hey!"

I didn't think it would, I mean, if he'd continued walking at the pace that he seemed to walk, and if he was going that way then he'd be *roughly* directly under us, but I didn't think it would. It did though. It appeared. The man's behatted head appeared. He was leaning out, his back over the railings, his face pointing up. "We're not bad," I shouted. "Here!" I dropped a Tiger Bar from my top pocket. He pulled his face out of the way and the chocolate went right down into the sea. "No, catch it!" I shouted. His face reappeared. "Catch!" I held another one out, I think I even took the wind into account, and I dropped it. I don't know what was wrong with this guy. Whether he was being blinded or he was just stupid or something, but the chocolate hit him in the face and knocked his hat off and both items went down towards the sea. He didn't even attempt to catch it. He disappeared then reappeared. Not his face, the back of his head came out over the railing, because he was looking down this time. His hat still hadn't... now it had. His hat hit the sea.

I leant out as far as I dared. Held my arm out as far as I could and threw the last sample Tiger Bar at an angle, so it'd land on the platform below, but it hit the railing and went down into the sea. With the samples gone I shouted for Simon to throw me something from the machine which I could throw at the man.

"What do you want?" said Simon, picking up on my urgency. "MelonyLemons?"

"No, Moonbeams," I said and he threw them and I didn't catch them and they went out over the railings and down into the sea. I looked down. The man looked up at me. He looked incomplete without his hat. I went to say something and then didn't. We looked at each other for a moment. I'm not certain he could see my eyes. I may have been simply a candy-firing silhouette to him. I could see his eyes. Mine were once again locked on his, and only disengaged after I slowly reversed myself so I couldn't see him anymore. I went over to Simon.

"That was nice of you," he said. He was nodding at me like I'd just done a good thing.

I quickly closed the machine without saying anything and gave him the box to squash and then, without waiting for him, I started up to the roof, only occasionally checking back. Simon caught up with me on the next level and I sat on the empty boxes on the pallet so they wouldn't blow away. I felt terrible about the man's hat. What if it was his lucky hat? There's a good chance it had been important to him. Maybe given to him by somebody special in his life. Somebody he never got to see because he lived at the Fish Market, scraping a living.

"They can fish it out," I told Simon when we were back in the Lady and I'd hung my mask up so it could dry.

"Fish what out?"

"His hat." I rubbed my face to erase the marks left by the mask.

"Whose hat?"

"Yeah, they'll have a net or something." Talking it through with Simon made me feel a little bit better but I was still shaky. I could have done with a Tiger Bar. "He'll get it back," I said. Simon didn't disagree. He always gets it. I really need him.

───────

We flew to the college with the windows open, which made any loose paper in the cab fly around. I looked through the dictionary. I'm on Bs again. There are some cool words that begin with the letter B, but soon the dictionary got boring so I bequeathed it back to the glove box. "Okay?" I asked, just for something to say. He turned to me.

"Why do you keep asking me that?"

"Just something to say."

"I'm okay. Are *you*?"

"Yeah." I felt okay too.

"Good talk," said Simon. "Hold on." I held on to the armrests as the Lady dropped down into the stream of traffic below.

"Ready to see your girlfriend?" I asked.

"Don't bother."

"You've gone red."

"That's very amusing," said Simon, but he wasn't amused.

"You are adorable."

"Hold on," he said as we swung left. We flew under and around, then through and over new layers being constructed and the battery factory. The City was never going to be finished. It would be nice if it was, well, not nice. The City was never going to be *nice*, but at least it could be finished. It was never ever *not* going to be a construction site, and they were constantly making it worse.

"Damn!" said Simon when he saw the delivery bay was full. I think he said it because I'm usually annoyed when we can't park immediately, but for whatever reason I didn't really mind and we set down by the astroturf, on the other side of the parking area. It was quiet. Peaceful. That would change pretty soon because it was nearly lunchtime. We'd messed up going to the Fish Market first, and we couldn't do the college in the afternoon or we'd be late back. "Do I smell?" I asked. I was still getting wafts of fish.

Simon looked at me and tilted his head up slightly.

"Yeah."

"Thought so."

 "We could run it off," said Simon.

"Okay. I'm feeling energetic."

"Really? Are you messing with me?"

"Nah." I was messing with him. I didn't feel *that* energetic. "I mean yeah, I am messing with you." I stood and stuck my head out of the window, leaning on the sill. There was a warm breeze and the plastic grass was inviting. I closed my eyes and turned my face as far as I could towards the orange sun. It warmed my left ear.

"He's not here," said Simon. I ignored him until my head was back in the cab. I looked through the Lady's windows for the guard who went mental at us last time we'd gone running. What a dick! We hadn't left a mark on the track. I couldn't see him and it was a big college. He could be anywhere. "It'll get rid of the smell, let's do it," he said.

"Nah."

"You scared?" asked Simon.

"I am, actually. I'm pretty much terrified of everything," I said and then laughed to show I was joking. Simon was up and opened the door. I saw a truck leave the bay. "The bay's free," I shouted but he was already outside and then he was in front of the Lady. Beckoning me through the windscreen.

"Come on, one lap! Tempered steel!" I went down the ramp and stood with my hands on my hips. I pushed my hips forward, to stretch.

"He's definitely not here?" I asked. Simon scanned again.

"Can't see him."

I *did* want to do a lap. It was the perfect day for it. I just needed a little bit more encouragement. I needed Simon to persuade me a bit more, even though I wanted to do it, what's that about? It's good that I knew he would continue to persuade me. He wasn't going to just give up. He knows how I operate. "Nah."

"One lap."

"Not today. Next time," I said, acting like I meant it.

"Come on, just one," said Simon, shaking me by the shoulder.

I paused before I said no, this time. "Nah."

"Yeah, come on."

"I don't know," I said. I *did* know, and Simon knew what I meant.

"Okay, one lap."

"Just one. Quick," I agreed. I started for the track.

"Maybe two," he said.

"Forget it," I said, stopping and pretending to be on the verge of turning back to the truck.

"Okay, okay, one lap!"

"One lap," I repeated, and he clapped his hands like a big mental angular seal. I had another look around. The guard had been *such* a dick last time I couldn't believe it. You'd think he'd personally paid for the track. You'd think he owned it! He spoke to us like we were kids who he'd caught messing around. He'd threatened to tell our boss. It's weird to care about your job as much as the guard did.

Simon held up the chain so I could get under without stooping and we stepped onto the running track that went around the astroturf. We both had a look around and then I climbed up onto Simon's back. I know which parts to put my feet on. He locked his arms, his hands on his lower back, my thighs through the loops his arms made.

"Ready?"

"No! Wait there," I said, slightly panicked. One of my testicles was caught somewhere between my underpants and my overalls. I repositioned it. I then repositioned myself so that I was safe and comfortable. I bounced a bit. It was never *that* comfortable, but there was a way of sitting so you avoided any corners and sharp edges. "Okay."

"Ready?"

"Yeah, quick," I said and Simon set off. Slowly at first. As we rounded the bend, I held his neck tighter because I knew what was coming up when we hit the back straight. And then we hit it and *WHOOMPH!* It was what, a hundred metres long? Two or three seconds it took us. A second of accelerating so hard it nearly ripped my face from my skull and my arms out of their shoulder sockets, a second of calm, before a second of being crushed against Simon's back. Then we rounded the bend at a steady pace, and I was able to laugh and gulp in some air. It wasn't like he went around the bend slowly, if I'd fallen off I'd have gone flying, but on the bends I could laugh.

"Again?" he shouted as we hit the straight. I couldn't answer and *WHOOMPH!* Simon had gone past where we started. I knew he would. He loves it. Back straight. *WHOOMPH!* My laughter altered in pitch depending on the speed. On the bends it was a scream. We did five laps and he stopped. I climbed down, half fell, and lay down on the prickly turf, still laughing, knees steepled. I was laughing while moaning because it did hurt. It hurt a lot. You could easily break a rib, but it was worth it. I liked the way the points at the end of the plastic grass stabbed the back of my head. I looked up at the blue sky. At Simon who was looking around the track, reliving his effort. I had to stop myself from lacing my hands behind my head, instead I extended my arm and shouted, "Oi!" and Simon helped me to my feet. I had to bend double with my hands on my thighs because of a big dizzy spell. I guess one day I'll have one that will get more and more intense and that will be it. There are worse ways to go.

I walked alongside the truck, my hand on it like I was guiding it. I wasn't, Simon was flying it to the bay which was now full again. Simon stopped behind a small tanker which was collecting or delivering a liquid. Or maybe it was a gas. I passed the time by mouthing obscenities through the windscreen at Simon. That had been quite hard to explain to him, at first. How insults worked. How sometimes they were friendly. Context. He kind of gets it now, I think.

The tanker blocking our progress was fully automatic so didn't hang about, but I still gave it a thumbs up when it undocked and backed out of our way. I like them, they're cool and silver and a bit like rockets. I like how the world reflects off them. Even the Lady would look cool if it was chrome. Simon would look cool if he was chrome. To be honest I'm struggling to think of anything that wouldn't look better chrome. A baby, I suppose. Or food. I pretended to look over the pallet Simon had produced, but before we headed to security I sensed that he was looking at me. I looked around a bit and then to him. He *was* looking at me.

"What?"

"Protocol violation, Michael," he said with his eyebrows raised.

"I checked it," I lied, looking down at the pallet and pretending to check it again. Simon continued to look at me, smiling slightly. "What? Are you okay?"

"You know!" he said.

"I don't, what?" I asked.

"Your overalls are undone," he said, his smile increasing in scope. I looked down at my chest and sure enough my overalls were unzipped a cool amount.

"Hmm," I said, "must have happened when we were going around the track."

"I don't think it happened then," he said. He probably shouldn't have, he should have accepted my explanation. He knows I don't like to be accused of lying when I'm telling lies. Anyway, maybe I'd unzipped my overalls a bit because it was hot and I was trying to cool myself, not make myself look cool. It's not like I wanted to look cooler in front of the college kids. That's crazy. Simon's crazy.

Then we heard it. Simon did first. I could tell he was listening to something, his smile had gone and his head was motionless. Only his eyes were moving, but he wasn't looking at anything unless his eyes met mine, even then he'd only hold my gaze for a moment before looking down. I thought he'd heard the guard coming. Then I heard it. The scream of the scooter.

I'd been waiting for it, I realised. You dread stuff happening. Have nightmares about it, but when it's happening it just happens. That's why I didn't just throw myself onto the ground and curl up into a ball. I started walking over towards the running track. Simon followed. We didn't talk and the scooter was coming. The surprising part was he'd try something like this in the open. Or was it? Maybe it wasn't. I didn't know what rules applied to Jeff. The speed limit obviously didn't, and that was one of the rules in the City which was strictly enforced. I held out my arm and found Simon as we looked towards the rising screech coming from our right, coming from Central.

"I see it," said Simon. I couldn't but it wouldn't be long and for the first time that day I wasn't scared. I saw it. There were multiple.

"Go Gary!" shouted somebody from above us. Above and behind. I looked up at the people hanging out of the college's tower block. Five or so windows had people leaning out. One had a homemade banner. Looked like it was made of a bed sheet. It had 'Go Gary!' painted on it. There were more shouts of Gary and some whoops, and then I couldn't hear anything but the scooter which was now far too low and far too close and heading for us. I dropped to the floor and curled up as best I could as the first one passed over us. It was no more than ten metres above us and the displaced air punched me. Before I got up, I was hit with four more blasts of hot air.

"It's okay!" shouted Simon, who hadn't thrown himself onto the floor because he can't. He helped me stand up straight. I stood next to Simon. If my head was below his then I knew I was pretty safe.

"What is it?" I asked. I couldn't see them but Simon's gaze was following something, presumably them.

"From what I can gather a person called Gary is driving around..."

"Like a dick?"

"Yeah, being pursued. There are four Patrols chasing him." If Simon's theory needed confirming, then the whoops of Gary's name from behind did just that.

"They'll kill him."

"If they catch him," caveated Simon. "He's coming back."

It took me a while to find him because of the jumbled backdrop, and I only spotted him when he was near and the sky was his only background. This time I cowered against Simon and watched with a mixture of awe and incredulity as Gary, to the delight of his audience, did three loops around the playing fields. And then he was off towards Central before the Patrols even passed over us. Machines don't get tired, that's a good thing about them, but the Patrols seemed to be flagging. Maybe it just seemed that way because they couldn't match the scooter's pace. They didn't need to.

Watching them I just about saw the explosion. It must have been near Park East. The Patrols, at least a kilometre behind, disbanded before any of the smoking arms from the centre of the explosion hit anything beneath.

"Crash?"

"Missile."

"Oof," I patted Simon, "what an idiot." Simon was looking out towards the crash site. "They're going to remember Gary's name for a while." I looked at the run track and saw that there were lumps on the bends. *Had they been there before?*

People were still shouting his name as we quickly made our way to the pallet. "Had a crazy dream last night." Something had made me remember my crazy dream. "I was stuck in it. It was like you, when you won't boot because of your bad sectors."

"That's horrible," agreed Simon. "It's like..." and then Simon did some acting. "It's like you're going to go," he extended all his pistons and grew bigger, one arm extended forward a bit, then he instantly went back to a slightly crouching position. "But you're..." he said, repeating this movement a few times until a group of students, heading somewhere with books, stopped and clapped in time with Simon's movements. A few, with whoops unused from the Gary incident, whooped. Simon pretended not to notice and spun around, then went backwards while his arms were moving like he was going forwards. More whoops.

That's right kids, overalls unzipped a bit or not, we're still cool.

"I might grow a moustache," I said as I pretended to check the pallet again. I'd forgotten I'd already checked it twice. Simon said he thought a moustache would be a tremendous addition to my face and we headed through security. It wasn't the guard who had got us on the track that time, it was the nice one, the one who never says a word.

"Do I smell?" I asked, while the guard held the scanner over my hand. The guard looked at me, so I nodded towards Simon.

"Yeah. Less than thirty percent."

I sniffed Simon. "You smell of cooked fish now."

"Is that better?"

"Oh yeah, much. Probably should have come here first though." That would have worked, just about, coming here first. We'd have had to double back a bit, but yeah, even though I was looking cool I didn't feel good about smelling in such a crowded environment. And if we'd have gone to the Fish Market second, then the chances were the handsome man wouldn't even have seen us, and even if he had there's no way that whole scenario would have played out the same way. With the sweets in the face. And the hat. Everything had come together at the wrong moment for that to happen. Well, it was done now.

I believe that. That every thing that every person does changes the outcome of absolutely everything. The kids clapping at Simon, outside. They had been held up and distracted for a few seconds. Their entire lives will now be different because of those few seconds, and then every person *they* interact with will have their life changed from what it would have been. Etcetera. I would have studied stuff like that if I'd gone to college. Interesting stuff. That or architecture.

The door buzzed and we were in.

Young people don't irritate me as much as all other people irritate me, but they still irritate me. Especially when they're a bit too happy. Stupid happy. Laughing and joking about anything. Tragic really. Naive is what they are, and you just want to shout at them and ask them what they're so happy about. Haven't they seen what's out there in the real world? What's in store for them? Or if they're not howling morons then they're too miserable. Too far the other way. Glum and gloomy. Depressing everybody with their morose faces. And what have they got to be miserable about? *Nada.* They don't know that their life right now is as good as it's ever going to get. Wait until they're me, you know? Then that's an excuse to be all miserable. They have nothing to worry about, and you just want to shout at them and tell them to wake up because, well, this is it! The ones in between annoy me too. Nondescript. Maybe I just like shouting at kids? Maybe. I could see myself as a teacher.

"Have you seen her yet?" I asked. The college contained a lot of young people who didn't move out of the way as we made our way along the corridor to the first machine, but I didn't shout at any.

"Don't be a..." managed Simon, before a miserable kid came over and stood right with us. Stood there next to us. Stood too close as Simon was unlocking the door. I ignored the weird kid, looked at Simon with one of my eyes bigger than the other, then hunkered down. I heard Simon say hello to him. I didn't hear his reply. I was ignoring him, the kid. Trying to. I tried but I couldn't, and when I couldn't not look at him any longer, I did.

"Yes?" I asked.

"Krench," he said, thrusting a hand downwards towards me. The hand was holding a token. I looked at the token and then at the open machine, and finally, back to the kid. That was my way of telling him that the token (I'd looked at) wouldn't go into the open machine (I'd looked at) and therefore the kid (I'd looked at) couldn't get a Krench. Not yet. It didn't work, he still had his hand out.

"You can't wait two minutes for us to finish?" I asked, and he dropped his hand but that was all. The kid just stood there. Didn't back up a single centimetre. I'm saying kid, but this guy was taller than me and had tufts of stubble all over his porky cheeks and round chin. I filled three rails before I could take no more of his presence. I handed him a Krench and took the token which was warm and very slightly sticky. He thanked me, which was nice.

Simon was looking at the artwork on the hall's walls as kids streamed past. That meant I had to keep my eye on the pallet as well as doing absolutely everything else. Thanks Simon! I didn't make a fuss. I didn't voice my displeasure, I just got on with my work. Quietly. Quickly. Efficiently, hoping Simon would continue to stand there gawping so that when I was ready, I could shout him over and he'd say sorry for holding me up. I was rushing. To finish. Before he turned back. So he'd feel bad. I failed. He sauntered back across the hall before I'd finished. "Don't worry about me. I think some kids stole a box of Big Bens." Nobody had stolen anything.

"The pictures are new," he said, but I ignored him because one of us had to do some work and I was filling the last two hoops. "They're new." He clasped his hand to the token box which fed the tokens into his compartment while his eyes fluttered, then he unclipped.

Before Simon came along, the worst part of the job was getting the token drawer out. It would always get jammed. It wouldn't slide back in smoothly. Yeah, those drawers had been a major source of frustration. I put the sticky token into the slot and typed A6. The Krench all advanced one place so that the front of the machine looked good and right. I closed the front and pulled it, and looked at how neat everything was behind the glass.

"Don't say anything," said Simon.

"I won't," I agreed. The pictures on the walls *were* new. You wouldn't think students could do them. I could see they were proper art. People see me and probably think *yeah, he looks cool, he's weathered but handsome, but he drives around with a robot all day filling up Vems, there's no way he could appreciate art,* but they're wrong and narrow-minded, about the art appreciation bit.

"Really, don't."

"You have my word," I told him. It was stupid anyway. I wasn't going to embarrass him in the canteen. It didn't even make sense, but the first time I'd said it everybody had laughed. I'd said it a few times since and people still chuckled, but I wouldn't say it today. It wasn't even that funny. It was stupid.

"Is that one good?" asked Simon, pointing out a picture as we went down the corridor.

I stopped in front of the painting. Kids passed me on either side. It was splodges of dark, earthy coloured paint. A few lines through it. "Hmmm," I said. I decided to go with my gut. That's the thing with art. Initial impression. How it hits you. "I don't *love* it," I said, "I can see what the artist was *trying* to say." I tilted my head. "Not sure they pulled it off." My favourite paintings and drawings are when they're photorealistic. They're my favourite. When they look exactly like photos but have been drawn by a human. I don't like the realistic ones that robots do. What's the point of that? Good art, to me, must have taken a very very long time to do. That's what makes it good. That's what I like to see in my art. Patience. The sense that the piece must've taken a fucking age to make. Even if it's rubbish, if it took ages then, you know, it's got *that* going for it. That's why I'm not so keen on the splodgy ones

"What do you think the artist was trying to say?" asked Simon. A good question.

"Well, what do *you* think?" I asked, flipping it around, and Simon looked at the painting and tilted his head the same way mine was tilted. A kid bumped into Simon and went spinning off laughing. He'd been pushed into Simon. The kids who pushed him also laughed. Simon said, "Hello," to the giggling cretins before turning back to the art.

"I'm getting..." said Simon as his fans kicked in, but that was okay. "I'm getting..." he said, and his fans were louder. Too loud, that wasn't fucking normal. No way. It sounded like he was going to take off.

"Stop!" I said, then held my breath, hoping the noise would subside. It took a few seconds before his fans began to spool down. I breathed again.

"I don't know," he said.

"The artist was trying to say they were in a hurry, didn't have time to do a proper painting and threw colours at a square. It's shit. There's nothing to get." I was angry at the painting and its artist for making Simon overheat. "Is that yours?" I asked the girl who I only now noticed was standing with us. She had a face bowl haircut, the one where the bowl is put over your face and the fringe is cut that way. I like the other bowl haircut better. The girl didn't respond. "Actually, I do quite like it now." I'd judged it prematurely. This painting had a lot to it, I now pretended to notice. I tilted my head the other way to how it had been tilted earlier. "I'm getting... space... space jungle and train tracks."

"Grief," said the girl.

"Oh yeah," I said, leaning into the picture a bit more. "Grief." I pointed at the picture. I was going to point out a certain part of it and comment, but it was just one big fucking mess. I withdrew my arm and rubbed my chin. "It's, erm, powerful." I'd been looking at this painting longer than I'd intended to look at it. I looked and nodded, then looked at the girl out of the corner of my eye, and then back to the picture. I looked all over it, from corner to corner, and I was thinking, *this painting is so bad it's making me feel grief for the death of proper pictures*. Maybe that's what she wanted. "I like it. Good for you," I said. The girl didn't thank me. Simon was still staring at it. "Do you want any sweets?" I asked, just for something to say. To end the awkwardness. "Free sweets? Me and him give out free sweets, don't tell anybody though," I said, looking at her and smiling.

"No."

"They're all safe."

"No."

"Well, if you change your mind, we've got a truck full of sweets outside. The, erm..." I pointed at the picture. "Yeah," I said while smiling at the girl one last time, then Simon and I went down the hall, around the corner and through the big doors. "What a horrid little goth," I said to Simon and the way he didn't react told me she was still there, on the other side of him. I stopped and pretended to do my shoes up. We went to the left, to the canteen. She didn't.

Most of the kids were still in classes. It was still pre-chaos and those taking art were working on how to do painstaking pictures, I hoped. We'd once been in at lunchtime and it was bedlam. I'd practically had a nervous breakdown. I'd been badly jostled, and a lot of confectionery had vanished when some kids distracted Simon by pretending to be interested in his capabilities. Never again at lunchtime. It was nearly lunchtime. We had less than half an hour. We really should have gone to the college first.

The machine in the canteen was double fronted. Simon's girlfriend was also here, but I'd promised him I wouldn't mention her. And I wouldn't.

"Don't!" whispered Simon, shaking his head ever so slightly when he saw me looking over at the chefs. One chef in particular.

"He's here to see his girlfriend!" I said, cocking a thumb at Simon. The woman behind the counter laughed while Simon shook his head at me, on the diagonal. "I had to say something, it'd be weird if I didn't," I whispered.

"Well, she's here if you want to get it *on* for ten minutes!" said the chef behind her counter. She pointed at the PPPP. The Portable Potato Processing Plant. I laughed a lot at her joke. Too much really.

"Hello!" said Simon, polite as ever but downbeat.

"Go on, Simon! Do it!" I said, patting his back and pushing him. He didn't move an atom. I looked at the woman and laughed more.

It had been sheer luck we were in the canteen when the PPPP was installed, a few months earlier. Or maybe a year ago.

Maybe longer. A crowd of canteen workers had gathered around it when its installation was complete. We'd just happened to be there and it seemed to be a big deal for the canteen, maybe for the whole institution.

"Insert potato!" it had said in a woman's voice, after it was switched on for the first time, and people had made impressed noises. And I'd said, even though I didn't know anybody and I was behind everybody, not even part of the crowd, and I'm surprised I did it, but I'd said – and this wasn't planned or anything, I just said it, spontaneously – I'd said, "Hey, Simon, you could put *your* potato in her!" and everybody had laughed, even though it made no sense! Simon didn't have any potatoes. It was just a joke. Still, we'd all laughed long and hard as Simon smiled politely and nodded. I'd patted him and shook my head and I'd noticed the chef laughing, and our eyes met for a moment and I'd given her a thumbs up. From that day forth it was a thing. Not a big thing. Just a thing that I said, or referenced, not every time. But often. Yeah, no, every time we were in the canteen and there was somebody to hear me.

That might make me a jerk in Simon's eyes, saying the joke even after he asked me not to, but to me it's just playing the cards I was dealt. One day it wouldn't be funny anymore and then I'd stop.

The PPPP needed a hoist and two lifters to move. Maybe it's called a PPP.

Simon opened the machine and my knees clicked as I hunkered down. I thought I could feel the woman's gaze warming my back and I restocked the machine with as much brio as possible. Simon was annoyed, I could tell by the way he'd dropped the pallet. But I also knew he'd get over it soon enough. Simon doesn't hold a grudge, that's another way he's better than me.

The double fronted machine looked doubly good when it was full.

"Hey Simon!" I said, squashing a box. You could hear how much effort it was for me, if you were close, because when I was squashing the box I made a noise in my throat. But you couldn't *see* how much effort it was, because I was putting as much effort into not showing any effort, as I was actually putting *in effort*. The boxes weren't messing around. They were well constructed. He hadn't responded. "Simon!"

He looked at me and I nearly didn't say it. But then I did. "Why don't you go and kiss her good-" I looked over at the PPPP, and then the counter. The woman wasn't behind the counter. I was disappointed.

"Why don't you go and see your dead wife?" asked Simon. I looked at him.

"Sheesh! It's just a joke," I said. It wasn't very funny if there was nobody else to hear it. I didn't look at him, even though I knew he was really looking at me.

"What?" I asked, sweeping boxes over to Simon with my foot. I'd squashed enough. He can squash them with no effort. It was a theoretical question which means it wasn't a real question and I was not expecting a reply.

"I asked you not to."

"Jeez, where's your sense of humour?"

"I don't have one," he replied.

"Come on," I said. The place was going to get overwhelmed soon and we needed to be out of there.

"Just be nice."

"I am nice. I'm a nice guy," I explained. "Come on."

"I don't think you get to bestow that title on yourself."

"What?" I looked around. I didn't want to have this conversation in public.

"You say you're a nice guy-"

"I am."

"But you can't just say you're something. That doesn't make it real."

"Okay, whatever," I said. It really wasn't the time to do this. What with lunch approaching. And I knew what I'd done wasn't totally cool. I knew that because I'm a nice guy. A complete jerk wouldn't even register what they'd done. "Stop being belligerent."

"You can't just say you're a..." Simon looked around the canteen. "A sauce bottle."

"I get it. I'm sorry. I took a risk. Come on," I said.

In the hallway we saw the bad guard, but working together we managed to avoid him. It was good the bad guard showed up. Without him the resentment might have simmered over and we'd probably have done the rest of the college in sulky silence. Maybe lunch too.

---

"Buenos dias!" said Simon again and I howled with laughter. Really proper out of control laughing. Squid attack laughing. I just couldn't believe it. How had I not known Simon had different voices? I couldn't even see the manual anymore and just crumpled it in my lap to not drop it. I couldn't see anything. I had to sit there, my hand over my eyes, shuddering with laughter.

When I was nearly under control he said it again and I was gone again. Without looking I knew he was smiling as we flew from the college to the towers. I really should have concentrated during the induction.

Tall guy. What was his name? Will? Bill? Balliam? Something like... Valium? You could shorten it. Malcolm! That was it, but he was known as Mal. I hope he called himself Mal and that we didn't all just decide to shorten his name because we're assholes. But yeah, Mal. He was a good guy. He ran the Hub back then. Back when Simon first arrived and because Mal had previously been a rep himself, he was far more human than those that came later. He understood us. That's what you need.

When he told us we were getting Pilots he did it correctly and apologetically. He knew that people didn't like change and he listened to our grumblings and even appeared to agree with them.

People were worried about the tracking. That's what they thought. They thought the robots were being brought in to keep track of us. Like we were children that needed to be kept track of. That's what annoyed people, and people didn't hide their feelings. I didn't, anyway. I grumbled more than anybody. I did most of the grumbling. A lot of the others weren't that bothered, really.

Yeah, looking back, travelling around the City on a shuttle doesn't sound great and it had its problems, but you got used to it. We were used to it, and at least you were independent. On your own out there. It was how we did it and it worked, so to suddenly find yourself being Piloted... the loss of autonomy. Loss of freedom. I hadn't been down with that *at all*, but Mal explained it was going to happen, it was progress and couldn't be stopped. He explained apologetically and that went a long way. He also said he knew about the tokens I stole. That wouldn't be an issue with the new Pilots and the sealed token boxes.

I could have taken a different job. Half of them did, but after all the grumbling I'd done I wanted to stick around, see how badly it turned out so I could go up to Mal and say, 'I told you this would happen.' And he'd say, 'Yeah, you were right, Michael, I'm sorry, I should have listened.' And I would have said, 'Ah, don't sweat it,' because Mal meant well. 'Listen to me next time, though, yeah?'

It was summer when they arrived. Seemed like the hottest week of the year and we'd had to go out in the morning and spend each afternoon in the horrible sweltering depot, listening to a guy with the world's most boring voice tell us how the things worked. Yeah, they were supposed to make things simpler and yet you needed a diploma to take one out. A week to learn, how's that simpler? I brought that up a lot during that week. To whoever was sitting next to me in the shadow of the pristine LD-950s. Us sat like school kids on fold-up chairs. And we had that horrible uniform that made us look like fucking idiots.

Some days there was nobody sitting next to me. I was always at the back, my legs stretched out in front of me and my arms crossed across my stomach. The others at the front, sat forward, taking notes. Losers. I tutted when there was nobody sitting next to me. When there was nobody who I could ask, 'Why do we have to do all of this if they're supposed to make things simpler?' I just tutted loudly.

The official answer is it's because they're nuclear powered. You needed to attend this induction to be certified to fly with one. You didn't need to be certified to travel on the shuttle.

That week the units had stood in a line, in front of the new trucks, like sentinels. Apart from the demo unit which the boring man would use for his demonstrations.

The boring man had told me off. To complete the image of us all being large hairy children. About halfway through the week I'd been moaning to Pete about what a waste of time it all was, and the boring man had asked if we were listening! I know. It was like being at school. Pete was a nice guy back then. He sat next to me and listened to me moan.

"So what was I saying? This is especially important," the guy had said to me, all condescending.

I glanced at Pete's notepad. "You were talking about the…" I twisted so that I could see Pete's writing. Lovely neat writing, if I remember correctly. "Emergency shut down," I said and winked at Pete. That was all Pete had written, even though the guy had waffled on for a while. He'd written it at the top of the page and underlined it. <u>Emergency Shut Down</u>. There was nothing beneath it. I couldn't blame Pete, I hadn't heard a word the man had said either, because I'd been going on about the waste of time it all was.

"Yes, well, I hope you wrote that all down," said the man. "Hopefully you'll never need it, but if you do, it could save your life."

"Will you be going over it again?" shouted Pete at the boring man.

"If we have time," the drone droned.

"So they're dangerous too!" I said to Pete and rolled my eyes. "It'll be in the manual," I told him. It would *all* be in the manual. I crossed my arms and stretched my legs out in front of me. The chairs couldn't have been less comfortable. Well, yeah, they could have been. They could have been lumpy. Or had spikes, but for normal chairs they were horrible to sit on and you couldn't even listen to the man's voice if you wanted to. It merged in with the other industrial sounds. It sounded like an air conditioner but didn't work like one and I'd sat there for a week, sweating in a damp T-shirt.

For five afternoons the man had spoken. Made units do things which he seemed to think were impressive. They could count tokens instantly. Wow! Amazing! He'd spoken about them like they were peak tech and engineering. Looking at them lined up they looked more like they were made from forklift truck parts. Made to look human with a rudimentary face. I wasn't impressed.

We weren't allocated a unit until the last afternoon. I guess it was Friday. We were to take them out. Solo!

"Get your unit!" the man had said with as much emotion as he could muster, it hadn't been much, and then he'd started clapping himself. "Tell it your name!" he shouted, still clapping himself. Mal had joined in the clapping and others did. I didn't. I sat there as the sound of clapping turned to that of scraping chairs, and people sheepishly approached the units like they were at a dance. *You can take any of them! They're all exactly the same! Why rush?* I'd thought. I didn't move. I sat with my arms crossed and my legs stretched out in front of me as I watched the others go over and make embarrassing introductions.

Mal pointed at me and then to the units. I stood and rubbed my forehead. Two hadn't been claimed. I looked at them both, then went over to the one that was nearest, because it was nearest.

"Michael," I said and I looked around, embarrassed that I was being forced to talk to a machine.

"Hello!"

The other robot, not this one, the other one which hadn't

been claimed was looking over. Smiling. Then it looked straight ahead. "Actually, I'm going with that one," I told the unit I'd introduced myself to. There was something about the first one I didn't like. I went over to the other unit. "Michael."

"Hello!"

"Yeah," I said. Then I stood near it, until our LD-950 was lowered.

"After you," I said and followed it in, shaking my head. "I didn't listen to any of that. I don't know how you work," I told it as I tried to work out the buckles of my harness. The as-of-yet unnamed robot pointed to the manual. The solid pristine manual wrapped in cellophane.

"You know what to do?" I asked. It powered up. I buckled in as best I could but one strap was baggy. The Pilot leant over and pulled the right strap. "Okay. Thanks. What's your name?" No response. "I have to give you a name?" You're supposed to be making things easier, and now I have to think up a name?" I exhaled a long *f* sound. *What's a name?* I thought. "Simon? That's a name, isn't it? You don't meet many Simons these days. Got a problem with Simon?"

"Hello!"

"You're Simon."

"Hello!"

And we'd taken our test flight which just to some predetermined coordinate. Out to the flags or somewhere. I don't remember. The whole flight had been undertaken in silence but by golly, Simon could fly.

That very same manual was now pretty fucked up. I'd stopped laughing. My throat hurt. Oh Jesus, voice twelve was called Antipodean Mature (F) in the manual.

"Voice twelve," I said and whined a bit. I twisted the manual in my hands like I was trying to rip it. Simon nodded. "Okay?" I asked.

Simon looked at me, then out the windscreen, then back to me. "G'day!" he said in a female Australian accent and we both laughed more than we'd ever laughed before. We laughed until we landed on the tower. "That's how you're talking from now on," I told him. "All this time you could have been a woman robot."

"Strewth!" he replied and no, I couldn't take any more of that.

"Voice two, confirm." I put his voice back to the default. "I wonder what else you can do?" I said, flicking through the book then putting it back in the glove box. There was nothing in it about cracked remembory cases.


"Sorry about before, in the school," I said. "I really don't know why I do things like that when people are around."

"I forgive you."

"I mean, you're a dick as well. You should be sorry. Give me the sandwich." I extended my arm and clicked my fingers at him.

"When am I a dick?"

"When you don't give me my sandwich." I clicked my fingers some more. My extended arm was getting tired.

"I threw it away," said Simon. I dropped my arm. It hit the platform quite hard. We were on the second-from-top service platform of Tower 3. Sat with our backs against the Lady. On the side of the tower sheltered from the wind. We were in the top ten highest things in the City at that moment. You weren't really supposed to go up there, but nobody had ever said anything.

"Why would you throw it away?"

"For a funny joke!" said Simon.

"Where did you throw it?"

Simon paused, turned to me and said, "In the sea?"

"No you didn't."

"I got you!" said Simon, launching my lunch to me. The foil wrapped burrito was very hot, and I juggled it then let it fall to the white plastic floor between my legs.

"Thought you didn't have a sense of humour?" I sat forward a bit, opened my knees while keeping my heels together, put the package down between my legs and carefully opened it so it would cool a bit. I had to lean back because of rising steam.

"Maybe you're just not funny?"

"Time is it?"

"Nearly one."

It was nearly one o'clock.

"How high are we here?"

"Seven hundred and twenty-three metres."

Even though we were seven hundred and twenty-three metres up, and on a deserted platform that encircled the towers, I still had a glance around. "I keep expecting to see him," I said, looking down at the steam rising from the tortilla. "You know, expect him to turn up, bandage on his head. All, *hello boys!*"

"I thought he was Gary," said Simon.

I nodded. "Be nice if it was confirmed. Be nice if somebody announced that he definitely *ain't* coming back."

"Maybe they will."

"How can they?"

Simon thought. "I don't know."

"They'd have to find him."

"Or a part of him."

"It would have to be a big bit."

"But we don't want that?"

"No."

"But also, we do."

"Yeah." I looked at Simon. He raised his eyebrows. I picked up the burrito. It was still too hot so I put it back down and shook my fingers for effect. "Your core unstable or something?"

"Have it cold next time if it's not good enough."

"It'll be alright in a minute. Clown."

"Old man."

I peeled the foil further open. "So, your remembory. Is it… do you remember everything?"

"I don't know."

"Think," I said. I picked up the burrito and moved some foil, then bit into the exposed tortilla. It was still too hot but I gulped air in as I chewed and didn't burn my mouth.

"How would I know?"

"You remember the time you ate a sweet?"

"Yeah."

"And the time Carlos put a glass on your head?"

"No."

"That didn't happen."

"Are you testing my remembory?"

"Yeah, you passed." Simon was following craft flying around the City using his eyes and small head movements. When one went out of view, he'd start following another one. "Julian said it was… but it'll… you know? Don't worry about it."

"Good?" he asked, without looking.

"Okay. Bit dry," I said, then I coughed, ejecting a small burst of tortilla crumb. My lower spine was a bit uncomfortable, pressed against the Lady. It crunched if I moved. I lowered my knees. My legs felt good stretched out. I forced my toes towards me and enjoyed the stretch as I ate more.

"Play pool tonight?"

"Nah, not tonight."

"Living life to the full!" he said quietly, still following trucks.

I wiped crumbs from my lap as I looked over the mess of the City. I took another bite of the food parcel, which had cooled to cardboard and was just a chore to eat. "Is that the prick from the Oasis?" I asked, pointing my burrito at the seagull. Crumbs fell out of the package, and seeing that made the bird dance excitedly on the edge of the platform. I glared at it. It watched me with its left eye. "What do you want to do tonight?" I asked. I expected us to then enter the infinite loop of him asking what I wanted to do, and me asking him what *he* wanted to do, and so on and so forth. That's how it generally goes, but he surprised me by saying something different.

"Something different."

"Something different?"

"Something different."

"What?"

"Something we don't normally do."

"Yeah, I know what *different* means. What do you want to do, the thing we don't normally do?"

"Anything."

"Oh, we'll do that then. Nice one. I'll get two tickets for anything. For something we don't normally do."

"It'll be good fun!" said Simon. He hadn't looked at me. He hadn't seen my face, so he was smiling. Then he realised I was staring at him and he stopped smiling. "What?"

"What is it *you* want to do?"

"Anything. I don't mind."

"Okay, I'll get two tickets..."

"Good," he replied, looking like he was about to smile, but then he read my face. "What?"

"I'm being sarcastic, about the tickets. How can you..."

"Oh."

"You can't just say you want to do something. You have to tell me *what* you want to do."

"You decide!"

"No, *you* decide." I balled up the foil and threw it at his head. It hit his head and, luckily, he caught it when it bounced next to him. You don't want to drop things from this height. "It's tiring."

"What is?"

"Me, always deciding what we're going to do."

"We don't usually do anything."

"That's because it's tiring, thinking of things. Thinking is tiring."

"Okay, I'll decide."

"Please do. Anything you want."

"Tonight..."

"Yeah?"

"We are..."

"Yeah?"

His fans came on. "Going to go..."

"Yeah? Where?"

"To..." his fans hummed.

"Where? It's not so easy, is it?" I was about to shut him down.

"The REP," he announced. His eyebrows raised and his mouth opened.

I looked away, shaking my head. "Nah, I hate the REP."

"You said I could decide. We're going to the REP!" I could

tell he was pulling that face again. Eyebrows raised. Mouth open.

"I know, I know, but I overestimated you and that's my fault. We're not going to the REP."

"Yeah we are, it'll be good!"

"It won't be."

"The Bounders are on this week."

"The Bounders?"

"Yeah."

"And how do you know?"

"I read about it."

"When?" I asked. I found it perplexing and unsettling whenever Simon knew a recent development which I didn't. I couldn't understand how it was possible for him to know something independently.

"I saw a poster."

"Well, we're not going. We'll go next week."

"Yeah, we're going tonight."

"No, we're really not." I turned to Simon and he did the face. Eyebrows raised and mouth hanging open in a dopey smile – the face he knew made me laugh. I laughed. "We're still not going, so..."

Urgh, just thinking about the Recreation and Entertainment Park made me anxious. Everything about the place was wrong. Everything. The smell of it was wrong. All the people who worked there were wrong. The machines there were wrong. It was *all* wrong. The floor was even wrong. We'd only been four or five times, and last time we witnessed the death of an elephant and I told Simon that was it for me, I wasn't going back. I understood it was just unlucky, an elephant could die at any time, but it's not like it was that event which forever clouded my opinion of the place. The elephant dying was probably my favourite bit. The whole place is just, urgh. It's just all fucking wrong.

"It will be fun."

"I'm not even joking but I'd rather go to an opera."

"Shall we go to an opera?"

"Nah, fuck that," I said. Simon closed his hand around the foil, then opened it and rolled a perfectly round aluminium ball bearing to me. I picked it up. He returned to watching the vehicles busily flying around. I watched the seagull some more. Rolling the ball between my fingertips. Daring it with my eyes to come and have a go.

We didn't talk for a while, we just sat there on the white plastic disc of a platform. I like that. I like that we don't have to talk all the time. I like that Simon doesn't feel compelled to chat. We're in a good place. I think I drifted off, or was just about to. I did one of those jumps like when you dream you're falling off something. "Back at it then," I said. It took me a while to fully stand up, the falling crumbs exciting the seagull. "Sea eagle."

"Seagull," said Simon.

"Yeah, but I wonder if they were supposed to be called sea eagles and somebody wrote it down wrong?"

"Seeeeeagle, seeagull. Maybe," said Simon.

"Seeagull," I said.

"Sea eagull."

We both took turns saying variations of that until we took off, leaving the seagull to feast. As we flew to the Stadium, I rolled the ball between my fingertips some more. It felt good.

The afternoon was largely drama free. At the hospital, as we were leaving, a group of people in gowns who seemed to be heavily sedated surrounded the Lady. Simon and I had a bit of a discussion from inside the gently swaying Lady about whether we should call somebody. I had the impression that the people were very slowly trying to escape. I guessed a door had been left unlocked or something. We didn't call anybody, I'm no snitch. Instead Simon took off really shuddery so none of them could hold on.

I didn't say it, but by mid-afternoon I was contemplating actually going to the REP. It wasn't totally off the table, but I didn't tell him that, so it'd be a surprise. A nice surprise. The other reason I didn't tell him was because there was as much chance that we wouldn't go. That we'd get back to the bunker and the thought of going out would be fucking abhorrent. That's how it usually goes. The nearer it gets to doing something, the less I want to do it. That goes for most things.

At Station 117 there were no Fatberry Bars. None. Fatberry Bars are new. They were only trialling them in stations. I went back to the Lady to check, but there were none. We called Pete, and Simon did that funny thing where he bleeps out Pete's swearing. So, yeah, anybody listening would have thought I was trying to talk to a fire alarm. From what I could make out from the garbled conversation, the Fatberrys had been discontinued a few days prior. When we were away. And we were to double up the Potzas! That explained why we had an extra box of Potzas! But it would have been nice to have been told before we left. "Cool!" I told Pete, and Simon bleeped for a good fifteen or twenty seconds solid before the communication ended.

On Tiler's Avenue the guy was there. The one who always comes out and talks to me about football. I know nothing about football but one day the guy had asked me if I liked football and, in the hope of ending the conversation there and then, I'd made the massive mistake of saying it was alright. Ever since, he'd thought I loved football and would seek me out to talk about it, while I had to think up replies that made it seem like I knew what I was talking about. That's the drop I dread the most, probably. The one with the friendly guy who thinks I'm interested in football. We got back to the depot close enough to five that we couldn't be sent back out. You get back at half four and there's a chance Pete will have an extra drop for you. You want to get back no earlier than twelve minutes to five, even if that means just sitting somewhere for half an hour. We'd done the job long enough to be able to judge it. We're damn good at what we do. Back in the bunker the idea of going to the REP was abhorrent. I told Simon we'd definitely go tomorrow.

# El Fin

It was seven months later. The end of November before Simon mentioned that the Bounders were at the REP again. We'd had the hottest summer since records reset, which had very quickly, over the course of a couple of weeks, turned into the coldest autumn. I put the squashed boxes in the box squasher, so they could get even more squashed, while Simon put the pallet on the pallet pile. Then he lifted the Lady into the stack while I joined the queue. Everybody was coming back. It was getting busy and there was a queue for the token deposit. The Pilots deposit the tokens and it flashes green and prints a ticket, which you take to Pete, and Pete looks at it, types the number into his terminal, then tells you to fuck off. It normally goes smoothly unless Shane's involved. You want to be ahead of Shane if you can, but I wasn't so fortunate.

Shane was a new dickhead. He replaced Carlos, who hadn't really been a dickhead to begin with. I hadn't seen much of Carlos since we got back from, you know, the time when we went away. I hadn't seen much of anybody. We hadn't left the bunker much, apart from working and eating. Carlos had knocked on our door one night and I'd nearly had a coronary, and then when he'd shouted my name I'd just ignored him. A couple of months ago Carlos was just gone and Shane arrived. Oh yeah, get this, Simon and I were banned from working at the college! They had tried to blame us for the damaged track or something, and some bullshit about trying to lure kids back to the truck. I never loved going there anyway so no biggie. Simon didn't mind either. I'd got my watch fixed too.

Today Shane was involved. His Pilot, after feeding in his tokens, was met not with a printed ticket but with a red light, and the queue groaned. A red light flashed on the token deposit machine and he started giving his Pilot abuse. Shane's a shit person. The machine printed a ticket, which Shane struggled to read before abusing his Pilot some more. I didn't want to get involved. Shane had fucked up. They'd need to go back to their truck and cross reference things. Find their fuck up. Find Shane's fuck up. Pilots don't make mistakes, but still Shane blamed his. Simon joined me. He watched them as they walked away. I tugged Simon's arm. We got a green light and a fuck off.

Simon hadn't mentioned the REP since lunchtime, and walking to the bunker I nearly told him that we'd go. It had been a good day and I was in a good mood. Nothing had gone too horribly wrong. I nearly told him, but as we walked down the hall I could hear something. I tensed my ears and didn't talk. There was a quiet clicking. I stopped walking and held out my arm to stop Simon.

"What's that?" I asked, cocking my head and holding my breath. There was a clicking coming from Simon. I looked at his face, in case he was doing it with his mouth. He wasn't. "What *is* that?" I asked. He just shook his head. Then I saw the side of his neck. "And what the fuck is that?"

"What?!" he asked, suddenly looking terrified, and he whirled around from the waist, his head turning the opposite way and his arms coming up to his neck where he waved them madly. He backed up and hit the wall, and the wall shook. Whoever was in that bunker got a fright. "Get it off me, get it off me!" he pleaded. I was ducking out of the way of his arms. One of those hit you and you'd know about it. Well, you wouldn't, actually, because you'd be dead.

"Calma!" I said, ducking again. "It's not a spider."

"Has it gone? Has it gone?!"

"It's not a fucking spider! It's... it's a light."

He stopped spinning but ran his hands over his neck as best he could. Then he flicked them towards the floor and vibrated. "There's no spider?"

I went over to his neck. "What's that light?"

"There's n-"

"No, shush." I listened and stared at him. There was a red light on his neck. Which lit with the clicks. The noise and the light stopped as I watched. "There was a light."

"A light?"

"Yeah, orange, or red. And clicks."

"I don't know," he replied, and I felt like he was lying. "There's no spider?"

"No!"

"Well don't point and say, 'What's that!'" His fans came on briefly. "In that scenario you're going to think, *a spider.*"

"There's no spider," I said, and then I pulled a horrified face and pointed to his shoulder.

"What?" he shouted.

"Nothing, nothing," I replied, before he could start spinning again and crash through the wall, and across a bunker, and out of that wall, before dropping a few hundred feet like an idiot. "Why are you even scared of them?"

"That's not funny. That's like me saying there's a... cactus on y-"

"I'm not scared of cactuses, I just don't like touching them. There was a light. A new one."

"Stopped now?"

"Yeah." We walked the rest of the way to the bunker. Simon was on edge. He kept trying to look at his shoulders and he was wiping himself. "There wasn't a spider." I was a bit on edge too. He'd given me a couple of frights over the last few months, and we'd stopped guessing distances because he was getting them wrong, but the last few weeks he'd been stable and I'd begun to relax.

As soon as we were in the bunker I hit him with the good news about the REP and the fact we were going.

"We'll see," he said.

"We are!"

"If we do, great."

I didn't blame him for his scepticism, but what he didn't know was that we were going out anyway, so, yeah, I'd take him to the REP. He deserved it. "Fuck, I've forgotten my... I have to go back to the Lady first, but we're going, so get ready," I said, going to the door.

"What?"

"Just something."

"But what, what have you forgotten?"

"I left my gloves," I said. My gloves were in my pocket. I didn't look down, I just hoped they weren't sticking out. He probably knew I had my gloves on me and I was lying, but it didn't really matter.

"We can get them on-"

"Just... mind your own business. Shut up. Get ready for going out. I'll be back in a minute."

"I am ready."

"Just... shut up then." I left the bunker and headed back to the hangar. In the hall I passed Shane. His fuck up must have been sorted. Our eyes met and I guess he was expecting me to say something. I didn't.

"What's your problem?" he shouted after me, after we'd passed. "Where's your friend?"

"Fuck off, Shane," I replied, quietly, so he couldn't hear me.


The stack was pretty much full. It was dark and bitter, which, incidentally, is the tagline on the Chocoal bars. I went up the ramps at the back. There's only a small gap between each truck, just for the wing mirrors really, and I could just squeeze through with the front and back of my big coat rubbing on Ladys as I stepped across the stack's frame. I was careful not to fall to my death as I opened the door. The door was stiff, and the hinges creaked in protest. *How long had it been doing that?* I didn't know.

You don't notice these things. My hood caught on something as I forced myself through the tiny gap, but it didn't rip and I twisted free. The interior of the Lady was a mess and I kicked aside some boxes. I leant on the dashboard and looked out at a delivery being delivered in the delivery bay. Pete was directing the pickers. You could see his breath. I sat in my chair, opened the glove box and found the tatty manual. I held it so the book was illuminated by the small bulb. It could have been Simon on the cover. I opened it to the index and found *Troubleshooting* and, without giving myself time to back out, I turned to that section. Blinking red light was one of the last entries. Not a good sign. *Fatal Error.* It's what I expected. *Shut Down Unit Immediately.* The light I'd seen was more orange than red, but there was no mention of an orange light.

The very last entry was entitled *Ducking and Covering.* I didn't read it. Things could be worse. I flicked through the dog-eared book and put it under the crap in the glove box. I looked down. It was just Pete. Walking around. Tidying up. It was nice up here. I felt like one of the screens in the security room. I was very tired, all of a sudden. I watched him for a while, trying not to drift off.

I stopped in the canteen and had a panini. It was okay. I sat on my own. A Table Clearing Unit ate most of my dinner.

"Did you get them?" asked Simon, unsure.

"Yeah." I pulled my gloves out of the pocket where they'd been all along, and threw them on the bed. I took my big coat off, then got my wash bag and had a quick shower. Simon raised his eyebrows when I came back. I got dressed then asked if he was ready.

"Ready for what?" he asked, playing it cool.

"Come on."

"Are we going?"

"You want to?"

"Yeah."

"Come on then! Before I change my mind."

I made him wear a scarf. I would have worn one too, so that he wouldn't look mental, but who has two scarves? We left the bunker.

"I knew it!" said Simon on the wrong platform, from his perspective.

"We just need to go somewhere first."

"Where?"

"Just... it'll take twenty minutes then it's straight to the REP."

"We're not going to the REP."

"We are."

"Yeah, *sure* we are."

An hour and three minutes later we were in Tower Robots. The man looked up from behind his counter as the bell above the door jangled. "Hi!" I said as I held the door for Simon.

"Can I help you?" he asked, and I was disappointed that he didn't recognise us. Yeah, true, it had been months, but I recognised him, so I was disappointed he didn't offer us the same courtesy.

"We got an eye from you… in the spring," I said, hoping that would trigger something. Otherwise, we'd have to start our whole relationship again.

He pointed over his shoulder to a sign that was on the wall behind him.

*No Refunds*

"No, the eye's great." I walked over to him, avoiding looking in any cabinets. I slapped my hands on his counter like I was trying to play bongo drums quietly. "I need a bloody new remembory now," I said. "For him. He's a money pit."

"Why?"

"Why? Because he's cost me nine pounds already."

"Yes, but why get a new remembory?"

"This one's... damaged." I put my hand on the back of Simon's arm, only for a moment, and then I went back to drumming. The man made a point of looking at my hands. I stopped drumming.

"And you want to replace it?" The man's mechanical eye focused. Maybe it focused. It turned with a whir.

"Yeah, if I can."

"Why?"

"Because... this one's damaged?" I was fairly sure I'd said that already.

"So you say," he said, proving I had already said it. "But *why* would you replace its remembory?" The man looked at Simon and his eye twisted again. "What exactly are you trying to achieve?" he asked.

"I'm trying to get this..." I looked at Simon. It was going badly. I had explained what I wanted perfectly well. The man badgering me suggested that what I was asking for was impossible. I was breathing through my nose as I tried to think of an even simpler way to put it. To put it in a way where the man would say, 'Oh that, yeah I can do that.' "I want this one to last for years," I said. I again touched Simon. "That's all."

"I don't think you understand how robots work," scoffed

the man.

"Well, I've worked with it for twenty years, so I've got some idea." I was happy with how I delivered that sentence. It was a good parry to his thrust.

"This is a remembory with a few motors attached to it. That's all it is, so why would you- "

"Because *I'm* attached to it. I want a new remembory put in this one and then I want the remembories from this one transferred over. Not necessarily in that order, but I want to end up with this one, but not broken. That's all. Should be simple for a man of your... of your..."

"And how would you do that? Transfer remembories?"

I laughed a little. "I was hoping you'd... you know?"

"I think you've been reading too much science fiction!" said the man.

"I haven't. I thought you could use a cable or something. Or radio waves, I don't know."

"It's not possible. You could possibly find a functioning remembory unit. Fit it to yours. But it would already contain data. I don't think you'd be able to tell the difference. These units were nothing special."

"Come on, mate, he's right here."

"I just mean there's nothing unique about this one compared to the thousands of others that were built. I'd just swap the whole thing, if I were you."

"That won't... I don't... I want a blank, you know? I guess, and then I want to transfer... I just want something to transfer him to. His remembory, anyway."

"Can't be done, I'm afraid."

"But you *do* understand what I'm asking? I'm not being

crazy, right?"

The man didn't say anything for a while. I hadn't expected the process of transferring Simon to be easy, not at all. But I thought it might be possible. In some form or other. "Do you even own it?" asked the man.

I looked at Simon and exhaled. "No," I replied, pulling the middle of my lower lip to a point. I let go of my lip. "Nope. But surely you could use radio waves to move it? Or something?" As I was saying that I mimed moving handfuls of me, from in front of my forehead, to his counter. I was just throwing it around really. "You can't do that?"

"There's nothing to transfer. What's on this will be the same as is on any Pilot from this batch. Do you understand?"

I thought about that. I didn't understand. "What do you mean?"

"It only stores location data," he said. I nodded at him while thinking. I began to drum my fingers on his countertop before I remembered he didn't like it. I started tapping my tongue against the roof of my mouth. It made a tutting sound which changed depending on how I shaped my mouth. "I'm sorry," said the man.

"Yeah, me too." Although that would have been the natural point to leave, I didn't. There was a solution that neither I nor the man had thought of yet. I was sure. The man began to drum his fingers on the countertop. I looked at Simon and then to the man. I pursed my lips and moved my small mouth across my face. From one side to the other then back again.

"Is there anything else?" asked the man.

"I'm thinking," I said, but I wasn't sure I was.

"Okay," sighed the man. "Just… there might be something," he said.

"Really?"

He didn't reply and came from behind his counter and locked the door, then marched back behind his counter and through the beaded curtains, which sounded like Simon shaking his arm when it's half full of tokens. I gave Simon a thumbs up. "We'll go soon," I said. "You're fine, by the way, this is, like, just in case," and the curtain shingled again. The man was carrying a tome. Is a tome a massive old book? If it is, then he was carrying one. It was open as he carried it.

"I can't guarantee this will work, but there *might* be something in here that could prolong the…" he said, laying it on the counter. He flicked back a few pages. I looked at the pages. It seemed to be written in some space language from the future. Shapes I'd never seen. Shapes I couldn't describe. "This book was written by the Engineers of Soul."

"Engineers of Soul? What, are they… magic spells?" I asked, appreciating how ridiculous that sounded.

"No."

"But you can *read* it?"

"Not this page, it's Korean. These units were built in Korea, did you know that?"

"I did not."

"I need to find the English." The man turned a chunk of pages, then another. "Here we are! English!" he triumphantly announced. I turned to Simon and smiled. He nodded. He looked bored. The man was really hunched over the book. He was rapidly dragging his finger down the page, then flicking it over and repeating it. The man's finger stopped but he remained close. And then he began to tap the page.

"Anything?" I asked, even though he'd clearly found something.

"Could be," said the man. I smiled at Simon again. He raised his eyebrows. "Now," said the man, standing straight, his palm pressed on the page. "This is the stuff they don't want you to know. I shouldn't have this book, I sourced it from a… well, let's just say I sourced it."

"I appreciate you doing this."

"This information isn't free, nor can I promise it will fix your unit."

"I have the wherewithal."

"Twenty pounds."

"*Twenty?*"

"If I told you how I came into possession of this book… you'd pay double, in a heartbeat."

"I wouldn't. I've only got thirty-eight pounds on me," I told him. I took my wallet out and, with eyebrows raised at Simon, I slapped twenty pounds down next to the book. The man took it and put it in his pocket in one squid-like move.

"According to the Engineers, your one hope is to…" the man found the line on the page. "Turn it off and on again."

"Turn it off and on again?"

The man was nodding as he stared at the page. I'm not sure what expression was on my face. "Turn it off and on again."

"Okay. I mean…"

"But wait! There's one more thing you can try."

"Oh yeah?"

"This may be something of a Hail Mary, but if turning it off and on again doesn't resolve the issue, then you should…" the man found his place on the page. "Yes, here, you should try waiting ten minutes. Before turning it back on."

"Okay. Is that it?"

"That's all there is about the computer."

"Are you going to give me that money back? Because that was all in the manual I've got, and-"

"No."

"You're not going to give me my money back?"

"No."

I nodded. I turned to Simon while nodding. I walked to the door nodding. The man unlocked the door. I shook my head for a bit but didn't say anything.

"God speed!" he said, and I nodded.

The Snake expelled its excited and goofy people at Station 17, but it was the shell-shocked faces of those waiting to board that told the real story of the REP.

Their faces were a grave warning, as easily understood as the sign that looks like a black propeller on a yellow background, which is stamped under Simon's serial number and means chemicals, I think. A warning that the REP was going to be, at best, a massive disappointment, and that's *at best*. It had the potential to be devastating. Things at the REP always seemed to be verging on complete fucking horror show.

Like the dead elephant on our last visit. People had whooped and laughed when the elephant kicked the big ball. They'd whooped harder when it fell to its front knees. There'd been cheers when it toppled onto its side. I'd cheered. Then jeers when the show was stopped, and finally tears when we were led out by crying clowns, wailing contortionists, and malfunctioning and overwhelmed stewards. Fucking hell. Grim, even if there are plenty more elephants where that one came from.

Yeah, it's a nightmare you can't easily escape by waking up, but still people went. We did! I guess it's like how people are sometimes drawn to abusers.

The REP is spread out over, what? A couple of square kilometres on the roof of District 17. And this is how mental the place is. The roof it's built on isn't, wasn't, nor ever has been level. It's a sloping roof. Not too steep, but who in their right mind would build a pleasure park on that?

Not that long ago it was a small thing. Low key. They held boxing or wrestling matches on a roof. Underground wrestling matches, but overground. It should have been underground. Deep underground, but instead, exposed to the air, it grew uncontrollably. It was like somebody drilled a big hole down through the Bizaare. Down through the lower levels. Right down to the ground, and then they kept going until they reached hell itself. And then, after this hole was complete, somebody threw in loads of explosives and ran away, covering their ears while chunks of anything and everything rained down. All manner of twisted man and twisted machine came blasting out of that hole, and it all splattered down at the REP. They put some coloured lights on the mess, where it landed, installed some huge speakers and hey *fucking* presto! It was done. Here it is! The REP.

Yeah, I'm not too fond of the REP. Simon loves it though so I didn't let my disdain show, even though they found a way of making it worse. It's not just bad enough that it's a noisy, smelly, dangerous and disheartening wonderland. Oh no, the REP's purveyors of misery came up with various methods of making it an incredibly *expensive* place to visit. You do well to leave with your shoes.

I had seventeen pounds in my wallet, Simon had nearly ten, and I would have happily put it all in the nearest bin and gone back to the bunker. But as I've said, Simon loves it, so I graciously put my feelings aside and we queued to get our hard-earned resources changed into Repcoins. I tried not to think about how many hours of work it had taken to earn those seventeen pounds that I was about to waste, because this was Simon's night, and I was determined to pretend to enjoy it. Because that's what friends do. That's what a decent person would do.

"Oh god, I fucking *hate* this place so much," I told him when we were twelve metres past the welcome sign. I just couldn't not say it. I really did try.

"You hate everything."

I looked at Simon's scarf and thought about having a look under it. I couldn't hear clicking. I couldn't hear much over the bass from hundreds of competing speakers. And I probably wouldn't have been able to see a small flashing light. Not with all the big flashing lights around us. And what could I do, anyway? If it was blinking? I left his scarf. "Look at that!" I pointed to three robots who were clearly once erectors, but who were now living their dream of being forced to be street dancers.

It's on the outskirts of the REP where the less established acts set up. Ones with begging buckets out, who just want to be seen. Some aren't even what you could describe as being acts. There were people just shouting on boxes. Brilliant. The fringe acts are generally shit, but the dancers had something about them. Sure, their movements were slow and limited, but, credit where it's due, they didn't let those limitations hold them back. And they weren't embarrassed. That goes a long way, for me. Doing something and not looking embarrassed about it.

"You could do that," I told him. He looked at me and smiled, and shook his head which was moving to the beat. I tried to start walking, holding his arm, but Simon didn't move and I was yanked. "We'll be here all night if you look at everything." He ignored me and waited for the song to end, while I bounced up and down, trying to generate some heat. I made sure I bounced out of time to the music, so nobody put a coin in my bucket. Upon completion of their routine the robots high-fived each other, which made a clanging sound. Simon went over, I thought just to get a closer look. I grabbed him and followed him. I was horrified when I saw he meant to put a coin in their bucket. "Woah!" I shouted.

"What?"

"Don't give all your money away." I held on to his arm. "We've just got here. Pace yourself."

"They were good."

"I know, but..." I looked at the dancers. They were being hosed down, and steaming and sizzling. One was looking at me, eyes narrowing as I spoke to Simon. I smiled and put a coin in their bucket. I got a raised hand in return. It was like a thumbs up, but erectors don't have thumbs. I nodded and pulled Simon away. "Nice one," I said when I was sure the dancers couldn't hear. "They're forced to do that, you know? It's basically slavery. Shouldn't be rewarded."

"Slaves shouldn't get paid?"

"Shut up."

"It looked like they were enjoying it."

"Well, they weren't. You'll have no money left for the Bounders." And just at that moment, really, just then, it really was a coincidence, at that very moment when I said the word 'Bounder', there was a pop in the distance and I saw one coming down. There were cheers.

"It doesn't matter if we run out of money," said Simon after we'd walked a bit deeper into the REP. It was busier, and the people and machines had formed into streams, the way walking people organically do, to get to where they were going next.

"Why's that then?" I was holding his arm, so we didn't get separated.

"I'll just..." Simon stopped. I let go of his arm, and turned to him and watched as he did some jerky dancing. It would have been weird if he'd ever done it in the bunker. I would not have liked it if he'd danced in the bunker. Too intimate. He'd never danced in the bunker, thank god. Out here, with all the people, him not giving a fuck, well, it was funny and I laughed out loud. Then he danced a bit more and it wasn't funny. He just did it for too long and I was a bit embarrassed for us both.

"Leave them wanting more, Simon," I said. "But yeah, in a few years I'll take you on tour," I said, pulling at him. Do you see what I did there? I said, 'in a few years'. I said that for myself as much as I said it for him. Years was optimistic, but if you say something it's probably more likely to happen. I'd have taken six months.

"I'd make a fortune!" he said, closing his eyes and doing some more. Only a little bit. Enough to impress people heading towards him and annoy people walking behind him. I'd have been annoyed too if a dancing robot was blocking my way. It was no place to dance.

"Okay, let's-"

"Robot Wars!" he nearly screamed, and we started moving again. I tried not to look at the Hammer which was over to our left.

Simon gets goofy at the REP, which is another reason why I dislike the place. I like calm. I like calm people.

I held his arm and followed him over to the Robot Wars arena. Arena! That glamorises it. It was a pit. The Robot Wars pit. Its edges are ramps and there are a few blocks in the middle which the robots can use to hide their fighters behind. The fights hadn't started so there wasn't even anything to look at. A large countdown timer was saying there were forty-two minutes until it began. Ages. And the first few fights aren't even that great, they're too one-sided. It's the last three or four when it all kicks off. That's when the best and most skillful robot controllers are left, and they can do crazy shit. Jumps and flips and dodges.

All we could see were the preparations. I tried to get Simon moving. He wasn't having it. He was taking everything in, and with the way the night ended I'm glad he did. He got something out of it.

The fighters were just people in motorised chairs holding padded poles. I'd always assumed they were diffabled people, but they were up and tinkering with stuff. I was surprised and yeah, a little disappointed.

Not long ago it would have been the robots down in the pit with humans driving them. Funny when you think about it. This makes much more sense. The best drivers driving and the fragile fighters fighting, not that it's real fighting. It is just a test of the driver's skill. The padded poles the fighters hold just register the amount of hits. It's not violent, but sometimes you detect a bit of an edge. Last time we were here one of the chairs had lost a wheel and the poor guy in it just got walloped for ten minutes straight. He couldn't turn and defend himself. The other fighter pulled up behind him and proceeded to unload as his chair was being moved left and right by his robot, so his swings had more power. We'd been at the back so Simon had lifted me up, but it had seemed to me like there was bad blood between the fighters. That was just a guess, based on the way the one getting hit was really twisting and thrashing, trying to get to the guy behind him. It had seemed like the one in front wanted to punch the guy behind him in his face with his fist. And that guy could have stopped hitting the stranded one, but he didn't. He hit him until his hits grew weak. The robot controllers had laughed through it all. They were cool with each other, even if their fighters weren't.

"We should do this," said Simon.

*Twenty!*

"Yeah, I'll just go and build a motorised chair with all my money. How much would a chair cost?"

Simon looked at me. If his fans were going, I couldn't hear them. "I don't know."

"Probably a lot," I said. One of the robot drivers passed on the other side of the netting, right near us. He didn't acknowledge us because he thought he was a big shot. I turned and looked up at the Hammer.

*Eighteen!*

*Seventeen!*

More of the crowd joined in the countdown. I turned back to the behind-the-scenes-goings-on-in-the-Robot-Wars-arena-pit. Drivers and fighters paused what they were doing. They were all looking up over us so I was just watching people watching the Hammer. I could hear the Hammer humming. Simon turned.

*Nine!*

*Eight!*

*Seven!*

I tapped Simon and pointed at the arena pit. "What... what would be our name?"

"Name?" asked Simon, turning to me. I pointed over at the drivers and fighters who were all looking up over our heads.

"Team name. What would be a good team name for us?" I knew he couldn't think of one. Even with his teraflops in order he wouldn't have been able to come up with a name. His teraflops were for driving, not thinking of names. I was just trying to ignore the countdown.

*One!*

I closed my eyes briefly and felt the rush of air and heard the crunch. I shouted over the cheers to get his attention. "Terror Flops would be an okay name."

"Flops?" he asked. His face pulling back.

"Yeah, maybe not," I agreed. Things behind the scenes in the Robot Wars arena grew animated again. And it was getting busier around us as fans arrived. Hardcore fans. People were pushing in and getting set up to stand there for the whole night, but there was still more than half an hour until it even began. Way too long and I needed to walk. My heart was thumping and it felt like the pounding music was adding extra beats.

I glanced over at the Hammer. The Divine Hammer™ isn't something that belongs in the REP. I'm not sure that it belongs anywhere. I'm really not sure that it should exist. But *if* it did belong anywhere, it should be somewhere serious, like a hospital, because *it's* serious. It's as serious as you can get.

Some people *want* to die. I get that and I've no problem with that, I don't know or care what other people have got going on. Who hasn't thought about suicide? It's the ultimate thing you can control, and what have we got control over these days? What aspect of our lives? And I'm not saying that like it's all bad. There's a lot of stuff I don't want control over. I don't mind being a worker. I really don't. Young me wouldn't have liked it, but he was an idiot. There's something okay about not having an ambition. The pressure's off.

So yeah, I can *sort* of get behind people having an option to give up. The option to be struck by The Divine Hammer. It's got its rules. It's got to be the most regulated thing at the REP. It might be the only regulated thing. You have to register at least a month beforehand, so it's not like you can just rock up and jump in, without giving it any thought. I think that's good and right. Things might get better and you might change your mind.

Sometimes things don't get better. Sometimes things *can't* get better. It's shit, but there you go, so I've no real problem with people choosing to get struck. It just shouldn't be at the REP and it definitely shouldn't be a game of chance.

If you've gone through all of that to get in it, then that should be it. You didn't bail out, you've said your goodbyes and put your shoes on the table. You're in it. In the compartment. The Divine Hammer is above you. You can look up and see it hanging there. Levitating. Humming. It's been up there for ages, hanging over you and the REP and then, finally, the countdown from twenty begins. It's too long, the countdown is. You've been ready for a long time and you don't need this last twenty count. They're longer than seconds. There's got to be three or five seconds between each number shouted, so you're stood there for almost a minute until finally, *finally* the polarity is reversed and The Divine Hammer drops. If you've gone through all of that then you'd want it at least to kill you.

But the Hammer might not hit you.

There's a chance the Hammer might miss you, and you're led out to applause and whistles, but you look embarrassed to be alive. If you walk in and out under your own steam you're led to a table and given back your belt and shoes. You might look back. Up at the front wall. The neon grid where it's showing red Xs on the compartments that got nailed. I don't know how that would feel.

You can bet on this. Audience participation. The ability to bet on the outcome. It's a lottery for those inside and out. There are sixteen compartments and the bottom of the dropping Hammer changes, supposedly at random, to hit a random number of boxes. Well, not boxes, but people.

Sometimes nobody gets out. This is from what I've seen and heard. I'm no big fan. I do know that once you're out you can't go back in. It's a one time deal. Why would you want to go back? You've been given a second chance!

There was a broadcast where they randomly followed somebody spared by The Divine Hammer. To see how his life turned out. And that person, a man of about my age, had embraced his second chance, but it was hard to know if that was just because the Hammer had made him somebody. He'd made a career just by being *that* guy, the one the Hammer chose to miss, and I wasn't even sure if there was a message to be learned. There'd been a spike in users while he was famous, even though he'd become quite evangelical about the sanctity of life. Then he was arrested for doing something horrible, but he was definitely doing okay for a while, and you had to wonder about the people the Hammer missed, the ones that hadn't been given fame. What had happened to them? Nothing good, I'd bet, but there was always a queue for the fucking fascinating thing.

The back of The Divine Hammer is a large tent.

I couldn't go in and have the chance of getting crushed if I wanted to because, if you consider my account at the Hub, then I have fewer assets to my name than when I was born. I had absolutamente nada when I was born and, half a century later, I've got slightly less. You can't go in if you've got a debt. But I wouldn't go in it anyway. I don't want to die. If people do then that's their business, I just don't think it should be at the REP. It's one of the five worst rides there and I kept away from it after we left the arena and headed in deeper.

"Are you hungry?" asked Simon.

"I ate."

"Did you?"

"Oh no, you weren't there," I said, detecting his concern.

"When?"

"Back at the... when I..."

"Without me?" asked Simon, pulling his face away from me once again. Staring. Offended.

"It was just a panini." I felt that was enough of an explanation. Just a panini. It wasn't. He was still looking at me. "What?"

"So this is it?"

"It?"

"You don't like me? You're eating on your own?"

"Oh yeah, that's it. I'm fucking sick of you," I said. He looked at me, squinting, and I fought my way in deeper, towards the Bounders. "How's your guessing game today?" I shouted. I knew the answer.

"My game is good," he said.

"You sure? Or is that a guess?"

"A guess."
"Yeah, well, let's see."

I'd spent seven coins before we got to the queue. Three of those on deep fried nonsense because it turned out I was still hungry. And I saw a missile, crashing satellite or a shooting star fly over the City. It had gone before I got Simon to look up.

The queue was huge but I could still just about see some of it if I stood on my tiptoes. I steadied myself on Simon. Balanced myself against him because standing on tiptoes on a sloping surface isn't that easy. "Do you want to get on my back?" he asked, noticing that I was leaning on him. I snorted and had a quick look around to make sure nobody had heard. Getting on his back would *not* be cool. Not in a crowd. I don't mind if he picks me up for a few seconds but I'm not a child. Anyway, he wasn't even asking me, he was just talking. The large orbs had his full attention. He had a better view than I did. I heard an amplified voice shout "Wobbly!" followed by a distorted laugh. I knew from experience it was the guy in the big hat.

The Bounders *do* belong at the REP. They're like the opposite of the Hammer. You bet on Bounders going up, not down, and they don't result in a splattered death. They are a scam, of course, because, you know, because of the REP, but it wasn't obvious how. And you *could* win. We'd won before by betting on a Bounder.

The Bounders. Five big spheres on springy legs. Each ball was as big as a Lady. A Lady is maybe a controversial thing to compare them to, being as they are spherical, rather than cubey, but they're about that size. Volume wise they take up about the same amount of universe. Maybe they don't. Determining the volume of shapes isn't my strong point. They probably have wildly different volumes. It doesn't even matter. The Bounders are noticeably big for things that run around and shoot up into the sky, is my point.

They're funny when they run. Comical. I do like them. Simon loves them and I like them. Not 'visit the REP just to see them' like, but if they're there, which they are a few times a year, and I'm there, then I'm not going to miss them.

"Ready to lose all your coins?" I asked as we moved towards the entrance.

"Blue," he replied and I got up on my tiptoes again. Walking on them this time, again using Simon to balance. For a moment I walked like that, but it was hard work and my calves burned so I lowered my heels. I couldn't see the blue one. I could see the tops of the red one and the black one. The crowd stopped moving and I tried not to blink. I could feel the Bounders shaking the floor and then the green metal ball went pop and flew up with a whistle. It lit up when it was airborne to make it easier to tell that it was green against light-polluted sky, and that Simon was wrong.

"Getting all the wrong answers out of your system?" I asked. "Good plan!" The crowd moved forward after each bound because a person through the gate, at a terminal, would have lost their last coin and would be forced by the tall thin men to shuffle out. Trudge to the station. The realisation of what they'd wasted crashing down on them like a...

We didn't get through the gate before Simon got the next twelve wrong, then one right and another one wrong. We funneled through and were at a terminal. And then it mattered. The terminals were spread out and it was nice to have some room after the queue. We were on stepped platforms so we had a good view of the game, not that seeing it really helped. The view and the extra room weren't worth all the coins it was going to cost us, but they did improve the experience. We were going to get poor with breathing space.

"Happy?" I asked Simon as the five massive balls on springy legs all ran around on the leveled platform. He was smiling. I fed a token into the terminal. They all stopped running around at the same instant and their springy legs compressed. Soon they began to shake. Tremble. Not all at the same time, but pretty much at the same time. Some shook more than others, but I knew not to be fooled. That's to distract you. Sow doubts in your brain. When they were all shaking, the round coloured buttons on the terminal lit up and we had to make our guess. Once the button was hit it was locked in, you couldn't change your mind because the buttons stopped working. We didn't have long.

"What do you think?" I asked. "Green?" Simon was staring out. "Green?" There was no advantage in waiting to the last moment, none that I could see. "Green? Simon! Green?"

If you put a coin in and for some reason didn't press the button before the Bounder bounded, then that coin was gone. It didn't go over to the next jump.

The man with the big, tall hat walked around his small stage laughing into his microphone as the Bounders shook. We didn't have long. The man stopped laughing, bent his knees and theatrically pointed at the balls and shouted, "*Wobbledy wobbly!*" into his microphone, and then he laughed like it was funny and it was the first time he'd ever said it. I'd heard him shout it twenty times already that night, and each time he'd laughed. He was creepy. Not as creepy as the slow-moving tall men with the long limbs who ejected people who didn't put a token in, but still creepy.

The Bounders shook more. "Green!" I said. Simon didn't reply. He was staring, like it would make a difference. He was taking too long and so I pressed the round green button. I couldn't really help myself. I slapped it. I didn't want to just lose a coin. The other buttons went dark and Simon went less rigid, looked at me and shook his head. He was right to be disappointed because the white one popped. Some unseen catch released within it, setting free the captive tension in the springs that were its legs, sending it whistling, soaring, illuminated, into the night sky, while the man with the mic squealed with delight. They go high. I don't know how high. Seven or eight Ladys high. It landed gracefully as people at a terminal behind us whooped. "Were you going to say white?" I asked, and the Bounders ran around. At the same time, the man on his small platform was pacing, repeating what he'd just done. Crouching, shouting variations of the word 'wobble'. Laughing. Walking to the edge of his platform, turning and walking to a different edge. Sometimes diagonally. Wearing a hat. A big hat, and sometimes walking corner to corner. And tall men were languidly dragging somebody away as that person clung on to a terminal, and Simon was talking to me but there was a bloom of kaleidoscopic shapes in the corner of my right eye. I tried to blink it away but it was spreading. Slowly spreading across my field of vision, and I held on to the terminal with both hands and tried to breathe. I was really blowing my breaths out. Short and sharp breaths. My cheeks fully expanded.

I wanted to tell Simon that it was my coin. He didn't have to worry, he hadn't lost anything. That's what I tried to say but different words came out. "Yellow... the..." I managed. I couldn't see anything but black and white zigzags. I couldn't talk. The wrong words were coming out. "Yellow." I could hear ringing and my heart, the music, Simon talking, and the man shouting 'wobbly!' I tried to breathe slowly. I tried to take deeper breaths but I could only do the same sharp bursts. I thought about trying to talk again. "Ye…" I was having a heart attack. Or a stroke. Or both. I hit Simon with my elbow. He said something I didn't hear and I hit at him again, and Simon put his arm across my back and under my armpit and we started walking. My feet and lower legs were filled with pins and needles that were spreading and he was holding me up.

"There's something... doesn't feel right," I said, rubbing the back of my head. That was where it didn't feel right. There was pressure there, all over the back of my head. I was still struggling to talk. I seemed to have to really think about what I was going to say, and then hope it came out right. Normally you think of what you want to say and you start talking and it's there, automatic. It was like... I had to do too much thinking to make words come out. Something was wrong.

"Eighty-seven percent probability panic attack," said the soothing voice. I rubbed the back of my head. "This is only an opinion," added a different voice from the same speaker.

"It doesn't..." I rubbed the back of my head more, to show the sensors where the problem was. You don't have a panic attack in the back of your head. It didn't feel right and the diagnosis didn't sound right. The pressure in the back of my head was most likely blood, leaking from my brain.

"Brain tumour," I said, carefully.

"Four percent probability brain tumour." And then, the other voice, "This is only an opinion."

"So there's a ch-"

"Do you require treatment?" asked the Medibox. "Prices are correct at seventeen hundred hours today," said the other voice. I looked at the price on the screen.

"Do you think I ne-" The screen went blank and the light came on. I fished in my pockets. All of my pockets, and I have six, just on my trousers. I had more trouser pockets than tokens. I rubbed the back of my head some more and gnashed my teeth. My head muscles were all wrong. I stood in the booth until the doors opened automatically. Simon was outside.

He nodded to me. I stepped out without acknowledging the woman with the large belly who barged past me. The booth shut and Simon and I were in a frigid moonlit square, the grey checker plate floor shining slightly. "What did it say?"

"Nothing," I said.

"Nothing?"

"It doesn't know for sure." I was very cold. I lifted the scarf which was around Simon's neck. Any red lights and I would have gently replaced it, but there were none, so I pulled it off completely, in a way which would have killed a human. Decapitated them. Because it got tighter as I pulled, and I then had to really pull the last bit to get it off him, before putting it around my neck. "Sorry about the Bounders." I shivered a bit.

"It's okay."

"We'll go next..."

"Yeah, don't worry, it's fine," said Simon. "Let's go home."

He was saying that because he knew I wanted to say it. I wanted to go home but I didn't want to say it, I'd ruined the night enough. It was better he said it. "Yeah, I don't..." I rubbed the back of my head slowly and winced. It didn't hurt.

"Come on."

I felt better in the quiet of the bunker. I'd begun to feel better before we were fully out of the REP. Maybe the Medibox was right. It could have been some kind of anxiety thing, I suppose. I hoped it was, that's better than a brain problem. But four percent, you know? I still suspected something serious and that was making me anxious. A vicious circle, if ever there was one. The thought of dying was making me anxious and the anxiety made me think I was dying. Thinking that you're dying isn't much better than knowing that you're dying.

My pillow seemed to press hard on the back of my head so I lifted my head, pulled the pillow out and dropped it on the floor. "Lights," I said, and Simon turned off the lights. "Are you okay?" I asked.

"Yeah. Are you?"

"Yeah."

"Goodnight, Michael."

"Goodnight, Simon," I said, and lay staring at the ceiling. It had been a bad day.

I opened my eyes and stared at the ceiling. The morning lights were on. I rolled the back of my head around on the mattress before opening my eyes. I still felt something. "Good morning, Michael."

I rolled my head over. Simon was next to my bed, then immediately turned and went over to where he normally sleeps, over by the sink. "Go away," I said, but he'd already gone. I got up on my elbows and rolled my head around some more. My neck sounded quite noisy. Crunchy and clicky and I didn't know if it always did that, or if it was a new symptom of my imminent death. "Did you stand there all night?"

"Yeah."

"That's crazy." I gnashed my teeth a bit then wiggled my lower jaw, then screwed my face up, transferred my weight onto my right elbow and scratched my left side with my left hand because it was itchy. Then I went back to leaning on two elbows. I looked over at Simon. "Turn around." He spun a three-sixty. "No, let me see..." I leant the other way then tapped the right side of my neck with my right hand.

"It's not on," he said, turning so I could see.

"Probably a loose connection." I didn't believe that at all, but it could have been, why not? "You know how we used to fix things like you?"

"Things like me?" he asked, pointing to himself, pretending to be offended.

"Yeah, things like you, if they didn't work, we'd just twat them."

"Barbaric."

"Good times," I agreed. I yawned with my chin pressed into my collarbone. "And it worked. Hitting you would reconnect the solder, if it had cracked." I tried to think of a time when I'd hit something electronic and fixed it, as I looked around for my pillow. I lay back down and tensed all my muscles as much as I dared.

I hadn't been sleeping well for months. It wasn't that I couldn't sleep, I just didn't want to. It was like I didn't want tomorrow to happen because I wanted today to last longer. If we went to work and got back to the bunker without any major disasters then I began to relax and it took until at least midnight to fully relax. Well, mostly relax. And then I didn't want to waste that by going to sleep and it suddenly being the next day where there was the potential of something really bad happening. I must have felt it unlikely that something was going to happen in the middle of the night, but then I had started sleeping in my clothes some time in the summer. Shoes as well. Just in case something happened and we had to get out. I wouldn't say I felt particularly anxious, though, and if I'd had the tokens to explain that to the Medibox then maybe it would have upped that four percent, because the back of my head didn't feel right. I got up and went over to the mirror. I couldn't look at both of my eyes at the same time, I discovered, and so I turned to Simon.

"Look into my eyes," I said.

"You going to propose?"

"Are they the same size? Is one bulging?" I opened my eyes wide and pointed my face at him. "That's a symptom. A bulging eye."

"They look the same," he said, and I turned back to the mirror and tried to look at both of my eyes at the same time again. I couldn't and so I rubbed the back of my head.

"Let's tidy up a bit," I said, still rubbing, and we tidied up the bunker a bit. I folded a few things. Simon tidied the table. Just cleaning up junk off the tabletop makes a big difference. That's where we get maximum results for minimum effort.


The canteen was noisy and I had toast and black bean butter. Before eating toast I cut it in half, on the diagonal, making two triangles of toast. I've always done it this way and couldn't explain to Simon why. He'd wondered why I didn't cut it in half across the middle and make oblongs. It had taken me a while to realise he was saying oblongs. That day, years ago, when we spoke about the shapes I was making out of toast, was probably the only time he has ever said the word 'oblongs'. He didn't comment on the shape of my toast today. We were past that.

I sat back and ate my toast, looking around the canteen at the tables full of the same thing as yesterday. The same loud people being loud. The same angry people looking angry. Maybe I enjoy the fact that with triangular toast each bite is different. The pointy ends have more crust, less spread. The middle has less crust and more spread. It spices things up a bit when days are all the same. Not that I'd complain about the routine. That's how I like it. Yesterday wasn't a great day but I'd take it again, given the choice. I knew how yesterday ended. Today, even though things looked the same, had the air of finally being tomorrow, the day I'd been so keen to avoid.


I could have told you the correct order in which people would leave the canteen. Up until we leave, that is. After we leave, I don't know what goes on. I looked around. Three guys who I knew would leave first made their way around the busy TCU. I looked at Simon. I didn't say anything. I was still a bit worried about speaking in case the words didn't come out. I finished the triangle of toast and then held the cold edge of the table. Pinched it, kind of. My fingers on top of the table and my thumb underneath. I let my hand hang there, then felt tingling. Like the onset of more pins and needles, so I let go of the table and clenched and unclenched my hand a few times. I touched the table again and there were vibrations. I was sure it was the table and not me. I looked at Simon and was glad to see that he was sensing something too. "Collapse?" I asked, and it came out fine because I hadn't had to think about it. Simon was still sensing. There was a rumble too.

I think I know all the noises that the Hub makes, and it makes a lot of noises. Mostly clangs. Clangs that you feel more than hear, when one of the support beams in the depot gets hit. Those beams run up through the entire building so when one gets hit, everybody knows about it.

It was unusual for this floor to rumble. That's why I thought of a collapse. When the vibrations got stronger and the rumbling grew so loud that the others in the canteen noticed, I was sure it was a collapse. Simon was looking at me. I didn't remember the procedure for collapses.

Run for it? But to where? If it was going to go, then it was going to go.

I swallowed the toast in my mouth and I stood up calmly. We were going to walk out calmly. Try to. Get to the yard, if we could, and take it from there. There was no point running. If we were going to make it out, then we were going to make it out. Maybe the canteen wouldn't collapse and the yard and the rest of it would, then we'd look stupid and crushed for running out there.

Most people had hurried from the canteen, giving the TCU room to clear the tables. The TCU couldn't sense danger. We were halfway across the canteen when people hurried back in, causing a bit of a melee in the doorway.

"What's happening?" I asked. Nobody responded. More people came back in. They weren't panicking but they weren't sauntering either. They came in, some with a hand on the back of the person ahead, not pushing them, but keeping them moving. They came in and moved to the side, keeping the doorway clear.

It wasn't a collapse.

There was a machine in the hall. A very loud machine. The front of it came through the canteen doors and the crowd around the door moved further inside the canteen. It was a scooter. I could see its nose and handlebars. It was massive and black. I could see the left hand of the person holding the controls. The bike made a roar and centimetred further in.

I looked at Simon, he was looking at me. We didn't say anything. We looked back to the door. The bike roared but didn't progress. It seemed to be jammed. It was too big to turn into the canteen from the hallway outside. The hand I could see came off the bars and the fingers on that hand clicked and pointed to people, then to the front of the bike. People went and started pulling the nose across. Some went out and, I guess, had to climb over the bike, to manhandle it from the other side. Twist it. The rider's hand was back on the left control.

I'm saying 'the rider' but it was Jeff. It was obviously Jeff. I hadn't seen his face but it was Jeff. People were now offering intellectual support as well as physical. Directing the bike and its pushers and pullers. It went on for some time and Simon and I didn't move. Eventually there was a crunching sound as the bottom of the door frame gave way. A peg or something had been stuck and when that was released the scooter was able to enter the canteen further. Still its nose had to be pulled and its tail had to be pushed. Jeff's right hand appeared and pushed on the door frame, but it was the efforts of those pulling the front of the machine which made the difference.

It was free and with a twist of the right control the bike roared, and with small controlled thrusts it was in. Jeff's face, red from effort and stress, was protruding from the front of his black helmet. The machine, the biggest scooter I'd ever seen, was now in the canteen. Simon and I were still still. Jeff held a finger up to me, a 'wait there' finger, and then, looking down and all around, he began to manoeuvre the bike, using its engine and his feet, around the canteen's tables. It was never going to happen. The tables screeched as they were wrenched from their fixings and pushed across the metal floor. A TCU, seeing its escape route disappearing because of tables being pushed together, reversed, spun, then went around the edge of the canteen four times faster than I've ever seen a TCU move. Turns out they can sense danger. Jeff was heading for us now, forcing tables apart. His scooter looked like it had every possible fairing and accessory bolted onto it. It must have cost a fortune. I liked that it had a combustion engine.

With a bit more scraping and revving, Jeff was finally next to us. "Boo!" he panted. He was out of breath.

"Nice entrance," I said.

Jeff turned, clicked his fingers at the people around the door, then waved his finger at the door. They got the message and left. He watched them go, then he turned back to us and started to pull his helmet up. It was tight. Its padding pulled at his ears, folding his earlobes up before they lazily snapped back into place when his helmet was high enough, and then it was totally off. I would have considered the idea that the removal of the helmet had removed Jeff's hair, had he not immediately rubbed his head with his hand which wasn't holding the helmet. He just rubbed his head. He didn't rub his head and go, "Ah! Where's my hair?!" before checking inside the helmet. He just rubbed the top of his head and seemed to enjoy the feeling. Then he placed his helmet on the scooter, between his legs. I had to resist the temptation to rub the back of my head. Us both rubbing our heads at nearly the same time would have been weird.

"You didn't expect to see me!"

"We did actually."

"No," he said, shaking his head, "you didn't."

"We really did, we've been talking about it every day."

"The look on your face!" he said and chuckled. His leather suit creaked horribly when he chuckled and leant back. It creaked with each movement he made. I didn't feel like my face had changed from showing no real emotion. I looked at Simon who looked at my face then shook his head slightly. Jeff was shaking his head.

"We're just disappointed, really," I said. Jeff laughed at this.

"You're a very bad liar," he said.

"I know." I held his gaze.

"Well," said Jeff, looking around the canteen, but he didn't immediately add to that. Instead, he lowered the zip on his black leather jacket and I felt the heat on my face as it escaped from his developed upper torso. He must've been really sweaty. "I'm surprised," he said.

"Okay," I said, and I could see his frustration that I hadn't asked him to explain.

"I'm surprised you're still going." He was talking to Simon. "I got you good. But look at you, up and about!" he said, waving a finger. "Nice eye."

"We're doing okay," I agreed. Jeff huffed a small laugh from his nose then nodded, turning his head away, then tilting it and looking at me through the corners of his eyes. Then he rolled his head forward again.

"I'm going to finish you this time," he said. Simon's eyes

darted sheepishly from side to side.

"You probably thought that last time," I said. "How did that work out?"

"Notice anything different about me?" he asked. He rubbed the top of his head again, and then slapped the side of his scooter. It made a hollow, plastic sound. I expected it to be metal.

"You're bald?"

"That's true."

"You've got no eyebrows and you look like a giant baby?"

"Anything else?"

"You're in a gang now? A bald baby biker gang?"

"A gang! That's good!" He held his fist sideways in front of his mouth for a moment. "No, as you can see I'm bigger, stronger and more aggressive now. Unstoppable. I should thank you." He turned to me. "That's what getting hit by an incredibly powerful beam will do to you."

"You're welcome."

"I've got a tattoo too." Jeff put his right hand around his left wrist and casually tried to pull his sleeve up. It was immediately obvious he was going to fail. He did look buff and his arms were big, but you can't pull up a leather sleeve. He pulled it up about six centimetres until it was jammed, and then he pushed it down again and smoothed it while the leather creaked and cracked. "It's a skull," he said. "With flames."

"Well, we're aggressive too, that's what having a dickhead pull yo-"

Jeff pressed the starter on his handlebars. His ride gurgled back into life. And then he revved it. He sat there in the canteen twisting the control on his handlebars, staring at Simon and me, while his machine gurgled and then screamed. He released the brake for a moment, sending the bike lurching forward, until he was level with Simon. He stood on pegs and leant forward and stared at Simon as he revved the engine. I took Simon's arm and pulled him and we made for the door, through altered gaps between tables.

The engine dropped to an idle. "You can't run!" shouted Jeff.

"We don't *fucking* run," I said. Jeff again revved his bike to what sounded like its maximum revolution. I heard more tables squeal and strain as he tried to turn. We didn't turn.

"Hey! Anybody out there? I'm stuck!" he shouted as we exited the canteen. There were people out there, in the hall. They'd probably been listening. They seemed to recoil from us. They twisted so they stayed facing us as we passed. I looked straight ahead and heard Jeff whistle. Sounded like one of those cool whistles you do with your fingers in your mouth. I can't do those kinds of whistles.

When the corridor was clear I tapped Simon's arm. "Fucking run!" I said, in a slightly warbly voice, and we ran along the corridor. My steps produced a dampened metallic reverb. We ran past the lift and all the way to the ramp. Going down the ramp I saw that the new units were out of their crates. They did look amazing. Revolutionary. Jeff had been right about that.

"The fuck are you doing?" shouted Pete as Simon started to bring the Lady down. He was chlunking towards us. I held my hands up. He stopped. "The fuck are you doing?" he shouted, seeing one of the new units standing in the stack's exit bay. "Out the fucking way!" shouted Pete. The new unit looked around, then pointed to itself as Pete waved his massive arms at it. It looked up in time to see the descending Lady. As it jumped into the air it somehow folded itself into a ball. It hit the floor and rolled with an electronic sounding whizz, before popping upright.

"When would that *ever* be useful?" I asked Simon, but he was concentrating. The Lady was down. Pete was asking other units what the fuck they were doing before remembering us. He'd lost control of the depot. He started towards us as we ran to the Lady. I pushed Simon inside first and saw Pete had turned back to his shed. I broke the rule about getting in the Lady while it was in the hangar.

As Simon spun the Lady, the massive hangar doors began to close with a rusted *reeee*. The doors weren't used to closing, and they moved noisily in protest. We had a chance, but that chance was getting smaller with every second we spent in the hangar. Simon lifted up over the mayhem on the depot floor. He spun until he was facing the narrowing band of light. Above us, to my right, a window exploded.

"Go! Go!" I shouted. The doors were closing really slowly, much slower than I'd thought, and we could have got four Ladys out, side by side. Yeah, that wasn't even close, but the building on the far side of the yard was getting closer. The building that we were heading towards at over one hundred miles per hour. I grunted as Simon climbed vertically over the yard. We'd never climbed like that before, pointing upwards. I wondered why. It seemed like something we'd have tried when we were bored. "Hngggh," I said, as crap from the dashboard hit me. The glove box held, luckily, or I'd have had a face full of manuals.

*Into the blue*, I thought, but Simon slowly levelled out and the City reappeared from the bottom of the windscreen.

"Don't slow down," I told him. "Go straight."

"Where?"

"Just straight."

We were heading towards Central. Off any sort of stream, but if it was dangerous for us then it was dangerous for anybody following. I checked my wing mirror. "You see him?" I asked, trying to look in his mirror. Simon lowered his head and looked in his mirror, then shook his lowered head. "Don't slow down!" I urged, and Simon somehow managed to extract more speed from the Lady.

"Hold on!" shouted Simon, and I looked around but couldn't see what he was trying to avoid because he threw the Lady into a twisted dive. I was pushed back into the chair and gripped the armrest as we headed down towards a roof. "Missiles," said Simon, and I was nearly thrown out of my harness and onto him as he evaded a small tower. We were no more than two metres off somewhere where they stored massive reels of cables, but before I could worry about crashing into anything we were going straight up again.

"Hggnnn," I said. "Raise..." I said, but my chest, empty of air, couldn't provide my vocal cords with what they needed to finish that. "Hggnngh," I said, and then I took the deepest breath I could and blurted, "raise your accuracy to one hundred and fifty percent and pretzel it!" I whined, as if it was one word.

"One hundred and fifty and what?" asked Simon. I couldn't repeat it. I wouldn't have replied if I could because he hadn't immediately understood the command. He hadn't immediately understood what I was asking. You *can* explain things to Simon, and if it's true he'll *eventually* understand, but it takes time and effort and you have to weigh that up. You have to really consider whether it's actually worth it. If it actually matters. Unlike myself, Simon will not be satisfied until he fully understands something. Not me. Explain something to me a few times and if

I still don't understand I'll just pretend that I do, by saying, 'Oh yeah, I see!' When I said about the pretzel, what I meant was I wanted him to fly around all twirly, so the missiles would sort of tie themselves in knots and crash into each other, and blow up as we flew through the last explosion unscathed, and their trail would look like a pretzel.

We were dropping down again and I couldn't even keep my head anywhere I wanted it to be. The G-force had a tight grip and was just twisting it this way and that as debris hit it from all angles. I was a doll. There was a flash just outside my window and I tried to cover that side of my face, but by the time I'd raised my hand we were flying down a street we barely fit through. Below us, people jumped into doorways and behind other people. There were twangs as we snapped through wires and ropes.

I thought that if we crashed now, at least we'd be remembered. Immortalised. People would remember the day they saw us tear through the City, the same way the kids at the college would remember the name of that guy, the one from April. Kevin? The one who hadn't been as proficient at missing missiles as we were. And then we burst out of the end of the street and we could see the Boulevard, and Simon climbed. Not quite vertically this time.

We flew straight.

"Where is he?" I asked in the sudden calm.

Simon checked both mirrors and shook his head. "No patrols either," said Simon.

"He's probably got his bike jammed somewhere. What was that even about?" Simon shook his head again. "How is he not smarter than that?"

"I don't know."

"Well, you're doing amazing. You're even better than I thought you were, and I thought you were great."

"Thanks. I was just jiggling the controls, to be honest. It was pure luck we didn't get hit or crash."

"It's because I bumped up your accuracy."

"That's not real."

"What?"

"I told you that you could alter my accuracy, so you'd play pool. I just let you win."

"Oh."

"Yeah, I just didn't try." He patted my leg before checking his mirror. "You're shit at pool."

"Whatever it was, it worked."

"So far."

"Yeah, so far," I agreed. "Can't believe you lied to me. You've gone rogue, huh?" I said and he laughed a burst of static. "You're a bit more human now."

"Is that a good thing?"

"It probably is. It's probably why those missiles missed us. They were aiming at something digital, but you were flying all analogue and they couldn't deal with it." Simon didn't humour me with a reply. Things had settled right down. "I prefer it when we can see him."

"Yeah."

"He's not scary at all when he's there."

"He's a little bit scary."

"Yeah, a little bit, only because he's mental. I'd still prefer to be able to see him." We were over all other traffic now. We should have easily been able to see if we were being followed. It didn't look like we were.

"Michael?"

"Yes Simon?" I looked at him. He checked his mirror then looked at me.

"So, am I going to die?"

I inhaled through my nose and looked at the glove box. "I don't know." It seemed quite likely. I think he knew. But the truth was I didn't know, not for sure.

I looked down from my window. I could see to the edges of the City. I could see the streams and HiWays that overlaid it. The City looked like a scab. "Bit high, aren't we?" We were still going up.

"Shall I descend?"

"I don't know," I said. It seemed safer up here. But we didn't normally fly this high. Why was that? I felt I knew the answer. It was on the tip of my top... the... top of my... the tip... "Is oxygen... here?" I slurred.

"Oxywhat?"

---

What's it called when you go all rigid and solid after you die? Rigger something? I did that. What they don't tell you about going all solid and dead is that, as well as being cold, it also really hurts. I could feel pain and cold in the blackness.

I could slide my feet backwards and forwards. I still had human form. I was extremely disappointed with Simon, he'd just gone up. This was avoidable. This was *easily* avoidable.

Being dead was one thing, but actually feeling the cold and

pain that came with it? Nobody had mentioned that was a possibility. Talk about from bad to worse. No wonder dead people are angry and scary. It was super-shit. Mega-shit, but it was what I expected. No tunnel with a delightful meadow and a warm breeze. Or even a station with dance classes. This was death.

My eyes were non-functioning, just colder when open and my eyelids fluttered. My feet were pain. My hands were difficult to move. I couldn't move my toes, not even a little bit. I opened my eyes, had to flutter my eyelids for a while, but I couldn't keep them open. It made no difference, everything was black. There's no way a dead person could run after you. If you're chased by a dead person just relax. Walk slowly away from them.

I could keep my eyes open for longer than a second. And soon after that I could blink, just about normally. I still couldn't see, but I was in my chair. And I could see the edge of the windscreen. There was definitely a straight black edge. Beyond it was black. Or was it, because I'd lost the black border which I'd thought was the edge of the Lady's windscreen. It was all black again. I turned to where the side window should be and I was sure there were differences to the blackness. I was sure there were geometric shapes of crushing black against just solid black. We'd just kept going up.

I knew what had happened.

"We're in space," I croaked.

"Where are we?" asked Simon's voice quietly. I looked around and saw nothing, so I fumbled for where the glove box should be. It was still there and my cold, solid fists gently punched around for the catch that held it shut. I had no dexterity but knocked the catch with the back of my forefinger and the door to the glove box fell open. The bulb inside produced enough light to illuminate my legs and part of Simon. "Where did you say we are?" whispered Simon.

"Where are we?" I whispered back. "Where's the light?"

"Did you say we were in space?"

"No."

"Space, where the moon lives?" he asked. I could see he was pointing up, through the windscreen. I couldn't see what he was pointing at because his partial reflection was the only thing I could see when looking at the windscreen with the glove box light on. His partial reflection and most of mine. "Did you think we were up there?" he whispered and then he did a quiet burst of static.

"Where are we?"

"I don't know, shush," he whispered.

"Why?"

"He's in the back."

"Who is?" Like I needed to ask. "Jeff's in the back?" I twisted in my seat.

"Yeah, shush. Keep your voice down."

"I don't like it when you whisper. It's creepy."

"Well..."

"I didn't know you *could* whisper."

"Did you *really* think we were on the moon? The *moon?*"

"Where are we?"

"You were asleep."

"I'll get brain damage eventually. You'll see, if you keep doing it. You can't keep doing it." That was probably what was wrong with me. It wasn't anxiety, it was brain damage. Simon had damaged my brain with the near-death experiences. "Why are the lights off?" I whispered.

"Why would they be on?" he whispered.

"Put them on then." Simon flicked the switch on the dashboard and the interior light came on, which made my eyelids flutter again. I closed the glove box with my knee. The light lit only what it lit. Our cab with us in it. We could have been in space, or purgatory, or down a big hole. Wherever we were in time and space, we were the only things illuminated. This was how small our world was now. "And put the heaters on. And my chair. I'm frozen." Simon flicked three switches and the fans in the dashboard whirred into life. They weren't much louder than Simon's. It took them a couple of minutes to heat and produce the stream of warm air you'd want to hit your face if you were walking towards the light.

It was a bit longer before I felt the heat from the chair on my bum and the back of my legs. Not long after that my chair felt too hot, even though my hands and feet were only slowly thawing. I don't like heated chairs.

Simon leant sideways, towards me. "So he's in the back," said Simon. I was staring straight ahead. We were having this conversation in the reflection of the windscreen. I didn't reply immediately. I was still trying to process that information and defrost at the same time. Simon moved himself back so he was fully upright.

I leant over towards him. "What? How do you know? Did you see him?" I was leaning at quite an angle. I had to put my left elbow down past the armrest so I could lean far enough over. "Simon!" I whisper-shouted. I could tell he thought the leaning was a prerequisite of talking, that it was a new rule we'd just established. It wasn't.

"I heard him."

"Heard him?" I asked, and with the help of my right fist on my left armrest I pushed myself upright. I turned to Simon.

"There was a noise from the back. It sounded like something fell over. A thud."

"Well, that could be anything, considering how you were flying. Like a dick."

"You said I was good."

"But something could have fallen over."

"There's nothing heavy in there."

"Part of the floor or something. We were upside down. That's probably it."

"We didn't go upside down. An LD-950 can't go upside down."

"Near enough. It'll be that," I said, but I was still whispering.

"Okay, but if you let me finish."

"Go on, but it was a panel or something. Dislodged."

"I heard a noise and, when you were asleep-"

"Unconscious!"

"*Quiet.*"

"Sorry."

"Are you going to let me fi-"

"Yeah sorry."

"It's rude to talk ov-"

"Yeah yeah, go on then. Hurry up."

Simon leant over slightly. "I heard the noise. You were oxygen starved." I nodded. I was staring at the glove box mainly. He sat upright. "I got out."

"Okay, you got out," I said. I was listening intently and nodding, and trying to picture what he was telling me because I needed to pick holes in his story, because how could Jeff be in the back?

"And the floor was weird."

"Weird?"

"Very weird. Not solid. Like a thick cloud."

"Okay, I'm getting bored of this now."

"You'll see. It took me a while to get down the ramp. It was wrong. I went down the ramp."

"You've said that. Look, my hands and feet are really hurting now."

"Why?"

"Because they're warming up. It makes them hurt even more. But you are making my soul hurt with your painful telling of this story. The ground was weird? What does that even mean?"

"Look." Simon flicked the headlight switch and a large circle of fallen snow, with us faintly superimposed on it, appeared on the windscreen. At the edge of the headlights' reach were the trunks of trees. He flicked the switch and it was just us.

"That's snow." I looked at the puddles in Simon's footwell. "You know what snow is."

"I know snow. But walking on snow? I had to believe there was solid ground under the snow. I went down into the snow, but it didn't seem to have an end, so I came back up."

"Have you been practising this story?"

"Yeah, a little bit."

"Does it go on for much longer?"

"No, listen, so I told myself to go down a bit further each time. I could only go so far and then I'd come back up," said Simon. I exhaled through my nose. "The seventh time down the ramp I went deeper into the snow and I found solid ground."

"Okay."

"The snow is, on average, sixty centimetres deep."

"I don't care."

"I went to the back of the truck, very carefully."

"Okay."

"And when I lifted my hand, to open the lock." Simon had stopped talking and after a few seconds, when it was apparent this wasn't just a pause, I stopped nodding along.

"Why have you stopped talking?"

"This is how *you* explain things. You stop explaining and wait for me to say something before you continue explaining. I was doing that."

"Yeah, I don't think I *do* do that."

"You do."

"Well... okay, you lifted your arm, and what?"

"I heard a laugh."

"A laugh?"

"A laugh."

"A laugh?"

"Well, somebody trying *not* to laugh. Trying to laugh *silently*, to be precise."

"You heard that?"

"Yes!" he whisper-shouted.

"You sure?"

"Every time I put my hand to the lock, somebody inside would giggle. But it sounded like they were trying *not* to giggle."

"Not to giggle?"

"It sounded like you do, when you try to stop yourself giggling."

"I..." I said, shaking my head, "I mean, I don't giggle." I was rubbing my chin with my left hand.

"Sometimes you giggle, and you try to stop yourself."

"I don't, Simon. I don't know why you're saying this."

"You do! You go 'tee-hee-hee', sometimes. If you've said something you think is funny."

"I do a manly, deep laugh. I bellow out laughs."

"Okay."

"But the laugh was from inside?" I asked with a nod.

"Yes."

"And it's Jeff?" I asked with another nod.

"*Yes.*"

"Definitely?"

"Yeah," said Simon, and his fans came on for a moment. "Ninety-nine percent."

"And where are we?"

"I don't have any idea where we are." His fans stopped.

"You flew here though?"

"We're north. Very very north."

"That's handy to know."

"Well, we're not on the moon, Michael, I know that!"

"Shush." I held my hand out and lifted it up and down slightly. My fingers were still basically fused together. "*You're* getting a bit loud there."

"We went over mountains. Big mountains."

"You would think he could break out, if he wanted to," I whispered. "If you can survive a Burrower, you would think you could break out of an LD-950."

"Well he hasn't."

"Are you sure?"

"Yeah."

"When was this? When *exactly* did you hear him?"

"Sixty-seven minutes ago."

"Sixty-seven?"

"No. Sixty-eight."

"Sixty-eight," I said, thinking.

"Sixty-eight and three seconds."

"Stop now. You haven't heard him since?"

"No."

"Maybe he's already broken out?" Suddenly the light in the cab didn't offer comfort. I could imagine what we looked like to anybody outside. "Turn the light off."

"The doors haven't opened. The light would come on," he said, tapping the dash before flicking the switch which turned the interior light off and drowned us in darkness. "And I would hear it."

"You didn't fucking..." I said, then realised I was getting loud. I took it down a few notches. "You didn't hear him getting in, did you, big ears? You didn't see the light then."

"There was a lot going on."

I scanned the total darkness until I could make out the edges of the windscreen again. Then I saw something where I knew the trees were. A glint. A red eye watching us. "You see that?" I asked. I heard Simon move forward, closer to the windscreen, and I saw the red light move. I turned to Simon and saw the red light on his neck. "Fuck," I said, and closed my eyes and held them shut.

"Sorry."

"Make it go off. It doesn't matter anymore."

"I can't."

"Fuck," I said. "Put the lights on. The cab lights." Simon did as I'd asked. I got up and limped over to the shelves on the wall at the back of the cab. The wall which was less than ten centimetres thick and maybe the only thing separating us from Jeff. The light only just reached back to the shelves. It didn't reach into the shelves, but my hands did and they found nothing, because everything had fallen out, I remembered. I looked around on the floor then limped over to Simon. "Seen the tape?" I asked quietly. He looked around and then found it. Jammed in a recess at the bottom of his side window. He handed it to me. I unreeled a strip and held my hands out so he could cut it. I stuck the cut-off over the light. "There, good as new," I said, before sitting back down in my seat and placing the tape on the tray on top of the glove box. I took my gloves from my pocket and put them on. I still had only limited finger movement. "Maybe he's frozen?"

"His clothes are thick."

"Yeah," I agreed. "I wish I had a leather jacket." I've never owned a leather jacket. If I ever did, I'd get a brown one. I began playing with my lower lip then realised my gloves didn't smell so good. I dropped my hand. "He could still freeze, even with that jacket. Or starve. Or he might be injured?"

"He was laughing," said Simon.

"Oh yeah."

"We should keep him locked in?"

"I don't know. How could we get him out?"

"I don't know. Should we move?"

"I don't know," I said. "To where?"

"I don't know."

"He'd probably find us again."

"Yeah."

"It might take him ages, though." I was basically just thinking out loud. "We should get him out. And then fly off."

"The other way around would be better," said Simon. I didn't get it straight away. I thought he was saying *we* should get out and Jeff flies off. That would *not* be better. If I had fans, they would have come on as I was trying to work that out. I worked it out. What Simon meant, I realised, was that *we* fly off and get Jeff out, somehow, *as* we were flying. That made much more sense.

"Oh yeah, splat! That would be better."

"Splat!"

"We can't open the doors when we're flying, can we?" I asked.

"No."

"Didn't think so, that's why I phrased it like that."

"I like it," said Simon. "You were saying you knew the answer but threw it over to me anyway."

"Yeah. That way I couldn't be wrong."

"Nice," said Simon, and I smiled. I wasn't anxious. We had something solid to focus on. I was still cold, though.

"Maybe we'll just keep him in the back, eh? Just never open the doors? Weld them shut." That had started off as a joke, but by the time I got to the end... welding the doors shut. That wasn't so crazy, was it? I looked over to Simon. My eyes narrowed.

He shook his head. "I think getting him out and flying away is better."

"Yeah, I wasn't entirely serious, just thinking out loud." I pursed my lips, held my still cold, but thankfully now begloved, forefinger from my left hand under my bottom lip, and sucked in while opening and closing my mouth. My gloves didn't smell that bad. A bit chemically. I made a baby-bird sound. I did this for quite a while. "What's behind us?" I asked, and then made quieter, quacky-chirps.

Simon leant over towards me as far as he could. "Jeff is."

"I mean behind the Lady. When you landed. Is there anything?"

"Trees. Many trees. And snows. Many snows."

"Just snow."

"Many snow."

I leant over to Simon. Our heads touched. I rested my head on his. "What about if we got out, right? Walked past the back of the truck, making noises, and we walked to the trees. How far are the trees?"

"Approximately fifty metres."

"Okay, we walk into the trees..." I stopped talking so he'd say something, so I was sure he was listening.

"Okay."

"We walk to the trees, then I get on you, and you reverse, as quietly as you can."

"Okay."

"And then we get in here and you'd be ready to go, yeah?"

"Okay," said Simon, nodding very slightly. His nodding made my hair crunch. The hair that was between my skull and his head.

"We open the back. He goes, 'Ah-ha! Footprints!' and he jumps out and follows them and..." I did an upward chopping motion with my hand held sideways.

"Okay."

"That's it, we've flown away," I said. Simon's head nodding was making my hair crunch slowly. "That could work?"

"How would we open the back?"

"Oh yeah." That was a good question. *How could we open the back?* I sat up straight and scratched my right eyebrow. "How could we open the back door?" I asked. I leant the other way. My right elbow on the right armrest. The heel of my right hand on my right temple, and I drummed my gloved fingers on the top of my head. "I know!" I said, then grimaced and held my breath.

"He knows we're in here," said Simon.

"I know, but..." I resumed whispering. I didn't want him even hearing us. Not yet, anyway. My plan wasn't fully formed, but already it involved some degree of Jeff hearing us. But not yet. I leant over to Simon, my face pointed at his. "String or... or cable or... string. That's how we do it!" I nodded at him to show this was a good plan. "Tie something on to the handle, because we have to pull it up... Okay, we go out to the back, and we're chatting and shit, it doesn't matter if he hears, then we carry on out to the woods, and then I climb on you and we *reverse* back, get the string, throw it over the top and then we get in, get hold of the string out of the window somehow and you get ready to fly, I pull," I had to breathe in, "I pull the string and the back doors open and Jeff jumps out and follows the footprints out to the trees and," I had to breathe again, "and we fly off while he's standing there like a fucking *dummy*." Our faces were close to each other. I gently slapped the side of his face. "What do you think?"

"That could work."

"It could, right?" I said, sitting upright.

"We'd need to have some string."

"Or cable," I said, because he was selectively quoting me.

"Do we-"

"No."

"There are straps in the back."

"Oh yeah, wait there, I'll just go and get them."

"What about Jeff?!" asked Simon.

"I'm not really going. I don't understand how he got in. Must've been at the hangar, right?"

"Must have been."

"Hey, what about the new units!"

"I didn't really see them," said Simon.

"They're revolutionary, I mean, they are. One turned into a ball. I couldn't believe it."

"Oh yeah, did it?"

"They're like gymnasts."

"Oh, that's fascinating," said Simon, holding the control stick and waggling it around. The Lady wasn't powered up, so nothing happened.

"I mean, they're not as cool as you. They're stupid. Rolling up into a ball. What's the point of that?" I asked, my face screwed up slightly.

"I don't know."

"You could throw one about a hundred miles. They couldn't throw you."

"It's okay, I'm not offended."

"They're too small as well, they're like humans. Waste of money." I looked at Simon. He smiled. "A waste of money!" I meant to shout that because, honestly, fuck Jeff. But it came out a bit below my normal voice.

"If I don't make it back, you've got my permission to work with one."

"Ha! Thanks but… I'm a one robot guy."

"I'm serious."

"Fuck off, Simon." I exhaled through my nose. It made a whistling sound. "We need a better plan," I said, and by the time we came up with one we'd turned off the interior light and I could see the tree line.

"This *can* fail. This isn't one of those plans that can't fail. This one can," I stressed from behind a plume of my breath. I stood straight and shivered as I tried to shimmy the sleeves of my jacket down further. I'd taken my gloves off so they didn't get wet, and my hands were pink and raw.

"I get it," he said, leaning forward and picking up the ball of snow I'd rolled. Simon can't roll balls of snow. That was something new we'd just learned. But he could fucking throw them after he'd compressed them and sphericalised them, which he did with vibrating hands.

I pointed to the trees with a horizontally sweeping forefinger. My finger went right first and stopped before I swept my hand to the left. Simon clicked as his elbows retracted. "Wait for it!" I urged, quietly. "That one!" I pointed at one tree in particular. Simon instantly fired and there was a hollow crack before the tree swayed drunkenly and lost a lot of its white topping. Simon hadn't missed one practice shot and I held up my palm. Simon slapped it as best he could. My hands weren't nearly as cold as Simon's. If I'd licked his hand then my tongue would have got stuck, for sure. I had never even nearly licked Simon's hand before, not even accidentally, so I'm not sure why I thought about it. "You are a weapon."

"Thanks." His weight had compacted most of the snow around the door, but further out and towards the back of the Lady it was still as deep as he'd said it was. Sixty centimetres or whatever. It was up to my knees. I crunched my way out to the soft snow and began rolling *the* ball. When I finished, Simon picked it up. I kissed it, for luck. That was probably the closest I'd come to accidentally licking his hand.

Simon shaped it. I stared at him until he nodded, then I

made my way to the back of the Lady. I had to lift my knees high to move. Simon was off to the side. Out of sight of Jeff until he got out. He had a clear shot and a direct route back to the cab. I would follow the path he made.

Yeah, it was a solid plan, but it could still fail.

I lifted my hand and heard the giggle before I touched the handle. I didn't know what Simon was on about, I'd never laughed like that. I looked over at Simon. I gave him a thumbs up. He raised the ball slightly and then I heard his elbows click. I lifted the handle too quickly and it took another attempt to fully unlock it, and I stumbled backwards. I didn't fall in the deep snow. So that part of the plan worked.


There was a chiming. A ding-ding-ding dinging. I was breathing heavily. They were the only noises that remained, the dings from above and my breath being pushed out over my teeth and lips. All the noises in the world had been compressed into the previous few seconds, and now they'd gone and left the dinging and my breathing.

We weren't moving. We'd experienced all possible movement and now it was still.

My legs were buried in snow and there was chiming from above, and I was breathing, and that's because Simon had been slipping. Simon's tracks had slipped on the ramp, and my pushing and shouting hadn't made any difference. His tracks had just spun on the icy ramp and he went sideways more than up. Eventually he had got in and taken off and then something had happened and now the Lady was chiming.

The Lady didn't normally chime. That was new. So was the fact that my chair was on the ceiling. The dashboard was up there too, and not down here with me. The windscreen was up higher than usual, the part of it I could see. The part which hadn't smashed and let in all the snow. Yeah, there was a lot of snow in the Lady. That was new. The snow filled a quarter of the cab. We were upside down. The truck was. I looked around. I wanted to tell Simon that the Lady *did* go upside down, after all. It was a day of firsts. He'd get a kick out of that. My harness, hanging from my chair on the ceiling, told me what angle we were at, and that helped me to get my bearings. We were at a bit of an angle. Upside down but not flat. My side was higher. This side was lower and badly crushed, from what I could tell. It was hard to tell because there was a lot of snow. Simon wasn't at the upside-down controls so I began to pull my legs out of the snow. The snow that had come in through the smashed windscreen, but it wasn't just snow that was trapping my legs, I found. There was something solid, and I dug in the snow until I revealed Simon's arm and solved the mystery of his whereabouts. His arm was preventing me from bending my leg. It wasn't crushing me, but I couldn't bend it with his arm there, and I needed to bend my leg so that I could use my foot to propel myself up. He was basically trapping me. "Simon!" I said, and I dug around some more. I couldn't fully uncover him while I was in this position. I was trapped and it was too hard to twist. I had to get free first. "Simon."

I pressed my hands around on the floor, which was once the ceiling, and when I found a place that wasn't too jagged I pressed down and I dragged myself backwards, using my palms instead of my feet. I had to move my hands around again, until I could place them down somewhere they wouldn't be sliced open. I kept my leg straight and slid back, ignoring that my trousers were getting snagged, and I pulled and slid until I felt the wall against my back. My lower leg was still under Simon's arm and I had to roll onto my side and really pull my foot, but at first it wouldn't come out. My foot hit Simon's arm and I did panic, just for a moment, and I really gave my foot a yank. It came free and my shoe came off and I slid around on my back for a bit until I could roll onto my front and stand up.

"The trappings of success," I said out loud, because I'd successfully untrapped myself. "The untrappings of success." I knelt, and after feeling my way up his arm, I dug into the snow where his head should be. Where his head would be. Where his head was. I knew I had to be fast. He was still only water-resistant and I wasn't sure if snow constituted water. It would be water if it melted, I knew that, I'm not thick, but snow itself? And Simon was warmer than snow, so I knew I had to be quick. I was quick.

His head was there but I found the top of Simon's head where I'd expected to find his face and that was *no es bueno*. I dug the snow away from around his head. *Yeah, that's not right*, I thought. I had to stop and blow on my hands and cross my arms across me, so I could put a hand under each of my armpits. I didn't do it for long as it didn't really help. The underarms of the outside of my jacket weren't any warmer than any other part of the outside of my jacket.

I needed a bucket or something and I knelt there, again with my hands under my armpits, and, like I'd done many times before, I looked around the cab for an object we didn't have. "Simon!" I said again as I pulled the snow off his chest with the unbending hooves which were my hands. "Simon!" I shouted. "Simon!"

He twisted. Thank fuck. The arm that had been over my leg hit the floor, which was the ceiling, and pressed down. This forced his chest up and out of the snow a bit, and I pushed the snow from his arm so that it fell into the hole under him. I grabbed my shoe and put it next to me. "Just... can you push yourself up a bit?" I sat back on my heels. "Just push yourself up a bit," I said. He didn't move. I was about to start digging again when the snow covering his tracks began to bubble. "That's it!" I said, "Just a bit." I dug some snow away from where his tracks were, careful not to go too deep and get my hand torn off.

Simon lowered both of his arms, which made his shoulders scrape up against the upside-down back wall of the cab. His head, which was at ninety degrees to where it should be, shuddered and rattled. I didn't like that and I winced.

It was dark in the corner where Simon struggled, but it was clear that something had broken. His head was loose and at a right angle to his body. It seemed to be just his wiring that was holding it on. The metal had snapped. Maybe it had. I couldn't see exactly what was wrong. Something had let go but it's not like Simon had a spine. My neck gets bent like that and I'm wearing a collar for the rest of my life. If I could afford a collar, which I couldn't. Simon's arms and tracks still worked because wires can bend.

He was getting no traction from his tracks under the snow, they were just spinning like they had on the ramp, but I saw a small crater form over where his left arm wàs, and he was, very slowly, moving up the wall. If he got a bit further, well, a lot further, I'd be able to push his head back. Then, what? A couple of bolts? That would do for a temporary fix. The tape! Until I could get him... well, first things first. Get him out of the snow first.

He was still centimetring up the wall. Maybe he was. His

shoulders were grinding up then falling back maybe a centimetre at a time. He'd reached the limit of how far his arms could lift him and I tried to press snow under him. The front of his tracks were exposed and spinning without much purpose other than splattering me and the interior with wet snow. "That's it!" I said with my hands flat on my soaked thighs. I put my hands back under my arms. "Bit more!" He wasn't really moving any more. "Bit more!" He wasn't moving but I could hear his motors. "Up! Up! Up!" I said, encouragingly, but his tracks slowed and then, as I watched, they stopped. "Yeah, take a break," I said. "That was good, though," I said. "Nearly there." I leant forward and slapped his belly then shuffled closer to him, on my knees, ignoring, or not feeling, that it was quite jagged, until I could reach his head. I put a hand on each side, to see if I could move it. I couldn't. It wasn't totally loose. It was still jammed and it was heavy. I sat on my heels then I curled up and made myself as small as possible with my face peering up, so I could see the top of his eyes which were facing his shoulders. "You okay?" I asked. He didn't reply.

"Does he look okay?" I didn't turn around. I didn't need to. I put a hand on the side of Simon's drooping head and I thought it was a fist that hit me. Something hit me just behind the ear. It was hard and sharp, like a fist, but a lot of the snowball fell onto my shoulder. Jeff hadn't thrown it hard. He'd tossed it at me. "Does he look okay?" asked Jeff. I turned around. He was leaning down through the hole where the side window once was. The window that had once been near the bottom of the Lady was now near the top. My side window. He was leaning against the outside of the Lady, his head and one arm inside the cab. The arm that had thrown the snow at me dangling straight down as he watched us. I turned back to Simon. He didn't look okay.

"Simon!" I said.

"You've really messed up."

"Simon!" No response, but that wasn't surprising because there was so much snow in here.

"Is he talking?" asked Jeff.

The snow was a problem. That was the major problem facing us. There was too much snow. It had come into the truck, through the smashed windscreen, and was all piled in this corner. The Lady had slid upside down for a while, forcing snow in through the windscreen and leaving the cab blocked with the stuff. There shouldn't be *any* snow in the truck. I had to remove the snow. Once the snow was out of the way, *then* I could tackle the next problem, but first things first, snow, because Simon was still lying in a pile of snow. Not quite lying, no, he was up on his arms. But about seventy percent of him was still in the snow. Actually, first I needed to put my shoe on, I realised, and so I emptied it and then quickly put it on and carefully tied the lace. Then I could worry about the snow.

"Is he talking?" asked Jeff.

The solution to the snow problem was simple. I just had to remove the snow, and for that, because we didn't have a bucket, I'd need a shovel. Not an actual shovel, we didn't have a shovel either. I knew that and it was okay. A shovel *type* implement was all I needed, and what is a shovel type implement, when you really boil it down? It's simply a flat thing and a handle. A flat thing and a handle and I didn't even need the fucking handle! I just needed a fucking flat thing. With my shoe successfully on, I sat back on my heels and looked around. Something with which to scoop snow was what I needed, and if I thought about it calmly, I knew I'd have absolutely no issues finding something that fit that description in the fucking wreck of the Lady.

"Hello! Is he talking?" shouted Jeff. I looked up to the window. My left hand was on my left hip. I gestured around the broken interior of the Lady with my right. And then I looked at Jeff again. "You've really made a mess."

"Just why, Jeff? Why?"

"Why what?"

"Just… fucking why?"

"Why did I choose your Pilot?"

"Fuck off." I looked down at Simon and had to clamp my lips together with my teeth as I breathed through my nose.

"You saw the list. Randomly generated numbers."

"Well, great." I looked around for something flat. I could hear the chimes from the dashboard. They were annoying.

"Is he talking to you?"

"Shut up." I placed a hand on the back wall and slowly tried to get to my feet. I got part way up, but some twist of metal was holding my trousers at the knee so I forced my leg up. It was also in my skin but I didn't hear that rip, only my trousers. I made my way up the rumpled metal hill towards where Jeff was.

"Uh-oh, here he comes!" said Jeff, sounding amused, his arm still dangling down. After a few steps I reached up, and on the third attempt I managed to grab the buckle from my hanging harness. Holding the harness helped, and I managed to monkey my way a bit further and grabbed the other harness, then, well, then I was sort of just swinging there. Only the balls of my feet on the ground. "What's your plan now?" he asked. I pulled down on the harnesses with a grunt. I'd thought that would lift me up, but it didn't. I'd thought I'd be able to somehow grab my chair and somehow get to the glove box, but I couldn't. If I bent my legs, my feet came off the ground, but I was still just basically hanging there. The chiming sound was still coming from the dashboard. My plan had been to get to the glove box.

I could maybe, with a swing and a jump, grab Jeff's hand.

I let go of the straps because my arms were tired just from that. "Will you open the glove box?"

"Is there a gun in it?" said Jeff, not waiting for my reply and leaning further inside the Lady. From his position he could reach it, at a stretch. He pulled the upside-down latch and most of my junk fell out. "Are you going to throw that book at me?" he asked, interested.

"Can you pull it off?"

"The door?"

"Yeah." I tried not to let Jeff know how out of breath I was. Jeff repositioned himself outside in some way, then reached in with both hands and, on his second tug, he pulled the glove box door off. He was strong. I lifted my hand up, and Jeff lowered the door before jerking it back up and away from me. I lowered my arm. Just holding it up was hard work. "Come on," I said, raising my arm again. This time Jeff let the glove box door drop and it bounced off my outstretched hand. I picked it up from the bloodstained snow and threw it towards Simon before carefully turning on the crumpled metal hill and following it over to him.

Just as I knew it would, it turned out to be an *excellent* implement for removing snow from Simon. "You okay?" I asked.

"What did he say?" asked Jeff.

"He said, 'Tell Jeff to fuck off.'"

"Charming."

I'd worry about Simon's silence after I'd got the snow away. The glove box door was a particularly good idea of mine. I just needed to keep having particularly good ideas. I could get a decent amount of snow with each scoop. The problem was, as soon as I'd cleared some, more fell in through the windscreen, but it wasn't an insurmountable problem. I just had to keep at it.

"That's not really working," said Jeff through the side window. "It's falling back in."

"Yeah, thanks, I hadn't noticed."

"Are you blind? Big piles are falling in," he said. I stood up straight and watched as a small avalanche buried Simon's tracks again. "See!" The snow-packed windscreen told me there was much more to come. I looked down at my trousers. They were wet, torn and bloodied. My arms hung at my side. I nearly dropped the glove box door. I nearly gave up, but I didn't. Instead I took a deep breath and went over and did some crazy digging. If more fell in, I just threw it over to the other side of the Lady. More fell in. I threw it. It was tiring.

After that burst of activity I again stood straight with my arms dangling by my side. "What happened?" I asked.

"I tied the strap to the truck before I got out."

"Oh."

"Yeah."

"He hit you, though, with the snowball?"

"He did," Jeff agreed. "I went flying. Decent plan. Kudos." Jeff brought his other arm down in through the window and clapped.

"*Could* we have got away?"

Jeff seemed to properly think about this before coming up with an answer. "No." He crossed his arms along the sill of the window, which was really the top of the window, and rested his chin in the middle. He looked stupid. He didn't look evil.

"Could we have done anything?"

"Hey, listen. You got an extra six mont-"

"Seven months."

"Even better. You should be happy."

I laughed out of my nose. "You're a fucking prick."

"Did you make the most of the extra time you had?"

"Partied twenty-four seven."

"Good."

"You are mental."

"Yeah, and you're a saint!"

"I'm better than you."

"Are you?"

"Yeah, I am." Only later would I give his question a lot more thought.

"Even though you've done…" Jeff dangled his arm inside the window and waved it all around.

"Yeah, I did this. You didn't, it was me."

"You did! Did your Pilot want to do any of this?" Jeff's face was lit by light bouncing off from the snow. That light originally came in through the part of the windscreen not blocked. It looked like a nice day outside, from the little I could see. "Hey, can I get in?"

"I'd rather you didn't. I hope you understand."

Jeff chuckled. "Okay, that's fair enough. Keep blaming me. I'll just wait out here, in the cold."

"Do you need to be invited in or something?"

"No. I've just got manners. I thought you might be ready. It's a bit cruel. I could take care of it now if you want."

"You're fucking insane." I shook my head and looked away. I was bored of talking to Jeff.

"You've got to wonder how much of that damage happened just because he was trying not to crush you," he said, and I looked at Simon and again my face nearly crumpled. "How did you survive?"

"That's just..."

"Selfish. That's what you are."

"I'm selfish?" I asked, placing splayed fingers on my chest and nodding. That pissed me off. I might be many things but I'm not selfish.

"You're *so* selfish. Did your Pilot really want to do all this?"

"Yes! He did, actually."

"Really? It's not just you? You dangling false hope? Trying to eke out a few more days? Because without your Pilot for company *you're* alone?"

"Go away, Jeff."

"So let me in, I'll sit with him. I'll sort it. It can drag on, this last bit, and it doesn't really benefit anybody, apart from selfish people."

"Well, I guess I am selfish then!"

"You're thinking he's going to get better," said Jeff. Said, not asked.

"He might."

"He won't."

"Let's see."

"He won't."

"If he does, we're going to kill you. You understand? And if he doesn't, I'm going to kill you."

"I go with him."

"What?"

"I go with him. It's the end for me too."

"He's not going-"

"I wouldn't like being like that. Would you?" I didn't even consider Jeff's ridiculous question. He'd started bombarding me with questions and it was preventing me from thinking. That was his plan. If I couldn't think, then I couldn't fix. I needed to think. "How are you going to get back from this? Have you thought about that?"

"Haven't thought about it. Don't care." I was looking around the Lady for inspiration.

"What did you think of the new units?"

"Thought they looked rubbish." I was getting ready to dig some more. Get rid of some snow.

"Would you do it again? The same way?"

"It hasn't ended yet."

"Soon you'll wish it had."

"Fuck off, Jeff," I said. Jeff unfolded his arms and then, by the sound of the squeal, slid down the angled side of the Lady on his front. He was gone from peering in. I looked at the glove box door in my hand and then to Simon. I dropped the door and went to Simon. "What a dick that guy is!" I patted Simon's chest. It was cold. "How are we going to get out of this?" I asked, and then looked sideways and listened. I could hear the chime from the dashboard. I leant in closer to Simon. "What's sixteen plus three? Simon?" I tapped my knuckles on his arm. "Simon! Sixteen plus three?" His fans were silent, of course, we were basically in a freezer. The one place he didn't need his fans to cool down his thinking, so that silence didn't actually mean anything. Nothing except that he was cold enough.

I somehow found his rain cover, it wrapped itself around my foot and I wrapped it around him as best I could. His arms prevented me from getting it all the way around, but it was better than nothing. I stood and put my gloves on and looked around. The truck was ruined. Absolutely ruined. That was a real shame. Pete could maybe get it fixed, but it wasn't going to be easy getting it back, not with Simon in this state. But that was all down the road. First things first, I still had a snow problem. I had to get the snow out. And then I had to get *us* out. I wasn't nearly agile enough to climb out of the window. Maybe if I were twenty years younger and an Olympic gymnast I could climb up, but not me, not now.

The dashboard chimed at the exact moment I had an amazing idea. I looked at Simon. It would have been good if he'd seen that. I tried to work out the timing, missed a few chimes as I nodded along, then I raised my finger exactly in time with a chime. It was pretty funny. "I'm going to make snow steps," I said, looking around for the glove box door. I couldn't see it. "Why can't I fucking find anything in this fuckity fucking truck?" I asked as I spun around.

"Ha!" I said, rather than laughed. I was amused, but not that kind of amused. "This is incredible." I stood there and marvelled at my third failed effort. That's right, *third!* "This is just..." It was just... I just couldn't understand how a staircase made of snow could be so hard to build. They're literally ascending. Lumps. Of. Fucking. Snow.

I dropped the glove box door and ran up the crumbled pile

of snow as fast as I could, hoping velocity would best gravity, but it just resulted in me mashing some snow, getting about fifty centimetres up the hill, and then falling knees first into the rest. I wondered why I'd thought I'd be able to make load-bearing stairs out of soft snow as I knelt in it. I picked some up with my gloved hand and let it fall through my fingers. "Well, that didn't work," I said, over my shoulder, to Simon. I'd wasted most of the day unsuccessfully building steps. There was probably a better use of my time, but I couldn't think of it. I slowly wiped snow from my thighs and looked up. I was in the shade now, the window of light cast by the window and light had made its way across the floor, which had been the ceiling, until it was nearly at Simon. There was no warmth in it. I knelt in the snow and ran my hands through it, my fingers digging patterns as the dashboard continued its dinging. It didn't bother me too much if I didn't think about it, but still, disabling it was on my to-do list.

I got up, slowly, and thought I could hear a gas leak. A hissing. Or it could have been liquid trickling. Neither would have surprised me. I don't know for sure but there are probably pipes in the Lady, somewhere behind the scenes, and they could well be filled with gas or liquid. The heaters probably used them. The heaters! I looked up at the dashboard. Would putting the heaters on be a good idea? If I could reach? I couldn't reach so I put 'Trying out the heaters' on the list in my head. I had to hope all the heat wasn't already gone, from whatever was leaking and making the noise.

Simon was making the noise. It took a while to determine that. Even when I was kneeling next to him, I wasn't sure. I had to put my head against his. He was hissing static. Very quietly. I tried to listen. "Bit louder, mate," I said and then listened harder, unsure if my harder listening was what seemed to make the static slightly louder, or if Simon had bumped up the volume. "I can't... what? What are you saying?" I pressed my left ear against his head, then moved it around, trying to find a better spot. I listened for about half a minute, my eyes moving from corner to corner. I sat back on my heels. "I can't..." The static did sound decipherable. I leant in again and listened. I was sure there were words in there, then Simon's klaxon crackled, the sound fragmented, and I nearly died. I banged my head on his as I tried to pull it away. The klaxon sound was fragmented. "Fucking hell!" I said, and then started laughing. "That was a good one."

Yeah, he was in a bad way, but he wasn't even nearly dead. I looked up to the window, half hoping to see Jeff's ridiculous head. It wasn't there. That was actually good, I didn't really want to see Jeff, and before I'd even turned back to Simon things got better still when I felt he actually started to move. His right arm was moving. He was lifting it. Trying to. At first just the right side of his torso dropped a little, which caused his shoulders to grind and me to grimace, but then, when his torso settled, his right arm left the ground. Slowly but deliberately he raised it up towards me. "You okay?" I asked as he held his hand up. "High five!" I said and slapped his hand. He didn't lower his hand and so I grabbed it and shook it. I couldn't actually shake his hand. I couldn't move his hand, but I shook my hand while it was holding his. Another fragment of klaxon blared and I held on to his hand until he began to lower it. He lowered it slightly and then raised it again. "You like that, huh?" I said, but as I was reaching for his hand the shattered klaxon sounded again. "What?" I asked. I thought maybe he didn't want a high five. I couldn't think what else he could want. "Do you want..." I stood up, using his raised arm for support. "I can't..." I said when I was upright and the dizziness passed. I pulled on his arm. I mean, no fucking way. "You're too heavy." I pulled again. Nada. I leant in close to his head. The murmurs of static were, I was sure, still going.

Simon lowered his arm. I didn't know what to do. "What do you want me to do?" I asked, scared he was just going to lower his arm and not move for several more hours. He lowered his arm until it hit the ground. Then he lowered it a bit more so his torso lifted and he wasn't so twisted. He began to raise his arm again. I reached for it but as I did, he lowered it. Quickly this time. It seemed to fall to the ground. "I don't know what you want me to do?" I said, as gently as I could. Over the next few hours Simon raised his arm three more times. I wrapped his rain cover around him a bit better when I got the chance, but I don't think that was his goal. And then it was dark.

I guess the Lady acted like an igloo because the next morning I was still alive. That was good because at some point during the night I'd come up with the solution. I was eighty-seven percent certain that I'd worked out what Simon was trying to tell me, and better still, when I woke up, I could remember it. And even if it wasn't what Simon was thinking, it didn't matter, because it was a good idea. It would take a bit of work but it *would* work. I needed to get out of the Lady to execute my plan. And no, my plan didn't involve executing Jeff. It also didn't involve *not* executing Jeff. If Jeff got executed along the way then so be it, but that wasn't my goal.

My goal was to collect material. Logs and things. I'd collect material and then, when Simon raised his arm, I'd just put material under it, and when he lowered his arm it would force him more upright. Eventually, with enough material under both arms, Simon would be upright. Then, hopefully, putting his head back on straight would be good enough. We'd have to get out somehow, but with Simon's strength we'd be able to do that. It might mean him ripping the side of the Lady out. And flipping the Lady over, yeah, I could see it. We could get a long tree for a lever, turn the truck the right way around, and hope it still works. It was still chiming so something in it still worked. This was all dependent on me gathering materials, and that was dependent on me getting out. The snow steps hadn't worked. I needed another idea. Just one great idea could fix everything and there had to be one. There was no sense to our situation. I needed to make sense of it.

Four days later I was considering giving up.

Eight days after that I gave up.

Two days after that I reconsidered and decided to have one more go at thinking up a solution.

The next day I gave up again.

"Do you want any more? Mikey! Do you want any more?" I didn't reply. I'd stopped replying to Jeff some time ago. I'm not sure he'd noticed. A chunk of hot meat hit the ground near my foot and sizzled for a second. It was seventeen minutes until Simon was due to raise his arm again. He raised his arm every sixty minutes and then he kept it raised for anywhere between one and three minutes, that seemed to be a decision he was making. He'd lower it slowly, and then sixty minutes from him first raising it, he'd raise it again. I spoke to him. Not as much now, but I still spoke to him. The Lady still chimed. Not that much had changed since I'd failed at building a staircase. Flying food had happened. A day or so after the stair fiasco, Jeff had started throwing cooked chunks of meat through the window. Apart from that, not much had changed at all. The solution sometimes seemed tantalisingly close. Sometimes there wasn't one.

I watched the meat cool on the icy floor. The floor which my walking and sliding had compressed into a mat of ice. I'd got good at not falling. I probably only fell seven or eight times a day. I'm talking about complete falls. Bum on the floor falls. I danced with windmilling arms and skittering legs more regularly, but I could usually hold them. Stay upright. I had extra motivation to stay upright because I'd noticed my buttocks getting smaller. Less cushioned. I could feel my butt bones when I sat on the floor and I could really feel them when I fell.

I stared at the meat on the floor. It had stopped sizzling. The Lady chimed and I wasn't sure if I could hear static from Simon. That may have stopped, but every hour his arm still moved. I could smell a fire and I could hear Jeff chattering outside.

It was a grey day. A white day. Some days the window was blue. Today it was white, and snow danced down. I could hear him scratching about outside. He was fucking about with the side of the Lady. This was new. Jeff hadn't tried to get in since that first day, and even then he hadn't tried very hard. I stood up and looked up, and tried to make sense of the noise. I blinked away any snow that hit my eyelashes. It crossed my mind that he might be positioning wood around the truck. He was whistling as he moved something. He sounded even more upbeat than usual. The tune he was whistling was jaunty. I thought I knew it. It could have been an old national anthem.

He was doing something. There was the unmistakable *scree* of wood scraping on metal. If he was piling wood around the Lady, which he then intended to set on fire, then it would explain his jovial whistling, but it still left some questions unanswered.

Would that kill us? With all the snow? I didn't know. Did I care? I thought about it. I didn't know.

I rubbed the fleshy part of my left hand, the bit between my thumb and forefinger, with the thumb and forefinger of my right. I could hear Jeff was near the window. "What are you doing?" I asked, but my voice was croaky. The words fragmented and quiet. I coughed. His head appeared.

"Nice beard!" said Jeff.

"What are you doing?" I asked, slightly stronger. I put my gloves on.

"I've got a present for you," he said, and immediately dropped a knife which bounced in a burst of tiny white ice chunks of its own making, and then clinked off Simon's leg and spun. I slide-walked over to it and when I was picking up the knife something much bigger hit the ice behind me. I tried to whirl, but as I tried my right leg left the ground of its own accord and went up. My right hand also went up. If it had been holding a handkerchief instead of a knife then that movement might have looked like a traditional dance. A national dance to go with Jeff's whistling. I had time to grunt before my other leg lost traction, and a split second after my back scraped against Simon's arm, I was on the floor. And that one *did* hurt. I didn't know how much it hurt, that would kick in after a few seconds. It was a cruncher, for sure, and I waved the knife while I established what was happening.

There was a bundle of wood on the floor. On top of the chunk of meat, which I probably wasn't going to eat anyway. It was bound with straps which I recognised as coming from the back of the Lady. I listened as Jeff's whistling faded. I shuffled over to the bundle on my knees. It was a bundle of small branches, about half a metre long or there about, and they were all roughly the same thickness. And they were bundled nicely. Jeff had done a nice job of bundling them together. You wouldn't think he had it in him. It's true that I'd only met the man three times, but not once did he strike me as the kind of guy who could bundle wood. It was possible his experience of getting blasted by the Burrower had made him more outdoorsy and pioneering, as well as aggressive. Maybe they were the same thing. I think Jeff was on steroids.

I spent the ten minutes until Simon was next due to raise his arm getting everything ready. All that really entailed was moving the bundle over to Simon. It took about fifteen seconds, and the rest of the time I spent periodically turning the bundle ninety degrees. Sometimes it seemed like the bundle would be stronger lengthways under his arm, with sticks running in the same direction as his arm. It made sense and I'd be confident, but then doubts would creep in. I'd think maybe they'd explode outwards, with all the weight on them, if I did it that way, and it'd be better to put the bundle crossways. I tried to picture it in my mind. What would happen? The wood exploded both ways.

When Simon lifted his arm, I pushed the bundle under his arm crossways. Then turned it. Then turned it again. "Gently!" I said. Frustratingly he held his arm up for nearly ten minutes before gently lowering it. "That's it, gently," I said, which was probably quite an annoying thing to hear when you're already doing something gently.

The bundle was about forty centimetres high, and all these figures are just estimates, but it was something like that. It wouldn't get him upright but it'd be a start. Proof of a *great* concept. The back of Simon's arm hit the top of the bundle and he stopped. "Careful," I said. Simon's servos whirred as his arm pressed down. The wood took the load. Spread it out as best it could within the confines of the straps. The bundle creaked, groaned, cracked and snapped. The top sticks snapped. Those below bulged and groaned, and Simon hadn't moved at all.

It looked as if he would just crush the bundle, and then what? It didn't look like it was going to work. Simon lifted his arm. Then he lowered it, and just before he touched the wood he raised it again. Then he repeated the up and down, slightly quicker. And then he did it again, faster still. I pulled the bundle out and his arm crashed to the floor. "Calm down," I said, annoyed. Annoyed that it hadn't worked. Annoyed that Simon now seemed frustrated with me. "Wood was too thin, that's all."

I only now noticed that Simon didn't have his usual dusting of snow. He usually had one that I'd wipe away with my hand. He was wet. The flakes that landed on him dissolved within a second or two.

The whistling outside had returned. I saw the knife on the floor and picked it up, then sat on the bundle of wood. That was nice. To sit on something. I sat there with my chest on my thighs and my chin on my right knee. I considered the blade that I was holding near my feet. Both sides of it. The scraping on the side of the Lady had returned. No whistling. I could hear struggling as I turned the knife over in my hand, and then I scratched the point into the icy floor.

I only looked up when I heard rustling inside. He was trying to feed a much longer piece of wood to the Lady. A big branch, or the trunk of a little tree. It was jammed against my chair. Another curse word from outside and then the wood withdrew a bit before being forced back in where it hit the chair again. Eventually, long after I would have given up, Jeff found an angle and managed to feed the wood in so it went in front of my chair. The end of the wood scraped along the dashboard and I was sure it was going to get jammed again, but he was lucky, and the end of the wood dropped down, the other end was still jutting out of the window. It didn't take him as long to feed the next similar sized branch in. It still took ages, just not as long as the first one. The second one, as it scraped along, knocked something on the dashboard which stopped the chiming, but I don't think that was intentional. I didn't know what Jeff was trying to achieve. Set fire to the inside? His head appeared briefly between the two big sticks.

I suddenly felt quite emotional. It had come and gone. Mostly gone, but every so often I'd find myself very nearly crying. My face would screw up and I'd choke a little. Not a pretty sight, and I'd kept it in check, but for some reason the fucking sticks set me off and I rubbed the heel of my hand on my forehead as hard as I could, trying to drive it away, as I stared down at the floor and scraped the tip of the knife into the ice. I was upset because I knew what the wood was for.

If you'd asked me what would be easier to build, steps made

from snow or an actual functional ladder made from wood and straps and tape, then I'd have said the steps, and I would have been wrong. Once I'd found a way of wrapping the binding, so that my weight on each rung pulled it all tighter, it had come together quickly. I was sweating. I didn't check what time I started to build it, but when I had about two thirds of the rungs in, I realised that Simon hadn't moved his arm, and I'd definitely taken more than an hour. The inside of the Lady had begun to drip. Constant dripping had replaced the constant chiming. I preferred the chiming.

I didn't really need to make the top three rungs. I could have pulled myself out, but I made them all. All the way to the top so it looked like a proper and complete ladder. Finishing the ladder meant I could, if I'd wanted to, stick my head out and look around. I didn't. I finished the ladder and climbed back down. I trod carefully but the ladder was sound.

"Check it out," I said, crouching down next to Simon. "I made an excellent ladder!" I could feel the heat on my face. I grabbed for his hand with both of mine and I pulled that ugly face. I swallowed. "I'm sorry," I said. I kissed the top of his head. "I'll go and see..." I pointed to my side window, which was up high because the Lady was upside down. Simon had been pointing to that window, on the hour, for days and days. I waited for a response. There wasn't one. I kissed his head again and then climbed out of the Lady. It wasn't quite an out of body experience, but when I was outside of the Lady I felt tiny, like I was looking at myself from the top of a tree, or the window of a passing transport, or the camera on a satellite, or from the frozen eyeballs of Floaty Bill.

I looked around. It had stopped snowing, but not before it

had buried whatever Jeff's camp consisted of. It was about twenty metres away. The fire pit was visible and black, but the rest, whatever it might be, was just pleasingly rounded mounds of snow. I could see where Jeff had dragged the wood but, like his camp, his tracks had been smoothed by the weather. I walked around the wreck of our truck. One rear door was missing, the other bent in half. It would have been a good shelter, but there was no indication anybody had been using it.

Trees closely surrounded us on three sides, but over on the side-door side, the most damaged side, which was buried under both fallen snow and snow we pushed up when we crashed, there was a clearing that went on to the horizon. I walked around the Lady twice. The snow was doing a good job of smoothing out its shape. You couldn't really tell that the thing under there had once been a cube, but massive shards of yellow told you it didn't belong.

"Don't go in, Jeff!" I shouted as I began to wander. I wandered over to the tree line, not expecting to find anything that could prop Simon up. And there was nothing. In the Lady I'd been able to picture perfectly sized large chunks of wood. Big enough to hold his weight, but not so big that I couldn't move them. Just lying about. Just fallen from a tree. There was nothing like that. With a saw I could have cut them myself, maybe. I didn't have a saw. I reached up and grabbed a branch that was about the same size as the ones Jeff had bundled. I expected it to snap off quite easily. It didn't, it bent so I let go of it and made a small blizzard.

I looked down across the treeless stretch of snow and decided to see where it led. I kept to the middle and ignored the narrower paths that appeared in the climbing wall of trees to the sides. I saw five animals. Three bounced away but two watched me. I didn't know what any of them were. Many more must have seen me.

The wide clearing didn't lead anywhere and it wasn't particularly wide when I decided to turn back. I'd go a little further each day. Or venture down one of the narrower routes that ran through the trees, but for today I'd gone far enough. I guessed I'd walked about three kilometres.

I wanted to be back before it was dark. Getting lost wouldn't end well. Nothing ends well. Everything ends the same way for everyone. You could stop a story at a happy point and call it an ending, but it's not the end. I turned and retraced my steps. I walked back even slower. It was hard work. I was tired and yeah, if I'm honest, which I'm often not, I didn't really want to go back.

I didn't see any wildlife but I saw that my footprints, at a couple of points, had animal tracks across them. Animals had darted across to the trees on the other side, after I'd passed. One didn't get there. Their tracks vanished and you could see the print of a large wing. I could relate. A woodland creature taking its chance to get to the trees opposite. It gets over halfway and thinks, *I'm going to make it!* Then the shadow.

Maybe the animal tracks had been there first and I walked through them without noticing.

I'd walked a lot further than I thought I had. Perhaps as far as five kilometres. I kept expecting to see the Lady but I was struggling to see my footprints in the gloom. I wondered if I'd wandered past it, but that was silly, because I was still following my footprints and there were green swirls dancing in the sky. The Northern Lights. Incredible. I didn't think they moved as fast for some reason. I thought they were clouds and hardly moved, but they danced. I wished Simon could see them too and then I did cry as I walked. Proper ugly pathetic sobbing, but nobody could see me so it was cool. I cried for a little bit, not too long.

I couldn't see my footprints and had to stop. I did a shuddery intake of breath and looked around. It was dark. I bent down but that didn't help, it didn't make it any lighter, and now that I'd spun, I didn't know in what direction I'd been going. I couldn't even see the footprints I'd just made. Wherever we were it got dark fast. I could have been blind. The clear sky had been short-lived and up was the same as down. There was nothing in any direction until I saw the speck of light.

I thought it was a fire I was walking to. Jeff's fire. When I was closer, and I could see the geometric shape the fire was contained in, I thought the Lady was ablaze. Closer still I realised it was just the internal light that was on, shining out through the window.

The light still working was cool. They really weren't messing around when they built those things and if we got it turned over it could probably still fly, I thought, and then closed my eyes.

The top of my ladder was still propped where I'd climbed it and I could feel the heat billowing from the hole before I got there. Large clumps of sludgy ice slid from outside of the Lady. It was a struggle to get up to the window. I grappled my way up and took hold of the top of the ladder. Jeff was at the bottom of it, across the other side of a puddle, sitting with Simon. It was tiny down there. Simon and Jeff filled most of it.

"I told you not to go in."

"I told you you'd want it to end," he replied without looking up. I didn't. I wanted to tell Simon about the Northern Lights.

Tell him how cool they were. He hadn't seen them. He would never see them. Simon would never see the spectacular aerial phenomenon that is known as the Northern Lights. He was about to explode. Jeff didn't seem concerned. Simon's chest plate was glowing red and was sunken. The sound of running water was inside the Lady, but I couldn't see where it was running to or from. I hadn't thought about this moment. I hadn't let myself.

That's a lie, I had. But I hadn't imagined it would be like this.

He had seen a rainbow.

Maybe if you lived your whole life up here you'd take the lights for granted and get excited over a rainbow. You probably got to see both up here, but if I had to choose one, just one or the other, and you only got to see it once in your life, then I would want to see a rainbow. A rainbow is incredible. They didn't dance, but those colours? Wow. We'd seen rainbows.

"You should go," shouted Jeff. He was sitting on the floor next to Simon. Sitting casually, his outstretched legs crossed over. A white-rimmed hole began to spread in the centre of the hollow in Simon's chest. It moved in a similar way to the dancing lights in the sky.

"Did he move? Say anything?" I shouted.

"Yeah, he said you're a dick," replied Jeff who then giggled at his own joke. "No, nothing." I nodded and swallowed. "This is it!" said Jeff.

I nodded. Small nods while I was breathing quickly through my nose. I swallowed, then opened my mouth and took a slow breath through it. "I'm here!" I shouted. "You can... you can conk out, if you want." I finished that with some very shuddery breathing. I thought Jeff might make fun of that, but he didn't.

"I'm just out here!"

I went across to the nearest trees. I stumbled on something which I think was part of Jeff's camp. I don't know what it was. The interior light of the Lady did nothing to light my way, and I waved a hand around in front of me until it hit something solid. I went past that one until I found another one. I went deeper into the woods. I picked a tree and felt my way down, then sat down in the snow, my back against a trunk. I hugged my knees to my chest.

It was at least two hours before anything dramatic happened, but when it happened it really happened. It was snowing again but none was hitting the truck, it was being waved up and away by the rising heat. I wasn't ready, but the light from inside suddenly grew brighter and whiter, and the Lady exploded. Three or four seconds, it took. Maybe five. From a safety standpoint I hadn't been far enough away because it was a big explosion. Using my hands, I covered as much of my face as I could. I made noises I couldn't describe. I don't think I cried much, but I made noises into my hands. There was no burning wreckage when I slowly lowered my hands. There was nothing. I curled up smaller.

I saw a green light moving through the trees. Its aura lighting up the trunks. I watched it flit around. The dot, and I thought about how much Simon wanted to turn it on but we hadn't got around to it, and then I did cry.

There were no trees on the snowy expanse where the Lady had been because it was a frozen lake, I discovered at first light. There was a pond and a thin milky crust was already forming. There were no flowers to throw on it. I stood and looked into the pond as the dot explored. Even in the daylight it cast colours on the snow.

# The End

*More by Jamie P. Barker*

A Year and a Day - Book One: Winter
A Year and a Day - Book Two: Spring
A Year and a Day - Book Three: Summer
A Year and a Day - Book Four: Autumn

GREGOR